STOCKHOLM SERIES: 4

IN A CITY TRANSFORMED

STOCKHOLM SERIES: 4

IN A CITY TRANSFORMED

A novel
by
Per Anders Fogelström

Translated from Swedish
by
Jennifer Brown Bäverstam

The Stockholm Series:
City of My Dreams
Children of Their City
Remember the City
In a City Transformed
City in the World

The fourth volume was originally published
in Swedish as "I en förvandlad stad."

Library of Congress Control Number: 2013951508
ISBN 978-1-932043-83-9

Penfield Books
215 Brown Street
Iowa City, IA 52245
www.penfieldbooks.com

Edited by Melinda Bradnan, Deb Schense, and Mary Sharp
Cover design by M. A. Cook Design
Cover photographs of Stockholm City Hall Garden circa 1940,
photographer unknown, and back cover photo by
Jennifer Brown Bäverstam

TABLE OF CONTENTS

The Author vii
The Translator viii
Translator's Note viii

I

IN A CITY TRANSFORMED 11
BEDBUG OUTING 14
MOVING DAY 22
CONTEMPTIBLE REVOLUTIONARY 30
THE QUIET STREET 37
AUTUMN MEETINGS 43
IN THE SPRING SUN 51
ON THE BARRICADES 57
ACCEPTANCE 64
YOUNG AT THE WRONG TIME 73
FAREWELL AND RETURN 80
SOLIDARITY'S DAY 88

II

THE BLACK BROWN YEARS 99
UNEMPLOYED 102
SHELTERED CORNER 108
UNDER THE STARS 114
WAITING 123
MARKED 131
SWIMMING AT KÄLLTORP 138
TO DARE TO CHOOSE 146
YET AGAIN? 152

OLD TRACKS, NEW PATHS 160
A BEAUTIFUL SUMMER 167
A TIME OF GROWTH 174

III

LIGHT AND SHADOW 183
BLACKOUTS 186
AMONG THE PINES 193
A TIME FOR CLEANING THINGS OUT 199
BORDERLANDS 206
SPRING OF VIOLENCE 212
A SUMMER OF GRACE 218
INSIDE THE DARKNESS 223
THE COOL HEAT 230
TO DARE NOT LEAVE 238
RETURN 245
EXPANDING BORDERS 253

IV

TURNING POINT 263
REMAINS OF TIES 266
DAUGHTERS 272
TAKE RESPONSIBILITY 279
DEFEAT 287
AFTER THE PARTY 294
THE MEMORY OF A FRIEND 300
BEACH IN AUGUST 306
THE PAST AND THE PRESENT 313
EQUALITY AND FRATERNITY 320
SPRINGTIME WANDERER 326
IN A CITY TRANSFORMED 333

THE AUTHOR

PER ANDERS FOGELSTRÖM is one of the most widely read authors in Sweden today. *City of My Dreams,* the first book in his five-volume *Stockholm Series,* broke the record for bestsellers. A compelling storyteller known for his narrative sweep, his acute characterization and the poetic qualities of his prose, Fogelström was highly acclaimed even before he wrote the *Stockholm Series.* Ingmar Bergman made one of Fogelström's earlier novels, *Summer with Monika,* into a film that is now a Bergman classic.

Born in 1917, Fogelström grew up in Stockholm and lived there his entire life. He was a vast resource on Stockholm's history, with enormous archives on the subject, and published much non-fiction about the city. He spent his early career as a journalist and, in the 1940s, he co-founded a literary magazine. His own prolific writing resulted in more than fifty books.

Fogelström's *Stockholm Series* has remained a favorite in Swedish literature among readers of all ages, and he continues to be greatly loved and respected as a chronicler of his people. Fogelström died on Midsummer Day, June 20, 1998, two days before the unveiling of a statue of him at the entrance to the hall where the Nobel Prizes are awarded in Stockholm.

THE TRANSLATOR

Jennifer Brown Bäverstam has traveled and studied languages all her life. She has translated several books and articles from Swedish and French. She holds a degree in French and economics from Georgetown University and has studied translation at the University of Geneva. She lives in Boston, Massachusetts.

Translator's Note

Swedish place names are generally one compound word with the proper name at the beginning and the kind of place at the end.

Because most of the place names in the book have not been translated, the following terms explain endings for names of streets, hills, bridges, etc.:

backen: hill
berget, bergen: hill, hills
bro, bron: bridge
gatan: street
gränd: alley
holm, holmen: island
torg, torget: square
viken: estuary

I

IN A CITY TRANSFORMED

The city that goes to sleep at night is a different city from the one that woke up that morning. Something has been built, and something has been torn down. Someone has been born, and someone has died. The changes go on without interruption, and what once was will never come again. But the dividing line between the old and the new is not short and straight. Instead, it is so winding and extended that we hardly know on which side of the knife-edge-sharp moment we have landed, if we are living in the past or in the future. To live: to dance on the edge with light and quick steps, so light that the knife does not cut, so quick that it does not have time to penetrate.

A short while ago, barns and pigsties still existed on the islands of Stockholm. Stables and rows of outhouses filled the courtyards in the center of town. A few steps from the office buildings and palatial business edifices on the main streets, tree-shaded, small cottages stood behind rickety fences, and tables were set for coffee in summer pavilions with gingerbread woodwork. Rumbling industries spewing smoke still operated in the center of town, and out by the tollgates, the fireproof gables of isolated tenement housing rose above tobacco barns and turnip fields.

That city was no idyll, but it had retained quite a lot of its small-town character, and if people walked down the right streets, they could find the peace and safety that a feeling of timelessness lends. People had been able to grow accustomed to the city such as it was. What people have come to know can be accepted, even what people would rather do without.

The present: a noisy, big city. Constantly expanding, consuming what was left of the idyll, and everything one had grown used to. The impoverishment of the outskirts, green with weeds, turned ever grayer; the slums of shacks gave way to slums of tenement housing. Furiously rumbling and eternally grinding traffic ran through the main streets, giving pedestrians a feeling of being without rights, of being legally hunted game. They clustered on street corners and waited for some car to show mercy and let them pass, or for some policeman to appear and for one moment stop the stream of traffic. They ran across the squares and found themselves suddenly surrounded, unnerved by angry beeping.

The buildings of the new city looked like buildings had never looked before, such as the city library's round canister on a square box. Neon signs with flashing bulbs blinked on and off, on the building facades facing the open plaza at Stureplan: *Our Home in every home. Runa estate-grown.* Electric trains ran in ghost-like silence between the lowered boom gates at Tegelbacken, and on across Järnvägsbron, the railroad bridge. And the radio apparatus with headphones told them about Charles Lindbergh, "The Lone Eagle," who had flown solo across the Atlantic.

Young people gathered to dance the Charleston and the Black Bottom, to see Josephine Baker dance, dressed only in a wreath of bananas, or to shout themselves hoarse at the stadium when Wide competed against Nurmi in running, or Djurgården opposed Stattena in football. And the young women showed so clearly that they belonged to a new era and a new city: shingled hair and knee-length skirts.

But along the quays in the middle of town, the wooden cargo boats still created whole forests of masts, and the smell of bark met the strollers on Birger Jarlsgatan and Strandvägen and the tourists on their way to the beautiful new City Hall.

She had recently smelled that fragrance of bark and freshly cut wood when she had been standing and waiting for the streetcar. Now the traffic was piling up on narrow Riddarhusgränd, where the lanes to and from Vasabron merged. A few young men with heavy handcarts were panting over their shafts. Truck drivers hung out of their cab windows; the car fenders rattled from the sputtering of the motors. The streetcar conductor on the number nine trailer car banged hard on the hatch to the smokers' platform to remind the passengers who had gotten on at Tegelbacken to pay. But it was so crowded out on the platform that he was obliged to unlock the door and come out himself to collect the fares: fifteen öre for a single ride and twenty for transfers.

Finally, the line of vehicles began to move again. The youths pulling the handcarts grunted with their efforts to get the wheels moving; the cars growled and followed behind them slowly; somewhere a horse whinnied anxiously.

Emelie, who was out on an errand for the store, held fast to the handle by the window near the platform. She looked out, though there wasn't so much to see just now, only the dirty walls of the old courthouse. Most of what she saw seemed either dirty or blurry lately. This was because of her glasses. She had been obliged to get them in order to see and read close up, such as in the store. For distance, like now, she was better off without them. Still, they stayed on. In the store, it was hard to constantly take them off and put them on. It was best to get used to them, even if it was a nuisance. Best to get used to having gotten old, fifty-eight years old now, in the spring of 1928.

That spring, Branting's successor as party leader, Per Albin Hansson, elected for the interim, had used a new and strange term in a preliminary parliamentary debate. He had spoken of the "people's home." It was a goal that had been set, urgent and difficult to achieve, as it appeared. However, it sounded more peaceful than the goal that Emelie had heard many times before—the revolution.

Times had gotten better; wages had risen. But unemployment was still high, especially among young people. And unrest increased, antagonisms grew. The liberal government had put forth motions that would limit the possibilities the strike weapon gave the workers.

At Riddarhustorget, a young man in a black shirt stood selling the fascist newspaper, *The Sheaf.* The sun had set behind Riddarholm's Church and stained the western sky red.

BEDBUG OUTING

David got off at the Folkungagatan stop. The day had been unsuccessful. He had hung out down by Central Station to find some "bumpkin" to swindle and had been driven away by the police.

He was well-known. He smiled suddenly, almost contentedly. Those country fools were in luck that the cops had come—otherwise David would have plucked them as clean as they plucked their own chickens. Because he knew the art, deftly and smoothly and with the right, well-oiled talk. It was just a pity that the cops knew about it.

His smile disappeared. He didn't even have enough money for a beer. He looked around uneasily; his thirst was growing, and time was short. The stores would close soon, and he had promised to come home, and Tyra would make an awful scene if he didn't show up.

The people closest at hand hardly gave him any hopes. Maybe this old lady … he took a few steps closer, politely lifting his hat.

"Might madam help out an unemployed man with a few öre for a coffee?" But she snapped shut both her mouth and her coin purse and moved away quickly.

More and more people arrived at the streetcar stop. And since David had already begun, he made the rounds, asking one person after another. He did not receive one öre, but an older man spat so that a gob of spittle landed between David's feet. And he regretted that he had made the attempt. There were too many in this area who recognized him, old devils with long memories who might still know him as Yellow David.

However, he kept on. The number four streetcar was late, but another number nine arrived, and several people got off to change cars. Among them was a man dressed in workers' clothes who gave him a whole fifty öre.

At last the number four arrived, and they boarded. David got on, too; he had a transfer ticket. A few of them sneered at him, as if it was so strange that someone who was begging could afford to ride the streetcar.

One man is as good as another, he thought while the streetcar screeched and turned along the edge of the White Hills, entered Skånegatan, and passed by Nytorget. Yes, he was smarter. Not as stupid as those poor blockheads that worked days on end for the hot dog money that was thrown at them on Fridays. He gave the worker who had just given him money a glance of pity: the poor dimwit. He, too, had just given away his hard-earned coins.

The man looked back at him, nodded. Was it just pure stupidity or had they met before? There was something familiar in the almost stupidly kind mug of that fair-haired man.

The streetcar reached Götgatan, and the man stepped off. David watched him thoughtfully. Yes, of course. That wasn't so good. But he hadn't seen him for many years. It was his brother-in-law he had been begging from, Bengt, Tyra's youngest brother. That was why he had gotten so much. Bengt had always been kind. In contrast to the other one, Erik, that Communist big shot who had threatened to punch David in the nose if they ever met again.

Previously, David had lived in the tenements above the garbage dump, with his parents. Now, for some time, he and his family had had their own apartment, smack in the middle of the cluster of buildings on the hill overlooking the inlet of Årstaviken, in "Negro Village" as it was called.

He got off, turned his back to the big, old-age home there, and walked across the deserted main road called Ringvägen. A lamppost stood like a black gallows against the evening sun. With enormous energy and display of force, the tenements' half-grown boys had managed to take off the whole lantern and bend what was left into a gallows-shaped arm. Unemployment was greatest among the youth, and they hung out there day in and day out with nothing better to do than to punch in at the employment office and get into mischief.

He walked past the store and picked up a couple of beers. The owner complained, of course, about his bill. Other decent guys who worked came in and paid on Friday evenings. Not even one box of matches would he get on credit anymore. But he had the money for two beers, so he got those. He stuffed the bottles into his jacket pockets, walked out onto the hillside and drank them after he pushed in the corks with the aid of a penknife. Across the water down below, they were building a giant railroad bridge to replace the old embankment up at Liljeholmen Station. He stood there a moment and stared and marveled at the energy some people had, that they had the energy to work so hard. But then they got a customer's passbook and money to buy things on the account with. Though on a day like today, at the end of the month, they would have to go to the tavern if they wanted to get anything. Or find a bootlegger. Not until Monday would there be a renewal of the passbook.

David Berg had not worked many days in his soon-to-be fifty-year-old life. And when he had worked, it had mostly caused him trouble, such as during the general strike of 1909. People still remembered, those with long memories who still called him Yellow David and spat as he walked by. But in the tenement housing, most people seemed to have forgotten and forgiven. This was thanks to Tyra, he well knew. She had made them understand that David had never taken work very seriously, and that no employer would find any satisfaction with David Berg. Not even during the general strike.

He was no moneybags, for sure.

His slightly contented smile came back. The beer he had drunk had calmed him and fortified him. He took the empty bottles and threw them one at a time down the hill, starting to laugh at the sound of the crashing and the tinkling glass. Those tight-fisted moneybags saved their empty bottles and carried them in bags down to the store. But David Berg didn't watch his pennies.

They were sitting around the dinner table when he went up. Gathered together, the whole family for once. Otherwise, there was almost always somebody missing. Ten-year-old Allan had been in a home for sickly children and then in a reformatory for juvenile delinquents. Eight-year-old Stig had also had problems with his lungs and been admitted to the sanatorium a few times. Seven-year-old Per and five-year-old Gun had been in the homes for children and infants when Tyra had lain in the hospital. David himself had been in jail a couple of times when he had been "nailed" and malicious victims had yelled for the police. But for the most part, they had gotten by pretty well, if one thought about what could have happened if everything that went on had been found out.

That their kids went into community garden plots around the hill and pinched apples and raided berry bushes was nothing extraordinary. People did that sort of thing. That they picked up wood at construction sites and made off with empty crates outside shops was also part of what was generally accepted. It was more serious when Allan tried to set the row of outhouses on fire and worst of all when a whole tobacco barn out by Tanto burned down after the little boys had been playing there.

Tyra served them fried smoked sausages and potatoes. That was the kind of food David liked, and he helped himself to plenty. Then—to everyone's astonishment—Tyra opened the pantry door and took out a pilsner. Even though they had not been able to get credit in the store for a whole week.

She still was a gem! He patted her rump gratefully. And she laughed delightedly, took the kitchen towel and wiped the streak of snot running from the nose of the youngest child. Gun always had a cold; perhaps she lay too close to the draft from the window. But they never got around to moving the bed.

"They have already been here and taped things up," said Tyra. "And they are coming back at the crack of dawn tomorrow."

"One's crawling up there!" cried Stig.

They followed his gaze: a fat bedbug crawled slowly along the hole in the ceiling where the ceiling lamp was fastened.

"Let it be," said Tyra a little wearily. Bedbugs were a constant problem in the tenements. But now they were going to be smoked out. That would make it better for a short while. It usually didn't last very long.

They ate.

"The picnic basket is packed," said Tyra. "It's just as well that we leave so that we get a good spot. I'll just gather up the rest of the food. We have to take it with us."

"It's too bad the accordion is at the pawnshop," David said. "Otherwise I could have made a little music."

But that's just the way it was. The accordion had been in the pawnshop for many years now.

On the slope near the water stood an old tenement that was no longer used for housing, now ready for demolition. Normally it stood empty, and a few windowpanes were smashed but temporarily patched with newspaper and strips of tape. These days, the building was only used when one of the other tenement houses was being smoked out, and the tenants who were temporarily homeless could move in.

It had begun to draw toward dusk, but in the west the sky still had a rosy glow behind the new railway bridge's half-completed arches and towers. Negro Village's many cats meowed and howled from the thicket alongside the road. It was their mating time now, in March.

Small groups came from various directions, families carrying baskets of food, potted plants and something to sleep on. Children had a hard time holding onto blankets and pillows; bedclothes trailed after them in the mud.

David walked at the head of the group, tried to balance his way there with two large ripped and stained mattresses, which he had placed on his head so that they would not drag. Behind him came the children and, lastly, Tyra, with the baskets of food. He sweated and swore—this was no better than working. Luckily, the way was short, and, as soon as he got there, he would lie down and catch his breath.

The children whooped and laughed behind him. It would be exciting to sleep away for a few nights, the whole family. It was an adventure in a framework of safety, something completely different from the forced transports to the hospital and homes for children. Those times they resisted, screaming and kicking—now they hurried to get there first and choose their sleeping places.

Tyra had them in front of her when they walked down the hill, the four children and her husband—who was the biggest child of all. David who had not done an honest day of work in his whole life, the children who had already begun to wander in and out of reformatories. But she felt nothing of sorrow or shame—just the opposite. This was her family and the people she fought and worked for. They were not like all the others; they were ungovernable and free. She was proud of the runny-nosed and hard-to-handle children and of the man who sometimes had his pockets full of money and sometimes not one öre. And she herself had not let herself be arranged among those who were useful to society; she also belonged to those who were free as birds. She sat like a rat in her hole in Negro Village and snapped at social workers and police when they stretched out their fingers to seize her children.

She swung the picnic basket, heard the bottles gurgle. What eyes David would make when she pulled out the half-liter and two pilsners. He would not ask her how she had set about getting hold of all this; he would forget to in his delight. He would never find out that she had crawled on her knees and scrubbed stairs for several days to put together the food and drink and the blood money that the bootlegger had demanded. But he would be happy. As would the children she had bought candy for.

They would truly celebrate the bedbugs' departure, really have fun on their outing.

Since many families preferred to sleep at home the night before the fumigation, the tenement was far from filled yet. That night each family could have its own room if so desired.

While David was out talking to people in the rooms next door and the children wandered around exploring the nooks and crannies of the tenement, Tyra set out the food on a newspaper she had spread on the floor. She placed out the bottles for herself and David. She had not brought along glasses; they would have to drink from the bottles. Then she poured out the sugar mice she had in a bag, counting them:

two for each child and one each for herself and David. She had bought ha'penny caramels, too.

She laid out the mattresses and blankets and nibbled on her sugar mouse while she waited.

The children arrived first and screamed with joy when they saw what they had been given. Perhaps David heard them and sensed something, for it wasn't long before he also came running.

He was almost dumbstruck he was so overwhelmed. He had to take a sip from the bottle first before he could believe it. Then he held his sugar mouse carefully by the tail and dipped it carefully into the liquor and tasted it delightedly. And the children wanted to do the same thing and, of course, they got to; a few drops could certainly do no harm. But Gun dropped one of her mice, and it lay and dissolved in the bottom of the bottle, and Tyra had to give the girl an extra caramel so she wouldn't begin to cry.

Finally, the children were asleep on their mattresses and patchwork quilts. Tyra and David sat leaning against the wall; he had his arm around her. He spoke in a low voice, talking about all his plans. She would see, everything would be better. There was something about bootlegging and maybe home distilling, too. She hardly listened, knew it all, had heard it so many times. She was probably a little drunk, too; they had shared the bottle. What David said didn't matter much. But she liked to hear his tone, to hear he was happy and that he liked her. It felt so soft and comfortable, soothing. Suddenly, she fell asleep in his arms.

The next evening, it was full of people and crowded in the tenement house. People had to move closer together. Since it was Friday evening many of the men had been to the tavern—now that they could not eat at home, they had a perfect excuse. Others had gotten hold of liquor by other means. But Tyra's little supply was gone, and even if she was clever, she could not work magic. David wandered among the rooms and managed to get a swig here and there.

The children gathered on the stairs outside. The boys talked about what Sudden Wahlberg had come up with to shout at the referee, and about Broarn Persson, who was the country's best halfback. Football season was about to begin and on Sunday AIK would play against

Djurgårdshof, and Westermalm would oppose Sleipner. The girls' legs in mercerized cotton stockings shone from the light of the lamp above the door. One girl had gotten a permanent, and they felt her curls—of course, it was pretty, but a twenty-five öre coin was a lot of money, too.

David staggered up the hill toward Negro Village, stood and looked at the cluster of buildings. Some lay dark and silent. Inside them, smoke and bedbug death now reigned. Tomorrow evening the family would get to come home again; then it would have to be aired out all the following day. And on Monday, he would begin in earnest, find someone who had a supply of Estonian liquor.

David Berg stood in the darkness and let his urine stream against an evergreen bush. He swayed as he smiled at the joy of the moment and the possibilities of the future. He had Tyra. And every opportunity to make money.

Gradually, all the murmurs and quarrels died down, the last lights were put out. David and Tyra lay in the darkness and whispered for a while. She told him that Emelie, who she had lived with before, was going to move. And that her youngest brother, Bengt, had gotten married. And David tried to be interested and answer, although he actually didn't give a damn about what any of the others did.

"Emelie doesn't drink, does she?" he asked, and Tyra had to laugh at the thought. But he continued: Emelie, who was self-supporting, ought to be able to get a passbook.

No, that was not even worth thinking about. Emelie would never give them alcohol, not even if she were to gain from it.

He sighed at the wickedness and foolishness of the world around them and fell asleep. Snoring was heard through the thin wallboards.

And then it wasn't long before the morning light began to make its way in. A few hours later, the windows in the fumigated tenements were thrown open by men wearing gasmasks.

When David walked over the hill, he saw the sun shining on all the open casements.

In the evening, they got to move home again. The outing was over. Everyone carried back their rags and their bedbugs.

MOVING DAY

Since the first of April that year fell on a Sunday, the moving vans had been in motion the whole Saturday before. Many took the opportunity to change domicile; if they were in luck, they could even get to live a month or so for free since the landlords were having a hard time getting places rented out. A lot of people enjoyed moving, thought it was exciting and fun to try something new.

Jenny thought so, had talked for a long time about their needing to find a new and better apartment. Now times were pretty good, even if there were still many unemployed. Emelie, of course, had a fine and secure position as manager of the large grocery store on Folkungagatan, and Jenny had had plenty of engagements for a while. Just now she was playing in "The Österman Brothers' Shrews" at the Mosebacke Theater.

Jenny, widow of Emelie's youngest brother, had for a long time shared a household with Emelie—soon it would be thirty years. First in the little ramshackle house on the hill where Katarinavägen now ran. The last twenty years had been in the large apartment houses on Åsögatan.

Naturally, it was quite difficult to live on the fifth floor without an elevator and with the outhouse in the courtyard. But they were used to having it this way. If Emelie had been alone in choosing, they would have remained where they were. Not because she liked it so much, she didn't actually, but because she thought that every change brought along a certain amount of insecurity.

Jenny saw only the gains to be made by the change, Emelie only the losses. So much and so many had been lost over the years that she became ever more anxious at the prospect of each change, just wished that everything could stay the way it was.

Things were quite good now. She and Jenny got along well together, despite their differences. And they had plenty of space. Besides the two of them, there was Jenny's youngest daughter who still lived at home—Elisabet, who would soon turn eighteen.

They had been so many before… Jenny and her two daughters, Bärta and all her children, and Gunnar. It was almost unbelievable that it had worked, that they had all had room here.

Gunnar was probably the one who had been dearest to her in any case. And when she saw him she felt like her life had had meaning. The time when she had come to take care of him, he had been just a little browbeaten, wretched creature. With her, he had grown up and become what he was.

Gunnar was also Bärta's child, of course, but he was something more as well, something his half-siblings were not: He was Emelie's brother's child. August and Bärta had met during the period when Bärta lived as a boarder at Emelie's mother's house. By then, August had already been adopted by the upper-class Bodins. But he had conceived a son with Bärta, though it had taken a long time before he himself found out about it. Emelie had known and taken care of Gunnar long before Bärta and her other children had moved in with her.

Now Bärta had been dead for many years, and her children were grown. But what had happened a long time ago had led to August once again becoming a brother, to Emelie's gaining him back.

Emelie could not leave the store; it was Saturday and there was a lot to do. But her thoughts were of home. Would they be able to pack the last things now without her? Gunnar must have arrived by now; he had promised to help them, and he had arranged for the truck as well. Jenny would make sure they got a little dinner, then she would have to rush to the theater. It was absurd that she and Jenny could not be there the whole time. But they had tried to get as much done as possible in advance; almost everything was packed and ready. Emelie had been up late every night preparing.

Not that they owned so much—but when it came time to move,

there was still a lot. Jenny held onto so much, too: theater posters and photographs, paper flowers, and old clothes. And Emelie herself had her souvenirs as well that she had put away in drawers. When the day came that she no longer existed, they could throw it all away.

Finally, it was seven o'clock, and she could lock the door. The shop assistant had promised to tidy up the shop so that she could leave as soon as they closed and the cash register was counted up.

Still, by the time she got home, it was almost eight o'clock, and Jenny had left long before. Elisabet had made coffee for Gunnar and Bengt, who had also come to help out. Emelie didn't think she had time to eat, so she made do with a cup of coffee. She inquired after Gunnar's family and heard that Hjordis and the children were fine. And Bengt being able to come ... newly married as he was. Well, he did want to help out. He had always been so kind and helpful.

Emelie talked to the two men, "the boys" as she called them. Elisabet was silent as usual. There was something a little aloof about her, as if she was keeping a distance. It had always been this way, and even though the girl had lived her entire life with Emelie, they were almost a little constrained with each other.

When Emelie looked at Elisabet, she could really feel that she herself had gotten old. Elisabet belonged so clearly to the new and incomprehensible era, with her boyish, short hair and dress that ended above the knees. And underneath she wore almost nothing; that was the way it was supposed to be these days. If she was sitting a little carelessly, you could see the goosebumps where her stockings ended. When Emelie was that age, she at least had been properly dressed.

Elisabet was surely behind all of Jenny's talk of moving. The girl wanted to live better; there was no one who despised the outhouse more than she did. She knew that there was a better way, and she did not want to go on living someplace she could not find acceptable.

While they were drinking their coffee, the driver arrived, a friend of Gunnar's, and he, too, had a cup. Then the boys began to carry everything down. There was not much furniture, and none of it was especially heavy. A few chairs, tables, and beds, a wooden kitchen sofa, and the little bureau that Emelie's mother had received when she got married. The bags of bedclothes, the boxes with household utensils, clothing, and linen. Since the truck was small, it was packed full anyway, but it only had to make one trip.

After everything had been carted away, Emelie walked alone through the apartment, lighting her way with a candle, looking in all the nooks and on the kitchen shelves. Nothing had been forgotten; they had scrubbed everything ahead of time. She had a rag left and wiped off the kitchen floor one last time. It didn't have to be any cleaner since there would be repairs made before any new tenants moved in. They would finally get done now, after the landlord had refused to do them for many years.

Here was where they had lived. Happy days, unhappy ones, too. She felt like she could see Bärta sitting in the shadow in the corner by the stove. Not everything that had happened here had been so good. But would she be able to get used to something new, feel at home? Though that was just the way she had felt when they had moved here, too, over twenty years ago.

Nothing had been forgotten. Emelie stuffed the rag and the stub of the candle in a bag, locked the outer door pensively. She walked down the stairs, rang the doorkeeper's bell on the ground floor and left the keys they had and said good-bye. So now there were no more keys, and, for an instant, it felt like she no longer had any home, as if all doors were locked for her.

Outside on the street, the moving van stood loaded and ready. They asked her if she wanted to ride, but she preferred to walk. It was only a few blocks away to Erstagatan after all. Even if they had moved, they had stayed in the same area; that had been her stipulation.

The building they moved into was not that new; it was not one of the many that had been built after the abolishment of the rent control law. Whole new sections of the city had been erected or were under new construction during recent years: Atlasområdet, Kristineberg. Five thousand to six thousand new apartments per year, August had said. He was a building contractor and knew.

It was not so fancy that they had an elevator, but they were only going to live up two flights. The stairway was light and wide, Emelie thought. She reached the door, which as yet had no nameplate. It stood open. Elisabet had gone ahead and opened it, and they had begun carrying things in. She felt like a stranger on a visit when she stepped inside. But, of course, she had been up here and looked around with Jenny once, before they had decided. It consisted of one room plus a kitchen and a little hallway; not much bigger than what they had had before, but lighter and more comfortable, of course. Elisabet stood inside the bathroom and ran water in the sink. For once, she was not silent and removed, but excited.

"Look!" she said. "Come and see how nice it is!"

And Emelie had to look at the water that ran in the sink and the toilet seat of white porcelain and the gas stove in the kitchen and the new kind of windows with double panes that were never taken down.

They would live with the same arrangement as they had in the old apartment, Jenny and Elisabet in the one room and Emelie in the kitchen. It was the most practical way. Emelie was the first one up, and she needed to make coffee for herself before she went to the store. If she slept in the kitchen, she would avoid waking up Jenny, who was out late in the evenings and preferred to sleep in the mornings.

Gunnar and Bengt carried the beds into the room—the beds that, with the help of pillows and coverlets, would be transformed into sofas during the day. The bureau went in the room, the wooden sofa in the kitchen—Emelie slept on that.

Emelie did not want "the boys" to be too late. Their wives might get worried if they were too long, she thought. So once they had carried everything up and helped put the furniture in place, they left. It was too late for hammering any nails in the walls, and besides Jenny would certainly want to be there and decide where her mirror would hang. It was her pride and joy that she had bought when the displays from the Panoptikon Wax Museum were sold off.

They could only satisfy themselves with putting in place whatever they needed to go to sleep. Tomorrow was Sunday and then they could set to the whole day. Maj, Jenny's oldest daughter, would surely come, too, and help them.

For once, it was truly jolly and easy to work together with Elisabet. She was happier and more approachable than she usually was. And Emelie regretted that she had resisted and not wanted to move for so long; it seemed to mean so much to the girl now.

When Jenny got home from the theater, they made coffee again. And they sat among the boxes and bags and talked a while. Emelie brought out the portrait of Olof, and Jenny asked if she could have it. She would go to a framer and have it framed. Emelie talked about the girl they had as a boarder once, Gullpippi, who had painted it on a leftover piece of cloth. Olof had only been seven then, but one could see that he already showed signs of his sickness, the tuberculosis that destroyed him.

Somehow, their sense of kinship felt stronger than usual that evening. And Emelie hoped this was a good sign, that they would like it there and live happily in their new apartment.

Maj came over on Sunday morning with husband, and child. Erik's taking time off was a surprise; normally he was always engaged in work in the Kilbom Party. In a way he was, of course, still engaged in it; it was the party he thought of and talked about. The other day, they had staged a coup against the Social Democratic Youth League, which was holding a meeting in Viktoria Hall. In spite of the organizers' refusing to hold a discussion, Gustav Johansson had jumped up and given a reply to Arthur Engberg's speech. And some enterprising soul had turned off the lights in the hall so the whole thing had ended in an uproar. Now the poor Socialists were completely hysterical; the Communist Youth League was in the process of taking over their entire "Stockholm Week" that they had advertised so widely. And then it was the waitresses at Feith's who did not want to organize. Someone should take them in hand and deal with them, commensurate with their wages—as boycott breakers.

Maj tried to calm him down. They had come to see the apartment and lend a hand, not to discuss politics. It would be best now if Emelie gave them orders so they could do something useful.

Elisabet was laying shelf paper in the kitchen cupboards. They had borrowed a pretty unsteady ladder, and when she was to do the cupboard highest up, she had to ask someone to hold it. Erik was closest and unoccupied besides, so she asked him. He sat on a kitchen chair and held the ladder. It started to sway, and he looked up and was startled at the view he got. Girls these days were the limit.

She was reaching and straining to get the paper onto the highest shelf. The ladder wobbled a little even though he was holding onto it. "You're not going to fall?" he asked, reaching up and placing one arm around her legs. And he wondered what she would say if he let his hand glide up under her skirt and into the open panty legs.

"Let me go. It's done now," she said quickly and came down a step. "Hand me what's on the table. They are going in here."

He stood up a little unwillingly and handed her the cans that were to go up there. He could not resist teasing her a little, had to ask if girls weren't wearing anything underneath these days. She grew angry and went to give him a sharp reply. But then Emelie walked in, and she kept silent and got down from the ladder.

The restlessness of desire irritated Erik. He was wound up from work and duties; there were constantly people waiting for him, demanding that he come forth with initiatives and ideas. At the same time, things were not really right between him and Maj. One thing led to another. The agitation made him restless, drove him on to new tasks that kept him from home, and Maj felt abandoned. And when things were like this, it was as if he could not take the time to make everything right again. Instead, he stayed away, seeking calm and desire that did not cost him as much. And Maj could well guess what he was up to, that he had his little affairs on the side. She pulled away, grew cold. She did not come out with any reproaches or harsh words, but her tone said enough. It was all very well to talk about "free love," but in practice it was bafflingly difficult. Love bound you, and just now he did not feel like he had the energy to be more bound than he already was with other responsibilities. Yet he did not want to let Maj go. Although it could happen so simply—since they had never really gotten married. That time, it was Maj who had wanted to be "free."

Their five-year-old son, Henning, came out into the kitchen. Emelie had promised that he would get stewed rhubarb purée. If he got that, he would sit still and eat it as long as there was any left.

Of course, Erik was fond of the boy; he was proud of his son. But now he didn't really feel like he had the energy for him either. He started to shout when the boy spilled purée on the oilcloth tablecloth. And Maj came and wiped it up. Though she did not say a word, every movement she made was a reproach.

"Well, I guess I had better take off," he said. "They are probably waiting for me at the youth club meeting this afternoon."

"Yes, you do that," Maj answered. "Henning and I will manage just fine home alone."

"So long then," he said and waved his hand to them all as he was leaving.

"Thanks for the help," said Jenny.

"It was my pleasure. You offer such a lovely view," he said and glanced sideways at Elisabet. She blushed.

"The view isn't that remarkable," Jenny replied. "But, of course, it is a little brighter and more open here than at the other place."

"Absolutely," he said. "Here you can see all the way up to heaven."

When he was standing on the streetcar, he fantasized about what might have happened if he and Elisabet had been alone. But you never knew how you were going to be received. If they were waiting and hoping, or if they were going to scream and call for help. They invited you and warded you off at the same time.

No, he was no harasser of women, not any kind of seducer. He was actually only tired. And starved for love. His body felt tense and hard, agitation tingled inside him. Without wanting to, he would go after one of the girls in the youth club. Though he longed for home, and Maj.

CONTEMPTIBLE REVOLUTIONARY

Even if circumstances had been relatively good for a few years, there was a sense of new crises ahead. Many employers tried to implement wage decreases and one workers' conflict followed another. Distrust grew; the city's police chief bought up machine guns that were to be used in the event of a riot. It was said that the money for the purchase was left by the Swedish-Finnish committee from 1918, the year of the Finnish civil war.

For many people, the Soviet Union stood as an ever-increasing danger, and the newspapers speculated about an armed Communist coup attempt. For some, fascist Italy was a model. There they had established solid order and even managed to get the trains to depart at regular times.

Uneasiness and increasing antagonisms gave the little Communist Party wide opportunities. It had managed to overcome the succession of party splits in 1924, and the number of votes and newspaper editions had increased. Now its members felt the wind in their favor and tried to take advantage of it; their industriousness grew ever more feverish. Strikes were fomented; a Russian-Swedish friendship committee was formed to help the striking Swedish mineworkers. The agreement was an idealistic one since the Russian workers would never be able to strike and demand service in return for the million they contributed.

Those who were in the party leadership and those who were in charge of the daily duties worked hard, sacrificed all their strength, time and money. Einar Olsson, who had become the labor union's chairman, kept up a continual round of parties, bazaars, and exhibitions. The activities irritated the strictest theoreticians who did not want to organize bazaars but revolutions. Could anyone imagine Lenin standing at the bingo table?

But the money that came in was certainly needed, so Einar Olsson got to have his way. As well as Erik, who also first and foremost had to work with organizing and bringing in money. He was a clever businessman; they had known that from the old days, and could accomplish more in this role than as a politician. He felt like they received the results of his industry and competence with a mixture of gratitude and contempt. The money was needed. But he who made it could hardly be an orthodox proletarian.

Kilbom, who had an understanding of the economic side of the work, could not be of much use to them now. He had overexerted himself and spent long periods of time in hospitals abroad.

Why?

Why did he tear himself apart and tear apart his relationship with Maj? Why did he destroy his health and his finances?

The answer was self-evident: for the sake of the working class and the cause itself, so that the proletariat would be victorious someday. He had been born into the proletariat, as one of the poorest of the poor, had been forced to support himself as soon as he had finished school. He could remember the years when he and his siblings had been able to eat their fill once a week—on Sundays when Emelie had them over for dinner. Hunger itself had taught him to hate, driven him to the party.

But sometimes he doubted, felt himself held in contempt by those he worked for. Then he did not know why he lived the way he did. Imagined that it had just happened, that he had landed in the hamster wheel and could not get off.

Before, he had been able to manage his own business on the side, had made deals and done really well. Gotten himself a big apartment, donated some money to the party now and then.

But they knew what he was good at and did not relinquish him until they had talked him into working entirely for the party. After that no one wanted to recall what he had given up and sacrificed. Then the only talk was of how badly the members would react if they thought that the salaried employees were overpaid.

Of course, he had resisted at times and threatened to quit. Yet it was not only out of solidarity that he remained there. Despite everything, he liked it when the work piled up and the tasks seemed impossible. In any case, he had to clear up what he had taken on, and then he would have to see.

But it certainly had demanded a lot. They had to move to a smaller apartment, and Maj had taken on extra work to manage their expenses. She knew how to economize and live cheaply. He did not; that he recognized freely. And his frenzied activity cost him, when he thought that every minute was vital for him to get everything done—when he took a cab instead of the streetcar and ate at a bar instead of at home.

He probably had sacrificed more than he had intended. And in truth, he was something of an egotist. He could not understand himself. Maybe it was all because he was too tired and driven to resist.

More and more he thought: If I find something good, I am going to leave all this behind. Still, he stayed where he was. Despite the fact that he understood he would never play any big role in the party. It was another kind of man they elected to Parliament and City Council, not someone who was busy with the contemptible business dealings. Others learned Russian and German, they attended congresses and secret meetings in Moscow, they came home with their information and were the ones to decide everything. They knew the order of the psalms for the day, if they were going to speak for the unification of the labor movement or for irreconcilable battle against the "Socialist Fascists."

He had to let them have their way; he took care of the day-to-day, such as, traveling out to General Motors to talk with the strikers and try to encourage them to hold out. The company had hired people from the Petterson strikebreakers' bureau on Rådmansgatan, twenty-five of "Dung-Petter's scabs." One day, when Erik got there, a fistfight was breaking out between the strikers and the strikebreakers. One of those willing to work pulled out a pistol and shot several shots. And Erik delivered a report to the party newspaper that the strikebreaker scum was firing with live ammunition. But in the bourgeois newspapers, they claimed it was only a starting pistol.

On other days, he organized ticket sales. The musical revue, "They Live It Up" written by Ture Nerman and Gustave Johansson, was premiering on Easter Eve at the Auditorium Theater. And then he had to prepare for the First of May, painting the words: *Down with attempts to divide! Down with the warmongers and the white executioners!*

There was always something that had to be done; there was never time to stay up and think over his personal problems. Sometimes, he could go days at a time without seeing Maj, even though they lived together. When he got home, she and the boy were asleep; when he woke up, she had gone to work and on the way there left Henning at her mother's. He would have liked to talk it all out with Maj and make everything right again. But he didn't dare, didn't have time. It was not so easy to explain everything that had happened, get her to understand that it didn't mean anything that he had gone to others. She was not unreasonable, but he had, of course, gotten himself entangled all too much, with all too many—out of desperation and exhaustion because he had not had the energy, had the courage or the time to talk to Maj.

Maybe it would get better in the summer, if they could find the money and the time to travel somewhere together. For a week at least. But then it was only a matter of beginning preparations for the fall's important election; then he would have to put in all his time and energy.

Of course, Maj felt bitter at times. Set aside, forgotten, betrayed. But she had known what she was in for, had known Erik so long, since they were kids. She could feel sorry for him, see how he wore himself out. She had been there when such periods of hectic work ended, with him collapsing and not having the energy for anything more, just weeping.

Despite everything, we still belong together, she had thought. Even if the party consumes him entirely. If nothing else, then for the boy's sake.

Despite everything, still, even if, if nothing else. The words revealed in some way the outermost position. Beyond that, their feeling of solidarity ended. But it was not only the outermost and last position, but also the first. With all these reservations she had moved in with him. She had been so well aware of how difficult it was going to be and how little she had to hope for. That was probably why she had not wanted to marry him; she had retained her possibility of retreat, wanted to be free. It was not he who had said no. He could have had his political reasons otherwise, or seen something petty bourgeois in marriage.

The way things had gone she had to wonder: Did they really belong together anymore?

She didn't know. Thought only that there must be some reason that two people tried to stay together, and they barely had one anymore. They tried to retain their composure and speak to each other in a friendly manner, but neither of them could avoid hearing the coldness in the other's voice, to feel their own coldness themselves. If it continued like this—would they then not freeze themselves and their feelings to death? And what joy would their son have from their staying together if they did it for his sake?

But it was difficult to come to a decision. What would happen afterward? Hard to get work, even supplementary work. The boy needed her; she wanted to stay home with him as much as possible.

So she tried to just go on living. Without really wanting to live like that, only since it had become like that, and that for the moment she did not see any other way out. Sometimes she thought she sensed he was waiting for her to say something that might pave the way to reconciliation, to a renewed effort. But she let the opportunities pass by, did not have the energy to take advantage of them, could not manage to believe in him one more time.

He might have come to her—but she sat silent and rigid and watched him leave. She knew that he went to others and that he did it because she would not forgive him without his asking for it. He was too proud to ask. And she was too proud to give it without his asking.

She felt like the room she was sitting in was charged with bitter silence; it was so tangibly present that it almost hurt to breathe. Mustn't the child feel it, be injured by it? How long would they have the strength to continue like this?

Maj did not share Erik's political ideas, was certainly not as much of a radical as he was. She thought he became too hard and caustic sometimes. He saw everything in black and white, or rather black and red.

But she voted for the party he belonged to and went with him to meetings sometimes, if she could find someone to take care of the boy. She preferred not to ask Beda since Erik was not really nice to his sister. It wasn't out of cruelty maybe, but he grew impatient and brusque and then Beda would become frightened and start to stammer. Otherwise, she spoke rather well now. Before, it used to be hard to get her to speak an entire sentence.

On the First of May, Maj walked in the demonstration anyway and participated in the rally at Norra Bantorget. She walked just behind the group of little Communist Pioneers who were carrying placards with slogans such as *Down with Corporal Punishment in Schools* and *First of May Holiday for All Working Children.* She gave a little start when she saw a twelve-year-old with a picture of a burning Bible and the text *Down with Christian Instruction—Separation of School and Church.* The boy did not have time to take many steps before the police stepped in and took both him and his placard away.

Was that placard one of those that Erik had painted? Had he coldly calculated that the one who carried it would be arrested by the police? Maybe; "the martyrs" were certainly of some use. And if it served "the cause," he most likely did not care what happened to the boy.

She did not like it, did not want to imagine that her son might be placed in the same situation in a few years. And despite the warmth of the spring sunshine, she felt the cold again, the bitterness toward he who was prepared to sacrifice even his own kin for the cause. That group solidarity frightened her sometimes; it forced people to take a stand before they were mature enough to do so. Instead of martyrs who were leading the way for what they saw was right, victims were created, uncertain poor creatures who had to answer for something they could not defend.

The demonstration wended its way along. Many of the young women were wearing light-colored trench coats that shone in the sun. They arrived at Kungsgatan, their red banners flying between the gray buildings and the hillsides that were not yet built up beside Kungstornen. Hawkers offered *Revolt* and *The Warning Bell* and sold red demonstration roses and carnations.

At Gärdet, they were using loudspeakers for the first time, and finally the speechmakers were relieved of standing and hollering like foghorns in the wind. Above the expansive, billowing light green meadow, a few airplanes floated like gray birds against the blue sky.

A few days later the large airship *Italia* flew over the city, on its way to the North Pole. Maj was in Vasa Park with Henning. She pointed out the vessel to the boy, and they stood and watched how the large cigar-shaped ship of shining steel disappeared into the west, toward Äppelviken, where it was to pass over the Swedish member of the expedition, Finn Malmgren's, home.

She was still tied down, to the earth and to a daily existence that was beginning to feel more and more unbearable. She envied everyone who was able to flee, slip away.

What she had long expected had happened, again. Erik was in a state of total collapse and had been obliged to take time off to rest for at least a week. It was not only the work and circumstances at home that had hit him so hard; it was also his colleagues' lack of understanding. He easily created animosity with others. Many were irritated by his arrogance and his general comportment. At the same time, he was easily offended, so sensitive to anything resembling criticism. He had often complained that his work within the party had not been met with enough understanding, feeling like they members held him in contempt. He exaggerated surely, was overly sensitive. Yet there must have been something to it.

He had wanted Maj to go along and travel somewhere with him. But he could not cope with the boy.

Had she dared hope for a genuine change, she would have tried to arrange it somehow. Now she had been promised a part-time job, and she really did not want to leave Henning behind completely without her.

Erik had to go away alone.

THE QUIET STREET

The street followed the slope from the edge of the White Hills down to broad Folkungagatan. Between high apartment buildings lay small dilapidated wooden shacks, woodsheds and an old stone cottage still standing in its garden. The fence enclosing the cosmetics factory's large yard ran along a whole block; leaves of shady trees spread their branches out over the top of the fence. And high above trees and small houses rose the factory's smokestacks that whistled every morning at seven o'clock.

One hour later Henning came here with his mother. Things had been like this since she started working. They rode the streetcar through the entire city, and Mama was always worried that something would happen to make them late. She would mutter bitterly to herself when cars and streetcars were backed up at the locks at Slussen, and once they had stepped off at the Folkungagatan stop, they would usually half run up the hill and up the stairs to where his grandmother, Mormor, lived. And then Mormor would barely have time to open the door before Mama was running down the stairs again, since she was going to catch the same streetcar on which they had ridden there. It would have turned around and been on its way back into town.

Once Mama had left, everything would be calm again for a short while. Mormor usually had not had time to get dressed before he arrived. He would play in the kitchen while he waited for her, a little excited. You never really knew what Mormor would come up with. Sometimes she would sneak up to the door and say "moo" like a cow, sometimes she would hide so that he had to find her. Mormor was not like other grown-ups. It was as if she was playing all the time. One time she got dressed up so that at first he thought a totally strange lady had entered the apartment. But when he grew frightened and was about to cry, the strange lady took off both her hat and her hair—and then he saw that it was only Mormor.

Now he was so used to her pranks that there was no anxiety in his excitement, only happy expectancy. He heard her turning down the door handle, sensed that the door slid open. But he waited, pretended that he had not noticed her. Then he heard a dog bark, and he quickly whirled around. There Mormor stood on all fours in the open doorway, and she barked and barked.

He jumped up on her back and got to ride around on the kitchen floor until she was panting with the effort. Then he had to go in the other room and hunt; she usually hid a candy that he would have to find.

She drank her morning coffee at the kitchen table. He climbed up on a chair and kept her company. Even though he had eaten at home, he got a piece of coffee cake and a glass of milk.

"Be a cow, Mormor," he begged.

"Naa," she demurred.

But he knew that if he asked long enough, she would eventually give in.

And she pulled up her hair so that it stood like two horns over her forehead and blew on him with her nose until he squealed with delight. The whole time her mouth was chewing, as if she were tugging and tugging on something that was hard to swallow. And then she swallowed—and stuck her nose in the air and mooed.

Someone rang the doorbell. And Mormor hurriedly patted her hair back in place—but he ran off and opened the door. It was the concierge who was going to look at the faucet in the kitchen.

"Was that the factory whistle that blew?" the concierge asked. "Though at this hour—"

"It was Mormor!" shouted Henning.

She quickly showed the concierge the dripping faucet.

While the concierge was working, Mormor shushed him and made faces; shushing so he would not laugh out loud and making faces to show it was not so serious. So everything grew sillier and sillier. And when the concierge was done and had left, the two of them were both so wound up that they almost exploded. Imagine that the concierge thought it was the factory whistle that blew!

No, now they had to calm down and decide what they were going to do, said Mormor. Should they go to the Uphill Park or to the Downhill Park? The Uphill Park was the White Hills, the Downhill Park the square on Folkungagatan. The White Hills had walks and winding paths while the park down the hill was a sandy desert with trees here and there. But today he had seen that there was a big sand pile down there so that was why he voted for the Downhill Park.

"Oh, yes," said Mormor. "We can jump in the sand."

He had not thought of that; that was a new opportunity for delight. And then he was in a hurry and admonished her for pretending to be so eager that she did everything all wrong, putting her hat on backwards and turning her coat inside out. Finally they were on their way in spite of all this, half running down the street, past the urinal that was called "Round Vic" and looked like a little fortress tower. A man who was buttoning up his fly stood at the entrance and gaped at them in wonder as they flew past.

The sand pile was truly enormous. Mormor would probably have liked to jump in herself—though, of course, she did not dare, for then people would really begin to wonder. But Henning climbed up to the top and jumped and jumped again and fell and sat down on his behind and laughed.

"Just watch out for your clothes," said Mormor. "Try to jump without falling. Otherwise Mama might be unhappy."

He must have been jumping for a whole hour while Mormor sat on a bench beside it and read one of her scripts. When he finally grew tired, he came over to her and got brushed off and was praised for not getting his clothes dirtier than that.

"Oh, for heaven's sake!" she said suddenly. "Your shoes!"

He looked down. And was horrified at the sight. His new shoes were completely ruined, completely scraped up at the toes.

"Mama won't be happy now," said Mormor. "But it was my fault, you couldn't help it. I should have thought of that."

"We will just have to buy new shoes," she said at last. "There is nothing else to be done."

A little downhearted, they walked along the street, crossing over to the row of buildings on the other side, as if the park scared them now. They got to the shop where Aunt Emelie worked. He called her aunt but actually she was really Mama's aunt. She came to the door and saw immediately how ruined his shoes were. Mormor and Aunt Emelie talked it over a little, while he stood looking in the window. He heard Mormor ask if she could borrow some money. Aunt Emelie went in and got it. When they were leaving, she called out that they should buy shoes as close to the ones he had as possible.

Exciting things always happened with Mormor. Now he would get to buy new shoes, too.

After shoe shopping, they went home to eat breakfast. Mormor made porridge, and he helped her set the table. Just as they were ready, Aunt Emelie arrived. She was panting, had walked as fast as she could. In reality, she had a whole hour free and could have taken it a little easier. Mormor said that often. But Aunt Emelie always had something waiting at the shop. She hardly took the time to sit when she ate; she stood and ate at the same time as she watched the coffee pot. And when the coffee was ready, she poured herself a cup and then ran out of the kitchen and put on her coat. Then she drank the coffee out of a saucer and was on her way.

But Mormor and Henning took it easy. They really relaxed afterward, once Aunt Emelie had left again, stretched out their legs and made no hurry to finish their meal. Mormor drank two cups of coffee and smoked a cigarette with each cup. She was the only lady he knew who smoked and that smoking was, of course, something that Aunt Emelie could not really condone. When she came home, she always opened the windows.

Mormor tried to blow smoke rings, but time after time, he made her laugh so that the smoke came out like a puff. Finally, she managed to form a ring anyway and he rushed to stick his finger through it and

Mormor pretended to cry over her torn-apart ring.

Then they went to the Uphill Park.

They climbed across the hills, across the grassy lawns, between the leafy trees. They threw themselves down on a hillside and spread out the blanket they had brought. Mormor had bought a newspaper to read. It was not the paper they had at home and that Papa wrote in, but another one, bigger and thicker. And there were pictures in it of the big airship that he had seen fly over Vasa Park last spring. He had heard that the ship had crashed on the ice up at the North Pole. Now it stood that they had found some of the ones who had tried to wander across the ice afterward. But the Swede who had been on the expedition was dead.

Since Mama was going out this evening, it was decided that Henning would stay with Mormor overnight. This happened from time to time, and then he got to sleep in a strange thing that they brought down from the attic. They called it the fold-out bed, and it looked like an accordion that could be pulled out to a bed. Emelie and her younger sister who had gone to America had slept in it when they were little.

Mormor went to the theater; she was playing at the Tantolunden now. He was left alone with Elisabet for a while. She had come home from the office where she worked. She was his aunt, but he understood that she was still not one of the real grown-up adults who made all their own decisions.

Elisabet made the meal, and when Aunt Emelie arrived from the shop, they ate. Emelie was no longer in such a hurry; she took it easy. She talked with him and wanted to look at his new shoes, and thought they had been really successful with their purchase.

Everything was so different together with Aunt Emelie, as if it had become a completely different kitchen. Aunt would never indulge in any practical jokes. But after the hubbub of the day, it felt nice and pleasant to just sit and talk. Though now it was Elisabet who was getting things going a little. She wanted them to go up to the White Hills and listen to the orchestra there and take some coffee with them.

A little unwillingly, Aunt Emelie gave in; she would probably have much preferred to stay home. But they packed their basket and took along a blanket. They sat on the slope alongside the small white music pavilion up on the hill behind the church. Below lay the factories and Hammarby Canal and the lake in the evening mist; everywhere on the hillside, families spread themselves out on the grass. And on the other side of the hill stood Ceder's Café where many passed through the gate in its red fence and took a seat on the verandas surrounding the four-sided open space.

It grew dark; the orchestra arrived and even more people gathered on the hillside. Elisabet got up and went closer to see and hear better, maybe looking for some of the friends from her schooldays who usually got together here. If she met up with them she would probably disappear afterward; she did that the last time.

When it got to be nine o'clock Aunt Emelie thought it was time to go back home. Henning should not be out too late. The music was still playing when they walked down the hill. Elisabet was nowhere in sight. Before them lay Sofia Church like a giant dark sugarloaf; lights shone from the community garden plots' small houses, and laughter rose in waves from the open-air theater beside the gardens.

Erstagatan lay quiet in the warm, late-summer darkness. There were no streetcars here like at home on the street where he lived, hardly any cars either at this hour. Only one or another wanderer on his way home or to one of the beer cafés.

Newly displayed election posters gleamed from the fences. One preached that the person who voted for the Labor Party voted for the breaking up of family ties, children running wild, and moral degeneracy. Plundering Cossacks illustrated these declarations.

He held Aunt Emelie's hand, tripping along, feeling rather sleepy now. It was nice that the fold-out bed had been made up before they went out.

AUTUMN MEETINGS

The workers would remember the parliamentary election that fall as the "Cossack election." Election campaigning became more violent and acrimonious than usual, and antagonisms were stirred up. The voters were driven to political extremes; the right and the Communists triumphed. The newly elected Social Democratic Party leader, Per Albin Hansson, had to record his party's greatest defeat of all time; fifteen seats were lost in the Parliament. The liberal Prime Minister Ekman was succeeded by the election's victor, Admiral Lindman. Since the remaining right-wing parties did not want to be part of the government, it meant a continued balancing act, a new minority government.

The victorious Communist Party, which had doubled the number of representatives in Parliament, also had reason to fear for the future. Opposition within the party was growing stronger, and "Hugo the fault-finder," as Sillén was called, criticized Killbom even more harshly. And for Erik it felt like all his work had been in vain; it was not worth winning outwardly when they could not be united inwardly. He began to be more and more tired of party work, to long for something else. Despite the defeat of the Social Democrats in this election, the labor movement was becoming an even greater force to reckon with; each passing year, the industrial workers grew in number and the trade unions increased in size. They should be able to take care of much that was for now left to private capital, start their own companies. And the day they did it, people like Erik would be needed, people with the right point of view, but who also had an understanding of business. One day his chance would come; until then, he would have to try to stay put and continue working within the party.

He dreamed of the day of transformation, the day when he would really mean something and get to direct an enterprise. Then his relationship with Maj would transform itself into something different as well. Did he long for things to become good between them again? Or for someone more amenable and less critical to stand by his side? It was as if Maj knew him all too well. Would she, who had seen him fail so many times, really believe that he had succeeded, if he actually had? And besides, could it be that he would need someone who was a more ordinary person than Maj?

For once, he had promised to pick up Henning at Jenny's. Maj was working overtime. He himself was going to sit at home and write. He took the streetcar up to Söder and grumbled over the fact that it went so intolerably slow. And here Maj sat on it and went back and forth two times a day to drop off and pick up the boy. But she had stronger nerves, of course. It was actually necessary for her to work, but he did not really like it. It emphasized his failure and made her independent of him.

Finally, he was there, walked up Erstagatan and thought that it appeared almost rural and hushed. The trees in front of the factory fence had turned yellow now; ahead of him walked the lamplighter and one lantern after another was lit and the lights grew into yellow balls.

It was Elisabet who opened the door when he rang. She stepped aside, a little startled when she saw who it was, and he did not know if it irritated or flattered him.

She called through the door into the room: "It's Erik." Then she walked across the hall and locked herself in the bathroom.

Jenny and Henning were sitting and cutting out paper dolls at the table in the room, long looping rows of them out of newspaper. Emelie came in from the kitchen and greeted him. They could not offer him any dinner because they were expecting company. Jenny and Henning had eaten earlier, and Elisabet and Emelie had barely had time to eat a sandwich. It was Emelie's brother, August, who was coming.

"Big company, then," Erik said. "The building contractor himself."

Emelie responded that August did not see himself as so important. He was really like one of them.

Erik pondered this and could not come up with having heard anything unfavorable about August Bodin. The guys who worked at Bodin's were known for belonging to "the old line," gray-hairs who could not be made much use of. But they, like the others, were probably taking advantage of the situation now. There was a lot of building going on, and there were a lot of opportunities for workers to lay down conditions.

Erik sensed that Emelie would have preferred him to leave before August arrived. And the boy should get home and get some sleep and he himself was going to write. Still, he lingered. To meet August or to look at Elisabet?

When the doorbell rang, Elisabet flew out of the bathroom. But Emelie opened the door and welcomed her brother. He had come in his own car. He had an Auburn with a high, narrow radiator.

August Bodin was going to turn sixty years old in a few months. He had gone gray in recent years; his hair was almost white. He had also grown a little heavier, not getting so much exercise, and his years of great vigor were over. Tranquility was not precisely what he had now; recent years had been filled with uncertainty in the construction industry. To be sure, the negotiations of 1924 and the devaluation of the krona had resulted in prices and wages sinking, but at least wages were rising again at full speed—partly due to the negotiations, partly, and not least, due to the workers' increasing skill at interpreting contract prices and settlements to their own advantage. If they did not get what they wanted, they stayed in their work sheds without working. The so-called shed sitters had become a real problem. You never knew which ones were sitting in the shed when you inspected building sites these days. And if you gave in, the rumor of the employees' victory reached other work sites and caused shed sitting in other places.

He talked about his troubles, how stressful things were, and how much time all these negotiations took. And Emelie thought it was too unfortunate that people could not be satisfied and stick to the conditions that had been agreed upon. But Erik thought it was about time the workers took back some of what they had lost during the ill-fated year of 1924, and now, when actions of the shed-sitting type got results, then it was foolish not to take advantage of the opportunities.

August explained that, of course, he wanted to pay fair wages. He had always done so and, thanks to that, he had a solid team of old, knowledgeable employees.

While he listened to Erik he remembered how he had sat like this many years ago and been verbally attacked. At that time, he himself had been young and quite insecure, just a little over twenty. It had been Thumbs, his parents' friend, who had attacked him then. And he had only been able to flee and afterward he could not meet with his siblings for many years. They were living with Thumbs and Matilda back then.

Emelie also may have been thinking of that day of the breakup of the family, long ago. He saw her anxiety, how she was trying to calm Erik down. But she did not need to be anxious; August was not feeling offended. He was too old and used to it, sat too securely. Words did not mean as much any longer.

He answered calmly, somewhat evasively, began to ask if Emelie had been out at Gunnar's place recently. And when it turned to talk of Gunnar's family—then Erik grew tired, noticed that it had gotten late and he had better take the boy home.

He said good-bye. And Henning was sleepy and fumbling and stretched out the wrong hand when he went to bow and leave. When Erik and the boy got down to Folkungagatan, an empty cab passed by, and he flagged it down. It was best that the boy be lying asleep when Maj came in, otherwise she would surely be cross.

Emelie wanted to make excuses. August mustn't take it the wrong way; he certainly knew Erik was a Communist. He calmed her down: He didn't care about what Erik had said. And actually it was not the demands for better terms that August had turned against. Rather, it was the fact that no contracts were valid any longer. If the construction workers pushed through better conditions at all the construction sites, it did not necessarily mean that it would affect the building contractors. It might mean instead that rents would go up. But in that case, it was important not to build so much that rents went down instead of up. Prices were determined by demand, of course.

The whole profession was just one big risky venture; that much he had learned. Right now, small apartments were most in demand, and so they were building these, even though they had a sense that larger apartments would be more sought after in a few years. The whole time they had to dread a surplus of housing that would make rents come down. And they could not keep the buildings they had built themselves unless as an exception. They were continually forced to free up their money for new construction. The deposits they had to make were large—and he wondered if any other branch of trade had been shaken by so many crises as the construction branch had.

Emelie felt sorry for her rich brother. What were the insignificant worries she had had through the years compared with those he bore? For her, it had been a matter of several kronor, for him, it had been tens of thousands. She put the coffeepot back on and persuaded him to drink a few more cups. And August got into a good mood and told stories about the contractors he had to deal with. Just now, he had a completely ideal project in the works: a villa for a millionaire that could basically cost whatever it took.

And then he talked about his family. About his daughters who were married now, all three, with men in quite good positions. Ida was completely occupied with visiting her grandchildren. And their son, Karl Henrik, had finally settled down and begun to get seriously involved with the company. August's dream had been that Karl Henrik and Gunnar would run the company together. Gunnar, of course, had the practical experience. But it never happened; the boys did not work very well together. And Gunnar had his own company; his carpentry business gave him a respectable livelihood.

Ten more years, at the most, if he lived that long. Then it was time to leave the company in younger hands. It might be time. He had led the firm for thirty-five years now, and it had been no easy job.

Emelie brought out the latest America letter, from their sister

Gertrud. Their sister talked about her family; several of her children were married to American citizens and were completely Americanized themselves. Rudolf had died a few years ago. He had been a collector on the underground streetcar line. Gertrud must feel very alone over there in that foreign land, Emelie thought. But Gertrud did not write that, and she had her children, of course. She lived somewhere on the outskirts of the big city New York, and did not get in so often to the tall buildings that were on the postcards she sent in the letter to Emelie.

They had grown up together only a few blocks from the building where Emelie lived, four siblings, children of a poor harbor worker who had died of consumption before he turned thirty-five. And after their mother's death ten years later, they had dispersed. August had already been adopted by the Bodins, Gertrud had emigrated, Olof died. Only Emelie had remained, close to their home and close to the material circumstances that had prevailed there. Still, much had changed for her as well. Sometimes she could hardly believe that she was living in the same city she had been born in.

And here they were sitting and reading the letter from the third member of what was left of their family circle. When August handed back the letter, he let his hand stroke Emelie's.

He put down his glasses, looked at the clock. So late already. And tomorrow would present many new problems.

"Thanks for this evening," he said. "It is always equally enjoyable to come here. One remembers so well here."

Emelie looked down on the quiet street through the window, saw how his car's headlights lit up, heard his motor start. And then August's car rolled away, to his world.

While Emelie washed the coffee cups, Elisabet made her own bed. She took off her dress and went to the bathroom to wash. Emelie grew cold just looking at the girl, could not resist asking if it wasn't soon time to dress a little more warmly. But Elisabet answered as she usually did—that she wasn't cold.

Elisabet locked the door behind her. Locking herself in felt liberating: Now no one could surprise her. Here in the new apartment, there was a light and tidy little room, the bathroom, where you could close yourself in and be alone. They had not had anything like this before, at their old place. Back there had been only the awful, foul-smelling earth closets down in the courtyard.

She used this new opportunity quite frequently and willingly. Would stand in front of the mirror in the little locked room and look at her image, as if she were searching for a secret. She would wrinkle her nose in annoyance. Otherwise, what she saw was pretty good. Her hair shingled and waved, her figure almost flat as required by the fashion. But were her legs a little too thick? Or too thin?

She demanded too much, was too critical, they said. She sought solitude but hated it at the same time. She had always gone her own way, had that slightly disdainful expression. Perhaps as a kind of protection against her mother's impulsiveness, against the friendliness that could be trying.

Always alone, she thought. Maj was ten years older and had had her friends; her mother had her theater world. Emelie was too old and could not really understand what was happening in this day and age.

Elisabet had not really connected with her classmates in school either. Now that school was over, she met up with some of them once in awhile—but then she was too critical. She thought that everything they occupied themselves with was so petty; they had no interests. The girls were giggly, and the boys only wanted to paw you and were clumsy and stupid.

She had begun to teach herself English, maybe mostly to have something to do. Maybe also to reach a goal someday: a better position. She worked as an intern in an office and had barely any salary at all. In fact, she was probably only an errand girl. But she would move on, and she would manage for herself. She was not going to have kids and not going to get married. She had learned that from her sister's fate if she had not grasped it anyway. Maj, who sat there with her son. And with Erik. Elisabet despised him. She would certainly figure out how to arrange things better for herself than Maj had.

Everything seemed easy and clear-cut. As long as she hung out only with some of the girls from her class. Even though they laughed and contradicted her when she came out with her views. Most of them could not think of anything more delightful than getting married and having children.

Then she had happened to run into a boy from her old confirmation class beside the music pavilion. They had left there together, and he had talked about the books he had read and about his plans for the future. It had been easy to talk to him, almost the first time she thought she had met a person it was fun to talk to, who had the same interests as hers. He liked theater, too, real theater, not the variety act her mother played in. They had walked for a whole hour and talked, and when they parted she thought it had felt like only a few minutes. She had met a boy who was different from the others, who was somehow like herself.

They had met again. Lennart had invited her to a café, and they had talked about Ingrid Undset's books and about Strindberg.

If one of the girls had seen them together, they would have believed that they were keeping company, that Elisabet was "in love." The girls comprehended so little. They could not understand that two people held interests in common and that was why they were meeting.

Besides, it didn't matter if her legs were too thin or too thick. It wasn't the intention that he look at her legs.

Finally, Elisabet unlocked the door to the bathroom, and Emelie, who had been standing in her nightgown and waiting a long time, got to go in.

"Good night," said Elisabet, and closed the door to the room.

"Sleep well," said Emelie. "And close the window so there isn't a draft on you."

But Elisabet let the window stay open, thought it felt nice to crawl into the bed and feel the coolness outside. Besides, her mother would hurry to close the window as soon as she came back. She was not at all as keen on fresh air.

IN THE SPRING SUN

The winter had been unusually cold and long—with boats frozen in and trains snowed in, coal shortages and firewood collections for the poor. At the end of April, winter was in full force amid enormous snowfalls. And on the First of May, the city was drowning in so much slush that the demonstrations had to be cancelled.

Perhaps that was why people welcomed the belated spring and the sun's warmth with greater wonderment than usual. For Elisabet, it was the first spring where she consciously felt she was young and alive.

She was still together with Lennart. They had begun to take a course in English together and, sometimes on a Saturday, they went to the movies. When the snow finally melted, they began to take Sunday walks, too. It was something new to her. Before she had usually sat at home on Sundays, possibly strolled a little through town or taken a ferry to Djurgården. With Lennart, she went beyond the tollgates and noticed—for the first time?—how close the big woods and the countryside lay. When you went past the warehouses and the community gardens on the outskirts, you were already away from most of the settled areas. The tracts with houses were only alongside some of the bigger roads and the streetcar lines.

It was like being liberated. Suddenly, there were wide open fields, big woods, quiet and solitude. It was wonderful to speak freely without somebody unbidden listening in and without having to think the whole time that she was being observed. But solitude also had its problems. Gradually, she came to understand that Lennart was not so completely unlike other boys, even if he was maybe shyer and nicer. At the same time, she was getting to know him so well that some of the shyness she herself had felt had disappeared. She began to find it quite natural for them to walk arm in arm, and for him to place his arm around her waist as they wandered along a country road back home to town, tired after a long day's exertions.

But she still drew a hard line that there would be no talk of anything other than friendship. If they teased her at home—Mama might use a word as ridiculous as "fiancé" when she talked about Lennart—she would become angry and lock herself inside the bathroom. And she would pretend not to hear when they stood outside and knocked and wanted to come in.

"No, thank you," she would say. "I don't intend to end up like Maj."

And then they would ask her for God's sake not to say something like that when Maj could hear it.

Mama and Emelie were so odd. Even they though were well aware of how hard things were for Maj, they still pretended that everything was fine. Not one bad word about Erik. The furthest they might go would be to say it was a pity for Maj that Erik was so busy. As if it would not be the best thing for Maj to be rid of him.

Elisabet could not comprehend this solidarity, this attempt to view those who were part of the family as benignly as possible. For her, it was more natural to judge those who were closest the most harshly. They were the ones she could find reason to feel ashamed of; they could become a burden.

Elisabet arrived home a little shaken up and unsure of herself, even somewhat unsure of what had actually happened in the almost overpowering sunshine. Hadn't he surely tried to kiss her, in any case? Only on the cheek and as if in passing, but still it was something new and something that she was not sure should happen.

She wanted to hide and be alone, ponder, not be disturbed. She had to decide if something had happened or not, if it was something she could allow, or something that should be blotted out and treated as if it never happened.

And there sat Erik's awful sister, Tyra, in the kitchen. Tyra would come by sometimes to say hello, as it was called, though she actually only came by to beg. Even for her, Mama and Emelie made up excuses, let her in and offered her coffee.

Elisabet tried to disappear into the bathroom, wanted to at least look in the mirror and somehow regain her composure and self-confidence before she said hello. But the bathroom was occupied. Apparently Tyra had one of her kids with her.

Elisabet was obliged to say hello, and Emelie poured her a cup of coffee before she had time to refuse.

David and Tyra had had an unusually tough winter she heard. The tenements kept out the cold poorly; it did not help to light a fire. The heat flew out, and the cold crept in through the boards in the walls. And still the cold was not the worst problem.

They had gotten a new social worker from the child welfare board over them. The one they had earlier they had somehow managed to wear down, as Elisabet understood, weakened him and rendered him harmless. And he had apparently only looked out for the children and not interested himself in David's life and loose living.

But the new one was filled with curiosity and a lust for efficiency. He had not been at all pleased with the occupations David could give as his attempts to support his family. He had even scared poor David so that he had even gone out for a few days on the snow-shoveling force. Though David did not have the strength at all for such work; he had his weak stomach to think of.

The social worker had probably wanted to send David to one of those "corpse tailors" that the child welfare center made use of, Tyra thought. But David had not been born yesterday, so he went to a doctor he knew of and got a paper saying he was not strong enough for heavy work. Thanks to that, he could stick the paper under the social worker's nose and get off, otherwise he would have been branded as a vagrant.

See, that was how they treated sick people, Tyra said.

Elisabet hid a smile of contempt behind her coffee cup. Not even Mama and Emelie believed in David's sickness. And she felt an immense desire to ask, "What is he, if not a vagrant?"

David had gotten off. But the social worker had taken both Allan and Stig away. Allan was not doing well in school, of course, had played hooky, had fallen into bad company and begun to steal. Had been arrested by the police. And through the efforts of the social worker, he had been taken to Hället, the talked-about and feared Eolshället boys' reformatory. Allan had cried with terror when they took him away; he had heard people talk about the many beatings given there.

Stig had been taken to a home for weak children. It was his lungs again.

Now Tyra was looking for work and asked if Emelie couldn't get her a job in the store. But Emelie could not. And Elisabet wondered if Emelie wasn't drawing a boundary despite all her efforts to understand and help. To her job, to the store—there she would not take Tyra in any case. Elisabet would have drawn the boundary a little tighter. If she had been in charge, Tyra would not have crossed their threshold, not received one öre. She would have liked to send the police after Tyra and David.

Tyra had to be satisfied with borrowing money. She could not get more out of Emelie.

David had given up. He felt crippled, did not even dare come into the vicinity of Central Station. If they had the least chance, they would take him in and place him in an institution. He had seen that in the social worker's eyes. This dangerous person had also shown himself to be dangerously informed about David's previous small dealings with the authorities.

Worry and insecurity were affecting his stomach. If before he had sometimes felt it all too well, his stomach pain was now a reality. In some way, this was a consolation, an opportunity for escape. Now the social worker could see for himself. Here lay David Berg, sick and miserable, persecuted and wronged. Who could require him to work, he who had volunteered and destroyed himself to go out to shovel snow? One could certainly not call a sick person a vagrant. So now Tyra could go without fear to the welfare bureau, tell them how hard a time they were having, take the doctor's certificate with her.

Actually, Tyra had never had much fear of going to the welfare bureau. She was used to dealing with the people there. But, of course, the paper came in useful. She went there and whined and argued till she got what she came for.

Tyra met adversity in a different way than David. She was not frightened by it. And she did not satisfy herself with just going to the welfare bureau. She took all the scrubbing jobs she could get. As she had often done in the past, she worked together with David's sister. They took stairways and stores, offices and workshops. Always the heaviest and roughest jobs, as if they were made for that. Others might dust and tidy up. Their equipment and their coat of arms were the scrub brush and the bucket.

Sometimes, when bitterness welled up, it could feel really good to scrub, to let the anger and sweat come out. Naturally, it was not David she was bitter toward, not the lice-infested tenements and the life they lived. No, it was society, all those people who did not want to let them live the way they did. Who came with all their demands that people should be all alike and well-mannered. As if it were a big deal if a boy took a few grubby toys from an overstocked store, or if a country bumpkin was fooled into spending a grubby ten bill for a no-good watch. That was more the way things should be anyhow: when some of the abundance from the tables of the rich was put to use by those who were living at the bottom of society. Then at least it would bring about some joy and good.

Red with sweat and anger, she would go home to the tenements. Her back ached, but she did not think about it. Now the important thing was to come home and make food, put the kids to bed, and look after David.

On one of summer's unusually fine evenings, he was sitting on the wooden steps outside, wrapped in a blanket. He shushed her, though she hadn't said anything, and whispered, "Smell that!"

She inhaled, thinking she smelled mostly food odors and also maybe a vague scent of earth and vegetation. Possibly there was a hint of something else, too, a more acrid smell.

"I'll be damned if they are not burning in a still," David said. "Down in the brewing hut, probably."

"That can never be good for your stomach," she warned.

"On the contrary, purely medicinal," he answered.

He began to laugh, full of audacity. Sat in the warmth of the slowly setting sun and drew in the ever-stronger smell of mash.

The social worker had not been seen for a whole two weeks. David began to feel better.

ON THE BARRICADES

Maj got one week's vacation and traveled to Trosa with the boy. Erik could not go along, perhaps did not feel like it either. As if he were afraid to be alone with Maj, afraid they would reach a decision if they found time to talk it through. He was completely taken up with things to do in town. Among other things, he had to get ready for Red Day, which was going to be an international demonstration for the solidarity of the masses with the Soviet Union and against the aggression of the Chinese imperialist government. The party had received much criticism from Moscow for not demonstrating on the First of May, despite the bad weather and despite the Social Democrats' cancellation.

But it was hard to work. More and more often it was happening that he felt handicapped. Everything that got done would still be under suspicion. In everything that happened, the party minority would find "right-wing bias" and hurry to report it to the Comintern.

And when he could not get enthused about his tasks, he could not get away from thoughts of his private problems either. Then he would just sit there in the empty apartment, sit there and feel like a failure, unhappy, abandoned. He, who had begun so well, who had felt like he had the right qualifications for succeeding and going far. He could almost remember the war years as happy years, when he had sold soap, been his own boss, and made big deals. And he and Maj had been happy; she had admired him then. But now? He sensed she despised him, now that he could not even support the family anymore. Though she did not despise him for that, he had to admit as much if he wanted to be fair. She was not like that. But she did for everything else, everything he could despise himself for.

Self-recriminations made him mad: Here he sat like a damned moralist and petty bourgeois. Instead of writing his lecture on China's assault, the "Social Fascists'" betrayal of the working class and the swindle of the Old Swedish Village refugees from the Ukraine. He was going to speak at one of the introductory meetings on Red Day.

Red Day did not really turn out to be the demonstration they had hoped for. Naturally, the party newspaper described the demonstrations on Norr and Söder as enormous mass meetings. They counted eighteen thousand demonstrators while the Social Democrats counted only two thousand. The critics in Moscow would believe more in the statements of the "Social Fascists," as they called the Social Democrats, than in those of friends of the party.

There were a few successes they could report, however. Twenty or so of the Old Swedish Village inhabitants wished to return to the Soviet Union. And, to be sure, they had not gotten ten thousand construction workers to strike as they had hoped, but they had still gotten some bus drivers on the suburban lines to do so. "Ten Directors and a Necrophiliac at the Wheel Yesterday," Erik reported in *The People's Daily.* "Unprecedented Outrageous Behavior by Police in Huvudsta. New Police Provocations Against the Strikers."

But everything was meaningless when the solidarity was lacking. Weld the Party Leadership Together! was the headline the newspaper had placed above a call to assemble—at the same time as the spokesmen for the majority and the minority were, at best, at odds with each other before the Comintern's leadership in Moscow. The Swedish party was one of the few that could show progress in recent years. But that did not help. In Moscow, they wanted the party to declare Sweden an imperialist country that in an impending war would break its neutrality and ally itself with the Soviet Union's enemies—for which reason the workers should affiliate themselves with the revolutionary left. The party majority refused and said that such a declaration would only harm the party's work in a country where neutrality was so highly valued.

In the beginning of October, the party majority's spokesmen were suspended by the Comintern. Erik was not prominent enough to be among those named. The following day, *The People's Daily* proclaimed that "The Minority and Ex-Revolutionaries Hold a Fascist Coup Against the Party."

While the party majority leaders sat in meetings with the delegation from the Comintern, the minority took over the Liberal People's Party headquarters on Torsgatan. There were only a few female office workers at the location. When Erik got there, the place was barricaded with the help of ladders, tables, and chairs.

He hurried out to get help. He gathered together a group that managed to push the door open a crack and force their way in. Projectiles of different types rained down on the intruders—weights, inkhorns, and stones. Sillén had a revolver and threatened to shoot each and every one who came closer. He fired several shots in the ceiling so that the plaster crumbled. With pieces of planking, the rest of them went to attack those who tried to come in.

Whoever it was who called in the police remained an untold story. Both sides strenuously denied turning to the henchmen of bourgeois society. But the riot squad came from two directions and broke up the fighters. The minority kept the party dispatch office while the majority locked themselves behind the iron gates to the editorial office and the printing press on Luntmakaregatan. The newspaper used advertisements to urge the people out in the countryside to address their correspondence to Luntmakaregatan after the "unprecedented violent treatment of the party headquarters."

The followers of Sillén did not get much pleasure out of the destroyed headquarters—they were turned out by their landlord, who did not approve of any revolutionaries.

So now, there were two Communist parties again, only five years after the previous party split when Högalunda had been thrown out. How long would their unity last now?

Erik had no exaggerated hopes. Of course, for the time being, things looked pretty good: A larger contingent of the party had followed Kilbom; they were freed of the tight bonds with Moscow. But still, there was so much worry and unrest left, of backbiting and intrigues.

He had felt like a revolutionary, preferred to talk about fighting on the barricades. But the only barricades he had gotten to climb were those that had been put up during the internal party fighting.

Fortunately, autumn brought with it a number of bourgeois scandals that made the party members forget some of the ignominy they had been exposed to. A major who had been carrying on affairs with young girls and a deputy director with a wife who had abused a waitress with a dog whip were exposed. The party quarrels could be moved from the front pages and be hidden farther inside the newspaper.

He was tired of all these heated disputes, had lost faith in the party being able to conquer society. He began to see the Social Democrats in another way from before. With them, there was none of this violent infighting and continually repeating scandals. Perhaps this was not only due to dullness and petty bourgeois values. To achieve any success, balance was required, calm and steady work. And the masses who gave the few at the top the possibility to act—this lent them power.

He had probably begun to lose hope in the masses being revolutionary. Not when there were somewhat decent living conditions, not if they got food. People, in general, wanted to live calmly and quietly and were afraid of the ones who made demands and wanted to force others to take positions.

He could see that in his closest kin. Bengt had been with him and worked for the party at first. But now, since his brother Bengt had gotten married, he was not around very often. Of course, he paid his dues. But still he kept away.

It was the same with Maj. She had the most objections to going along with the party. And Emelie—who had even lived through so much hardship and poverty. None of them wanted any revolution.

That was how his kinsmen were—and naturally so were most people in his class. And that was why they went to the Socialists and not to the Communists.

He himself would stay in the party for now. But pull out of the daily work more and more. There were signs that he tried to interpret. He had a presentiment that people would soon be growing hungrier.

The American stock market had been shaken by an enormous crisis. Such crises usually propagated themselves. If there were another period of crisis, then maybe the party would have the opportunity to play a role. There were a whole lot of capable people, even if they rarely had any occasion to show their mettle. The infighting had sapped everyone's energy.

But the years that had passed had taught him that he was no politician, and that he would hardly ever make one either. There were other possibilities. He had a good business sense. A difficult talent for someone who felt like one of the proletariat. It could lead to temptation and betrayal. But he could serve instead of betraying. And at the same time gain merit. Maybe in one of the movements that were allied with the labor movement but was run like a business, such as a cooperative or a tenants' building association.

Combine egotism and idealism? It did not sound quite right, not for someone who was used to always talking about solidarity. But everyone had to look out for his or her interests, and solidarity was really there to create better conditions—conditions which the egotism of the masses unified and elevated to something greater and finer. Didn't that also go along with materialistic perception? He hoped so. He had never had the time and enough inclination to study the prophets more in depth. But he did remember what Marx had said: "The distinguishing feature of Communism is not the abolition of property generally, but the abolition of bourgeois property."

He had never been bourgeois and did not intend to be so either. And for the time being, in any case, he would have to continue working for the party.

Maj had been working for over a year in the office of a furniture company, and was beginning to feel like it was a permanent position. She took care of part of the bookkeeping, and if the cashier was sick or had the day off, she would take over her job. The office was not so big, of course, but her duties still showed that Maj was recognized as a force to depend on.

Both the company and the office were old-fashioned; a patriarchal spirit reigned there. The wholesaler was God the Father and the old cashier his angel with a sword. She saw it as her responsibility to give and demand the most work possible. If someone stood up from his or her desk before she had closed the account book, it would be very much resented. The workday was officially from eight-thirty to six o'clock, but as a rule it ended at six-thirty.

Sometimes Erik encouraged Maj to protest, to leave as soon as the clock struck six, indeed to strike. But she knew it was not easy to find something new, and if she were to follow his advice, she would soon be out of a job. He was in no way to get involved, not to write anything. And for safety's sake, she told him as little as possible about her work. Once, long ago, he had betrayed her confidence, written about her work conditions. That was not to be repeated.

She had not yet turned thirty but was beginning to feel old. Her years of youth seemed so far away. Now she was on the treadmill, always in a hurry, always with a bad conscience about the boy who she had to constantly leave with others. Rush off to Mama with him, then to work, sit as if on pins and needles and wait for the cashier to close the book, away to fetch Henning again, then home, fix supper, make up the beds.

It was never more than that. Erik was gone every evening, came home late. Life became quite meaningless. Only on Sundays could she relax a little. Then she would ride to Skansen's open-air museum and zoo and walk around there with Henning. Although Erik really did not like that. Skansen was, of course, too patriotic.

The double commutes morning and evening were maybe hardest on her in any case, the constant fear of getting caught in a traffic jam and arriving too late. A lot would be simpler if they lived closer to her mother. But her relationship with Erik made it pretty futile to think of moving; you don't move a wreck. You clean house when you change domiciles. If she was going to move, it should be without Erik.

She still hesitated before making the decision, as if she wanted it to be Erik to announce it. She realized that he was not really as taken up with work in the party any longer. He had an additional commission that seemed to suit him more, which required him to place a lot of advertisements for the big exhibition that was going to be held the coming year. Now he talked more about the exhibition than about the party in the moments they saw each other. And she wondered if he would become different and calmer if he got into another job. But she did not dare to hope any longer.

She herself struggled bitterly and resolutely onward against the hurries and worries of everyday life. She felt how this battle was destroying her. And her certainty grew: Something had to change, had to happen soon. While she still had the strength to make the most of life.

Her steady job was the starting point and her only possibility. She had to manage for herself and the boy, could not become dependent on others. The necessity to work and the daily bustle had to and could give freedom and calm.

But maybe not until she had gotten away from Erik.

ACCEPTANCE

Surely people had never before torn down and built as zealously as they were doing now? When Emelie looked out the window over Erstagatan, she could see how the new buildings were rising up where the cosmetics factory had stood before in the middle of its big garden. The long high fence along the street and the trees inside it had disappeared. Åsögatan, which had once climbed out along the edge of the hillside, had been made lower and widened, and the small wooden cottages that remained looked like they had taken flight and gotten stranded up on the rocks, damaged by blasting, that rose high above the new street level.

Almost every year was a record year for construction, August said. Now they were at around eight thousand new apartments per year in the city. Mobility in the housing market also grew larger; on the first of October it was positively remarkable. They figured out that one hundred thousand people moved that day, approximately every fifth Stockholm inhabitant. Now they were building mostly small apartments of one room and a kitchenette, and a significant number of old-age homes and institutions.

Many old buildings were torn down; some of them, such as the main building of the cosmetics factory, were slated for eventual reconstruction on the city block that was being planned at Skansen Open-Air Museum. The old police station at Mynttorget was razed for a new government building; all along Götgatan's southern portion, shacks and workshops were torn down, and up on Tjurberget a big new school was being built. The old Owenska Building was torn down to widen Hantverkaregatan. On Hamngatan's incline, new temporary facades, in the functionalist style, replaced buildings that had jutted out into the street. Beside Sankt Eriksbron, a giant sports arena went up, and at the end of Sankt Eriksgatan, Europe's largest parking garage was built with space for twelve hundred cars.

Traffic increased even more. Because of it, streets had to be widened and new roadways laid down, such as Norr Mälarstrand, which now ran across the grounds where the military bridge platoon's barracks had been torn down. Many streets were asphalted. At the busiest intersections, they had begun to draw chalk lines to show where pedestrians should proceed. New buses and bus lines were put in place; Hammarbyleden motorway, and Årstabron, the big new bridge, were inaugurated. And the City Council decided that Söder and Kungsholmen would be connected by an enormous bridge that would be given the name Västerbron. But, for the time being, they declined an American proposal to build a subway under the city, with stations with elevators and escalators. There had to be some moderation and besides, such a plan was seen as impossible to carry out.

At the same time as the city was changing and being smartened up, the large exhibition was coming up alongside Djurgårdsbrunnsviken. It showed the way to a new city and a new style: the rational and the functional. All unnecessary embellishments were banned; simplification would go as far as possible. Even doing away with the capital letters of the alphabet could be rationalized. And the halls of the exhibition were neither palaces nor towers of spun sugar. Instead, they were unadorned geometric surfaces or naked constructions of iron and glass.

Many completely condemned the new style, denying that, everything taken into consideration, it was even relevant to architecture. Others were drawn in by the young architects' enthusiasm and belief in their work, capitulating to their war cries of: "Accept!"

August Bodin was among the undecided and waffling, and had a hard time choosing. He was attracted to both the old and the new—and at the same time felt some of the youthful tingling urge to try things out. As a building contractor, he did see the opportunities with the new style, how much could be done more cheaply, more easily, and more quickly. Light and air that would cut through the dark and old-fashioned neighborhoods, the clean surfaces, the simple proportions.

Whether they liked it or not, the new style would carry the day; that much he understood. That would mean that adaptation was necessary, and it would be dangerous to be one of the last to implement it. He could not count on things going calmly and smoothly during the years he had left. Even he would probably be forced to accept the changes as well.

As soon as the new exhibition opened, he was there. And returned time after time, as if he had to get accustomed to the new architecture and really figure out how it functioned.

It was not just a question of a new way of building. It was something more, something that was harder to get a grip on: a new way of living. He tried to make a note of each thing that could explain the new way of building but soon found that nothing lacked function. It was meaningless to try, equally impossible as cataloguing all the details of one's environment.

But it seemed to him that women played a significant role in the change. The fact that they were working more and more outside the home required that the apartments have another design than before, that they be functional in the actual sense of the word. And he thought that he got the best image when he compared buildings and women's clothing: the turn-of-the-century's well-wrapped, bedecked luxuriance and today's simple, straight lines.

Emelie was on vacation. During recent years, she had had one week off in the summer; now suddenly she had two. She almost felt it was a little irresponsible of the store owners; how would the shop assistants manage alone for so long? She had to wonder if there was something she should worry about behind this kindness—what if they were beginning to think that she was too old and they wanted to get rid of her? But it was growing more and more common for office workers and shop assistants to get vacation; workers usually only got a few days off around Midsummer.

Jenny thought Emelie should travel somewhere. But traveling and staying somewhere were expensive. And Jenny had had fewer engagements recently, so Emelie's money was needed. Besides, Emelie could not imagine traveling alone, in which case Jenny would have to go along. And then they would have to take Henning also. Maj would probably have a hard time finding someone who could take care of the boy. It would be too expensive. And it was probably also more peaceful and pleasant to stay home.

During 1909, the year of the strike, Emelie had gone blueberry picking in Trolldalen outside the Danvik tollgate. It was too early for berries just yet, but she still took a walk there on her vacation, bringing Henning along so Jenny could take the chance to run a few errands. She found that not much had changed since she had been there last. Trolldalen was still a bit of woods on the edge of town, seemingly untouched, but, at the same time, with traces of having been strolled through by many city dwellers leaving papers and bottles behind. But it was more difficult now for her to make her way than it had been the last time; she saw more poorly and was stiffer in the limbs. And then she had to be so watchful that Henning did not run away from her. He might get lost or go too far out on the steep rocky ledge above Svindersviken.

She sat down cautiously, spread out the contents of the picnic basket, and discovered that there were mosquitoes and flies everywhere. She was glad when it was time to go back; the country was not the place for her. Only uneven paths where branches hit her in the face, and moss and tall grass that hid small creepy-crawlies of every kind. It was good that she had not let Jenny tempt her into traveling somewhere. The comforts of home could not be had anywhere else. She was probably too old to get any greater enjoyment out of that vacation thing. Though, of course, it might be pleasant to take a few days off, as long as she got to stay home and did not feel obligated to go to the country.

But when August, who heard that Emelie had vacation, wanted her to go with him and look at the exhibition, she thought if would be a lot of fun to get out. Even if she dreaded finding the right clothes and looking all right, thinking that August would probably be ashamed to be seen in her company. Luckily, she had a few days advance notice, and, with Jenny's help, was able to go shopping for a new dress and coat. She had been saving for this purchase for a long time and now it had to happen.

August was standing and waiting for her at Norrmalmstorg where they had decided to meet. He was alone; Ida was in the countryside with their daughters and their daughters' children. They still had the summer house on the island of Stora Essingen, but ever since the new bridge had been finished this year, it was not really so rural there anymore. That was why they were mostly out on Värmdö at one of their daughters' houses.

August held his hat in his hand; the wind played in his gray curls. He greeted her a little formally as if she were a fine lady he was meeting. Emelie remembered that their mother had said with a certain amount of pride that the Bodins probably adopted August because he seemed so well brought up. Fifty years had passed since then, but, on that point, he had not changed.

The streetcar for the exhibition left from Norrmalmstorg, the number twenty-two. They stood inside the streetcar with waving pennants printed with the winged emblem of the exhibition. Soon they were rolling along Strandvägen, between gray house facades and trees coming into leaf. It had rained early that morning, but now the sun was shining and the small cargo boats carrying wood that were closely moored along the quay had raised their sails to dry—like an endless parade of white flags.

For a moment, Emelie felt a sensation like the streetcar was rolling back in time, to the exhibition of 1897. During that whole exhibition, she had stood and packaged soaps in one of the pavilions. It had been called the Perfume Bottle. It was as if she almost expected to see minarets and towers sticking up again, even though she had seen pictures of the new exhibition in the newspaper. It was not even standing on the same spot. The old one had stood out on Djurgården; the new one had its main location on the Östermalm side of the water. The streetcar continued, past Nobel Park and the elegant diplomatic mansions on the continuation of Strandvägen. Then it turned onto the turning loop and stopped.

All the flags of the world were fluttering from the white entrance building. And they walked along the road, between the transportation hall's enormous glass surfaces, on the one side lighted marquees and constructions jutting out, and on the other the Alnarp Garden's abundant greenery and floral profusion, and continued in the direction of the planetarium's shiny silver globe and the rows of exhibition halls along the main street. Above the festival grounds rose the steel skeleton of the exhibition's mast. It was crowned by the conquering pair of wings followed by a row of see-through neon advertisements for "the big four" magazines: *Weekly Journal, Everything For Everyone, The Whole World, Housewife.*

Blinking facades of eternity, steel, glass. Marquees sparkling with color, the play of the fountains over the inlet. And everywhere the constant flutter of the flags in the wind and all framed by greenery that seemed dark against the lighted glitter.

"Do you think it is as ugly as people say?" August asked.

No, she thought, it was light and beautiful. Hopeful. It was hard to explain, but it was as if the picture she saw gave a vision of a better world, a lighter, easier one.

Though when she saw the row houses, houses and apartments that were exhibited, she grew perhaps a little more doubtful. It was probably good, but she would not want to live that way. It seemed a little too cold, and some of the new furniture was probably more odd than practical.

It was always like that at an exhibition, said August. One was tempted to pare down and exaggerate. Some of the critics had only seen the exaggerations.

He himself had been very dubious at first, he told her. But he had not been able to get away from what he had seen and had returned time and again. Gradually, he felt like he was beginning to understand the thinking behind it all and see some of the beauty.

They went for coffee at the Bridge Café, sitting on the veranda and looking out over the exhibition area, the bridge, and the inlet where the funny water cycles moved like water striders on the shiny surface.

"Maybe only we who were born poor can really understand how necessary it is for the world to change," August said. "We who saw our parents go under do not have such an easy time romanticizing the past. We know how it was, not for everyone, but for all too many."

Only to herself could she admit that she sometimes wondered if August remembered. It was good to hear that he did.

Evening came, the day faded and the darkness began to fall. But at the exhibition, a new and fascinating picture was lit up; the fountains became a cascade of color, the neon lights began to bloom along the building facades and on the mast and were reflected back in the water of the inlet. All the buildings had long, shining rows of lights, on the field of the amusement park the waterfall sparkled, and the lamps shone around the small gondolas that swung in the giant Ferris wheel.

They ate dinner at the Paradise Restaurant, the large restaurant on the edge of the festival grounds. It was so elegant and expensive that Emelie felt quite anxious, but August did everything to lessen her nervousness, making her almost feel like it was natural for her to be sitting there. Then he ordered seats in front of the platform so they could see the festival play, *The Big Construction Site.*

A giant voice thundered from space, gray Michelin Men came bouncing in; it crackled and thundered from the big building under construction where the world advertising machine Fulgus-Victoria, the Psychic Institute, World Ready-to-Wear and other strange companies had their headquarters. People mixing with robots and world advertising machines appeared very unhappy. There was a young couple who could find nowhere to live, and Emelie felt especially sorry for them. Finally, the heavenly cicerone called down the genie of the future, Manyana, to help the people. She looked cold in the cold light—and no wonder, given how lightly dressed she was. All the frightened people asked her for consolation. They hoped it would not be all too cold and hard in the world. She did not have much hope to give—but gave them her little sisters, the dreams, who danced in.

Emelie got the feeling that whoever wrote the play probably did not really like the future that the exhibition was pointing toward. She looked around, feeling like the lights were colder now, as if the giant voice in the loudspeaker and all the commotion had frightened away some of the hope she had felt. There were dangers, too, in all the light and cleanness, something of coldness and ruthlessness. The young pair had not found a room in the big building; there was only room for the inhuman, the frightening. Was it like that in the city and in the world as well? Were they tearing down people's small homes to make way for World Ready-to-Wear and Fulgus-Victoria?

She was cold and started to shiver. The evening was quite chilly.

"We will get warmer when we walk," August said. They walked along the wide avenue, past the Planetarium, and out toward the entrance. And the warmth returned; the light was not so cold any longer. She had to stop in the garden and see all the flowers in the glow of the lights and the glittering water. Now Fulgus-Victoria was not so frighteningly close any longer. Maybe the play was more a warning than a prophecy. Maybe the steps forward would not have to be paid for so heavily.

Along Strandvägen, crowds of people strolled home from the exhibition. A little quiet and tired after all the adventures of the day, she sat by August's side and looked out through the streetcar window. He insisted on accompanying her to Norrmalmstorg and making sure she got on the other streetcar home. Then he was going to walk a little way back; he lived on one of the side streets off of Strandvägen. They had talked about moving, he said, getting something more modern and also maybe smaller now that all the children had moved away from home. Though he would probably wait a few years, till he had left the firm and did not need to think about representing it sometimes. Maybe he would end his work as a building contractor by building a house exactly like one he would want to live in. Another building contractor had had a real palace built for himself up on Stigberget. He had, incidentally, hired the same architect who had designed City Hall. Something that grand was not what August had in mind nor could afford. They would have something smaller to be sure.

He stood there and waved as she climbed aboard on the number six streetcar that would take her to Folkungagatan. Then she would walk the rest of the way. It would never occur to her to pay another fare to ride one stop, and now she had already taken advantage of her transfer ticket.

On Folkungagatan, there was still a long row of small wooden houses left, though a gas station had squeezed in on the corner facing Borgmästaregatan. The little cottages looked dirty and ready to collapse, but in some way cozy and human.

When she passed by them, she wondered for an instant how she wanted things to be, if she was so used to poverty and want that she was frightened by everything new and fine. But after only a few steps, she arrived at the store and then all her ponderings disappeared, then she had to see if they had put up the new window display and if it looked liked they were getting by without her. This thing with taking vacation was both fun and disquieting at the same time.

YOUNG AT THE WRONG TIME

While the colorful flags were still fluttering above the lighted pavilions of the exhibition, the crisis was closing in. Unemployment grew. It was most difficult for the youth. Some companies hired students who did not receive any pay other than the hope to one day get a permanent job.

Elisabet received a few kronor as an office intern, but was made use of mostly as an errand girl. Lennart, who had worked for four months in the warehouse of an electrical supply store, did not receive one krona. When he was called in to the boss and believed that the promise of a beginner's salary was going to be fulfilled, he heard instead that he was fired. They claimed that he did not fit the job; he guessed that a relative of the owner was going to get his job.

So he was without work at a time when it seemed impossible to find anything new. People were talking about cutting back everywhere.

A certain amount of toughness and energy was needed to push one's way forward and take hold of one of the few opportunities that were there. And Lennart was not tough; he was one of those who would rather back off than push his way forward. It had been like that already in school; he could not do himself justice. Despite the fact that he had probably read more and knew his lessons better than most, his grades were rather mediocre and that did not make it any easier for him now.

To see his worth, one had to have a clear eye and time to let one's eye see into him. Most saw only a slightly awkward and shy boy, a gray shadow who disappeared among everyone like him, among the growing train of the unemployed.

Elisabet had been in his confirmation class. Since girls and boys usually went in separate groups, she had had no reason to notice him. But they met later at some confirmation meetings that the minister had organized. She could not recall that she had more than nodded at him before they ran into each other in the White Hills Park. And the boy that she had seen as just one among all the other boys had gradually acquired his own features, shown himself to be a person who read and who thought, who had viewpoints and opinions. She had never had so much to talk to one person about, she thought. And now she found herself surprised that she had not noticed him earlier, that she had not seen how different he was from all the others. It was so evident, already in the features of his face, in every expression he made.

They had been going together for one year now. This was not a question of a quick and giddy falling in love. Slowly, they grew together, meant more and more to each other. It grew plain to see that they belonged together. It took a few months for him to kiss her, and even then, she was still not sure that she wanted him to, was still frightened by Maj's fate, and she held tightly onto her determination not to share that fate. With time, she began to see it differently. Lennart was not Erik, and Maj's fate did not have to be hers. He was allowed to kiss and caress her. But nothing more was to happen; they had no way of dealing with any accidental outcome that might ensue if they went further. She knew that and behaved accordingly—and Lennart had to accede to it as well.

His mother was a widow, sewed buttonholes and pockets in a garment factory. They lived in a one-room apartment on Danviksgatan, close to the candle factory and the tollgate. Outside, the streetcar squealed past on their narrow street.

Lennart was an only child; his mother's small salary was barely enough to support them. As soon as he had finished school, he had naturally looked for a job. He had been an errand boy for a while but been fired when he had collided with a box of china. Since then, he had only managed to get shorter part-time jobs and now the internship that he had just lost.

He had spent most of his free time before at the city library or together with the books he had taken out from there. Shyness had prevented him from making real contact with people his age; he had been quite solitary before he met Elisabet. He had often looked at her in their confirmation class. But had been scared by her appearing so self-assured and also slightly superior. He had viewed her as unattainable, believed that he would have to be satisfied with admiring her from a distance.

In the beginning, it seemed unbelievable that she could accept his company. He had only gone to elementary school, while she had gone to a girls' school. And it was even more unbelievable when he heard that she was the daughter of an actress. Then she told him that her father had been a singer, but her parents were divorced. She belonged to another class of society, he thought.

But once he had met Elisabet's mother and been in their home, he did not think the difference was perhaps so great. Elisabet's mother was not hard to talk to. And she had none of that slight remoteness that Elisabet had from time to time. Just the opposite. He had never become acquainted with and become good friends with a woman so quickly. And he was not to call her "Auntie," he had to call her "Jenny"— and that was easier than he imagined.

He used "Auntie" to her real aunt on the other hand, while Elisabet only called her Emelie. Later on, he learned that she was not actually Elisabet's aunt. Their relationship was somewhat complicated. Jenny had been married previously to Emelie's brother and later on to the singer who was Elisabet's father.

He recognized Emelie, had once shopped in the store where she worked.

Day after day he sat at the employment office's waiting room or hung about in the lines of youth that formed when some opening was being advertised. He hardly had any hope, but he did his duty, he tried, he searched. He went to the English course together with Elisabet, even if he could not really believe that he would find any use for his knowledge. And he constantly carried a book in his overcoat's inner pocket, and took the opportunity to read for a bit while he waited. He read without plan and without motive, not to learn, but because reading had become a way of living, sometimes almost a replacement for life. He wrote down words that he did not understand in a notebook with an index, and then looked them up in the library's dictionaries. But he did not dare use many of the words since he did not know how they should be pronounced.

And he did not get any job.

Apparently, such was life, one could certainly not ask for more. If there was nothing to be had—well, that was just the way it was. He was distressed by it, but he did not belong among those whom distress drove to revolt. Still, it was different with Elisabet; she could not accept the situation such as it was. She could grow furious, explode. Then she would hate the older generation. Those who by simply living and working became an obstacle for the younger, who seemed to fill the world so that there was not room for those who came next.

They had lived their lives, she said. Wouldn't it be better if people died when they were fifty?

You don't really want that, he would say calmly. Think of your mother; she would not have much time left. And mine would be dead already.

No, that's true—but still. We have to have a chance to live, too. And when there clearly isn't room enough for both old and young.

She was beautiful when she was angry, he thought. Looked so wild, so strong. Did not care if anyone heard her. There was no point in trying to hold her then, she would shake loose, could not bear anything that felt like a restraint.

He looked at her. Thought it was amazing that she could put up with him, that she was his. That he would get to hold her when her outrage had subsided, that he would dare to do so.

For he did dare. They were together and would stay together; they had said things to each other that he thought you only read in books and that they did not dare say at first except in the dark. Yet, they had seldom or never spoken about the future, nothing about their maybe getting married, having a home and children. No, this seemed too completely unattainable and distant. There was, on the whole, no point in talking about the future when there barely seemed any place for them in the present. A steady job and a steady salary that they could live on—to talk about or dream about that was almost ludicrous. The only happiness that was secure and truly existed was that which could be won from the impoverished present, such as the moments they met, the feeling of closeness and warmth.

There was not more than that. But what they had was already unimaginably big. If you have happiness in the present, you do not need to derive happiness from the future.

Though, of course, he wanted a job. Not for the sake of the future, but to get by in the present, to be able to pay for a home, buy a suit, take Elisabet to the movies.

They stood in the September darkness on Katarinavägen and looked down over the city. She was a little cold; once she had calmed down from her recent outburst, she snuggled against him to get shelter, and he placed his arm around her.

There were a lot of people out moving about, waiting. Some spotlights went on from Kastellholmen and swept quickly across the sky. Then, suddenly, there was heard a gasp of excitement, everyone looked up, someone pointed. And the long, shiny silver airship glided into the spotlight, in over the city.

The airship Graf Zeppelin had arrived.

Once another type of airship, a balloon, had lifted off to sail toward the North Pole. In a week or so, its passengers were expected back: The bodies of the members of the Andrée Arctic expedition had been found and were now on their way home after having disappeared for more than thirty years.

Here was a new technological wonder swaying at a low height over the city. And almost every week the newspapers told of foolhardy pilots who, in small sport planes, tried to throw themselves from one end of the earth to the other. Two weeks earlier, two Frenchmen had carried out the first non-stop flight between Paris and New York.

He begins a dance high up in the air,
Falling leaves with a shimmer.
The wind comes against him heavy as a bear,
But o'er this shock he does prevail.
He takes his glide, must soon go in,
Turns his tail
Does a spin.
But before the earth receives his kiss
He soars windward up on high.
For homeward bound on proud wings
Under the blue sky
An aeroplane swings...

Elisabet hummed the "Pilot's Waltz." And the airship above them glistened in the light.

The heavens had been conquered. But on earth the Great Depression spread from country to country. And political unrest grew as well. In the country from where the large airship had just come, the new Nazi Party had just recorded a landslide election victory. From almost nothing, it had suddenly become the German Parliament's second biggest party. And its leader, Adolf Hitler, had threatened that the day he took power those guilty for the treachery of 1918 would be punished; heads would roll.

Otherwise, no one knew what those Nazis thought or wanted. Elisabet had heard Erik say that Germany's workers, despite all their divisiveness, would probably unite when it came to stopping Hitler. Since she was suspicious of everything Erik said and thought, she wondered if that Hitler might not actually be a really good guy. But Lennart mistrusted him as well, and so maybe Erik was right for once.

There were a number of Nazis in Sweden, too, Lennart said. Those people dressed in black who they had previously seen selling the newspaper, *The Sheaf,* had just changed color, were wearing brown. But he did not believe that the Nazi movement could have any real importance, neither here nor out in the world. People could not be that crazy.

He followed her to her door. They lingered a moment before he watched her disappear up the stairway. Right across the street, the new buildings stood finished. People had moved in, and there were lights in the windows.

He turned in the direction of the tollgate, toward home. Without any hurry, there was no reason to hurry, nothing that waited the next day. He would just make the usual rounds and get the usual replies.

FAREWELL AND RETURN

The fall was gray and gloomy; it stormed and rained. The crisis and unemployment grew. If the exhibition had presented an image of a brighter future, the autumn wind had torn down the house of cards. They were on their way back; into the darkness. And the dark forces grew, seemed invincible. In Germany, the Nazis continued on victoriously. In Finland, people cowered before the terror of the Lappua Movement. And in Moscow, more and more "counterrevolutionaries" were arrested and executed.

But also in the darkness, they had to find their way, try to live their lives. You could not choose your era, your backdrop to play against. Private problems did not become any fewer because they had chosen an awkward point in time to appear. Though they might seem more trivial, completely uninteresting to everyone other than those they affected.

That fall Henning started school. The way there went across streets with quite a bit of traffic, and Maj did not dare let him walk alone; he had to be accompanied both to and from. She did not want him alone either the many hours before she got home from the office.

Jenny did what she could to help Maj; she met Henning at school in the afternoons and took him with her to Söder where Maj would pick him up as usual.

But the arrangement was not really a good one. For Maj to have enough time to get to the office, she had to leave Henning at school far too early—and worry about what he might be up to while he waited. And then she knew that her mother was hoping to have a part in Söder Theater's *New Year's Revue.* When rehearsals began, Jenny would not be able to help Maj any longer.

With Erik, things were as usual. Maj had known about his affairs with other women for a long time but still not forced anything decisive. Maybe because she knew that this time it would be definitive.

The difference from before was maybe not so great, but still it felt more difficult to know that he had a steady companion instead of more transient connections. It had become so useless to pretend any longer, so obvious that she was extraneous. He did not go out with girls from the Youth Club any longer, but instead was with someone from an advertising agency he worked for. They had surely been together for many months before Maj learned about it.

Of course, she could blame herself. Say that it had to become that way when she had made herself so inaccessible, had such a hard time forgiving, and done so little to keep him. She knew that he could not be alone. As far as work went, he was hard on himself. Demanded a lot. But not when it was a question of love, as if love did not mean enough for him that he thought it worth making an effort for. Was it just a way for him to relax, a little playing and entertainment after the serious matter of work? A soothing voice, a caressing hand. Something almost impersonal, closer to meaningless when it came to whose voice and hand it was?

If Maj was difficult and he did not get what he wanted and needed from her, he went to someone else. He chose the easiest path. It was not he who "kicked up a fuss" and grew bitter; it was she. He just stayed away to avoid becoming irritated.

Still, he had really been fond of her, perhaps he still was. But he was not made for adversity, was not one of those who stayed put if they risked being defeated. It was like that with everything he undertook. If he was met with opposition, he would put everything into a quick attack. As a rule, he would succeed that way. If not—then he would step aside, look for another path, move on. It was surely like that within the party as well, was probably why he seemed on the way out. If he did not receive enough goodwill and admiration, then he would go where his talents were more appreciated.

Now he had apparently found a woman who demanded less and who he was happy with. Someone who was prepared to overlook a lot, who maybe did not even insist on him leaving Maj and the boy.

He would avoid confrontation as long as possible. It would be Maj who would make the decision, admit her defeat.

She wondered if she was basing her decision on the fact that it was so difficult with Henning's going to school. What seemed to be the lesser of the reasons stepped up the process, required a quick solution.

Usually, she was asleep when Erik got home. When he saw that the light was on in the kitchen, he realized that she was sitting up awake and waiting for him, and he felt a desire to sneak off, just go into his room and go to bed or even leave again.

But he could not do that, had to pretend that everything was normal. He went into the kitchen with a cheery: "Aren't you asleep?" He thought of kissing her on the cheek, but she pulled away. Did she perhaps smell Irene's scent? Irene had a little bad habit of dousing herself too much.

Maj got up and took a few steps toward the window. She was slender, still so much a girl. The opposite of Irene.

He had to feel sorry for Maj, so small and pitiable with her short hair and boy's rump. He could remember how they had played together. She had been like a boy then, too, agile and swift, never whined.

But when she turned around, he saw that she had tears in her eyes now. And that she was not a girl any longer. Tiredness and bitterness had etched themselves on her face. She was older than Irene, actually, had turned thirty.

"We can't go on this way," she said. "Henning and I are leaving tomorrow."

"No, you can't do that!" He tried to convince her—but heard himself that there was no force in his words. Was it fatigue? He had just come straight from Irene's. Or was it because he realized it would be simpler if Maj left? Since she could not accept things the way they were.

Out of shame, he had to try to talk her into staying, had to say that the thing with the other woman was not so serious, that in fact under any circumstances he was going to leave the other. Only to show Maj that she was mistaken. In order to not make the defeat so ignominious?

He knew the whole time that what he said would not change anything. Once Maj had decided something, that was that. It was too late now. She had waited almost unnaturally long before she gave him her decision. Was it because she thought it was so hard?

But it was a point of honor to not give up all too easily. Then she might think that he did not care for her. But he did, despite everything that had come between them. She was his little Maj, the girl from his youth. And now he was going to lose both her and the boy.

He tried to feel sorry for himself, wanted to feel betrayed and abandoned. They had never gotten married; he had no hold on her, no right. Neither regarding her nor the boy. She had made sure of that.

But it was impossible to blame her. She did not spare herself either. She said that she had much to regret.

They sat there in the kitchen until it was morning, did not get out of their clothes that night. When he went in to look at the boy who was sleeping, he saw that the suitcases stood there all packed. Of the furniture, she only wanted her bed and the boy's bed and some chairs she had bought on her own once. For now, she was just taking a couple of suitcases. The rest could stay there for a few weeks. She had been promised a small apartment soon; until then she would live at her mother's.

She had everything arranged, prepared in advance. And by that prevented any means of retreat.

He did not feel like he had the strength to say good-bye to Henning. While Maj went in to wake the boy, he carried down the suitcases and placed them inside the outer door. Then he left. He wondered first if he should go to Irene's place but felt in some way that it was not right; she would not understand this whole thing, in any case. Instead, he bought a morning paper and drank a cup of coffee at a café. He sat and tried to sort out how he would manage on his own now, if maybe he would take the opportunity to break off with Irene too—so that he would be completely free. Or marry her and settle down. He would have been able to flip a coin over it; everything seemed so indifferent now. It was best to let a few days pass before he told Irene about all this. First, he had to know how he himself wanted things to go. Now that Maj was no longer there for him.

He would not have believed it could feel like this. So intense. So empty, so alone, so miserably meaningless.

For more than seven years, Maj had lived in Vasastaden. Now she had returned to the part of town of her childhood and youth. She noticed that she was someone else from when she had lived here before, that this part of town was also another one from what she had left. So much of the rural outskirts had disappeared; rocky outcroppings and wooden cottages had been replaced by heavy city blocks.

Maj had returned tired and worn out, unsure of herself and her decision. During the first days on Söder, while they were living with her mother and Emelie, the friendliness she was met with was mostly forced. She could feel all too palpably that they felt sorry for her, that it was a shame about her. But soon things were different and better, as if they had wound soft bandages around her wounds. Everything that had ached and itched in irritation gradually felt better; the wounds healed even if they left scars behind. She could accept their friendliness for what it was, not a sign that they felt sorry for her but a sign that they liked her. Closeness and conversation in the kitchen were able to have a calming effect; she did not have to think always about what had been, and she had people to talk to—people were always there and were ready to listen. Her tasks were not so numerous and time-consuming either, when there were several people. Emelie took care of repairing everyone's stockings and buttons; it actually seemed as if she longed for more to do, something more to think about. Jenny probably wanted to also, but she did not get so much done; she mostly talked and forgot what she had in her hands. Elisabet stayed out most of the time. Sometimes her boyfriend, Lennart, came up with her and was there and drank coffee. He was still unemployed. Maj felt sorry for them, maybe she felt sorry for all who were young—they were so dreadfully unaware of how cruel life was. She herself had lost her illusions; there was not much more than gray work, gray workdays, many small petty worries.

Of course: Henning. Naturally, she could not feel sorry about him, too. Without a father, a little scared and unsure, faced with so much new. After only a few months in his first school, he had to begin a new one, with a new teacher and new classmates.

Henning was her hope and joy; when she thought about him, her slightly curt, sober matter-of-factness could evaporate. Then she could believe again, even in the unbelievable.

Their new circumstances meant that Maj had more time for herself; more than before she was able to look critically at herself and improve what had been neglected. She began to wave her hair, bought new clothes. Truthfully, she could not afford it, but Emelie insisted she wanted to lend her what was necessary.

On the first of December, they moved into a building owned by a foundation that ran it for single women with or without children. It was an attractive and modern building; there was both central heating and a gas stove. The only disadvantage was that the lavatory was out in the hallway and was shared with several other tenants. One benefit was that they had access to a bath; there were two bathrooms in the basement that they could reserve.

Proximity to her mother and to Emelie made everything easier; they lived on the next block. And here Henning could walk to and from school alone. Even if there was a lot of construction, the area was still pretty quiet and cars few. Private cars were seldom seen here. Transport to the shops was done to a large extent by horse-drawn carts. Down along Folkungagatan, it was livelier, but around the school and the blocks adjacent to the White Hills, there was still some of the rural tranquility.

Once school was done for the day, Henning could be at his grandmother's as before. He went there, too, even when Jenny had begun rehearsals and was not always home when he got there. He had gotten his own key then. Though when he got to know his new schoolmates, he stayed out more and played with them. One of his friends had a sled made of boards and two pairs of old skates. With it, they rode down the hill on Bondegatan when the snow came. But since a car might come there, too, Maj made him promise unwillingly to only sled in the park.

Since Maj got home late and their kitchenette was small, they still ate at Jenny and Emelie's. It was easier and cheaper, too. And during the winter, Maj had to count on working overtime. At the time when they did the books and inventory, she often had to stay at the office until almost ten in the evening. Then Henning went home alone after he ate. Emelie wanted to go with him, but she was not allowed to. He wanted to show that he could take care of himself now.

He would be in bed when Maj came home, but all too often he was still not asleep. Of course, it was nice to talk to him a while, but it would grow too late for him. He would get too little sleep and was always just as tired in the morning.

Their situation was far from worry-free; a lot of the old bitterness and want was also there. But still, she had a lot to be happy about.

She had dreaded the move, dreaded that she would not achieve anything more than emptiness and loneliness. She had not dared believe in more than the possibility of survival, had worried about regret and thoughts about what had been. But then she found new and unexpected opportunities and even a new lust for life. Together with Henning, she had her own home. And at the office, she had been informed that she could consider herself a permanent employee.

Had Erik not meant more than her really beginning to bloom when she gave him up? Of course, he had meant a lot; of course, she still missed him and even loved him. But she also found that it was not only that she could not live with him, but that she could live without him. That, in spite of everything, she lived better now.

The years with Erik bore the stamp of his agitation. Maybe for the first time now she felt happy in her environment. Maybe in this happiness there was almost some resignation. But it was a relief that not every day was a struggle in the same way as before. The struggle had lasted so long that she experienced the final defeat as liberation.

Now she did not have to always be on the run, could take a little time for herself. Henning had gone to school. She had time to look in the mirror before she went to work; she had not always had time for that before. Was it only this year's fashion that made the coat and dress she had bought have softer, almost more harmonious lines? That made quite a lot of that boyishness disappear.

SOLIDARITY'S DAY

Unemployment and the crisis resulted in terminations of contracts and demands for wage reductions. Right after the new year, thirty-three thousand textile workers went on strike in protest against lowered wages.

The upheaval of the Communist Party and infighting had caused many workers to lose faith in the extreme left. Under the pressure of the crisis on the job market, people were searching for the party that could be expected to give the best protection and the strongest resistance. The provincial elections out in the countryside during the fall had yielded large victories for the Social Democrats, mainly at the expense of the Communists.

In Stockholm, the vote was not going to take place until the nineteenth of March. The situation seemed ideal for the Social Democrats. The members of the Communist Party were at each other's throats; there was opposition between the liberals and the freethinkers. And then a split within the right-wing party occurred; a group called "The Free Right" broke off and obtained *The Evening Paper* as their mouthpiece.

Such opportunities had to be taken advantage of. The unrest was being whipped up harder than usual and more consciously as well. People felt their strength, dared say that it would be a scandal to lose: The labor movement has had mud slung at it from day to day—answer the outrages with the voting ballot. The bourgeoisie want to drive the workers back to the misery of the old days. It is our duty to be victorious.

The agitation was being banged out on the big drums, swirling on tightly stretched skins. A few days before the election, enormous torchlight processions wound through town, from Norr to Söder.

They made their way eastward, but not out onto the large meadow at Gärdet, instead straight into what could be considered the bourgeosie's own lair, Östermalmstorg. Their red banners shone in the torchlight, the echo of their battle songs resounding off the walls of the buildings. And a few days later, they could triumphantly claim: *The bourgeois blockade has been crumbled to pieces. Municipal election landslide in Stockholm. Social Democrat majority.*

Erik had left the Kilbom party. It was not only the capitalist buyers of labor power who were reducing wages; the party had set a good example. One hundred kronor per week was the highest salary a party functionary could receive. He himself had not received more than half since he had had another job on the side. He could manage to get by on as little as Flyg could manage to get by on a functionary's salary. But Flyg was part of the highest leadership and for him they had had to make an exception.

Erik had hardly any political ambitions within the party any longer. And staying in the old party could be an obstacle to his new plans. He wanted to get away from the whole thing.

He should be somewhere within the labor movement in any case. Without any great enthusiasm, he had left his application for admission to the Social Democrats. He had still not received any answer. He had seen the torchlight procession from a distance but not joined in. He had not known if he was welcome. And then he did not want to risk being seen by any of his old comrades from the party.

Just now he was living at a juncture. Between women, between parties, and between assignments. Maj had gone, and he had not let things really be settled with Irene. He had left the one party and as yet not been granted entry into the other. And he had quit his old job without more than a vague hope of a new one.

He had never felt so unsure of himself before. It was probably for this reason that he seemed more assured than ever. Now, when he did not know if he had any worth at all, he would sell himself for as much as possible.

What happened out in the city and in the world did not concern him anymore in the same way. Several hundred unemployed had marched from the People's Hall to City Hall to deliver their demands. They had tried to force their way in, and the police had been called. If things had been like before, he might have been one of the organizers of the whole event. But he would have probably done it a little better, gotten more people involved. It was probably Sillén's followers who were behind it this time; they pushed with their "class against class" theme and added fuel to the fire wherever they could get at it.

On the First of May, it was raining. And since he did not really know where in the procession he should go, he stayed home. It was the first time since his boyhood that he had not participated. He felt a little bitter and nervous; that day reminded him of the day Maj had left. He felt abandoned and betrayed, like the one who gets kicked out of the community.

They had gone—and left him. No one asked after him. He had still not received an answer about his membership application; he had still not gotten the position he was hoping for. And he had not heard from Maj. She could at least have called and told him they were well. He did not want to be obtrusive; besides, she had never wanted him to call her at the office, and she did not have a telephone at home.

There was Irene, of course. But that seemed to make her worth less.

Then he finally got an answer: He could start on the first of June. It was a cooperative company, and he was to be in charge of sales and advertising. Luckily, there were people there who knew what he was capable of, who had seen him in action. He felt how he came to life again; A desire to work streamed through him. They would have no cause for regret; he would give everything he had.

While he waited to embark on it, he stayed at home and planned, almost completely forgetting the world outside. No newspaper arrived in his mailbox; he no longer received *The People's Daily,* and he had not gotten around to subscribing to anything new yet. He had beer, coffee, hard bread, and butter, and he could get by on that until evening came; then he would go out and eat at some restaurant. Irene called one time, but he answered rather curtly that he was working.

He would not arrive at his new assignment empty-handed. But he would still take it carefully to begin with, so he would not commit anything stupid and lay himself open to criticism. Gradually, he would begin to test and make use of his ideas, bring them out like a magician pulls one rabbit after another out of his hat.

Life could be worth living again. But the apartment looked abandoned and untidy since Maj and the boy had gone. He took a break from his work, walked through the rooms. Actually it was a dreary apartment. They had moved here when they were having the hardest time economically, leaving the large and pleasant one they had had earlier. He would like to have it back now, that one or another like it.

A large apartment needed a woman. Well, even a little apartment did, he saw now. It wasn't enough with someone who came and cleaned sometimes; it needed someone who was there picking up every day. He had always wanted to have order around himself; Maj used to say that he was a perfectionist. But it took too much time to do it all himself; he was hoping that his time would be expensive soon.

If everything went as planned, it would also soon be time to settle down. It had to happen sometime.

Maybe it would happen that he married Irene in the end. She wanted to, of course, was waiting for it. And a boss needed to be happily married, not getting involved with secretaries and office girls. Conventions one had despised could still turn out to be practical—once one was a little older, calmer.

He was beginning to feel hungry. It was probably just as well to go out and buy a newspaper and get a bite to eat.

And see if anything new had happened. Strikebreakers had been put in place in the sawmill district and that, of course, had brought along demonstrations and fighting. Most likely, it would end as in Halmstad recently, when the scabs at the lumberyards had disappeared after a period of riots.

There were a lot of people standing around the newspaper stand and already from a distance he saw that the letters of the news placards were unusually big and black.

Five Shot to Death in Ådalen. Military Shoots Demonstrators' Parade.

His hands shook as he pulled out the money to buy a paper. He took that day's edition of *The Social Democrat,* read the giant black headlines running across the front page.

It had gone that far. The military had been called in and shot the demonstrators as they came with banners and a marching band. Among the victims was a young woman who had not participated in the demonstration at all.

And he was no longer a member. Now, when this had happened! He had been sitting there with his little suggestions and ideas, having a good time with his cleverness and dreaming of his private future. While they, his comrades, had been shot down.

He stood there by the newsstand and tried to comprehend what he was reading, tried to understand what had happened. Those in power had sent in the military; such a thing had surely not happened since the food riots during the war. The weak Ekman government had given in to the employers.

The county governor had given the order for the strikebreakers to be sent away, but the sheriff had not conveyed the message to the demonstrators. If they had learned they had won, they would never have needed to demonstrate.

Had they wanted to shoot? Had they decided to "teach the workers a lesson?" Should they show that he who did not give way was risking his life?

In that case, one had arrived at "class against class," the irreconcilable conflict.

What could he do now, where was his place? He did not belong anywhere anymore. He felt doomed to stand powerless and watch at the moment when he felt the need to show his solidarity more than ever.

But here was something: Stockholm's workers and other citizens who condemn the military bloodbath of Ådalen's workers ... are gathering this evening at six o'clock at Norra Bantorget. The procession was going to take the same route and in the same order, as on the First of May, to the meadow at Gärdet.

He could take part, everyone could take part.

He pulled out his watch and checked it; it was already past six o'clock. But he had to catch up with them. He began to run from the newsstand on Odenplan, up Upplandsgatan, and then down toward Norra Bantorget.

It was twenty past before he arrived, just as the demonstrators' procession began to move. He had never seen so many people on the First of May; they were spilling in from everywhere to join, running from buses and streetcars. It did not matter so much where he stood in the procession, as long as he could join in. He almost stumbled in.

The band played Chopin's "Funeral March." Black mourning veils waved over the red banners in the gentle breeze. And during the muted music, an enormous, heavy silence was felt.

Like a black tidal wave, the procession flowed into Kungsgatan; more and more people who had not gotten there in time hurried to join. When they reached Gärdet, there were maybe one hundred thousand, the mightiest mobilization of people the city had ever seen.

When Erik walked home several hours later, he still carried inside him the mood and the experience of fellowship. For the first time in many years, he had not needed to represent something or someone, he had been able to join in completely anonymously. A nobody at all who got to be absorbed into the world.

He had never felt so strongly before that he belonged. And as he walked through the streets in the pale spring evening, he recalled his memory of childhood, all those hungry years, his mother, his skinny and ragged siblings. In fact, everything that he had almost forgotten during recent years when he was so taken up with looking ahead.

Naturally, he would continue, take the job offered him, settle down, and get married, and do whatever one does. It just was like that, one did things like that.

But even if he appeared to distance himself from his origins, he would never forget where he belonged. Not as an organizer and an employee any longer, but only as one of the many.

That feeling returned of having betrayed, of being a defector. At the same time as he wanted to settle down and attain some sort of prosperity, there was also that lingering wish to stand among the oppressed and hungry at the outermost flanks. Although he felt he could see through his old friends and the old beliefs, it felt like committing treason to leave them. Why? Wasn't it natural that over the years one changed one's views, became sensible, somewhat calmer, not such a flaming radical? It could not be that it was only honorable to change one's views when one stood to lose by doing so, could it?

His old party, would never claim any major success; that he understood. Of course, there were a lot of good people in the leadership, but there were too many weak and dangerous ones. And they were squeezed hopelessly between the masses of the Social Democrats and the more acrimonious intensity of the Sillén faction. Ådalen was part of the Sillén stronghold; they would know how to make the most of what had happened. In those regions, the old party comrades did not have much say.

He grew ashamed of his thoughts, that he could see propaganda value in a tragedy.

It was not until he got back home that he remembered that he had actually gone out to get something to eat. His hunger had disappeared in the face of what he had experienced. Now it was creeping back. But he felt no desire to go out and sit down at some tavern. It did not fit in with what had happened today.

He went out to the kitchen and took a few pieces of hard bread from the cupboard, opened a pilsner. He sat down at the kitchen table and felt how some of the solidarity was still there inside him. But also the knowledge that he was on his way out of the daily political work, into the business and advertising world and everything it brought with it. It was a government cooperative he was going to, there was a connection. And yet.

The day the funeral took place in Ådalen, all machines were

silenced, all wheels stopped. The clock struck twelve and for five minutes, the city lay as if paralyzed. People poured out into the streets everywhere, standing still with bared heads in the sudden and frightening silence.

But somewhere a bird was heard chirping.

II

THE BLACK BROWN YEARS

Those years were the black brown years, the years when hope withered away and want and tyranny grew.

During the good years before the big crisis, there had been people who had talked about "Sweden's second period of greatness." Now there was nothing of greatness left. It had been pierced through by the shots from Ådalen and now the last shot in Paris. The man who more than anyone else had symbolized the period of greatness, Ivar Kreuger, "the match king," had committed suicide. Now he was being called a traitor. There was a stock market panic when the stocks in his company were sold off. Those who had relied on him or borrowed from him fell. Some committed suicide. His mansion on Villagatan, with all his furnishings, bed linens, and clothing, was sold at auction before a sensation-hungry public.

At the same time, unemployment and poverty increased. Countless advertisements offered compensation to anyone who could offer work; please reply to "Anything at all." The lines of hungry grew outside the soup kitchens at the Salvation Army and Filadelfia, in the Södra People's Park, and at the locations of the society for feeding the poor. The harvest failed; iron ore exports sank. The value of the krona diminished daily, and the gold standard was abandoned.

Out of desperation and hopelessness, hate and violence grew and the belief in new doctrines of salvation. In countries that had been hit even harder by the crisis, hate swelled like mighty boils. In Stockholm, the Munck Corps was exposed, a "defense corps" armed with weapons smuggled in from Germany. The Nazis in the country were organizing, and the veteran Furugård spoke to an audience of six thousand out on Hötorget, although most of them were opponents. More and more youths with brown shirts and leather straps and boots were seen on the streets. The Communists began to wear uniforms, too.

Unemployment among the youth seemed on the way to driving a whole generation to becoming tramps and loafers. It was mostly those who were somewhat older who got the jobs created by the unemployment commission and relief work of various types. And it took a while before it began to be understood how extensive and devastating youth unemployment was. Young people who were neither supporting their families nor were union members never made it into the ranks of the unemployed and remained uncounted on the periphery.

The black brown years were the years that should have been youth's best and perhaps most active period. They should have learned a trade, built a home, created a foundation for their futures. But over the years, they were forced to while away their time in the waiting rooms of the employment offices and on the stairs of the offices where a position for an errand boy had just been announced.

In the beginning, they really wanted to protest, felt affronted at having to be packed in with the numerous beggars and tramps in the dirty waiting rooms of the employment offices. The atmosphere weighed down on them, robbed them of all human worth. Gradually, they grew used to it. They sat there for hours, spat their gobs into the spittoon in the corner, clicked the tiddlywinks game that stood on the table, and waited. Not for work any longer, but for the stamp. The one that would give some of them the possibility to get some cash support and that for everyone would mean that they had stayed there in line.

It was worst for those who had come from the countryside, maybe in the hope that the opportunities would be greater in the city. Those who lacked relatives and friends, lodging, and a union book. For those, even the people who lived in unheated community garden cottages were somewhat upper class, and bachelor housing was a luxury beyond them. They tried to arrange bedding with paper and sacks in barges and sheds and made their way in dirty, ragged groups to the dump to ferret about. They tried to live on garbage, felt like garbage, were treated like garbage.

To begin with, it had mainly been the workers who had suffered. Afterward, unemployment permeated the middle class as well. Many firms that had been shaken by the Kreuger crash shut down; others tried to survive with diminished personnel. The unemployed office workers grew more numerous, began to squeeze into the lines, came in overcoats and low shoes to shovel snow.

The election in the fall of 1932 was lively; for the first time the politicians got to appear on radio broadcast and propagandize to the people. The government parties suffered a devastating defeat when Prime Minister Ekman, despite his denials, was shown to have received subsidies from Kreuger. Per Albin Hansson became prime minister in a Social Democratic cabinet. In an explanation of their program, it was stated that the new government's primary duty was to find ways to help the victims of the crisis. It was, of course, what one would expect—but could they succeed? Many did not have the ability to believe in words any longer.

A few months later Adolf Hitler became the German chancellor.

UNEMPLOYED

They ended up sitting next to each other in the employment office's waiting room. They said a few words, mostly just to say something about the hopelessness of it all—and the hope for a good snowfall. Then they went out to the street at the same time and looked around at a loss, as if they did not know in which direction they should go.

The younger of them, a skinny, dark-haired kid, started to laugh.

"It's equally meaningless whichever way we go," he said. "Sometimes I wonder why one doesn't simply go out and walk around the world instead of just wandering around here in town."

"Shall we get a cup of coffee?" asked Lennart.

"Don't have a nickel," the other one answered.

Lennart had enough so they could each have a cup.

"Let's walk around a little," said the dark-haired one, who wanted to save up his pleasure.

They walked, a little listlessly and slowly, as unemployment had taught them to walk. There was nothing to hurry for, nothing to arrive for.

It was Lennart who led the way so they walked southward. Sooner or later, he would take a look in the city library's branch on Götgatan. There was a café in the same building.

Although the ranks of the unemployed continued to grow, a surprisingly large amount of work was going on in the city. Far out on the inlet of Riddarfjärden, tall wooden platforms were being constructed above the water. They were preparing the casting of the pillars for the new bridge, Västerbron, that was going to be built. Groups of barges with workers and material flocked around the structures. And at the locks at Slussen, they were filling in the old Polhem locks and digging a new sluice where the statue of Karl Johan had stood. Along Katarinavägen, some of the buildings had been torn down for the new streetcar tunnel that would run under Katarinaberget and

Götgatan, the subway. The hill on Götgatan looked the same as before, but when they walked down it toward Folkungagatan, the whole of Götgatan was an excavated ditch. At Björn's Garden, the entrance to the tunnel stuck its nose out from under the hill. The entire old garden there had become a storage place for boards and beams; digging machines were at work behind the high fence.

They stood there hanging out a while even though the wind was cold. Work was so close and tangible. But they were among the ones shut out, the ones who always came too late, who never made it there before the sign, "Work crew filled," was put up.

At the café, the dark-haired boy, whose name was Sigvard Strand, said that he had been going around town for close to a year and came from Norrland. Lennart had realized from his dialect that he came from the countryside; despite a brave effort, it was not completely a Stockholm dialect yet. Sigvard was nineteen years old and so far had not had any real job, just temporary jobs.

Lennart thought about it; could he call any job he himself had had anything more than a temporary one? The longest one had been for a few months and never anything that could really be called an occupation. And he was, after all, twenty-two, had ruined three years more of his own life. He had had time to do his conscription, of course, but now there was talk of cutting back on military service to save money. So maybe he had lost there, too.

"If one at least had a broad to live off of," Sigvard said. "Someone who earned a few kronor, who could give you a cup of coffee sometimes and had a bed you could crawl down into."

Just the thought of lying in a real bed, if there were a broad in it or not... When Sigvard got a couple of kronor together, he usually slept for a few nights at the old Dihlström Institution on Glasbruksgatan, "the seventy-five öre paradise." Now he was hoping to get a place for a week down at the *Ark,* the houseboat Filadelfia had bought from Gröna Lund amusement park and fixed up. It lay on Klara Lake. During the days he usually stayed around the warming shelters that the city had set up; he could both half-sole his shoes there and mend his pants. There were tools and materials there.

"I left home because I did not want to be treated like a pauper," he said. "And what do you become here? Here, you have to stand in line for hours and on top of that sing hymns for hours in order to get a bowl of soup. If you at least had a union book so that you had papers to show you belonged somewhere, that you were a jobber and not a loiterer."

What did the authorities know? Could even the labor representatives comprehend what it was really like? Those who sat in Parliament and the government lived in another world. If they had ever been in something that was like this situation, they had surely forgotten how it was. Maybe they were working for a better future. But they were not managing the here and now.

Lennart had not given up, not now. Though he did wonder how things would have gone if he had not met Elisabet. The thought of her forced him to keep on going. But sometimes it made the circumstances harder, too; it became even more shameful and unbearable to go around like this when she existed. He had to wonder if she wasn't going to get tired of waiting for him, someone who did not get anywhere, who seemed doomed to end up on the outside.

She had learned to type and was not just an errand girl any longer, but was an office apprentice for real. She had gotten a foot in the door; she would probably manage to keep herself there. Now it was she who paid most often when they went out. It was kind of her, but still it did not really sit well with him.

If Elisabet was the dream that held him up, then his mother was the more commonplace reality, the everyday foundation. Thanks to her, he did not have to be on fireguard duty or sleep on the barges like Sigvard did. She gave him a little money now and then so he could go out for a cup of coffee or buy a new shirt. His old, worn-out mother supported him; she was apparently still worth something from the employers' point of view, she had work. It should have been he who helped her instead of the opposite. But he did not even get the chance to try. He almost envied Sigvard, who at least took care of himself, however mediocre it was.

Since they had sat at the café as long as they could, they went upstairs to the city branch library that was on the floor above. Sigvard had not been there before. He did not really know what he wanted to read, only that it should be something exciting. Lennart got hold of *The Three Musketeers* for him, and, with that, Sigvard sat down in the reading room. But even though the book was as exciting as anyone could wish, he did not have the patience to sit, wanted to go down to the *Ark* and hear how it was going with getting a place for him to sleep.

Lennart stayed sitting there. The years of unemployment had taught him a fair amount, such as organizing his reading. At first, he had only taken a book from the pile, preferably by some author he had heard of. He had read without a plan. Then he had begun to get a sense of context and looked for links, made his way forward, discovered books and writers that he had never heard of earlier. He found that he had to know more about background and ideas. Just now, he was sitting there with a little book whose foreign words and untranslated citations caused him some trouble—but which still gave him a feeling he was handling dynamite. It was called *Civilization and Its Discontents,* and something was said there that cut to his core, or perhaps that cut him free from dreams and illusions? Much of what he had thought and believed seemed to fall like scales from his eyes, and he felt both liberated and frightened, as if naked in the rain.

Religion was a falsification of the truth that people had come up with in order to have the strength to live. To believe that life had a goal was perhaps only a result of people's unbounded overestimation of self-worth. And that "neighbor" the Bible spoke of was not just someone to love, but a temptation, a victim that people wanted to take out their sadism and aggression on.

Yes, of course, it was like that—that happiness "is from its nature only possible as an episodic phenomenon," that no path can lead us to everything we desire.

It was difficult, but it was also fantastic—that happiness was only an episodic phenomenon, that one perhaps loved through inflicting pain and through suffering. More difficult to comprehend and perhaps less meaningful was the part about man becoming a "prosthetic god" and about dwelling houses being a substitute for the mother's womb. Then it was even more troubling to read that the sex life of civilized man was a regressive impulse—the enforced restraint felt like a danger.

One word hit him especially hard, ate away at him as he walked toward home: We are never so defenseless against suffering as when we love. This was something he could see in his mother's face, something he had known the whole time but still remained unconscious of. The truth rendered life fragile and unprotected, what he had possibly believed to be protection itself was instead a lack of protection. For the first time, he felt like he understood how costly and how hard it was to live. To live was to love, to love was to stand unprotected against suffering.

Unemployment had given him something at any rate; maybe he would never have had the time and the reason to read otherwise.

During the months that followed, he got together with Sigvard quite often. Sometimes one of them had work for a few days or weeks. Then they would get together some evenings, until soon they were back in the same old groove again, at the employment bureau. But not to the library. Sigvard had apparently had enough of that. He preferred to be outside. When spring arrived, they climbed up to the lookout on Fåfängan, crawled through a hole in the fence, and lay out on the hill opposite the Saltsjö windmill and watched the boats as they came and went.

For a short while, they could almost forget their unemployment. Such as when they ran into some boys with a football down by the Lugnet industrial area; they also were unemployed. They divided up and had goals between some piles of scraped paint from the boats at the adjacent wharf. But afterward, Lennart felt ashamed, thought he had betrayed himself and Elisabet. He should have been pushing his way up some stairway, trying to get some of those jobs that led nowhere and that, in any case, were not attainable. He did not have time for playing. And, at the same time, he had nothing else but time, empty time.

Before, it had been said that time was money. In that case, he should be rich by now. But time was evidently only worth something when one did not have enough of it, when it became as rare as old stamps with errors. Now everyone was out there offering his time, and so it sank in value, so low that it had to be thrown away since no one wanted it.

Despite Lennart's reading in recent days having probably pulled him further and further away from religion, he decided to visit one of the ministers in his parish. His own confirmation minister had moved to another parish, but the one who had succeeded him was supposed to be very decent, Elisabet had heard. He had helped a whole lot of unemployed youths get into the folk high school. There were possibilities of getting stipends, and the parish also had some funds to draw from, of course.

Naturally, it was more sensible to try to learn something than to just let the time slip by, more effective to study following a thought-out plan than to sit at the library finding his own way.

After a few visits to the pastor's office, he received the news: He would get to begin at Sigtuna Folk High School the coming fall.

Of course, it was going to be difficult to be able to see Elisabet regularly. And he would worry over missing a chance to get a job while he was going to school there. But still, it was something good to anticipate.

SHELTERED CORNER

There was actually no reason to expect so many guests, absolutely no reason to celebrate. But Emelie knew they would come, they kept track of her birthday and came to pay their respects even in the years when her age was not a round number. Now she was turning sixty-three, and she really did not think there was anything special about that. But, of course, it was fun to get together, and certainly those who remembered her were kind. She might find it impossible to understand why, but it was as if her birthday was the most important one. They might forget others but never hers. Even though she was embarrassed at having such a poor excuse as an ordinary birthday, she had to bring home plenty of coffee cake and cream and leave the store as soon as the door had been locked behind the last customer.

Maddeningly enough, even one of her bosses, old Director Lundin, remembered her. He had things to do at the store on Söder and had brought with him some Easter lilies in a vase. He had happened to see that it was her birthday as he was shuffling through some papers, he said. She didn't really believe him; he had an unbelievably good memory and ever since her sixtieth birthday, he remembered her birthday every year. That was not really good; she would have liked him to forget how old she was. So that he would not decide that she was beginning to be too old, that she would need to be replaced by someone new. He was, in fact, approaching seventy himself, but for owners, the same rules did not apply. They could remain as long as they themselves wanted and were able to.

Still, she could feel pretty much at ease; she saw how Director Lundin enjoyed himself in this store. The best branch, he said, always attractive and well run. Almost too well kept—it was truly a pity to expand. But nevertheless, they were going to do so this summer; it was going on ten years since they had done it last. The demands of time, he said. And they had rented the property next door, where a small shop had shut down. Now the adjoining wall was going to be removed so they would have more space.

Emelie thought how a bigger store meant a bigger rent and that would require in her turn increased business, more customers. It was as if she would become responsible for the directors' plans. A lot of new buildings had been built in the area; she would take the opportunity to ask August if there were going to be any more. For August would surely come this evening; he usually came.

Henning walked home to Mormor's right after school. On other days, he might tarry along the way, play with his classmates, take a detour through the White Hills Park. But today he had tasks to carry out. He himself was going to turn ten in a few weeks, and he was looking forward to it. He was asking for a real yo-yo, a "ninety-nine."

Mormor had put out a glass of milk and some sandwiches. She had time off now for a little while but was counting on getting engagements at an open-air theater in the summer. He had gone to see her perform a few times but thought she was even funnier at home.

Now she was really agitated, all red in the face. She had promised to tidy up and set the table, but she had made more things messy than she had straightened up. It was lucky that he had arrived, she said, so the whole thing could be put in some semblance of order. He, as a man, should take charge now; she was only a poor ordinary woman who failed at everything. Even though he might agree with her, he knew that she was only joking; she had messed things up a little extra just to please him. She had put a bouquet of flowers in the coffee pot on the table and placed her slippers on the hat rack. The hat she had put on the floor.

There was no one as silly as Mormor, who could come up with so much and go to such great lengths for a laugh. Mama would never put her good hat on the floor; Mormor would stuff hers in the garbage pail if she thought he would find it funny.

He ate his sandwiches, and she talked on, in that eager way she had when people arrived, as if making up for being alone and silent for several hours. What was it now that they had to have time for? Oh, yes, he should begin with fetching two chairs from his apartment. So there would be enough for everyone they could think might be coming.

No matter how much they goofed around and no matter how much Mormor thought up that prolonged their work, they still had time to set the table and get everything ready and put out the food in the kitchen, whatever could be eaten cold, and even the big bouquet of flowers. It was from Emelie's brother August. On the card was written that unfortunately he and Ida could not come but asked to drop by another evening.

Emelie read the card when she got home. Even if she would have liked to see August and Ida there, maybe it was still good that they waited till another evening. Partly because it would be crowded and partly because the others grew a little quieter and more timid when August was there, no matter how kind and friendly he was.

The little apartment filled with people. Emelie counted them to make sure there would be enough cups. People who lived there, Henning and Maj, were included among them. Then Gunnar and his half-siblings, all except for Erik, who, of course, could not come since he and Maj had separated. But Bengt and his Britta were there, and Beda had come. Even Tyra had surprisingly made an appearance with her oldest son, Allan. Gunnar had come alone; Hjordis had to stay at home with the children. And then Mikael had come, Thumbs' son. And Elisabet's Lennart, of course.

At one time, Emelie had believed that Jenny and Mikael would become a couple; they had seemed to get along well together. But Jenny had, of course, been married twice. Maybe she thought that it was enough. And Mikael had had a hard time finding a job, did not really have anything to get married on. Besides, he had certainly developed his bachelor ways, for fifty-eight years now.

But there had been something there; maybe he had hoped for something... It was nice, in any case, that he had begun to come round again. It had been a while since the last time.

It was crowded—but they seemed to be enjoying themselves. Jenny grew lively when she had an audience and got them to laugh time and again. Even Elisabet laughed; she did not otherwise seem very pleased when her mother "played the clown," as she said. But she had grown more cheerful and easy to talk with during recent years.

Emelie sat down and looked at all those who were honoring her. She had lived with almost all of them for a longer or shorter period. With Mikael and his parents, long since dead, in the house on Åsöberget, back when they were young. She had had all of Bärta's children with her, and she had let Gunnar sleep in her bed for many years, a poor little skinny and frightened boy then, a big and secure man now. It was only Tyra's son, Bengt's Britta, and then Lennart, who had come along later, that she had not lived with. And Tyra's Allan was the only one who seemed a bit of an outsider here, rather tall and heavyset for his fifteen years, not so many words. Emelie was ashamed of what she thought, but guessed that Allan had come along to eat his fill of coffee cake; it seemed so. He had recently come home from the reformatory, Tyra had told them. Now he was supposed to find work, but there was no work to be had.

Tyra's family had moved closer. The bedbug tenement houses in Negro Village had been torn down and the wreckage burned so that the bedbugs would not move on to other dilapidated housing. It had been a terrible sight, since the fire had been close to leaping over to buildings that had not yet been evacuated. There had been many fires for the firemen to keep under control since the kids in the tenements had taken the opportunity to light some little fires at the same time. Naturally, they had tried to lay the blame on Tyra's boys. But this time they had not succeeded; she had the two oldest at the reformatory at that point and the youngest was down with the measles. It was what you call an a-li-bi, said Tyra.

They had gotten an apartment in one of the apartment buildings just a few blocks from Emelie. So now they were nearby again, in their old haunts. And Negro Village was gone. But by Rosenlund some of the old tenement buildings were still standing. David's parents were still living in one of them.

In the slightly condescending tone that she had used toward Beda since they were small, Tyra asked her sister what sort of employment she had. Beda was sharing a room with a friend, and they were both seamstresses, managing quite well. It was not until Tyra had gotten this response that she seemed to notice how Beda had changed, that she was no longer the pitiful stuttering and anxious little girl.

"Well, my goodness," said Tyra. "You look like a real lady. But, of course, you don't have a husband and kids to keep in order."

Beda had sewn her dress herself. The women admired it, the men moved out into the kitchen to smoke and cool off at the open window. Allan had a cigarette that he dug out of his breast pocket and lighted. Lennart and Bengt did not smoke, but Mikael pulled out a cigarillo, and Gunnar scraped out his pipe.

As the men sat there and talked, they realized Gunnar was the only one among them who had a job at the moment; he had his little carpentry workshop, which employed himself and one other man. But Lennart went without work, and Mikael had been on unemployment commission work and built roads for a while but had come back. Bengt, who was an electrician, had suffered from reductions in personnel at the company where he had worked for a few years. And the youngest, Allan, had not gotten anything yet.

They realized that the women had managed better. Jenny sort of didn't count, otherwise they all had work: Emelie in the store, Maj and Elisabet in their offices, Britta at the factory. And Beda sewed, and Tyra scrubbed.

Unemployment commission! Mikael spat out the word. Unemployment commission was, in any case, better than poor relief. At least the money did not have to be paid back. One had worked for it. Or gotten it as public assistance since they had no unemployment relief jobs to give. He had built roads, together with people who had never held a shovel or a pick before, weaklings who collapsed under their loads of gravel. He himself had done some heavy work after he had stopped going to sea. And he had worked in the harbor as a youth, so he could stand a fair amount. But there could never be any contracted work in such company. And a hell of a life they had had in the barracks at night with all the people who had been scraped together from all directions and sent to some damned deserted spot where there was not even a beer café to get away to for a while. But some had stills—so there was something to drink for those who wanted.

The worst had been the filth and the lice. Some slept in their boots and clothes, too tired or drunk to take them off. And when they got the fire going in the stove, the foot sweat rose up like a vapor from all the wet socks. To live like that and work hard for almost no pay... no, he had given up in the end. But he, who did not have a family, could not count on public assistance. Though—he got by, things always worked out somehow.

Gunnar sucked on his pipe, found it was burning now. He knocked it out, said, "We are building a house. I have a job for you for a week or so if you want to take it."

Lennart felt a stab of envy; he never had any such luck. But Mikael and Gunnar were old acquaintances, and besides Mikael had the book that was needed, the union book. It was worse when one had not even come so far as to have that.

No one mentioned Erik that evening, despite the fact that all his siblings were there. Perhaps out of consideration for Maj, perhaps because no one had contact with him any longer. In one way or another, he had caused offense to most of them. Tyra and Elisabet could not tolerate him for various reasons, he had annoyed Mikael with his self-assurance, Gunnar had been called a petty capitalist Social Democrat by him, and he had always snapped at Beda.

Even though it was certainly calmer when Erik was not there, Emelie missed him anyway. He belonged there; these were his closest kin. She would have liked to gather them all together, but could not keep the peace, and so it was easiest the way it was. But she could not approve of it; one belonged where one had grown up. And Erik belonged here.

UNDER THE STARS

Sparkling, crackling stars shot from the sky in cascades. Every night the workers had been in full swing cutting through the iron girders of the elevator footbridge. Tonight it would be completely demolished. Now the Katarina elevator was going to be dismantled, and those fifty-year-old layers of rust and paint gave the onlookers who came hurrying to the spot a brilliant spectacle.

Small men sat crouched between the giant girders high above the street, working with the precipice beneath them. The gates to the footbridge entrance from Mosebacke had already stood closed for several weeks. The bridge railing had been detached and taken down, the boards that had once formed the walkway also had disappeared, and what remained was a skeleton of slippery iron beams. Beside the elevator shaft, and at its point of connection to land, were immense tackles with thick cables running down to the winches on the ground. And where the neon signs once blinked off and on stood the Hedlund Brothers' big sign. It was their company that was running the performance that was drawing more and more curious onlookers.

Tonight, the hundred-ton footbridge was going to be slowly lowered down to Katarinavägen, once the girders had been cut through and the bridge left hanging by the cables. During this time, the traffic toward the eastern side of Söder had to take detours, and the streetcars were replaced by buses that ran up Götgatan.

People on their way home from Friday evening entertainment stopped on the streets and overlooks alongside. Others came out of their homes with sweaters and thermoses to wait out the event. Already by ten o'clock, there were large crowds, though they knew it would still take hours. But the evening was warm and lovely, a red full moon hung over the big Konsum building beside the elevator. The elevator that was the pride of this section of the city, but whose dismantling they were still celebrating with joy.

On a Saturday evening like this one at the beginning of the month, many people were drunk. Yet things proceeded jovially, even when the police drove away those who had placed themselves on Katarinavägen. They could not stay there; they might get in the way of the work. But there were good vantage points on the terraces descending from Mosebacke and on the new plateau beside the old Brunns Park, where the streetcars to Mälarhöjden had a turnaround while the Slussen area was being rebuilt.

Now the streetcars used for assembly work were arriving, and the men began to loosen the overhead lines. Some of the streetcars were from horse-drawn days and were pulled by powerful, aging draft horses. Mr. Hellgren's horses were fed with pieces of warm sausage by the most drunken spectators; a large number of sausage vendors had made their way to the location. When the dismantlers began to loosen the cable fastenings, sparks flew around them. It looked dangerous, but the streetcars were well-insulated.

It was twelve-thirty by the time the net of wires was lowered to the street and driven away. And a half hour later, it was time for the big fireworks, when they cut through the massive weight-bearing girders of the footbridge. They began out by the elevator tower; the bridge had to be cut away there first so that the weight of its span would not cause the tower to collapse.

Bengt had waited a long time in vain, waited to get a position as electrician in the streetcar garage. Instead, he had now begun as an assistant in the overhead power line division. Even if the starting salary was low, it was better than going jobless; he had been doing that long enough. And if he could only get the job it would mean a certain amount of security and safety for the future; the streetcars were part of a semi-municipal enterprise. Although even that had been hit by the crisis, and for the first time in many years, it had not been able to distribute any dividends to its shareholders.

Now Bengt had participated in lowering the overhead lines. And he really ought to go home and sleep a few hours before it was time to put the lines back in place again. But he too had been curious and interested; it was hard to leave the show when the most exciting part was about to begin. Imagine if the cables did not hold, if the tower could not bear the weight, if the elevator bridge did not sink down as slowly and neatly as the engineers had calculated... If he were lying in bed and sleeping while something happened that the whole city would talk about for years to come.

Britta was not expecting him; he had said he might stay there. She was probably asleep. Otherwise he preferred to stay home in the evenings. He had not had a proper home as a child, now he had one. "Homebody," she might say jokingly when she had the urge to go to the movies or go out. But for the long period when he had been unemployed they had not had the money even for cheap entertainment. But they had managed to get by and now he had work again, now everything would be better. Maybe they could even dare to think of having children.

He stepped back a little, closer to the onlookers, to see better. Someone called his name. It was Erik. Elegant, in a light-colored summer hat and well-pressed suit. Bengt wiped off his hand on the back of his pants before he greeted him, feeling simple and ordinary. Despite Bengt being wider in the shoulders, and there being only one year between them, he always felt small in the presence of his brother. Erik had always decided things, Bengt had obeyed. It was Erik who had led the games and the undertakings, it was also he who had brought Bengt into the party. It was Erik who had taken care of Maj. But now Erik had left both the party and Maj. Erik was living in another way, faster and harder, he used people and ideas. While Bengt held onto what he had gotten and stayed where he had landed.

Now it was Erik too who took the initiative. He was the one who asked the questions. Bengt answered.

Yes, both Maj and the boy were doing fine, as far as Bengt knew. And Emelie was working as usual while Jenny did not have any engagements this summer.

Erik had not seen Maj and the boy for a long time. He felt like it was best to stay away. There could easily be upsetting scenes if he tried to stay in touch. And a child should not have to be part of these things, would feel best to live in peace and quiet with the one who took care of him.

Maybe it sounded sensible and good, but Bengt probably thought that Erik seemed rather detached. Erik talked about his new job and all the plans he had. That he had changed apartments and was married. Erik probably did not have time to take interest in those who in any way belonged to the past. He had always lived so completely in the present.

But the encounter with Bengt seemed to please him. And in the encounter, there was no reproach or unease, they did not owe each other anything, there were no conflicts to remember. In fact, they had never argued or not gotten along, not even as boys. Maybe because Bengt had always given in.

Erik felt lonelier than before. Since he had left the old party, he had lost most of his friends, and since he had left Maj, he did not see any of his relatives anymore. Now, of course, he had colleagues at work and a wife—but that was not really enough. Besides, Irene was expecting a child and was not as lively as usual; she wanted to rest and be at home. If Erik was to be at home, he wanted to have people around him, life and activity. If there was only a woman whining that she felt sick, he would rather sit alone at work. It had gotten so that he stayed at the office as long as possible. There was always work. And he had been successful. He had been recognized for his contributions, he was making good money, and it was going to get better. So he had excuses to give if Irene complained about sitting around alone. In such a big fine home as she had…

But on a warm and beautiful Saturday night like this, he, of course, could not stay in the office. Irene and he had eaten dinner out, then she had gotten tired and wanted to go home. He had gone with her, but once she had gone to bed, he went out. As an old Stockholm townie from Söder, he had to be there when the elevator was torn down, he said.

They stood silently a while; the summer night was unusually warm. The star-like shower of sparks was still falling over the street by the hill. The hissing sound of the many cutting flames blended together like sighing.

The area around Slussen was one huge demolition and construction site. Giant pile drivers stuck up between half-poured columns and endless planking. Tunnels gaped in Katarinaberget; the subway was to be ready by fall. Something approaching a pattern could be discerned, but it would take several years before the new Slussen with viaducts and underpasses would be ready. The buildings below and closest to the elevator had been torn down. In their place would soon be built one new building to be combined with a new elevator.

Bengt fetched his thermos and invited Erik for a cup of coffee. Just recently, the water and sky had been united in one deep blue hue that made the lanterns and lights along the strand glow a sharp yellow. Now it was as if their glow was being fed at the same time by the first streaks of morning light slipping across Kastellet and Östermalm. Dawn was already breaking. The short night had barely provided any coolness; one could imagine that it was the heat from the cutting flames that was reaching them.

But now the sighing stopped; the showers of sparks were no longer falling. The one-hundred-ton bridge span was hanging by tackles and cables, and was slowly being lowered. But it was almost four in the morning before the span was resting on the ground, and the workers could begin anew, now to cut the girders into pieces. The iron scrap was to be driven in trucks to the railway cars that were waiting at Stadsgården.

Bengt went and found out when it might be time to set up the overhead lines again. The earliest they would begin would be around two o'clock.

The show was over. Erik wanted Bengt to go back with him and get a late-night sandwich, and Bengt obeyed, even if he was beginning to feel tired and would probably have preferred to go home.

They walked through a dead city. Now it had grown completely light. Windows stood open everywhere; it was as warm as midday. But empty and silent, only a few street sweepers with brooms and horses and carts.

Erik lived in one of the buildings on Norr Mälarstrand that had been built a few years earlier. The apartment was light, spacious, and beautiful. Even if Bengt knew that Erik had been successful in life and had totally different circumstances than his own, he still was taken aback. It was unbelievable that they were brothers, that at one time they had lived in the same pokey hole. That Erik dared live like this; he himself would never dare do it. But he did not have to worry about that either.

No, he did not want to sit down in the fine room. He had his work clothes on, might get it dirty.

"Then we will sit in the kitchen," Erik said.

He opened the window; maybe it would be a little cooler that way. Then he got beer and snacks. A schnapps. Bengt only wanted a schnapps; he was going to go work again.

The conversation grew a little halting now. They were beginning to get tired, and Bengt also got quieter in the unfamiliar surroundings.

Then the door opened. A dark, rather buxom woman came out into the kitchen and took a few steps toward Erik and the window. She was dressed in a thin nightgown that revealed her body's soft round contours. It was a moment before she caught sight of Bengt and quickly turned around—while Erik burst into roars of laughter. She came right back in, having put on a bathrobe. Now she was laughing, too. Although Bengt felt even more unsure of himself and clumsier than usual, he had to take part in the general laughter.

It was so warm, she complained. She had not been able to sleep. Erik poured a beer for her, and she took sips from the glass. She did not want to have a sandwich.

"She's expecting," said Erik, even though he had already said it earlier. "But womenfolk usually like herring when they are in that condition." And he took a little piece on a fork and held it out to her. But she did not want any.

Irene was her name, and it was clear that Bengt was expected to say it. She said Bengt; it sounded as if it was not difficult for her to do it. But for him it was harder, and he avoided saying her name or the familiar form of you.

Gradually, he came to realize that she was after all just an ordinary person, and had worked in an office before they got married. And apparently she liked having company, as she talked on. It would feel good to go out and take a swim somewhere. But Erik worked all the time; Bengt could not imagine how unbearably hard-working his brother was.

Yes, he knew. Erik had always pushed himself.

Altogether too much. What was the point of earning money if you gained no pleasure from it?

This was something for Bengt. He had never come so far. For him, it had always been a question of earning enough to eat and to live. But if the beautiful Irene was alone here all her days, then she at least wanted companionship in the evenings.

Erik made coffee and offered cognac, good cognac. And Bengt, who should have left a long time ago, stayed where he was. It had become very pleasant. It seemed as if Irene had not been able to talk for several weeks and was making up for it now. She grew so lively, was so ready to laugh. And it only grew warmer, despite the open window. The air was trembling with the heat. Irene's bathrobe fell open more and more without her seeming to notice it. He caught unsettling glimpses of her beneath the thin nightgown, hurrying to pull his gaze away. He looked instead at Erik, who had thrown off his jacket and opened his shirt at the neck.

At around nine o'clock in the morning, Bengt left. And on the way home through the city, he thought about his encounter with his brother and maybe even more about his encounter with the beautiful

Irene—would they ever meet again? Maybe. But that would probably be completely by chance then as well; they lived so differently.

When he got home, Britta had just woken up. He sat on the edge of the bed and told her about his night's events. But she was more interested in Erik and Irene than in the elevator bridge. A little envious when she heard about their fine apartment, perhaps a little jealous when he talked about Irene. That a person could walk around in that fashion... that she did not cover herself properly when she saw that Bengt was there.

"She was much more attractive than I am, of course. In a silk nightgown and everything...." She sat up in bed, displaying her own nightgown.

In that moment, he made a big and difficult decision that would cause him much worry: She would have such a nightgown. He would go into a store and buy one.

He washed up at the sink, changed into his Sunday trousers, and sat down at the table by the kitchen window and read the newspaper he had bought on the way home. He heard Britta's quick, barefoot steps cross the floor but did not have time to look up before she pulled the newspaper away from him. Then she sat down on his knee and threw her arms around his neck. For propriety's sake, he glanced at the window although he knew that there was only the empty party wall outside. Once he had ascertained that this was still the case, he took hold of her, stood up, and carried her into the other room.

It lay in shadow; the shade was rolled down but flapped a little in the cross breeze. Streaks of light slipped in and out and sometimes sparkled. Like the starry sparks last night, almost.

And he felt a great happiness at the thought that he had Britta, and time and time again, he had to assure her that she was much prettier than anyone else.

They went out a few hours before it was time for him to return to his workplace. A thermometer in the shade showed it to be almost thirty-five degrees centigrade. This was the hottest day the city had experienced in more than one hundred thirty years.

Britta was red from the heat and hung a little heavily on his arm. And they looked in the display windows; there was so much they would have liked to buy now that he had a job. But when he pointed to an especially thin and low-cut nightgown, she protested almost in consternation. She should have one just like it, he thought and laughed to himself.

It never happened. First of all, it took a while before he had enough money, and then they found out that Britta was expecting a child. There was too much else that it became necessary to buy.

But sometimes he dreamed that she came walking in a shimmering and transparent garment like that one. And around her fell a shower of stars.

WAITING

The longstanding crisis crippled everything. Even city life grew immobile, became paralyzed. It was especially noticeable after a halt in construction ensued, and consequently even more people were unemployed. There were not nearly as many cars on the streets as before, streetcar traffic diminished, the harbors lay empty. Newcomers to the city were fewer than ever before, and the number of inhabitants stagnated.

The banking system showed, however, a record rise in reserves. But the money was not put into use and into jobs, and instead the idle capital just piled up in the bank vaults. Interest rates sank once more.

The whole summer had been wasted. There was still no sign of light at the end of the tunnel. The construction workers apparently did not intend to yield.

August Bodin sat in his large and beautiful room in his office but did not feel any of the usual comfort. He had not turned on the lights even though it was beginning to grow dark. In the dusk, he was looking for someone unknown, his opposition, maybe his prosecutor. The one who had to be convinced, be prevailed upon to understand that August Bodin was not any sort of ruthless extortionist, but rather an ordinary decent person, in fact, a worker himself.

He tried to give the unknown a face, features he recognized. It was easier to argue then, if he had an idea of how the response would sound.

The face he was looking for existed in the past. It was from there the worst accusations came: from his origins. In other words, from himself? He had no guilty conscience; did he feel like an extortionist?

No, of course not. He had nothing to reproach himself for. Everyone knew that construction workers were among the best paid. All the other groups complied and went along with lowered wages, as the crisis demanded. But not them, not the ones who had it best.

The other day he had seen a drawing by Chatham. It showed how small, ordinary people had to stand in the dark chasm of the crisis because an enormously fat bricklayer was filling the opening toward the sun and happiness: "The way is blocked until he has squeezed the bacon through it."

The caricaturists had created a scathing stereotype of a bricklayer in their pictures: a fat guy with an enormous rump in britches hanging from suspenders, with a droopy hat, and a droopy mustache, and a beer bottle.

Did Knut look like that now?

Knut, or Knutte, as they called him, was a son of Thumbs and Matilda, August's parents' friends. Knut's older brother, Rudolf, had married August's sister, Gertrud, but they had emigrated in 1909 and Rudolf was dead now. August saw Mikael, their younger brother, sometimes at Emelie's, and Mikael no longer heard from Knut either. Besides, Knut was living in Göteborg, far from Stockholm.

But Knut was a bricklayer. And bricklayers were the toughest among the opposition.

Knut had been rather broad already in childhood, a husky fellow. He might look like the caricaturists' bricklayer now.

The bricklayers were an upper class among the working class. For this reason, they were naturally often the object of other workers' jealousy, and this jealousy had been fed. It had yielded results as well, such as the municipal workers taking it upon themselves to lay the tiles in the "subway" at the cost of the city—to the fury of the bricklayers, who claimed that the work was more expensive for the city than if they themselves had done it for their asking wage.

If Knut had been sitting there on a chair in the twilight, August would have said, there you have it! Not even your own workers feel solidarity with you. You have demanded too much, provoked their sense of justice.

And the independent negotiations have led to pure blackmail, he would say. Total anarchy reigns at the workplaces, just think of the work shed meetings. It just cannot continue this way; we have to have proper contracts and a certain amount of order.

Look at the levels of salaries in other professions, he would say.

There, the workers have found themselves with much greater wage reductions than we ask of you. Even though their starting positions were worse.

But Knut would surely sit silently. No justifications were eating at him. No justifications had eaten at his father once upon a time.

It is, in any case, better to have a lowered wage than to go without work, August would finally threaten.

But even if Knut said nothing, he meant to say: You are a traitor to the class you have come from. Don't try to claim that you would satisfy yourself with a bricklayer's salary. What you employers suffer from most is that we bricklayers sometimes manage to earn some money without working ourselves to the bone.

You want to have slaves. Municipal workers do not understand what is in their best interests. They do not realize that bricklayers are fighting for them too. We go before—and we do not give in. Instead of envying us, they should strike until their own starvation wages are raised.

But we are in a time of crisis—now is not the time.

But the time is convenient for you. You are earning from others' misery, exploiting the crisis in order to force down our salaries. You believed you could break us—and when we do not give up, you hate us. Look at the drawings, admit it: You hate us. You laughed when you saw that drawing of the worker in the chasm, you certainly remember that one.

No, August assured him, of course not! Maybe I laughed—but I didn't hate. I have not forgotten my origins, I wish all people well. The only thing I ask for is understanding when there are difficulties. And a certain amount of order.

August suddenly realized he had spoken aloud in the twilight, as if Knut had really been sitting there in the twilight.

A little angrily, he turned on the light, scaring away the shadows. Was he beginning to grow old?

Knut would never understand. Just as little as Thumbs had understood. And the bricklayers would not consider giving up even though both the government and the Trade Union Confederation were trying to get them to compromise. Furthermore, the general contractors did not intend to go along with any compromise. If anything, they demanded capitulation.

August was a member of the employers' association. Some of its members had been traitors. They were mainly those who had not gotten their construction jobs done on time and let their workers stay on after the first of April and work for a previously agreed upon salary. In this way they had avoided the strike. He could not operate that way, had been part of the organization for too long, was good friends with many, and had to show solidarity. Whether he wanted to or not. Probably he could have gone along with keeping the wages the same. Even though they were too high. But the free negotiations had to be done away with; They had caused too many problems. There had to be regulations in the profession, clear rules, and strict standards. He agreed with that. It felt like better regulations were part of the inheritance he wanted to leave his son. Karl Henrik needed the support that better regulations could give.

August did not have many years left; soon, it would be time to hand over the responsibility. And he knew his son's weaknesses. A conflict could only be settled through calm, work could only be led with assurance. Karl Henrik was rather hot-headed, got into arguments easily. If nothing else, fixed contracts and central negotiations were needed for his sake.

These last few years, August had wanted to do his utmost to stabilize the company. And time just passed without anything being able to be done. His last and, therefore, most precious time.

He got up and walked over to the window. The October afternoon was gray, a woolly mist lay over the street and the roofs of the buildings; the cars drew faintly shimmering trails in the asphalt.

He looked at the clock. He had promised to pay a visit to his adoptive mother. It was time.

Annika Bodin had turned eighty-seven. She felt the weight of the years, how they threatened to break her. And also how light they were, like dried leaves that whirled away. It grew so empty around her. All the people she had known would soon be dead. All her life experiences as well.

Sometimes she thought that the only thing she had left was her memory. She had always had a good memory. But not much worth remembering.

For thirty-five years, she had been a widow. But, in fact, she had been quite alone before that; poor Fredrik had not been much for company those last years. It was actually when August had gotten married that the loneliness had started. She had never quite been able to forgive Ida for taking August from her. Everything would naturally appear to be fine between Annika and her daughter-in-law. But it was not really fine. Ida was always just as kind and friendly when she came over—but she came over quite seldom. And the grandchildren practically never now that they had become their own people. Could it be Ida's fault?

Annika Bodin had always needed to hold onto people to get them to stay with her. If she let them go, they disappeared. All those countless housekeepers and maids.

Fredrik's relatives that she had not heard from for many years now. All the friends she had had—but seldom for more than a short period.

Now there were, in fact, only two people left. The old faithful servant who was too old to be able to leave. And then August.

The only thing in her life that seemed worth remembering had connections with August. With August—also even before August. His father, who she had known when she was young, the harbor worker. Henning, who had probably been a little fond of her for all that. But she had wanted up and out of the squalor and poverty, and when she met Fredrik, she also had met her opportunity to succeed.

She had succeeded, but not until afterward did she understand how much it had cost her. To succeed had cost her her happiness. If there was now any happiness to be found in the world.

August had become a replacement. For Henning who she had let down and for her own children that she had never had. She and Fredrik had adopted August after Henning's death. But August's mother had lived for several years afterward. He had siblings; he had gotten married. Annika had never been able to have him completely, had always had to satisfy herself with part of him. And it had been difficult at times to feel how large a part of him was still there in that impoverished little home on Söder. It was something that he had hidden from her, a part of his life that he kept locked away.

The church bells were tolling out there now; she could just discern the light in the large church windows between the as-yet bare trees. A burial. The same bells that had tolled when Fredrik was buried; they would toll for her, too, one day rather soon. She did not like the bells; they were a constant reminder. She should have moved a long time ago; now it was too late. Yes, she could just as well sit here as anywhere else and wait.

The faithful old servant came in and told her that August had arrived.

"Sofi can tell the building contractor to come in," she said.

Worriedly, she looked him over. He looked much too old and worn out. That terrible strike was apparently hitting him hard. Every time Annika Bodin thought of the strike and the unreasonable workers, she would flare up, feel how the blood rushed to her head, and had to really force herself to calm down. She would not let them be the death of her!

"You have grown old," she said. "You work too hard."

"I am old," he replied. "Several years older than Father was when he retired from the firm."

"Well, that was another case with poor Fredrik."

But she did not want to talk about Fredrik now. In fact, not even about August and his family, although she naturally asked how Ida was and how their children and grandchildren were. It was herself she wanted to talk about, and her affairs.

While she was sitting here alone, she had thought about her possessions that had been collected during a long life. When she had met

Fredrik, she had not owned more than the clothes she had on her back. But Fredrik had inherited quite a lot, of course, and they had bought and piled things up over the years that had passed. Now, these possessions worried her; she felt responsibility for how things would be preserved. She wanted to decide who would have what. Sofi, her faithful servant, would need August to be kind and find her a suitable living arrangement. There was money put away for her and what Sofi had in her room she could keep.

Otherwise, August and his children would get everything. But a piece of gold jewelry she had once bought she thought August should give to his sister Emelie, as a token that old Annika had appreciated her. And she wanted to give something to the little Henning Nilsson, as a memento of a friend of August's biological father. August must help her to find something appropriate.

While it grew dark outside, they sat in the old-fashioned furnished room and conversed. And he felt once again how lonesome and unhappy she was, how she desperately tried to cling fast to life and to people. She wanted to give away something that would make them remember her, that would make it possible for a little something of herself to remain and survive.

Of course, she was aware of how strong her selfishness was, how her whole life she had thought mainly of herself and acted accordingly. His father had not had it so easy, nor August himself either. They had had to bend themselves to her wishes in the long run, always been a little afraid of her. She had made herself alone and now the big emptiness frightened her. There was not so much he could do for her, not much more than sit here and listen.

As he walked home, he thought he could feel her loneliness ache inside of him.

The rain still lay like a large cloud of fog over the city. No drops fell, but his coat grew slightly damp from the light moisture. He took the route across Drottninggatan, maybe to relive the memory of how he had walked from his home to his office a long time ago, before he had gotten married. He remembered a morning when he had seen six hired coaches drive through the streets, in one of them Hjalmar Branting, who had been fetched from Långholmen Prison by his faithful followers. Those were other times; Per Albin certainly sent no one to Långholmen now.

And here was where Ida had worked. They had not met for several years, and then he had suddenly seen her just as she stepped onto the horse-drawn omnibus, the one with the white horses.

So long ago, another city and another time.

Now the lights outside the picture theater were glittering. He passed by Skandia Theater, which was showing "A Night in Smygehus." The evening papers' placards were displayed outside the tobacconists', telling about the trial over the burning of Parliament in Germany, and the police hunt for "Beautiful Bengtsson," the robber-dynamiter.

A tall thin fellow said hello to him a little guardedly and reluctantly, and August lifted his hat. It was one of "his" bricklayers, a capable man who he hoped would come back when the strike was over. There was a risk of losing the core crew one had built up. And, once again, he felt his impatience—may the conflict soon be resolved so they could begin to work again for real. There was nothing so irritating as just waiting and waiting.

MARKED

Many of the city's youth felt driven away. Some of them went off as hobos through the land, half-starved, lodging in barns, picking up odd jobs from time to time. Others landed in jobs created by the unemployment commission, cutting peat and building roads. A lot of them turned to crime and were put in institutions or were broken by hardship and sickness and ended up in the sanatorium at Uttran. Some were lucky.

In one way or another, the years of crisis left a mark on most people. These years would not be forgotten but rather dwelt on. They would be blamed for future failures, for someone not getting the start one had a right to have gotten. These years would be remembered as the impoverished and hungry years. But still, they would be bathed in a glow, perhaps precisely because they had cost so much.

Lennart was well aware of his belonging to the privileged ones, and he was happy at the folk high school in Sigtuna. He got to read and to learn, he gained clearer views, his horizon broadened. Although he seldom took part in the lively debates himself, he liked to listen and take note of things. It was not until afterward, if a few people were sitting and talking, that he might come forth with his own opinions.

Despite all this, he longed to get back to the city. It was, after all, where his home lay. The future and opportunities lay there; it was there he had to defeat any opposition. Everything else was wasting time. It felt that way even if he hoped the knowledge he gained would make it easier for him later.

And Elisabet and his mother were in the city, they who were closest to him. When he could afford to, he traveled home during days off. On Saturdays, Elisabet would go directly from work to the station to meet him. They had found a newly opened snack bar in the center of town where they could eat pretty cheaply: ham hock and mashed turnips and potatoes for sixty-five öre, or a Wiener schnitzel for seventy-five.

Usually, it was Elisabet who paid.

Then they would walk home through the city toward Söder, passing theaters and movie houses. *The New Moon* with Margit Rosengren and Lars Egge was showing at Oscar's. Jan Kiepura sang "A Song for You" at the Göta Lion. But they could seldom afford any entertainment.

Most of the time, they went to Elisabet's place and drank coffee. They would sit together with her Aunt Emelie in the kitchen. Jenny was performing at one of the small theaters. It was pleasant but still felt like doing something other than what he actually wanted to and should be doing. At his place, there was always his mother, at Elisabet's always her aunt. If they wanted to be alone, they only had the streets. And the doorways where he could hold her a little while before they were separated for the evening.

Christmas drew near. The newspapers began the collections to provide food for all of the city's poor and needy. The "bus Santa" traveled around and collected Christmas sausages and Christmas breads that would then be distributed. Charities held bazaars and gave clothes and shoes to poor children. Two of Tyra's sons were among the lucky ones. They got to dance around the Christmas tree at the Stockholm Guild and were photographed by the newspapers.

Tyra brought along the clipping one Sunday evening to the apartment on Erstagatan and proudly pointed out her boys. She had brought along the older one, Allan, too. It was probably not only for the sake of the coffee cake that he had come along. Emelie felt regret now; she had been unfair. Of course, the boy ate as much as he could get hold of—but that was not so strange, they barely had enough at home. Still, it was chiefly to be with Tyra that he had come. He reminded one of a large and clumsy but faithful dog that would rather not stray from his mistress' side.

Of course, it was good that the boys had been given suits, Tyra said. But she had wanted to get something for herself and David as well. That did not go over so well. She had gone to the poor relief and showed them her coat: Look at how torn it is. Must I go around like this? But the person had answered that one could still keep a needle and thread in any case. As if it was worth repairing this old coat!

Lennart could see that Elisabet did not like Tyra's prattle. To Elisabet, Tyra's exposing herself this way was disgraceful; for Tyra it was natural.

Elisabet could not dissimulate, not humiliate herself. She felt almost ill seeing others do it.

With Tyra, there was something of a professional humiliation parade with a beggar's offensive cheekiness. Tyra could reveal anything at all of her miserable home life; she made an exhibit of her drunken husband, her institutionalized kids, the bedbugs, the rags.

It was so clearly visible what Elisabet was thinking that Lennart was amazed that Tyra did not take offense. But she pretended not to notice anything, perhaps because she had come to borrow money from Emelie.

But Emelie quickly began to tell about how they were expanding the shop where she worked. Then they learned that old Annika Bodin had died a few days ago. August had said his adoptive mother wanted Emelie to have a piece of jewelry she had. Henning also was going to get something as a memento of a lady who had known the first Henning, Emelie's father, Henning's mother's grandfather.

Fifteen-year-old Allan treated the five-year younger Henning as an equal and as someone the same age. If he had not been out of cigarettes, he probably would have asked Henning if he wanted one.

Allan was big and strong, and his voice had become rough. To look at, he was almost a man. But also still a frightened child who anxiously kept as close to his mother as possible. Sometimes he dreamed they were coming to take him away to the reformatory again; then he would scream in terror and wake up. And would not calm down before he had crawled into his mother's bed and hidden there, safe in her warmth.

She was strong, the only protection he had. But against "them"—the dangerous people, society, the reformatory—her powers were not enough. If they wanted to take him, then they just took him, even if she tried to resist. Deep inside was always the terrible knowledge that life was without mercy.

He belonged to the completely unprotected, to those who must fail. He had learned this. Already his manner of movement condemned him. He was so clumsy, dropping everything, bumping into everything. He could never avoid drawing attention to himself; they would catch sight of him. And once they had caught sight, they would catch hold of him and put him in the reformatory. There, he would bear the blame for everything that happened. The clever and cunning ones would hide behind him. He would be beaten, both for what he himself and others had done.

That was why it felt safe and good that Henning was smaller, for then he was probably not dangerous. And he seemed nice, too. Henning had a little sticker album with stamps in the pocket; they were duplicates.

"If you want, I can get stamps," Allan said. "I know where you can find them."

They made a plan to meet the next day when Henning was done with school. Allan was still without work so he did not have anything special to do.

"Shall we build with matchsticks?" Henning suggested.

They sat down in a corner. The goal was to build a tower, stick by stick. They took turns placing them, and the one who placed one so carelessly that the tower fell had to take all the sticks that fell. The one who used up all his sticks first won.

Allan was no worthy opponent. But he lost patiently and without giving up. Henning won time and again without Allan getting into a bad mood.

Maj sat and watched the boys, how Henning seemed to take the lead. Sometimes he was too daring. He had not run into any adversity yet, was still unmarked. She had managed to protect him; the divorce from Erik had not left any wounds. Naturally he missed—and would continue to miss—a father. But there was nothing harrowing, no crisis or scene for him to remember.

He did well in school, apparently got along well with his classmates, too. But his successes made him maybe too confident and, therefore, easily vulnerable when setbacks were to come. She did not know if she was cheered or worried when she saw Allan and Henning get along so well.

But it was hard to be afraid of Allan; He looked so harmless.

Lennart was going back to Sigtuna. Elisabet went with him to the station. They were the first ones to leave.

She grumbled half-aloud to herself as they walked. About Tyra, who had no shame, and about all of them at home, who let themselves be fooled into lending her money they would never get back.

Because Elisabet was the way she was, life had to be more difficult for her than it was for most, he thought. She suffered from things that others did not even notice. She listened for tones of voice that might express contempt, suspected that every kindness was an expression of high-handedness. She was more sensitive than anyone else he knew, easier to hurt and wound.

It also could be difficult for him. He had to try and calm her and then she believed that he was not reacting at all to what had upset her. Of course, he was. But not so strongly and not in the same way. While she saw flaws in people, he sought to see them in the context of their circumstances. It was maybe not so strange that Tyra had become the way she had become, nor Allan. They had been handled so roughly in life; they did not have the strength to react differently. They were maybe more weak than bad.

But for Elisabet, weakness and evil were almost the same thing.

Allan was standing and waiting in the Sofia schoolyard. Since he himself had gone to Högalid School, he felt pretty safe, was not troubled by any dark memories.

Henning came through the school door. He immediately caught sight of Allan, waved to his classmates and left them. Proud, of course. It wasn't everybody who was friends with such a big guy.

"Let's go home to Mormor and get a sandwich first," Henning said. Of course, it was fine; Allan would also get one. Mormor had promised.

All the warnings he had received to not go along with anything Allan might do that was foolish or wrong—he kept those to himself.

This suited Allan just fine. And Jenny had to fix twice as many sandwiches as usual. She sat and looked at the unmatched pals, calling them in her mind lighthouse and caboose. Though the lighthouse seemed to act more like a caboose. It was Henning who took the lead from what she could see. But once they had gotten out on Folkungagatan, he had to stop—it was Allan who knew where you could find stamps—he had to show the way.

Yes, indeed, he had figured something out. Actually, it was his mom who had come up with it. People threw away so much that could actually still be used. Allan would wander around town and pick one thing and another from trash cans. Bottles and such that you could sell to the rag-and-bone men.

Though there was a difference between trash cans and trash cans. You chose the place according to what you were looking for. If you wanted leftover food and bottles, it was best to walk through residential areas. If you were looking for paper to draw on or stamps, then you should go to where the offices were. Along Skeppsbron, for example. There were a lot of firms there that sold things abroad and received a lot of letters. There were loads of envelopes in the trash cans sometimes.

Allan showed Henning the way into the small, dark, back courtyards. Sometimes Henning had to stand guard and watch in case any doorman showed up. It was important to have an escape route; it was best to have at least two entrances to the courtyard. Then they could easily slip away when someone came.

Henning kept himself a little apart to begin with, having not dug through trash cans before. But in this neighborhood, they were pretty neat, containing mostly paper, sometimes coal and cinders from the stoves. They got hold of some large bundles of envelopes, and he saw immediately that there were plenty of stamps that he did not already have. He grew more and more excited.

Allan had a bag with him and gathered up some bottles, too. Henning tore off the corners of the envelopes with the stamps and stuffed them into his schoolbag. Both of them were quite dirty before they were done. They walked home tired but proud.

Christmas came, and Henning received his present from old Annika Bodin. In fact, he was quite disappointed. An old pen and ink stand. But they told him it was very fine, of real silver. Surely worth a lot of money—though he would keep it as a memento.

Lennart had vacation and came home for Christmas and New Year's. A few days before Christmas, he got part-time work as a bicycle delivery boy. In that way, he earned a little money and could afford to give Elisabet a Christmas present. It would be a new book, he decided. And he chose a newly released poetry collection that was called *Barefoot Children* and was by Nils Ferlin.

You have lost your word and your paper slip,
You barefoot child in life

he read aloud. And it could be thought of that way, it was really like that. He did not have much to offer, there was not much he could hope from a new year. The future seemed just as gray, though there were optimists who claimed that they could detect the first signs that the crisis was going to ease up.

SWIMMING AT KÄLLTORP

As if by agreement, the neighborhood's delivery boys all arranged to go home and take with them their big and heavy delivery bicycles. Three-wheelers with cargo platforms in front or back, two-wheelers with a little front wheel under an enormous baggage rack.

They parked their vehicles outside their doorways and hurried in to grab a bite to eat. The other boys from the building began to gather around the bicycles. They had to stay there if they were going to be able to go along.

The summer day had been hot and sticky and the heat still held. Most of the windows in the big tenement houses stood open; fumes from food cooking rose in small gray clouds through the kitchen windows. Men with bare torsos or dressed only in white undershirts leaned out over streets and courtyards. Sweaty women went between stove and kitchen table.

The delivery boys began to gather around their bicycles, squeezing the tires and pumping them up a few times, shoving away small boys who were getting too close. It almost looked like they were getting ready for a race; the delivery boys were filled with the sense of worth that privileges and the right to decide can give. They determined who would get to go with them, they decided, with or without permission from the bicycles' owners, over the bicycles.

Two girls stood hanging around a little way from the pack of boys, waiting to be invited. Each one had a cardigan over her arm. They were whispering and giggling, trying to look blasé and interested at the same time.

It was a perfectly fine evening to ride to a lake, Källtorpsjön, and swim. But only a few of the many would get to go along.

Even a "dancing dandy," a twenty-year-old who was too old for these kinds of escapades, took a few turns past and maybe wished himself back a couple of years in time. But he pushed his bowler down more securely on his pomaded, center-parted hair, stuffed his silk necktie inside his jacket lapels, and sauntered slowly away, with his pants slapping at his heels.

Allan had been working for some weeks as a bicycle delivery boy. He rode a three-wheeler with a large metal platform in front. It had already been decided which ones would get to go with him: his brother Stig, and Henning.

Allan pushed his way over to his bicycle. Somehow, he was always too big: for his age, for the spaces available, for the clothes he wore.

The girls had to sit on the platform of another three-wheeler; it was ridden by Hjalle, who was the oldest in the group, and the least shy with girls. And then Hjalle yelled, "Let's go, boys!"

Slowly and bravely, they began to tramp on their pedals. The heavy and heavily laden bicycles rolled toward Bondegatan where the hill lay steep and long before them. Once they were there, it was only a question of letting it roll; the biggest worry was keeping their speed down. Someone could come along on a cross street, though they did not give too much thought to that risk.

Hjalle went first with the girls; they clung on tightly and shrieked like sirens. And then the whole gang followed, six or seven fully loaded vehicles with hollering boys and tinkling bicycle bells.

Maj heard them and hurried to the window. She had been set against Henning going along—but he had been so stubborn. Now she regretted that she had given in; they were riding like idiots. Not least of all Allan; His entire bicycle was wobbling as he hurtled downhill. She tried to call out, but they heard nothing, were yelling too much themselves. There was nothing to do now, just wait and hope all went well.

Beyond the folk high school, the street narrowed and went uphill a little, past Myrorna's second-hand salesroom, before it turned and ran between the long fences of Tegelviksgatan. Then it was downhill again, and they whizzed onto Danviksgatan. The last ones in line were about to crash into the streetcar that had to jam on its brakes while the conductor clanged the bell angrily.

Allan laughed recklessly at the danger, taking the turn with two of his three wheels, and was about to tip the whole vehicle over in front of the brake-screeching streetcar. But his passengers were not completely unprepared and did their bit to right themselves. On the hill up toward Danviksbron, they had to jump off and walk alongside.

Beyond the tollgate, calm descended. There were not so many onlookers to impress here, and no downhill parts to pick up speed. The cyclists panted and pedaled persistently. Now they felt how warm the evening was after having been cooled off by their recent rush of speed. The long upward route toward the bridge over the railroad track at Sickla was taking its toll; the passengers once again had to get off. The cyclists hopped off and pushed their heavy vehicles up the hill. But then they could ride again, past Diesel's engine factory and the yeast factory, and on down the road that slowly descended all the way to Nackanäs and the bridge. Then it was a little upward slope again, on toward Nacka windmill.

Finally, they were rolling along the path to Källtorpsjön. Branches brushed their faces, the three-wheelers jolted between stones and tire ruts. The boys let off their passengers and brought the bicycles together in a cluster.

The sun had gotten quite low in the west, but it still lit up the inlet where they had stopped and the high rocks along the eastern shore. The boys had their usual swimming spot where they immediately went. The girls went a little off to one side. Since they had not been sure they were going to get to go along, they had not taken their bathing suits with them. It would have been mortifying to be left standing on the street with their bathing suits in hand. But since it was so hot, they were still going to take a dip. They went far enough into the bushes so that any rustling would warn them in time if someone was coming.

But the boys seemed to have forgotten about them for the joy and delight that swimming gave. They dove from the rocks, yelled and whooped. When the girls came out from behind the branches, they saw the whole gang from a distance: a dozen boys between the ages of eleven and seventeen. So clearly a group, maybe with temporary solidarity, yet still a collective against the girls' solitariness. Only one of the younger ones had landed a little on the outside. He had not undressed, but instead wore his shirt and shorts at the edge of the water and was getting his feet wet. It was Allan's brother, Stig, and they knew he had phlegm in his lungs. He was not allowed to swim.

But Allan was splashing around so that he made giant swells around himself, and those who were close by shouted and swore. And they swore even more when he clambered up onto a rock and, big and spread-legged, stood and pissed into the swimming water.

The girls giggled at crazy Allan who so unabashedly showed everything he had. Then they swam in among the branches and sat down to dry before they got dressed again. Allan and the little guy he had with him swam a race just beyond them, but were too caught up in their contest to notice the girls' nakedness.

The little boys stayed down on the beach; those a little older climbed, together with both of the girls, up onto the edge of the rocks where there were fine ledges for sitting and where the last of the sun's rays reached.

The ones who had cigarettes pulled them out, taking a few puffs after their swim. Hjalle, who acted as leader, had two cigarettes and gave one to one of the girls. He put an arm around her neck, pulling her toward him. She giggled a little again but let him have his way.

The other girl felt alone and abandoned; without a cigarette and rejected by one of the few boys who was actually older then a young whelp. Closest to her sat crazy Allan. But he had cigarettes; she had caught sight of half a pack of Bridges. So she leaned over, saying: "Can you give me a smoke?"

Allan fumbled around in his shirt pocket and let her take the pack from him so he would not crush all the cigarettes.

She stuffed it back in his pocket, and he saw into the open sleeve of her blouse where a tuft of hair glinted in the sunshine. Before he had never actually been interested in girls, thought they were mostly full of rubbish. But now he felt something new and unsettling: an urge to stick his fingers into that armpit. He stared a little embarrassedly at Hjalle to see how those who were older and more experienced behaved. But they were just sitting there completely ridiculous, cooing with their heads together.

Once Daggan had lit her cigarette, she moved a little closer to Allan, leaned her back against his side, and blew out the smoke voluptuously.

"God, this tastes good," she said.

She sank sort of deeper-softer in toward him, and he was made uneasy by her closeness. What was he going to do with her, what was she expecting? Now he regretted that he had not stayed with the little boys.

Some of the others were evidently beginning to grow tired of sitting still. They made their way down to the inlet and skipped stones they found. A couple of the bicycle owners got ready to ride back to town. Stig wanted to go home and got to go with one of them. But Henning wanted to stay and skip stones.

Allan also would have liked to throw some. But he did not think it would work to leave Daggan, who was leaning against him. Though now, if he just let her sit there, it was just as bad; the whole neighborhood would laugh at him. If he tried anything with her, there was the risk of failure. Something had to be done, if he was to believe everything he had heard. He did not know what.

"Just get straight to the point," Lången at the reformatory, Hället, had said.

He stared thoughtfully at Daggan, met her gaze.

Why forsake one quiet little flirt,
The moment may never come back,

she sang teasingly and peered at him with her brown eyes. It was a challenge, an invitation. He had to attempt something.

Suddenly, he grew desperate, angry at her and angry at himself. Indeed, at the whole situation that was so complicated, at everyone who laughed at him and teased him.

Straight to the point, straight to the point, Lången said. The moment may never come back. She had wanted it, so she would get what she was asking for.

Frightened and angry, and without truly realizing what he was doing and why, he suddenly let go of her, sticking his clenched hand hard and recklessly between her legs.

She screamed loudly in pain and fear, tried to kick him away, began to scratch him. He felt how it began to burn over his eye, put his hand up—it turned red with blood.

Hiccupping with sobs, she flew up.

"You are crazy!" she screamed.

"Take it easy, for God's sake," hissed Hjalle, who did not seem to like being disturbed when he had gotten so far with Ansa.

But it was not so easy to calm Daggan down.

"He is crazy," she sobbed the whole time. "He is crazy."

"You have some terrible way with the girls," Hjalle sputtered. Now things were ruined for that evening. Daggan was not going to stop until she got to go home. And Ansa had certainly cooled down and begun to think twice.

The boys who had gathered around them wondered what had really happened. And they teased Allan, who silently and sullenly walked to his bicycle. He would have liked to ride away from them all, but had to make sure that Henning got home. He had promised.

The girls would ride with Hjalle, the same as they had come. Daggan, who was still sniveling, lagged behind the others as they walked to the bicycles.

Slowly, they began to make their way up the narrow path to the main road. The bicycles felt heavy now; the path was hard to navigate in the twilight. And now they felt like it was mostly uphill.

They had arrived as a group, bicycle after bicycle. But some had gone on ahead and now the caravan was thinning out even more.

Hjalle was lagging far behind with the girls.

Daggan told Ansa what had happened before they separated.

"So what?" Ansa answered. "You don't have to make such a ruckus because of that."

While Allan pedaled heavily toward home, worry grew inside him. He thought of Daggan's dad, a big and angry guy. He hoped nothing worse would happen than that he would get a thrashing. Some vague ideas about possibilities for running away from everything ran through his head. On a boat maybe—or hitchhike along the roads. If they wanted to catch him they would probably manage to, no matter what he did.

Henning wanted to talk, ask him what had happened. But he soon noticed that Allan did not want to tell him. And then he grew quiet, sat silently on the rattling metal platform, almost nodding off. It was beginning to get late, and he was a little worried, too, about what Mama would say when he had been out so long.

They helped each other push the vehicle up the steep hill on Bondegatan. When they reached the house where Henning lived, in the middle of the hill, they stopped and nodded silently at each other. Henning looked up—his mother was standing in the window.

Allan pushed his bicycle though the entryway to the courtyard of his building. He walked up the stairs, as if to his place of execution.

He sat down quietly at the kitchen table—though, of course, he was in the process of dragging half the table with him. At the last minute, his mom saved his dad's half-drunk half-liter of beer. His dad was sleeping with his arms across the table; his siblings were sleeping in the other room.

His mother caught sight of the wound over his eye, and Allan said he had run into a branch in the darkness. She washed the scratch left by Daggan's long nails without asking more.

Though he knew that his mother was the only one who could understand and help, he said nothing. Most of all, he would have liked to crawl down into her bed and fall asleep there well-hidden under the blanket.

"You are tired," she said.

"The bike is so damned heavy."

"Have a sandwich and then go to sleep."

It was not so easy to fall asleep; the worry of what might happen was all too great. What could they do?

The next few days he tried to hide from Daggan's dad; for that very reason, of course, he ran right into him. But the old guy only grumbled something like "oaf," and Allan was not unused to hearing that. It sounded harmless. It seemed like Daggan had not told on him. The social worker did not show up. Still, he did not dare be really calm. Maybe what he had done had been so bad that they had to take time to prepare the punishment.

It was not until long after that he dared ask Daggan if she had said anything.

"You are crazy," she answered him then. "You don't talk about that kind of thing."

But he did not go swimming any more times that summer.

TO DARE TO CHOOSE

The longstanding crisis had shaken people; many felt like they had lost their faith in the future. In the city, the mortality rate exceeded the birth rate. It also had happened eighty years earlier, when sickness and hunger had tipped the scale. Now it was more a question of a conscious strike on the procreation of children. The year's most discussed book was called *Crisis in the Population Question.*

Still, it was increasingly evident that the economic crisis was easing up. Traffic increased again, residential construction picked up speed, though there were plenty of empty apartments; wheels that had long stood still began to roll.

But beyond the borders, the world outside was still as dark. The black brown wave was rising. In Austria, Dolfuss destroyed the labor movement and was then murdered by Nazi agents. In Spain, it seemed like they were getting closer to a civil war, and in Italy, Mussolini went on the rampage against Abyssinia. In Latvia and Bulgaria, dictatorships were established. In Germany, SA Stormtrooper leaders were executed without a hearing and a verdict, and in the Soviet Union, hundreds of members of the opposition were executed or deported after Kirov's murder. In Marseille, France's foreign minister and Yugoslavia's king were murdered by Croatian fascists.

Was this a world one dared to live in, that one dared to give birth to children in?

Hatred seemed dense, violence had become normal. And much of the paralysis of the time of the crisis still remained for many. They could not believe there was any work for them, did not have the strength to try again, did not dare to believe in a future. And even if the work opportunities were more numerous than before, there was still great unemployment. As it began to be somewhat easier for the young, it became more difficult for the older, those who had gone without for several years and now suddenly were too old to find something new. A worker over forty was not especially sought after on the job market.

Lennart had counted on returning to the folk high school when the second year of study began. But then he got the chance for a job that looked like it could be secure. Sigvard Strand, whom he had met at the employment office and then spent time with, had gotten a position at a printer's that was going to expand. They were going to take in some younger men who would be trained in hand typesetting. Lennart's year at the folk high school was a strong point there, though he, of course, would have to count on using some of his free time for job training.

He weighed the opportunities, although he had immediately decided. It was unthinkable that he would dare let slip the chance for a steady job. He was already twenty-four, after all. It was high time he entered a more settled situation. His mother was not going to have the strength to hold out much longer, then he also had to think of supporting her.

When he applied for the job, he got to take a tour of the workplace. He began in the printing works itself, where Sigvard stood, and he was a little frightened by the giant presses, the roar, the blackness, the weight. Everything was in such stark contrast to the schoolroom's light and the library's quiet. He felt how unused to it he was, almost a foreigner to the world of work. It demanded courage and overcoming his trepidations to go in there, where he had longed to go all these years. For a moment, school and the library felt like a salvation, something to flee to in order to escape reality.

But the typesetter's had another character, lighter and calmer. Of course, the presses could be heard beneath, but at a distance now. And there was the industrious clinking of the typesetting machines. But it was still completely different from the printing works. If it had been the printing works he had had to choose, the choice would certainly have still been a given—but harder.

And he got to begin, as an apprentice, somewhat advanced in his years.

It meant a change in his life. Even if the salary to begin with was low, he was still earning something himself now. And suddenly, there was also a future; he was going to educate himself in his profession, and his salary was going to go up. One day he would be able to get married.

But he did not have time to read as much as before, naturally; he had his evening courses for typesetting to attend. The school and the library faded away, became memories. Of a difficult time but also one of hopes and dreams, discoveries and subjects for rejoicing. After a while, he almost had a hard time believing that it was he himself who had lived like that once. The new, so recently strange environment became everyday, the norm.

He had been able to adjust, had dared to choose to. But he knew that he also had chosen to let go of a dream he had. Of course, he could read some in the evening when his courses were finished, but a truly organized course of study he would certainly never have the opportunity for again. It was like cutting off a piece of his life. But unavoidable.

So he resigned himself, did what he could to learn his new profession properly.

The question would always remain: What might have happened to him if he been able to continue his studies? How much had he lost?

He had chosen. But, in fact, there had been no choice.

On weekdays, he had his courses; on Saturday evenings and Sunday evenings, he got together with Elisabet. If the weather was at all decent, they liked to take walks in the woods on Sundays. When it rained, they walked in the city, seeing how new large clusters of housing grew where previously it had only been small cottages, meadows, and woods: on Kungsklippan, on Gärdet, in Traneberg. Just opposite Central Station, an enormous office building was being erected, and where the 1930 exhibition had stood a group of museums appeared.

One Sunday they walked across the new bridge, Tranebergsbron, that had been inaugurated a few months earlier. It was seen as a giant leap—perhaps into the future and the city of tomorrow. Nothing had ever been built like that here before, not with such frenzy. It reminded one of a giant stallion, an animal that raised itself up, threw itself between the high hills over the water deep below. Far below, the old bridge still stood, laughably small and primitive.

It came as a surprise that there was such force in these times. He had, of course, felt mostly paralysis, insufficiency. Västerbron, that was still under construction, showed the same force. Maybe it also existed in the huge spirals of the new Slussen that was emerging more and more. A new form and a new scale, the creation of a new city.

They walked down the slope beside the bridge, stood and looked up at the enormous arch. They had to ask themselves if this was their era, if they belonged in it. Recently, they had talked about the day they would be able to afford to buy bicycles. They felt it was a big and distant goal. The bridge seemed to lead to a city with completely different demands on engineering.

During the weeks that followed, he could not forget the image of the bridge, the sensation of the rain driven by the wind as they walked up on it. So high, so free. As if he had suddenly noticed he lived in another era from what he had believed, been awakened by the rain that hit him in the face. He had to ask himself: Would he have made that discovery if he had not had a job? If he had not been wrenched into life again?

Indeed, he was standing right in the middle of life. Yet still—not quite. The hunger for Elisabet's body felt like a cry inside him. But the crisis and unemployment had frightened them, forbade them to take the risk.

That he had a job maybe did not change the situation. It would still be a long time before they could support a child and think of getting married. But despite everything, something had changed: It felt different. He was no longer such a failure. His self-confidence had grown and with it the strength and desire.

It became harder and harder for him to let her go, to hold back. The feeling was explosive, irrepressible. But it was released in confusion and without any appeasement. And he asked himself how much they could risk in not choosing to take the risk.

The autumn had been unusually warm; the snow and cold were late in coming. Though it did not look like it, Christmas was approaching. The trees that were being sold in the city had been chopped down by men in their shirtsleeves.

But on Christmas Eve, the snow arrived, as if it had been ordered. Already by early morning, the whole city was white, and the hills on the outskirts and the parks were filled with children who had taken out their sleds, toboggans, and skis.

Since Christmas Eve fell on a Monday, a lot of offices and workshops had closed that day. Both Elisabet and Lennart were free and had decided to meet in the morning. In the evening, they would celebrate separately at their homes.

They had an errand to take care of, had to go down into town. They walked down Katarinavägen and saw the city lying white in the whirling snow, as if half hidden behind a heavy drapery. Some boats were sounding their wailing horns from the Baltic; beyond the long narrow footbridge over the Saltsjö railway line, the ferries were tied opposite Karl XII Square. Their smoke rose up quickly. Down at Slussen where the sleet had free rein, they took the new walking tunnel that had been opened only a few days earlier. "An elegant thoroughfare of tile," it had been called.

When they had finished with their errand, they walked slowly back beneath Regeringsgatan's shining Christmas stars while the snow still fell on them. Now and then, he felt the little package that stuck out inside his jacket pocket. Really expensive, so expensive that they had decided not to give each other any Christmas presents.

They had decided to go a step further, give a confirmation that they dared believe in the future, their future. They were going to get engaged. But not before New Year's Eve.

By then, all the snow was gone. The evening was unusually warm. The restaurants and cinemas tempted with New Year's vigils. There were New Year's premiers at Södran and Folkan theaters. Södran had engaged so many big, well-known artists that Jenny, who had surely hoped to be included in some corner, had not gotten any offers. Lizzie Stein was there singing "Sun over Söder," Thor Maddén was appearing there, and Edvard Person and Åke Söderblom. The unemployment relief workers "air transport" at the Flatenbadet's open-air beach construction was a popular number:

When the boss came
With a little air
And asked us
With a little air
To take some time
With a little air
Every other day...

But Lennart and Elisabet had decided to go to Skansen Open-Air Museum. An entrance fee of seventy-five öre was about what they thought they could spend.

Despite the warm weather, it was not a particularly nice evening to be out. The fog lay thick over Strömmen and the Baltic, the air felt damp and raw. The promised "big illumination" of Skansen almost disappeared in the mists. Anders de Wahl, who was to read *The New Year's Bells,* had not dared go out in the raw weather. They got to listen to Uno Henning instead.

When the reading was done, they drew away from the crowd. They got to Håsjö Bell Tower with its open arches and view over Djurgrden's Canal and Östermalm. He pulled the little boxes out of his pocket. And then they took the rings that glowed dimly in the darkness and slipped them on each other's fingers.

And so they were engaged.

YET AGAIN?

Tyra came more and more often to Emelie's. Several times a week, she rang the doorbell and asked if she could come in for a while.

Of course, she could, even if it perhaps was not so convenient every time. Emelie had to make coffee and sit at the kitchen table and talk, even though there was so much to be done. But even worse was that she was afraid Tyra's visit would drive Elisabet out of the house. Fortunately, Elisabet was not home all the evenings Tyra came. She was taking a course, or she was out with Lennart. Still, it felt like Emelie monopolized more of their home than she felt she had a right to—when she sat there with Tyra and Elisabet disappeared out somewhere.

Tyra was not quite herself. Not as bold and booming as she usually was. She had grown thinner, too, seemed paler and more tired. The years had probably done their work—but still, Tyra was not more than forty. Though she had toiled, done heavy work for many years. Ever since she had moved together with David and had both him and the children to support.

Gradually, Emelie realized that there was something that Tyra wanted to tell her, though for once she had difficulty getting it out. And then it began to unsettle Emelie, too; it could not be good news. Surely, it was something that would mean worries for Emelie, too.

It grew so that Emelie jumped whenever the doorbell rang, that she suddenly felt faint. She thought: Now it's coming. And I cannot help her, I don't have the strength any longer.

But once Tyra had come in, it felt different, not so difficult anymore. Then Emelie was ready in another way, ready to help as well, if such was required.

What could it be that was bothering Tyra? There was a lot to choose from. David was falling apart more and more, and now had been put in the institution for alcoholics again. Allan, who never got any stable work.

Stig, who was at the sanatorium again. And Per and Gun, who continually played hooky from school and were up to all kinds of mischief.

But all that was just normal, what Tyra had always had to deal with before. Her daily struggle that she had fought with such strength, a struggle that perhaps had given her this outright strength.

There was something else. For the first time, Tyra was afraid. She had never been before, not that Emelie had seen. What would have scared most people had only irritated Tyra, made her fight.

Now she seemed defeated.

Finally, she talked about it.

She was sick, incurably so. Cancer. Even if the doctor had not said it straight out, she understood anyway that she could not live much longer. She felt it. It was too late to do anything.

Too late. She should have gone in earlier, had felt that something was wrong. But it was so hard to be away from home, how would they have managed if she had been admitted to the hospital? Someone had to be at home, someone had to take care of everything. And now—now—

What would happen to the children? And David. It would be best if they put him in the institution for the rest of his life. For the first time, Emelie saw Tyra cry.

Emelie sat silent. It was worse than she had feared. A blow, also a blow against her own life.

It was too much. The misfortune too great. She could neither comfort nor help Tyra; no words were enough. She was too old now, could not take care of all those who would stand unprotected if Tyra left them.

In spite of everything seeming hopeless, her thoughts still looked for some possible solution. The boys were seventeen, fifteen, and fourteen. The girl only twelve. Maybe the boys could take care of themselves somehow, if only Allan got a job. They could live with their father. David would maybe behave a little better if he felt that he had the entire responsibility. But Gun?

There must be some way out, Emelie tried to say. Maybe it is not quite as bad as you think. Maybe the doctor can still do something.

Tyra didn't think so.

They sat quietly. Tyra had crumpled in her chair. But then she stretched, wiped her eyes with her knuckles, looked at Emelie, and suddenly smiled a piteous little smile.

"Maybe they can come here and eat from time to time," she said. "Like we got to do once, when we were little."

Emelie could see how Bärta's children had sat around her table. Though Tyra had not been with them very often. It was probably her siblings who had been happiest to get to come. Tyra had gone her own way early on.

"Of course," Emelie said. "Of course, they will come." She hurried to promise this. It was something she could manage.

"We have to really think about this," she said to Tyra. "Maybe we can come up with a solution. And maybe, in any case, it is not as dangerous as you believe."

Tyra's troubles gave Emelie a bad conscience. It was against her nature to say no when somebody asked her for help. Time after time, she had to ask herself if she was shirking her duty, if she somehow couldn't manage to do something more.

She tried to talk to Jenny about the matter. Maybe Emelie needed to hear someone else say that she could not manage, have it confirmed.

Jenny's view was that Emelie had really done her duty. This time the problem had to be solved in another way. Emelie had to understand that Emelie herself had grown old. She had to permit herself a little rest and peace. She could not carry all the world's troubles and sorrows alone.

If Emelie was having a hard time saying no, she could blame it on Jenny and Elisabet. That would maybe make it easier. She could speak the truth that they did not want to have Tyra's family living with them. David had to try to get it together and give the children a home.

If they came and ate once in a while, that was a completely different thing. They could help each other to cope with that. But Emelie should go no further than that.

Her bad conscience meant that Emelie tried to help Tyra with money as best she could, perhaps actually more than she could. Tyra had often received loans before. Now it could no longer be a question of a loan.

It became a small sum every time Tyra came. What Emelie could spare from her salary quickly disappeared, including the ten-kronor bills she entered into her post office savings bankbook as well. Soon she found that she had reached the point where she was many years ago, when Melinder's cosmetics factory had dissolved, and she had gone without work. She had to take the one bill after the other out of the envelope containing her funeral money.

When she had taken out of this envelope before, it had frightened her. It felt like stealing. This time, it was strangely enough not as difficult. As if she had gained something of an assurance that everything would take care of itself that day anyway. It was more important that Tyra get what she needed than that the money be there the day Emelie herself was dead.

"You should let the poor relief bury me," she said to Jenny and Elisabet.

"Don't worry about that," Elisabet said. "Do what feels best—though I don't think it will help to give anything to Tyra. At least not now."

"But what will she do?"

In her case, poor relief should step in and take care of everything, was Elisabet's thinking. There would never be any order among those people anyway. Just as well to have them living in an institution, every one.

But then Emelie and Jenny, too, had to protest. It was not that bad. Allan, who was so nice to Henning. Stig, poor thing, who was sick. It was not so extraordinary if the children had a hard time getting by. However hard Tyra tried, they still had never had a really good home. Elisabet shrugged her shoulders. She thought what she thought. About sacrificing energy and money for hopeless situations. Just as long as they didn't take in Tyra's family, because then she would move away from home.

Of Bärta's children, Beda had been the one who, after Gunnar, had lived the longest with Emelie. As a child, she had seemed backward, with her difficulties in speaking. Gradually, things had cleared up for her. From being a difficult case, Beda had become a completely normal and maybe even unusually well-balanced person. She lived together with a friend; they were both seamstresses. Beda often came to visit Emelie as well.

When Emelie told her about Tyra and her worries about the children, Beda said that Tyra's daughter could certainly live with her if needed. A twelve-year-old girl could not be so much trouble to look after.

Emelie hesitated to tell her that perhaps Gun was not so easy to steer; they would have to talk about it when the day came. If it came at all. Tyra was maybe worrying needlessly. Emelie did not want to believe that things were the way Tyra said.

In any case, she decided to begin by inviting Tyra and her children to dinner once a week. They came every Sunday. That was a good arrangement since then they could get together a little earlier than on a weekday and besides, Elisabet was usually out with Lennart. Emelie had hoped that Elisabet would eat at home as she usually did, but she did not. And she locked her dresser drawers and took the key with her when she left.

So, once again, Emelie had a flock of children around her table. As if time had melted away and Bärta's children were sitting there again. She saw them so clearly before her. It was truly difficult to keep then and now apart. She would call Tyra Bärta, she said Bengt when she meant Per. They were just as hungry and lively; forks fell on the floor, and milk glasses were tipped over. And when they were done eating, there was hardly a breadcrumb left in the breadbasket or a spoonful of stewed fruit purée in the bowl.

Emelie had come through the crisis and years of unemployment rather well. But now it was growing more difficult for her. She had to borrow money and pawn things—the fine piece of gold jewelry she had received from Annika Bodin she could no longer keep at home. And she would not be able to stay at the shop more than a few more years. By then, she would be too old. But the task she had at hand pushed away concerns for herself.

She fretted a lot about Allan. He was probably the one who was most dependent on Tyra, anxious and afraid. If nothing happened, he could maybe be saved from the reformatory. He had such a hard time keeping a job, and when he was loafing around, the risks were numerous.

Emelie wondered if she could talk to August. But August had helped Gunnar and thereby done his duty. Gunnar—that might be a possibility.

She traveled out to Gunnar's one evening. A little nervous and unused to it, she got off in the underground station at Götgatan and took the train to the suburbs out to Skarpnäck. Gunnar knew she was coming and was standing at the stop waiting.

They walked down to Tistelvägen, where he had his house that he had built himself. Now trees and bushes had grown up, and there were no signs left of it being a newly developed area. Gunnar opened the gate to his yard; Hjordis and the children stood on the porch. The spring evening was light and cool. A thin veil of mist lay over the fields and gardens, and from a pile of raked-up branches and leaves a narrow column of smoke arose whose top shifted in and out in the mist.

In Gunnar there was so much calm and strength. He had put on a little weight these past few years, and it seemed to underscore the assured calm. When Emelie told him about her errand, he sat there silently and weighed it all, saying neither yes nor no. But when the answer arrived, it was a clear decision. Such was he. Emelie knew him well.

There was a lot of construction underway again, as Emelie was well aware. The building office had calculated that an increase of around eleven thousand residences was needed per year during the coming decade. That meant entirely new areas of housing, and there would also be stores and offices. Gunnar was working mostly with commercial interiors these days, but he also had built a number of houses, and he would be building more. There was a lot to do, but naturally he made use mainly of skilled craftsmen. But he would give it a try. He wanted to first see where Allan could fit in. That clumsiness and awkwardness in the boy might go away. In any case, he would try with him.

He gave Emelie a paper where he had written down where and when Allan should present himself. It was at a construction site for a house that was about to be started, and first some work for the foundation was necessary.

Emelie could feel a little more at ease as she sat down on the streetcar to go home. Gunnar had met her expectations. Clearly, she understood that it would be a little difficult for him to say no; he had to think about the fact that Emelie at one time had taken care of him and now she was asking him to do a similar favor. Maybe she had pressed him too hard. But if anyone was going to be able to help Allan, it was Gunnar. He was patient and calm; with quiet tenacity, he would lead Allan until the boy could go further on his own. If Allan now would put out a little more himself and had not been completely ruined by his father's bad influence.

For David, Emelie held no hope at all, even if she did not say it out loud to anyone.

So it was arranged for Allan and Gun. Stig would remain at the sanatorium for a longer period. The littlest of the boys was left. Maybe David's sister could help them some. She was apparently quite a reliable person, scouring and toiling hard with Tyra as she had. Tyra had to talk to her, since now Emelie could not think of anything else.

The streetcar reached the tollgate. Up on Hammarby plateau, where it had previously been spotless countryside, they had begun to build big new clusters of rental apartments. The city was in the process of passing beyond the tollgates; it just kept on growing. Sometimes, Emelie was frightened by this activity; it was liable to make her feel like a stranger. But just now it made her happy; many new buildings meant a lot of work. For August. For Gunnar. For Allan, too, she could hope now. They would be building just as much for the next ten years, Gunnar said. In which case, he would be able to teach Allan.

The subway station under Folkungagatan that had seemed so foreign to her when she had stepped on the train a few hours ago, now felt familiar. She knew which way she should walk to come out and tramped boldly up the stairs. Of course, she had grown old—but she was not finished yet; she could still be of some use.

OLD TRACKS, NEW PATHS

He shook himself drowsily awake, pushed his hair off his forehead, yawned. He lifted the bottle: There was a splash left in the bottom still. He set it to his mouth and drank it down, gave a jolt as if he had a cramp and grimaced. He wiped the back of his hand across his lips, smiled suddenly, and sang:

In Svartsjö, I was in a robbers' ring
And in the granite I carved so many marvelous things.
I lay among fops and false barons,
Among thieves and rogues of various nations
Who on unknown seas have foundered—ta-ra-ra boom.

The Svartsjö song. The hated Svartsjö Prison. Which now suddenly almost felt like something of a home, safety. There were friends there, cronies. And no demands. No one who believed in anything.

All the fear came back. Sorrow and longing.

Tyra, Tyra… He could only mumble the name, the sobs caught in his throat. Tyra who they had taken to the hospital, who herself did not believe she would be coming back. His Tyra, his life. What was left if Tyra did not exist? The kids. But that wasn't enough. The kids without Tyra were nothing, barely existed. They were only a part of her, as far as he was concerned.

His sister, Dora, had just left. Or not just; maybe he had slept with his arms on the table for an hour or so. Dora and Tyra had talked things over at the hospital, decided how they would arrange things for David. Had agreed that it would probably be best if he and the boys moved in with Dora. Dora and her daughter lived with his father in one of the tenement houses that were still next to Rosenlund's old age home. Their mother had died a few years ago.

It was not appealing to move back home. David was a little afraid of his sister, of her strength and stubbornness. She was as strong as Tyra. But Tyra had loved and forgiven him, understood. Dora understood him in a completely different way, suspected all his small ruses, exposed him. With neither love nor forgiveness.

Still, he would, of course, move there. Take his punishment. For Tyra's sake, since she wanted it and since she was going to die. It felt right to subject himself, to submit to the torment. He would probably try to find a job, too, if anybody wanted him. Not immediately, there was not that much of a hurry. Now he had received a tip about a completely harmless deal. Tyra did not have to worry; he would not take any risks. Only rake in what there was.

Besides, Allan had begun to work for one of Tyra's brothers. And in the spring, their youngest boy was finishing school and maybe he would get work, too. The boys should be able to actually take care of their father in a pinch. Stig was still in the hospital, Gun had already moved in with Beda.

I have lain among fops and false barons…

Maybe he could even get his accordion out of hock. But, no… He would never be able to play again if Tyra died. Then everything would be over.

…among thieves and rogues of various nations.

Before he had played and sung for her; she had liked it. The Kungsholm's League's parade march. And the Eira song:

But girls, do not sorrow over what you have become,
Let us break out into a merry laugh,
For one only lives a single life
So I think it should be lived joyfully.

Tyra liked that particular verse, at least she had before. He had sung it when they had drunk together and then they had laughed together. Then Tyra would change the words from girls to boys—so that it was like they were encouraging each other not to sorrow. She had many funny ideas, Tyra. And she had not sorrowed, she had taken the day as it came. Except for the last time. And that was probably not because she was afraid of dying, but because she was anxious about him and the children.

She had never been afraid for her own sake. And she had never been ashamed of living together with Yellow David either; she had silenced the old gossips.

Tyra, Tyra...

He snuffled, tried to swallow his crying. He caught sight of the empty bottle. Everything was meaningless.

Allan ought to be able to get a little advance from his job, now that he was working for a relative. But the earliest it could be would be tomorrow. And he had solemnly sworn to Tyra not to go see that Emelie in the grocery store. Otherwise, he would surely have been able to tell the old lady some story and get a bit of cash. They sold pilsner, of course, in that shop, too. Just think: Someone he almost knew sold pilsner and he sat here whimpering from thirst. Life surely was strange.

He collapsed over the table. There was no help any longer. Not for Tyra. Not for him. For him, the path led back to the tenements on the hill above the garbage dump. And then? Back to Svartsjö Prison?

Gunnar had made up his mind to have patience with Allan. First of all, because he had promised Emelie. But gradually also because the boy got him to recall his own youth more and more. Or rather, his childhood, the years before he had come to Emelie. While he still lived with his mother and his stepfather, the chimney sweep apprentice Johan.

Allan's home was probably somewhat like that home. Fathers who drank, mothers who did not have the strength to hold the whole thing together. As for himself, Gunnar had gotten away rather quickly. But his younger half-siblings had lived on there. He could remember how ragged and hungry they had been, like small wild animals. No wonder

Tyra had become what she had become. But Bengt and Erik had gotten by and even Beda, who had such big impediments, had managed.

Emelie's help must have meant a lot for them. But Emelie could not help Tyra's children in the same way, even if she tried. If Allan was to be able to become a decent person and fit into society, it depended on Gunnar. He had the responsibility.

Sometimes Gunnar wondered if it was too late. Allan had already had time to drift pretty far away, been institutionalized a few times, was certainly a little timorous regarding work as well. And childish, not mature for work, even though he had turned seventeen. Gunnar had come across him standing and building dams in a ditch instead of digging for the house foundation.

And then he was clumsy. One did not dare place someone like Allan on a scaffolding; he would fall. Nor could he do a more refined task, interior decoration details and such. So he mostly had to push gravel, dig and carry stones.

In this way, Allan got Mikael as a boss. Mikael had stayed working for Gunnar; there was a lot to do now. And Mikael, who had been a sailor earlier, had no professional training or experience in carpentry. He preferred to do heavy work. Letting Allan work under Mikael was a pretty good solution. Gunnar had to move around, be at different worksites. But Mikael stayed at the same place. Besides, he was calm, did not grow irritated with Allan's bungling.

During the first days Allan had seemed afraid but at the same time contrary. As if he believed he had landed in a reformatory again, some sort of work camp. He did not do more than he had to, slipped away or stood and idled on his spade when he thought that no one saw him. Mikael neither scolded him nor shouted, but instead talked about the agreement, that they were a team and the faster and better things went, the more there would be to share between them all when it was time for that. It was during breakfast break that they talked about it, and Mikael offered Allan coffee from his thermos. The boy only had a few dried bits of bread with him.

Allan did his best afterward. But it was noticeable that he was unused to organized work. He had a hard time holding out; suddenly, he would be standing there hanging around again. Then Mikael would give out a really rowdy whistle so that Allan almost fell over with the spade. The boy would set to with his work again.

Gunnar came by and asked from time to time, wondering how things were going. Mikael said that they would likely go well eventually, one could not be impatient.

But actually one should send the kid to a doctor. For clumsiness.

Gunnar laughed. Doctors had not helped with that before.

But Mikael was stubborn. There was something wrong with Allan, with his balance. He swayed when he walked, almost as if he was drunk. But he did not smell like alcohol and did not act in any other way as if he had been drinking.

That was true, there was something to what Mikael said. Gunnar had also seen how Allan bumped into everything, took unexplained steps sideways sometimes. It might look only like clumsiness, but was maybe something that could still be helped.

"Let's wait a little anyway," said Mikael. "I think he is afraid of doctors, afraid of most things. Let's let him get used to things, till he knows us a little better."

Some mornings, Allan arrived late. Mikael admonished him. But it did not help much. It was simply that there was no one to wake the boy up.

But he had to observe the schedule. To get used to that was also to fall into necessary habits and tracks. Mikael could not find any other solution than to buy an alarm clock for Allan. He handed it to him when they shared coffee from the thermos as usual. The boy was a little abashed but grateful as well. He had certainly not been spoiled by presents.

In the future, he arrived on time. And every day he had the alarm clock with him in his sandwich bag. He did not dare leave it at home. His father could always get beer with the clock; if he got thirsty enough, there was always something to replace with beer.

Despite the difficulties, everything seemed to work out anyway. Allan drifted along more and more with the everyday rhythm. He became Mikael's faithful shadow; where Mikael was, Allan would also be. He admired his adult colleague, followed his advice, put in an effort.

But one day he did not show up.

When Gunnar came, Mikael told him that he had not heard from Allan. The boy might be sick. They decided to wait and see. But in the evening, Mikael walked over toward Rosenlund anyway, thinking he would find out what was going on.

Children were playing on the hillside; some old men lay with cards and bottles on a grassy spot. Mikael was shown the way by some of the children; they went along with him and waited steadfastly while he rang the bell. A girl of about twenty opened the door.

No, she had not seen nor heard from Allan since yesterday evening. She hesitated, as if she did not want to say more. But then she asked Mikael to come in. It was unnecessary for the whole building to hear them.

She removed some pieces of clothing from a chair, pushed it forward for him, sat down herself on the unmade bed.

"The cops took away his dad yesterday," she said. "And the old man too—Farfar, Allan's grandfather. David had filled up the whole kitchen sofa with bottles of bootleg liquor so there was no denying it."

"And Allan?"

"He always gets the wind up. He thinks the social workers are going to come and take him back to the reformatory."

Mikael gave her the address of the room he rented, asked that Allan get in touch with him if he came.

It was unnecessary; He ran into the boy a little way from the house. Allan tried to sneak away.

"Don't let them take me," he said.

He was dirty and tired, had tried to hide himself in a shed, had lain there and watched when they took away his father and grandfather. And the bottles with Estonian alcohol.

"No one is going to take you away," Mikael said. "They don't take away people who are behaving and have jobs. As long as you didn't participate in the bootlegging, of course..."

No, it was his father and grandfather who took care of that business. Allan would not have been allowed to do it even if he had asked. He was not good enough for such dealings.

"Do you know where the social worker lives?"

Yes, Allan knew.

"Then let's go there right away."

Allan wanted to flee. But Mikael held onto him.

"We are going to clear all this up now," said Mikael. "Then you won't have to be afraid in the future. You can't run away anyway. Whatever you run away from is always there, waiting for you. The only way to get rid of something troublesome is to clear it up."

But the social worker... Allan was sure that the dreaded one's only desire was to place him in the reformatory again.

The social worker would probably see at least that Allan had a job and was taking care of himself. They did not place people in institutions because they wanted to have the institutions populated.

Allan did not dare believe what Mikael said. Still, he went with him, had given in. In a workers' shop on Södrabantorget, Mikael bought a shirt, pants, and shoes that Allan had to put on. Even though it was the simplest clothing imaginable, Allan felt like he was in his Sunday best, as if prepared and dressed for his sentencing.

Even though he felt like he was being led right into misfortune, he followed Mikael without any attempt to get away. There was no one else in the world to rely on now that his mother had disappeared. No one else to cling to.

A BEAUTIFUL SUMMER

Ascension Day, the thirteenth of May, the city suddenly lay covered in snow. It felt like something of a shock: Was summer not coming?

Yes, it came. Sudden and overwhelming, with such intensity that people talked about "the perfect summer."

For Tyra, it was not perfect. She suffered from the heat—that which like fever and sickness spread inside her, that which summer brought. Silent and angry, she lay among the many sick in the public ward. Swore at those who complained about the draft as soon as a window stood open. If she had been able to decide, they would have let the cross draft flow through the room. So what if someone was finished off from it?

She could not feel at home here, not be part of the group. More than before, she felt how she stood outside. Since she could not get well and come out of here alive, she wanted to hide and die.

Kill me instead, she would hiss to the doctor who made his rounds. I know the story. No point in fooling with me any longer.

In truth, she did not want any visitors. David and the children should not be drawn into this hostile world. With Emelie, it was different; she somehow belonged in it. Not exactly in the hospital world, but still in this humdrum community.

Emelie was welcome to come; indeed, she was the one Tyra longed to talk to. She could forget her pains when she got to talk about her children and hear that they were managing quite well. She was especially happy to hear how well they ate, and Emelie always had to meticulously report what she had given them to eat. Then Tyra would close her eyes and smile. She could see how the kids had dug in and felt good.

In spite of everything, of course, it was nice when Allan came. He came every Sunday. He was the only one of her children who went to the hospital. David would have scarcely come even if he had not sat in prison. Stig was still at the sanatorium. Per and Gun were young.

Allan was the one who was closest to her, who she worried most about after David.

She thought the boy had changed. She could not really decide if it was for the better or not. The change somehow took him away from her, in among the enemies: those who fit in. Allan was probably on his way to becoming one of those nose-to-the-grindstone types, as David said.

At first, it irritated her; the old feeling of outrage flared up. She lay and swore to herself when he left, over that damned reformatory. They whipped the children into mush there, broke them whichever way they could. They had ruined Allan, frightened him into a busy bee.

Afterward, it felt different. Not regarding the reformatory, only regarding Allan. Maybe what had happened to him had occurred despite the reformatory. Maybe what had happened to him was something good?

For Allan was not of her or David's kind. He did not have her strength, nor David's resiliently tough resistance. Allan was too afraid to become someone proud and happy and free as a bird. He was no rebel. In fact, he was probably most like her brother Bengt, kind and compliant.

So he had been rescued if he had become a nose-to-the-grindstone type. So he would escape being one of those who society set tax money aside for. In contrast to her two youngest. They were probably more like her and David, could not be tamed. She lay there feeling pride over them until the pride changed over to worry: How would they fare?

Now Allan was living together with Mikael, he told her. He had been able to move into the room that Mikael was renting. And Mikael had arranged it so that Allan could buy a bicycle in installments. They bicycled to and from the different construction sites out in the residential areas.

Tyra had met Mikael at Emelie's a few times, but knew him very little. She felt some kind of jealousy toward the one who had replaced her. Still, apparently he was a nice guy. He had been a sailor, and that maybe meant that he was not quite as narrow-minded as people in general were.

Allan was happy to recount his description of how he and Mikael had gone to see the social worker. Just think, the social worker was really friendly. And Tyra felt a barb: She had never been able to manage that. Her conversations with the social worker had been more like full-blown arguments.

Others could help Allan, not she.

Had everything she had done been all wrong? She had been forced to choose sides, to become one of those who were called asocial. There had hardly been a question of choice at the time. At that time, there had been only David. At that time, they had had no children yet. Now it was different, like choosing between David and Allan. She could very well have forced Allan to move home to the tenements, to hand over his money to David. That would have meant that it would not be long before Allan gave up his job. He would not have been able to stand it if he had not been able to keep one öre.

Even though it felt like a betrayal of David, she said: "That's good. Try to behave so that you can stay with Mikael."

And when Emelie arrived, she continued the betrayal: "Don't let David get a hold of Allan. He would take every öre from the boy, force him to run his errands instead of going to work."

She questioned Emelie closely about Mikael: What sort of man was he exactly? What did he want from Allan?

Emelie answered that Mikael was just a decent and ordinary person. He was a good fellow worker.

Fellow worker... She lay there and mulled it over. Not really a good word, it had certainly been fellow workers who put the yellow stamp on David because he had been a strikebreaker.

Fellow worker... As for herself, she had never been able to get solidarity to be enough for more than David and the kids. Now she had to try and believe that others had more of that item. Though it was clear—Mikael was certainly gaining something from this. Allan had to pay his own rent.

"Talk to Mikael," she asked anyway. "Tell him not to let David take Allan's money or force the boy to go back. But... he can't hit David, that he can't do."

It was as if during that time of loneliness and torment, she saw her life in another light from before. Before, she had only had time to fight for life. Now, when fighting for it was of no avail, she could see it from a distance, observe it critically. Although, of course, there was a lot to regret, much that she could now wish had been different. But, for sure, they had had a lot of fun many times, and she did not want to reproach David for anything. He was the way he had to be. And he needed her. How would he get by now? Had she done wrong when she asked Emelie to prevent him from exploiting Allan?

No, that was the only possibility. The only way to save the one she could save. David would take everything from the boy, his money, his job. He took whatever lay closest, it just was that way, he did not have the capacity to do it differently. Tyra knew what kind of strength it took to handle David. Allan did not have that strength.

But poor David... So thoughtless. If she had been home, he never would have been allowed to place the bottles of moonshine inside the kitchen sofa. She would have helped him hide them someplace where a person could not prove that David had had anything to do with them.

David would not have gotten any help from Allan anyway. Only the little money the boy could earn and which, in any case, would not be enough for David. Allan was not enough. But Per would be, when he got on in a few years. Though Per was too strong, would not give anything willingly. Possibly Gun, then.

But she could not wish on Gun the same life that she had had. However bitter it might feel, Tyra still realized it would be best if David were abandoned. No one could really help him. Without being pulled down themselves.

There was one who might be able: Dora. But she would make life hell for David, scold him to death.

No, there was nothing to be done.

Something might be regretted, something blamed. But more could be missed. In moments when she did not really know if she was awake or asleep, the memories would come back: David sitting on the stairs with his accordion and singing. Joy, pride, togetherness—she would not have wanted to live differently. Not with anyone other than David.

Emelie came, on an ordinary weekday. She was on vacation. She had been out at her brother August's for a few days at his summer house on Stora Essingen. It was no longer the country; you could get there by bus. Emelie thought it was good that way, not at all like the real country. But August talked about tearing down the old wooden house and building an apartment building. He would rather have a summer place somewhere farther from the city.

August had actually intended to retire from his company, Emelie told her, but since he was not really sure that his son could handle it all, he felt obligated to stay on a little while longer. He was probably not really sure that Karl Henrik had the steadiness that was needed.

And she had been out at Gunnar's, too. Gunnar was so pleased with Allan. And Gun had been able to go out to Children's Island this summer, so she was having a good time.

Per had finished school but not gotten any job yet. But things would surely work out for him, too.

Tyra nodded; she knew more about Per. More than she wanted to tell Emelie. Dora had complained. The boy hung out at home with girls. Like Rut, Dora's daughter. Rut was twenty-three and a hussy. Tyra did not like to think about Rut and Per hanging out there alone.

But Tyra had grown worse; she did not have the energy to worry anymore, hardly even be engaged. In any case, she could do nothing any longer. What was to happen would happen.

While Emelie was sitting there, she fell asleep.

Still enveloped in the atmosphere of the hospital, Emelie came out to the street, and jumped back when a car quickly shot past right in front of her. Silent traffic had been established only a week ago and sometimes she had a hard time remembering that the cars no longer honked and warned you as before.

There was not much left for Tyra. It would surely be over soon. There would not be so many more visits. She would have liked to have more and better news to give. So that Tyra could die in peace.

There was no problem with Allan, and she had not exaggerated, not much in any case, when she told how pleased Gunnar had been. Troubles with Gun she had kept quiet about. Beda had received a letter from the children's colony. The supervisor out there was not at all happy.

Although Emelie knew that they would prefer to take care of things on their own in the store during her vacation, she took a look in as she walked past. There was always something it was best she see to herself.

Then she went home and sat down to have a cup of coffee with Jenny in the middle of a weekday afternoon. This time of day one should be working. It felt self-indulgent, almost indecently so. But Jenny laughed and thought Emily was too ridiculous, actually poisoned with work.

Jenny took everything lightly, so enviably lightly. It was Emelie and not Jenny who thought that it was a little worrisome that Lennart and Elisabet were out camping together. They had bought those bicycles they had talked about for so long and gone to Gotland.

Emelie seemed to wonder if it was proper, they were not married yet. But it was not worth saying that to Jenny; she would just laugh herself silly. It was surely because Jenny was an actress; she saw everything in a different way.

They had received a postcard from Lennart and Elisabet. A postcard with ruins on it.

Imagine that they were so far away. Emelie pulled out Elisabet's old student atlas to be able to really see where they had gone.

"You should go somewhere on vacation, and not just hang out here at home," said Jenny.

She had said this many times before.

But Emelie just shook her head. It was impossible now that Tyra was sick. Besides, it was nicest at home.

Tyra died at the end of August, the same day that the newspapers announced that the former Swedish princess, Queen Astrid of Belgium, had been killed in a car crash at Vierwaldstätter Lake. And therefore many flags flew at half-staff the day Tyra died.

A TIME OF GROWTH

The city was thought to be growing faster than before, the new parts gaining ever-greater dimensions. Was this not overconfidence, had they not taken on dimensions all too big? Mighty Västerbron was in the process of completion on the westernmost edges of the city, where traffic was not especially heavy. All these new residential areas—where Bolinder's row of machine shops had once clung to the sides of Kungsklippan, tall apartment buildings were rising up. A whole new city was growing up at Gärdet, another by Fredhäll. The new buildings were so numerous that a glut of apartments followed. Many stood empty; rents sank.

In the middle of October, Slussen's giant traffic cloverleaf was inaugurated—"a piece of functional furniture in the style and spirit of our time." In front of the Swedish Cooperative Union's new building on Katarinavägen, the new elevator stood finished. It seemed rather spindly compared with the old iron colossus. One month later, Västerbron was also ready for its inauguration.

Even over on Erstagatan where Emelie lived, innovations had been set in motion. Once Västerbron was done, the streetcar lines changed their directions. Line six was extended to Folkungagatan, up the previously so quiet Erstagatan and down toward Sofia School. Suddenly, big streetcars began to rattle past outside the windows, and automobiles increased, too. Now one could not sled down the hill on Bondegatsbacken anymore. The last small wooden cottages had disappeared, and the outskirts were no longer outskirts.

Sometimes, Emelie wondered if she was dreaming. Was it really possible that this was the same street she remembered from when she was a child? Then it had been a pot-holed and uneven country road, edged with wooden fences and small low houses.

To better remember, one Sunday morning she walked along Åsögatan out toward the hill. There also, a lot of new things had been added. The street had been ground down into the rock, its southern side built up with apartment buildings. But on the north side, it was like before; the cottages still lay in their gardens, trees without their leaves rose above the fences. Even the house she had lived in as a child still stood—how much longer?

Here, where she could see her childhood home, she felt more strongly than before how irrevocably vanished the past was. How far away. And she herself—another person. Memories of her parents had faded; their features had become harder to capture than before. She would have liked to have a photograph of them, but it had never happened that one was taken.

As if the city was peopled by shadows, life was just one quick shadow play sweeping by. A few more years, and the people who were now walking around would be gone, remain as memories in time, then rubbed out and completely disappeared. While the city continued to change, buildings were torn down and built. As if stone contained more life than a person; the person was only a shadow that fell across the stone for a moment.

But when she walked back toward home, the vision of shadows sweeping by disappeared in exchange for reality's concrete beings. In an hour, she would have them sitting around the dining table, hungry, lively. Bärta's..., no, Tyra's children. Though apparently only two of them, Allan and Gun. And then Mikael and Beda and Maj with Henning. With Jenny and herself, they would be eight for dinner. Elisabet was going out, as usual. And Per would surely not come.

Maj usually helped prepare the food; she and Henning came earlier than the others. He was wearing his school cap with its insignia; he was attending Katarina Real School in his second year. This insignia gave cause for some teasing, showing, of course, that he was a schoolboy. Maybe that was the reason he was wearing it. Of course, he was not the rowdy type—but he was tenacious, stood up for his rights.

Maj borrowed an apron. She was still so slim that Emelie had to admonish her every time she saw her. But she was happier than before. Liked her job, got to live more tranquilly than before. And she had accepted, did not mourn Erik any longer. Though she sounded a shade bitter when she talked about how well things were going for him; director was how he was listed in the telephone catalogue. One of the labor movement's directors, a capable guy who had to be paid if they were going to keep him.

Then Beda and Gun arrived. Beda's self-appointed Sunday task was to do the dishes after dinner, but now she helped Emelie set the table as well. Jenny sat and talked with Gun and Henning; she thought it was better that she keep the children calm than run around in the kitchen. Gun was, in fact, not so easy to talk to; she barely answered. She preferred to sit and read a magazine, and there were some there. It was Jenny who bought them.

Last came Mikael and Allan. Heavy and powerful, a little noisy in voices and movements. Allan seemed to be taking after Mikael, tried to act like him.

Allan had been to the doctor. They knew there was something wrong inside a little labyrinth in the inner ear. It was there the sense of balance was directed, Mikael explained. Allan was to go back to the doctor; it was a question of a minor operation. Nothing to worry about. But there was every reason to hope that much of what was perceived as clumsiness would disappear.

Allan was smiling when they talked about his ear, delighted over the attention.

"The doctor is a nice man," he said.

Then he went into the other room to talk to Henning. He wanted to invite Henning to a movie that afternoon. There was a funny film showing at the Södra Kvarn movie theater.

Having his own money was a new experience for Allan, and the whole week he had thought about being able to invite someone to go to the movies. Now he was in charge of his own affairs, paid for his portion of the room and the food, bought what he needed. His salary gave him a new confidence, a feeling of importance.

When Gun heard that the boys were going to the movies, she wanted to go, too. She would not give in until Beda had said yes and given her the seventy-five öre that a ticket cost. But she had to promise to go with the boys and go straight home when the movie was over.

Beda washed up, and Maj dried. Emelie brought out the coffee cups. And Mikael sat and talked to Jenny.

While they drank coffee, Beda told about her problems with Gun. She was doing poorly in school, and she had skipped school a few times. Gun was not stupid, she should be able to follow along. But she was not interested; the only thing that really interested her was collecting those Diva pictures that were found in chocolate bars. Beda could not understand where the girl had gotten all her pictures. She would never have been able to afford to buy so many chocolate bars.

And what would happen to Stig if he was coming home from the sanatorium soon, Maj wondered.

Emelie had gone and talked to Dora. Stig would get to live with Dora and his grandfather, like Per was doing. And as long as David wasn't home, things went well. It would be worse if David was set free again.

It was a little strange—but for the boys, it was evidently best if their father sat in prison. Now that Tyra was gone, there was no longer anyone who could influence David, not anyone who could help him either. And so what happened was that he took advantage of those who were closest to him and were the most defenseless.

Things were going well for Allan now.

They came out of the theater, stopped a moment outside the bicycle shop on the corner of Renstjärnasgatan, and looked at the used bicycles. Allan ran into some neighboring boys and went off with them

Henning and Gun walked together up Skånegatan.

It was the first time he had walked alone with a girl. He did not really know what one talked about with girls—but they could always talk about the film they had seen.

She hardly replied. But she looked at his cap, made a face and said, "You're a schoolboy!"

"Maybe I am," he said.

"You like to study?" she asked him after a minute.

"It's okay."

"You doing well?"

"Yeah."

"I'm not," she said, and laughed as if she had something funny.

They grew quiet again, trudged on.

"But I don't give a shit," she said in a low voice.

He jumped at the word. He thought that girls did not use such words.

They arrived at her door. She took some steps into the street and saw that the light was on. Beda had apparently already come home. He thought he would just nod and go on, but she stopped him.

"Do you collect Diva pictures?"

"Not really…" He had a few actually, but he really collected stamps.

"Stamps. How boring."

He did not agree. You learned a lot about different countries when you collected stamps. About animals and kings and …

But she was not interested in what you could learn.

"Do you have them with you?"

"What?"

"The Divas, of course."

He dug in his pockets, found the little bundle held together with a rubber band. He handed them to her. She rifled through them eagerly. Three of the pictures evidently interested her especially. She laid them on top of the pile. He reached out his hand to get the cards back, but she pulled hers away. She wasn't going to steal them?

"I can take these three," she said. "The others I already have."

No, he did not want her to. Even if he didn't really collect them, he did not think there was any reason to give them away.

She drew back a little into the darkened arch of the doorway. He followed her to guard his possessions.

"If you get something..." she said.

Maybe mostly to get away from her—some classmate might just happen to pass by and see him standing here with a girl—he said hastily, "Take them then."

Before he had time to stop her, she was on him and her wet lips were pressed against his. He pulled himself free, smelled the stink of violet candies; she had had a box of them that she had eaten at the movies without offering any.

If he had only guessed that this was what she meant he would get in exchange for the pictures, then she would have never gotten them.

"Here are the rest," she said and threw the pictures that she already had at him.

And she disappeared into the darkness, up the stairs.

He stood a minute as if paralyzed, felt so confused that he did not really know what he should do. She was nuts! It was so gross.

But as he walked along, he thought that he must have had a real adventure in any case, that maybe in fact it was worth the pictures. To have kissed a girl was still something pretty exciting. And, of course, he did not collect Divas.

III

LIGHT AND SHADOW

The shadow grew with the light. At the same time as prosperity continued to grow in Sweden, unrest increased out in the world. The dictatorial powers pushed forward step by step without meeting any real opposition. The Italians occupied Abbyssina, and Mussolini had Victor Emanuel crowned as emperor of the new allied kingdom. The Germans occupied the Rhein zone and annexed Austria. In Spain, a civil war broke out after General Franco took the lead for a military revolt. Japan attacked China. In Moscow, new trials ended with new death sentences; "the old guard" was being weeded out.

Amateurs and idealists stood up against the professionally carried-out violence of the dictatorships: barefoot Abyssinian bands, Columna Durrutis' anarchists, and the Socialists of the International Brigade. The large democracies seemed to be gripped by a paralytic distaste for action; their attempts to stop the attacking nations amounted to nothing more than vague gestures.

In the shadow of the threat of war, entrepreneurialism blossomed; the economy boomed. In some trades, there was now a shortage of qualified labor. Construction surpassed all previous records. A law for twelve-day, universal vacations was passed. The recently so impoverished Sweden was beginning to be seen as a leading country, an example for the nations of the world. Big transatlantic liners lay moored in clusters along Strömmen. Many tourists were coming to observe.

The city was growing once more; newcomers arrived in wave after wave. Out at Bromma, a new aerodrome was opened; new parts of the city grew up at Ängby and Abrahamsberg. Lilla and Stora Essingen were developed with apartment buildings. On Söder, a huge new traffic route was begun, Södergatan, and the old tumbledown buildings on Södrabantorget disappeared to make way for a civic hall. Beside Vasabron, the Strömbadet public baths were torn down; the new Vanadisbadet baths were opened.

The winds of change… But they also brought with them the stink of blood.

One day at the end of August, smoke from a fire lay thick over Stockholm, and the wind carried it farther to Värmland. Everywhere people searched and scouted for the glow of the blaze. But it was burning far away in Russia. Enormous forests were being burned down so there would be better defense capabilities in the event of an anticipated invasion.

That fall, 1938, Henning Nilsson began his last year at Katarina Real School; if all went as expected, he would take the real exam in the spring. He had turned fifteen, as old as Emelie's father had been when he came walking into the city in the year of steam, 1860.

Emelie looked at Henning, found it quite difficult to imagine that her father had been no older when he came here. Alone, forced to fend for himself. She had to wonder if this boy could manage the same thing, thought of how worried they grew if he was out on his own and happened to come home a little later than usual. How Maj would admonish him, help him with his lessons, was his support.

They said that children were maturing earlier than before. Naturally, they knew a lot more, had to go to school longer, read newspapers, listened to the radio. But still… in her father's time eight-year-olds had worked in factories. She herself had been twelve when she had stopped school and begun at Melinder's cosmetics factory. Even if their knowledge was less than that of today's youths, their responsibility had been bigger. And wasn't it responsibility that gave true maturity?

Emelie had plenty of time to wonder now. Since last spring, she had been free, a retiree. She felt like she would have had the energy to continue. But they did not want such an old person as a supervisor. They had been very kind and friendly; she had even received a little pension. Kind—but unshakable. They did not think they should take advantage of her past sixty-eight, they said. Now she was worth her pension.

But ever since Emelie had stopped, they had had to change supervisors a couple of times; things had not worked out so well. So then they got to see that it was not only age it depended on.

Now she would like to have something to do again, some task outside of her home. She felt that she possessed strength now that was just disappearing instead of being put to use.

And it would no doubt also be necessary for her to earn a little money besides her pension; Jenny had not had many engagements lately. Still, Jenny had gotten a telephone so the theater directors could reach her more easily. It was a huge luxury, Emelie thought. Especially since it did not seem to help; no directors called. But Jenny called and talked to all sorts of people, and then the high bills would arrive.

Emelie borrowed Jenny's telephone catalogue, looked for Konrad Melinder, who, at one time, had been her boss at the cosmetics factory. The last time she had seen him had been fifteen years ago. He had been selling paper. Now he was not in the catalogue; maybe he was dead. He would also have grown old, of course, by this time—old and superfluous. Although she still thought of him as "young Herr Melinder."

Emelie stayed sitting a while in the evening dusk and cried by herself, about herself. But then she got up quickly and turned on the lamp. In the cold exposure of the lamplight, she could not give herself over to sitting and pitying herself, she felt.

BLACKOUTS

On Monday, the fifth of September, the national air defense exhibit opened in Meeth's old, fire-damaged warehouse. At the Mea, the military equipment store, they were selling the civilian gasmask, Fatra C—think of gas protection in time! Every day, the newspapers gave new blackout advice.

As if without resistance, people were driven toward the war, into the war's atmosphere. It felt like there was nothing to discuss any longer. All that remained was to prepare oneself. The impossibility of the war had been accepted.

At ten o'clock on Tuesday morning, a state of war was begun. But it was not until Wednesday that the citizens of Stockholm saw anything happen; the air force was holding an exhibition at Gärdet. Otherwise, the day was spent "under the emblem of blackout paper, thumbtacks, and sore thumbs." The blackout was not going to start until two o'clock that night, but many had their windows ready by afternoon. The lights of the taxis were painted mostly black, so that only a little slit was left open for light, then rain arrived and washed away most of the paint.

Thursday was completely a war day. Warning sirens wailed, and damages of various types were simulated on the city streets; shot-down planes, holes from bombs, fires. An explosion on Riddarfjärden killed thousands of fish that floated to the surface with bellies up and gave a good excuse for a hasty fish catch.

When the alarm went off, all vehicular traffic stopped, all outdoor work stopped, and people sought shelter against building walls as instructed. They stood pressed there and searched the skies until the siren, which got to be called "Hoarse Fredrik," gave the signal that the danger was over. But not one plane had sailed over the city; the flights had been prevented by clouds.

Toward evening, the sky cleared; people could count on a blackout in the moonlight. Movie theaters and restaurants had transformed their entryways into dark passages where visitors were passed through.

But for the pilots, the situation was difficult, despite the fact that it appeared to be excellent flying weather. The runway was covered with an impenetrable ground fog that prevented the bombers from talking off. Only six fighter planes could take off and simulate attacks on the dark city.

By the hundreds of thousands, people streamed out onto the streets to experience the darkness of the streets, a moonbeam promenade with something of the atmosphere of a Sunday in spring.

Cars glided slowly forward, like dark prehistoric beasts with light shining dimly from their eyes. The black-clad windows of the streetcars looked like a row of mourning veils in a funeral procession.

People bumped into each other in a friendly fashion in the darkness, spoke excitedly, laughed. They felt a little tense; there was something ghostly about the town in the light of the full moon. As if the picture might attract those unknown beings called enemies, as if foreign planes might be drawn like moths to the streams of light that the searchlights swept across the skies.

A drill, a game. Somewhere behind it all was still reality. A deeper darkness, without moonlight and without mercy.

The French lay fully prepared for war at the Maginot Line. Hitler was practicing blackmail on Czechoslovakia with his demands for the Sudetenland. Something could happen—at any time.

Large streams of people wended their way down toward Slussen and the center of town, stood along the quays, looked out over the water and at the play of searchlights in the sky. When the sirens sounded, a huge dark wave of people washed away from the quays and up against the walls of the buildings, or into the passageways of the locks' labyrinth. The roads lay almost empty, shone dead in the moonlight.

A single plane was caught in the searchlight, glided out of it, was spotlighted again, disappeared.

Henning had begged to be allowed to go out and watch. When the sirens wailed, he moved along with the wave of people, away from the friends he had been with. It was hard to find them again in the crowds and the darkness. Finally, he gave up, began to walk toward home.

But there on Katarinavägen some people he knew were standing. It was Allan he noticed first; his laugh was unmistakable. And then Stig.

Allan was twenty now—but still just as childish, Henning thought. At the least silliness, he laughed so that he howled. But Stig only smiled, almost sadly. It was probably because he had been sick so much. He was two years younger than Allan but seemed many years older.

Henning joined them; they stood there and kicked at the stonewall and talked. Allan about his job, how many buildings he had participated in laying the foundations for. Stig was something between an errand boy and a security guard at an insurance company, but his big interest lay in playing the trumpet. He and some other guys had gotten to borrow a room in a basement to practice in. He could not play at home, had tried sitting in a closet, but they claimed he still drove them crazy with his tootling.

Stig spoke in a low voice, eagerly. His dark hat jutted out over his face, which seemed paler than usual in the moonlight. Under his jacket, he was only wearing a white shirt that was unbuttoned at the throat, but he did not seem to notice the evening chill. Beside Allan, he seemed slim and almost elegant.

"Playing..." Stig said. "That is life..." Truthfully he did not think he had time for his job; life was short. Not least of all his life. He sensed that. But his job was still necessary anyway. If nothing else, he had to pay off his trumpet. Though he hoped that he would soon be able to live off his playing. That was the only important thing.

Henning could not understand Stig's ardor, his suffering. But he had an idea. Maybe Stig and his guys could come to the club and play? It was a boys club that met in the parish hall.

Stig promised to come. Every opportunity to test the prowess of his band was welcome.

Allan was almost forgotten. He was nice but not so much to talk to.

Suddenly, they noticed that Allan had company. Two girls had stopped and stood there joking with him. Henning thought he recognized the girls. Weren't they the two who had been on the outing to Källtorp several years ago?

Allan promised to buy them all coffee at some café. When he got going, he was impossible with his wanting to treat people.

They made their way up Götgatan. It seemed normal somehow that they went in that direction, were drawn to the lights. Even if they were off now. There were not as many people out anymore; they had seen enough darkness. But it was pretty filled in the café, and they had to squeeze together in a corner.

Henning stayed beside Stig. Allan was completely occupied with the girls. When they came into the light, Henning saw how Stig took stock of the girls—and apparently rejected them. He turned to Henning again and continued to talk about his band. Allan had to take care of Ansa and Daggan himself, and it seemed he did it gladly, especially Daggan. He had taken a scarf from her that he stuffed inside his shirt.

Allan ordered: five cups of coffee and almond cakes.

The crowded and smoky café felt like a safe hiding place against the great darkness outside.

It was time for Henning to go home. Stig followed him.

They walked through the dark streets that ran alongside the main thoroughfare, silent and empty now. Sometimes the moonlight cut through from between the roofs.

It was Stig who did the talking. About his years at the hospital, the feeling of being disconnected from life, forgotten by life. And about his new home; he felt like he was a stranger there, too. His father was still in Svartsjö Prison. He and his younger brothers were living in the tenement housing with his grandfather and his Aunt Dora. Rutan, Dora's daughter, hung out at home all day. She was over twenty-five now but had probably never lifted a finger to work. She must be doing a little prostitution. Dora could deal with others—but never with Rutan.

Actually, he had no home anymore since his mother had died.

He was going to get out of there as soon as he could. Maybe move in together with one of the guys from the orchestra. As long as he stayed out of the sanatorium.

Henning had certainly heard one thing or another about Stig's family and circumstances, heard them talked about at his grandmother's. At those times, he had never thought much in particular about what they said, never tried to imagine how things might really be. Now he felt like he was learning about a world different from his own, which he had always thought was the only one. Maybe instead the other was the world, real life? And he himself had led a sheltered life, hidden from reality.

"Of course, I should not be playing a trumpet," Stig said. "With these damned lungs of mine. But when it is what I want to do, then I feel it is what I have to do."

He turned and left and was blotted out quickly by the darkness.

But Henning could not forget the narrow, pale face that had protruded from under the hat rim, the voice that had something of hoarse disdain and heated engagement.

Life, he thought, real life. And he felt how a breath of cold and death blew into his safe world.

Allan had a problem: He wanted to get rid of Ansa but keep Daggan with him. It was hard to arrange. Since the girls lived in the same building, there was the risk that both of them would disappear if he saw them to the door.

He felt like Ansa ought to be able to see that he was gravitating toward Daggan, that she could have the sense to go. But she was probably afraid to walk alone through the dark streets.

So then he had to leave with both of them. He took a detour down toward Ringvägen and Hammarby canal and then up through the White Hills Park's most distant parts that were dark even when there was no blackout. He led them onto the narrowest paths and laughed with a devil-may-care attitude when they squealed at how dark it was.

He pushed Daggan up the hills; there was every possible opportunity to hold onto her. But Ansa felt left out and treated unfairly and began to whine that she wanted to go home.

"Now let's have a smoke," he said when they reached the slope beside the music pavilion. He threw himself down on the lawn, pulling the girls with him. He pulled out his pack of cigarettes and offered them. Ansa became somewhat mollified and crept closer to him so he could give her a light more easily. And he stretched out his arms and held them both by their shoulders, a real pasha.

Daggan wanted the scarf back that he had taken. She managed to get a hold of it and tried to put it in under her coat, but then he was on her. And under her coat he felt her breast, which was rather large.

But Ansa wanted to go. And then Daggan said, too, that it was probably time.

He followed them to the door. He had hoped that he would be alone with Daggan a moment. But they fooled him, both of them, and disappeared inside the door and closed it quickly behind them.

He jiggled the handle a few times, gave up. Sure, he had been fooled—but still pretty satisfied.

Mikael was in bed and reading when Allan came in. Allan got ready for bed, sat for a while on the edge of his bed with a sock dangling from his hand and bragged a little about the evening's events. What babes he had run into!

"Take it easy a little," Mikael said. "So that something doesn't happen to you, like paying for a kid, for example."

"Oh," said Allan. "There was nothing like that. They took off, both of them!"

And then he laughed till Mikael had to quiet him down. He might disturb the neighbors.

"Let's turn out the lights now," said Mikael. "So long."

"G'night."

Allan lay snuggled down in his bed, thought about how he would meet up with Daggan again. It would be a little different if Ansa was not along. He almost dared believe that Daggan liked him, he had felt it. And otherwise she would have protested against all his shenanigans in the park.

He had to laugh to himself in the darkness.

Mikael heard him chuckling. He smiled, maybe with a shade of envy. Allan was young, meeting girls, having fun. He himself had aches in his limbs and was stiff in his back and had not bothered to go out and look at the blackout.

AMONG THE PINES

On the hill in the woods, high up among the pines—that is this fall's rental trend.

During lunch break, Elisabet read about the new residential areas. Enormous advertisements promised "the pleasure of country living and the comfort of city living."

She would like something like that. Now that they were getting married, she wished that the change would be properly observed, wanted to clear away all of the old ways.

Without really wanting to admit it, Elisabet knew that it was she who was going to get to decide. Lennart did as she wanted; it just turned out that way. It was not that he was "henpecked," it was only because he did not wish for things as strongly as she did. For him, one suggestion was as good as another. Sometimes this irritated her; she might have liked him to have a pronounced opinion. He had one when it came to books and politics, for example—but not when it was something that concerned them more personally. Then he was satisfied with whatever she decided. Worriedly, she would wonder: indifferent? But that could not be so; she knew, of course, that he loved her.

She would have liked to move into a completely new home, in a house where no person had lived before them, where no one had gotten it dirty, no one made love, no one died. Where everything was as nice and clean as a pair of newly ironed sheets. And where there were no houses right across from it with people who could look in. Instead somewhere one could be free, have a clear view.

That was what the houses in the advertisement looked like: clean, straight lines, open around them, a few green pine trees by the corner of the house.

The print shop where Lennart worked was in Klara; her office was on

Kungsgatan. It would not be farther to the hill in the woods than it was to Söder. Not much farther, at least. It was Traneberg they had in mind.

It was not Traneberg that they chose; the road between the houses and streetcar stop seemed quite long and arduous. But in Fredhäll, they found an apartment in a new building. There was a view of Lake Mälar from the living room window. Many apartments in the new buildings stood empty; there was a lot to choose from. They signed a contract beginning the first of October but received the keys right away without paying anything extra for the remaining two weeks of September.

During the preceding years, they had put away a sum every month for a home. Now they walked into furniture stores and home goods stores to pick out what they needed. They did not have much to bring from home. Jenny did offer Elisabet the mirror that once had hung in the Panoptikon Wax Museum, but Elisabet did not want to take it, partly because she knew how proud her mother was of it, and partly because she did not like it. Lennart had some books, which he, of course, wanted to bring. Most of them were unbound and pretty worn and would maybe look a little out of place among all the new things. But it couldn't be helped; it was different with books.

They were up in the apartment practically every evening putting things in order. Jenny and Emelie came a few times as well to help them. It had to be on Sundays since Jenny had finally gotten an engagement.

It was terribly far away, Emelie thought. Fredhemsplan was already a great distance, where she had not been for many years. And the streetcar just kept on going, out to areas where she had never before set foot. They lived, in fact, just as far from town as August did when he was at his summer place.

"Though actually it is the same distance from here to home as from home to here," said Jenny. And it was not longer to their workplaces than before, according to what Elisabet said.

Söder was still different, home. Emelie would never be able to feel at home here. Though Elisabet and Lennart were young, of course, thought maybe that it was exciting to live like this. Elisabet had always been so intrigued by everything new.

They were married on a Saturday afternoon a few weeks into October, at the home of the minister who had helped Lennart get into the folk high school. Afterward, they ate together with their closest friends and relations at Jenny and Emelie's.

They were forced to do it all on the early side so that Jenny could be included. She was playing in "The Kitchen Cavaliers" at Moseback Theater and had to be there in plenty of time to change and make up before the show began at quarter past eight.

They were not going to take any honeymoon; everything had cost so much after all. But they took a taxicab out to their apartment and felt almost solemn at the thought of this luxury they were allowing themselves. They could confirm that the way there was indeed long when they went to pay the driver.

Lennart placed the key in the lock, lifted up Elisabet, and carried her into the dark room. He stopped in front of the window, set her down. And for a while, they stood silent in the darkness and looked out over the black water and the lights that glimmered along Alvik and Stora Essingen.

Then he went and removed the bunch of keys he had left in the lock on the outside of the door. Elisabet turned on the light, put the flowers she had with her in water.

They felt a little lost, unsure. It was not much more than seven-thirty; they had eaten and drunk coffee. And everything was so prepared, nothing to be done

He had bought a little bottle of port and put it in the pantry, and he opened this, set two glasses on the coffee table, lit the floor lamp, and turned off the overhead light. She straightened the sofa pillows they had received from Jenny, ran her hand over the fabric of the sofa and thought they had made quite a good purchase. The sofa bed was the most expensive piece of furniture; had cost a little more than three hundred. More than one whole month's salary, she ruminated.

They sipped the wine, said a few words. A little nervous, as if before a test. Something they could not help thinking of but avoided talking about.

For once Elisabet felt unsure of herself, of what she actually wanted.

She had wanted to come here: to their new and own home, to independence from those at home, to Lennart.

Then it became more difficult, more unsafe. With Lennart? It was, of course, part of it all now as well, what still remained to be done, in spite of the many years they had been together. It felt more difficult and more important just because they had waited for so long. The so extremely tangible closeness and joining—the importunity, the invasiveness, something that seemed to her as a giving up of her very self. A surrender, almost a defilement. She felt like she could see eyes glowing through the dark window, hear how they whispered. Waited, knew.

"You have made up the marriage bed, haven't you?" Mama, who was not very careful about what she said even when others could hear, had asked.

"I'm not going to fold out the sofa bed before I go to bed," she had answered.

"Why don't you see if you can get any music," she asked Lennart to silence the voices.

He went over to the new radio that they had received as an engagement present from Gunnar's family. He turned it on, waited a little. There was some musical comedy that was on. He turned the dial, could not really see what foreign station he had gotten, but it was dance music at any rate. He pulled her up off the sofa; it was a tango, and they glided a few slow turns around the room before the song was over. They stood there and held each other, kissed. He unbuttoned the back of her dress; his hands rested against her skin.

"Shall we make the bed?" he asked.

"Yes, maybe," she answered. "It has been a rather demanding day. I'm actually really tired."

As if she had to hide behind other excuses. As if she had to be evasive.

She disappeared from him, out into the bathroom. He opened the top of the sofa and pulled out the beds. The radio was emitting static; he turned it back to the Swedish program. It was old dance music now. He turned it down, dampened the boisterously leaping polka.

Elisabet was especially proud of the bathroom. With its bathtub and ceramic tiles and everything else that was not found at home on Erstagatan. She was longing to try it out.

She looked in the mirror, saw the little expression of uneasiness and perhaps dissatisfaction that was there. Wasn't she happy and pleased, now that she had gotten everything the way she wanted it? She had to be. Both because there was reason to be and for Lennart's sake.

She tried to smile at her image, coax out a smile.

She looked at the bathtub and could not resist turning on the shower, let a little cold steady rain fall on her outstretched arm. She kept her arm there even though the water felt so cold that it almost stung her skin. It would feel lovely to take a real shower. But Lennart must be wondering what was keeping her, was waiting.

When she finally came out of the bathroom, he was sitting in his pajamas on the edge of the sofa; he had hung his clothes on a chair. He stood up quickly, walked toward her, opened his unbuttoned pajama shirt and pulled her to him.

Maybe it was more difficult than they had expected, maybe easier and better than they had feared. The long wait, fear of failure, nervousness, unaccustomedness, and uncertainty—there were so many reasons for it to be difficult. But there was also love and a long-standing familiarity with each other; there was warmth, consideration, and understanding. A wish to give and to help, not just take and demand. For this reason, he dared come back despite his unsuccessful attempt, and she dared let him come to her again, despite the pain. The way was constricted and the door narrow, and closed. It eventually gave way, and she cried from the pain.

Finally, she fell asleep in his arms on the narrow sofa top. In the faint light from the streetlamps, he lay and looked at her narrow and pale face, could glimpse the sheen of tears in her eyelashes, feel the warmth of her breath on his chest, the coolness of her leg against his.

But on Sunday morning, it was she who woke first. When he opened his eyes, he found that he was lying alone. He looked around. One of the beds was still unused, but her nightgown lay across the arm of the sofa. The pajama shirt that he had thrown on the floor last night lay neatly folded on the pile of his clothes. And now he heard how the faucets in the bathroom were turned on, the stream of water.

He got up and went over to his clothes. But he changed his mind, continued instead to the bathroom door, tested it and found it was unlocked. She was still standing under the shower with her back toward him and her skin was glistening with small drops of water. He retraced his route a few steps, looked in the pocket of his jacket that was hanging under the hat rack. He pulled out a little box, opened it, and hid the contents in his hand.

She had turned around, looked at him. Now he climbed out of his pajama pants and stepped into the bathtub with her. But she did not say anything, not even when he carefully turned her around so that she stood with her back to him. He hung the chain with the little jewel around her neck, clasped it in back.

"Oh," she said, and held the jewel in her hand. "It is so beautiful. See how it shines." Then she threw her arms around his neck and kissed him.

While the cool, steady rain fell on them, while the water streamed between her breasts and washed over the little sparkling jewel.

"Do you remember when we walked across the bridge over there?" he asked, and nodded in the direction of the room's window. "In the rain. Isn't this just like then?"

Almost like then. But much better. He had barely believed he could be so happy.

But during those days while they had set up their home and gotten married, a world war was closer than ever. Bomb shelters had been dug in London's parks. Europe's leaders had gathered in Munich to negotiate—and parcel out Czechoslovakia to appease Hitler's demands. Swedish conscripts who were going to be discharged had been retained in preparation.

So fragile was the foundation they were building on, so close to the precipice was the happiness they had found.

A TIME FOR CLEANING THINGS OUT

So, Elisabet had finally gotten married.

Erik smiled as he thought of her. She was probably, in fact, a real tough little customer. The guy she got a hold of would probably not have it so easy. But she had been good-looking, at least before, during the time he used to see her.

It wasn't so often that he heard anything from his relatives and his circle from before. It never came about. But he sent money for the boy regularly as he had promised.

By sheer coincidence, he had bumped into Maj. He was just going to step into a café and get a cup of coffee between two meetings—and she was just sitting there having lunch. She had looked to be really well off, almost like before, though she was probably a little rounder. And it suited her. She had been pretty skinny.

He asked her how she was doing and heard a little about what had been happening. His son was going to finish school in the spring, Maj said.

The years passed, eight years since he last saw the boy.

"I didn't want to cause trouble," he said. "Thought it was better to stay away." But now—he wanted her to allow him to see Henning from time to time; maybe he could be of some use. He, of course, had certain contacts that could be good when it came to looking for a job. And then it would be nice to see what Henning looked like.

"He is your son," she said. "I have never tried to stop you from seeing him."

"No, I know," he said. "It was me, of course."

"You can call my office and say when will be a good time," she said.

"I am still at the same place. We don't have a telephone at home."

She was probably not as unaffected as she sounded. It was visible in her face, the stiffness of her movements. And she didn't have any ring on her finger now, as before. She still lived in the building for single, self-supporting women—so she had not gotten herself a new man. Might she still be attached to him? Though she was the one who had left, had ended it.

"And yourself?" she asked. "Are things going well?"

Yes, they were. A lot to do, of course. But he had been successful. Gotten a lot of commissions within the party as well. Now that the Socialist Party had splintered once more, most of his old cronies had become his party comrades again. The whole Kilbom old guard had returned to their "father's house." Soon it would be only Flyg and his Nacka gang who were left in the Socialist Party. But Flyg had to have gone completely crazy; he had defended Italy's attack on Abyssinia. And now, no doubt, he was beginning to even understand Franco.

As for himself otherwise, he was married and had two children, girls. And a wife at home and a nanny. Plenty of womenfolk.

Irene had filled out a lot, he thought. He would tell her that he had seen Maj, who was as slim as before. It would annoy Irene to hear it; she needed something to stir up her stomach acids. She went and lazed about, like some kind of indolent house pet.

"And you are still unattached?"

She made a face.

"You could say so. But I have frankly not advertised."

So Elisabet had gotten married in any case. He returned to that, also to the thought that she was quite pretty. Not that he had any intentions, but it still felt as if his existence had become somewhat less rich in possibilities. As if he had wished that everything would remain the same and wait for him. Such as Maj?

Though she very likely was not waiting for him. More like she had been burned, did not wish to risk making the same mistake again. Otherwise she would not be lacking offers; in fact, she still looked like a girl. Though she had turned—yes, she was thirty-eight, was the same age as the century.

Maj stood up.

He took her hand. It was slender and cool.

"Then I will call," he said.

He sat there and watched her leave. Straight and lithe, the boyish derriere. So unlike Irene. Had he chosen right? But he and Maj had somehow not been able to deal with each other. She had so much will of her own. Like himself.

Out on the street, piles of trash were heaping up. The big drive to clean out attics was underway—up to your attic and clean, I have done mine, bellowed the cars with loudspeakers. For the sake of the air defense, if there was a war, despite or because of Munich. Day after day, giant bonfires burned in Valsknopp out toward Nacka.

He walked between the piles. He was irritated by the thought that Irene would probably not give up until he had been up in the attic and pulled something down. She had so much time that she did not really understand how busy he was. She had given him a slip of paper to put in his wallet, wanted him to buy movie tickets. To "The Kiss of Fire" with Viviane Romance. He who had not even given himself time to ride out to Råsunda and watch when AIK beat Landskrona in football, 7-0.

But one day he would call Maj and arrange to see the boy. Henning, fifteen-and-a-half years old. He had a certain amount of responsibility in any case. It was foolish of him not to have asked what the boy's interests were. Then he maybe would have had an easier time of figuring out some appropriate occupation for him when he finished school in the spring. It was perhaps just as well to speak with Henning directly.

A few weeks passed without anything happening. He had a little trouble deciding where and how the meeting would take place. He did not want to go to Maj's nor take the boy home to Irene either.

So much was happening. It distracted him. Riots in Germany since a Jewish boy had murdered the German diplomat, vom Rath, in Paris, synagogues being burned, stores being looted.

The Germans were crazy. There would probably be a war anyway. And then nothing would matter anymore.

But he wanted to meet with the boy. Could not come up with any other meeting place than his office. He called Maj and arranged it, reminded her that he had changed his name. He was not called Karlsson any longer, but rather Karge. But she knew that, of course; it was on his money orders.

Henning had never heard his mother say anything disparaging about his father. The only one who said anything was Elisabet, but he could not remember what her actual comment had been. Maybe because they had silenced her so that it had been more a question of her tone than the words that had been pronounced.

Henning usually received presents from his father for Christmas and his birthday. But he had not seen him since they had moved to Söder.

Still, he had an image: a lively and dark-haired man who grew angry if one caused a rumpus, but who was otherwise quite kind. But who let him and Mama live on their own, and who, to be sure, sent his money, but who otherwise did not care about them.

He had no special desire to see his father, instead felt uncertain, wondered what could have happened, what this meeting would bring.

He was not exactly worried; he would probably do just fine. But he felt a little shaken when he saw that his mother had been crying. Was there something that was frightening her?

He prepared for opposition. With a spark of antagonism deep inside, he did as he had been told: He went up inside the big office and asked for Director Karge. He had to wait a few minutes; his father had a visitor.

Then he came—and now the sight of his father merged together with the picture he had in his memory. This was Papa! For a moment, it felt like a shock, he grew unsure, almost so that he felt small again. He did not really know what he was supposed to do, how he should greet him. But there were people close by; he did not want to show his feelings. So he took the outstretched hand, bowed as to a teacher.

Erik clapped him on the back, placed his arm around him, and led him into his office.

"How big you have gotten," he said. "It is so great to see you. It has been a long time..."

Henning kept quiet.

"Maybe you think that I have behaved strangely since I have not been in touch," Erik said. "It is probably hard for you to understand. But when Mama and I realized we could not live together, I thought it was wisest to not come and see you both. It was easier for you two to be on your own, for us not to meet and be reminded of all the old stuff. But now that you have gotten big I wanted to be able to see you, get to talk a little, too. About what you think of becoming, what you want to do now that school is almost finished. It could be that I can help you."

Henning had to admit that he did not really know what he wanted to be. Maybe he had not believed either that it was possible to choose, that you had to take what was offered.

At his father's request, he reported his grades. Not without a certain amount of pride.

"You should actually continue your studies," Papa observed.

Perhaps it did not sound entirely appealing. Sometimes he had longed for school to be done so that he could begin to earn his own money.

"If Mama can do without your earnings, maybe I can take care of the expenses and books," Papa said.

He took Henning to the café next door for a soft drink and a pastry. And before they parted, he said that he would think about that school idea and then call Mama and talk about it.

It had become something of a principle: Do not upset, do not stir up the past, best that Maj take care of everything herself, she knows, after all, how she wants things.

But now, if he has a son who is a gifted student, then he still ought to give him the chance to get an education. His son won't be able to say that he had a father who had the resources but did not bother with him. Maj's son would get the same opportunities as Irene's daughters. The boy could not help it if his parents could not manage to stay together.

He himself had never had any opportunity to study—if he had actually wanted to. He was not completely certain. But society had changed since he himself had been young. Not enough, naturally. There were still many obstacles left. It cost too much in general for people to let their children get an education.

If Irene had anything against this, then let her. He grew a little tired of her sometimes; she could not see farther than the end of her nose. She went around at home and tried somehow to spy on his world, as if she were jealous of his work and the people he met.

He was truly not a sadist, but sometimes he felt an irresistible urge to torment Irene. As if spiritually and physically she was made for it, asked for it. Her jealousy, her flabby flesh. As if she did not feel good from having it good.

He called Maj from the office. Met her during lunchtime again and talked about Henning. He would have preferred to go to a restaurant but she had so little time.

Maj was in favor of Henning studying. She had actually entertained thoughts in that direction herself. She was prepared to take care of her share of the burden of supporting him. If Erik would pay for school fees and books.

He reprimanded her a little gently that she had not gotten in touch and told him how things were going, how the boy ought to continue with his studies.

She had not wanted to demand anything, she said. Erik had delivered what he had promised and had his family to think about. But as it had turned out, now that he himself was offering to pay, she was grateful.

So it was decided. It was easy to come to an agreement with Maj. She knew what she wanted and gave clear, quick answers. She would be an ideal secretary; the secretary he had talked too much.

And Maj still looked good. So good that he might feel like... But that was not to be thought of. What Maj had once ended was to remain over. It was very principled—but a little inhuman.

She was probably all too unrelenting. If he had not happened to run into her, Henning never would have had a chance.

Though he could have called her himself sometime, of course.

Maj had to run, could not get back too late since she was in charge of the cashier's office. He stayed sitting there waiting to pay, leafing through the newspaper. His eye was caught by some lusciously illustrated legs beneath a fluttering dress. That fashionable wrong-side-out stocking—like powder on the leg.

It reminded him of Elisabet again. She had stood on a ladder one time and—well, offered herself was certainly too strong to say, even if the sight was inviting. Strange that he remembered just that girl and that time so well. For, in fact, nothing more had happened than that she had stood there on the ladder.

No, he had in truth other things to do than to sit here. He rattled his coins irritably on the table top and finally the waitress came and he paid her.

And then back again, to his many duties: Director Karge shall kindly call here and call there, a visitor who was waiting, an answer that had to be delivered. And in the middle of all this surely a call from Irene, who had come up with something to take care of on the way home.

At times, he wished he could push everything aside, get away from it all. Out somewhere, around Europe, get new ideas. Though then it would hit him that he had not been able to study, he should know some languages.

It was right to let Henning continue his studies.

BORDERLANDS

They still got together at Emelie and Jenny's every Sunday afternoon. The apartment, so silent on weekdays, filled with life.

Emelie felt almost like it was Sundays she lived for. Then, for a while, she could feel like she was not completely cut off from life, then she still counted for something.

Now even Elisabet and Lennart came. As if Elisabet more easily acknowledged Tyra's children now that she herself no longer lived at home.

Yes, Sundays were happy days.

Allan was the center of interest that Sunday—it was the first time they had seen him in uniform, and he looked quite funny in his gray trappings with blue collar and high blue helmet. In addition, he had received a gray cape that was as big as a tent.

He had gone through his recruit training on barracks duty. There was still something a little wrong with his sense of balance in spite of the operation, and he was flat-footed as well. As a barracks duty recruit, he had had to join up at a different point in time from other recruits in general, right after New Year's. Now he was going to do the half year that followed.

Because he had not been granted leave before he had learned to fall in and salute, a few Sundays had gone by since he was there last.

Emelie had wondered how Allan would deal with the drills, if he would be frightened and the anxiety and insecurity from before return. But apparently no greater harm had come to the boy. Even if certain similarities might exist between the barracks and the reformatory, he knew his worth now. He had his steady job, he took care of himself—in which case he could take his military service as something unavoidably annoying and not a completely devastating misfortune.

"But that bit with drills..." said Allan. Turn to the right and to the left and turn about and raise the hatches and whatever it all was called. Of course, they had given up hope of being able to teach him. And the same with badges of rank. The sergeant had screamed at him that he was a blithering idiot.

Allan laughed the whole thing off. He had heard too many earfuls before for them to sting. They didn't scare him, more the opposite. They were the means of the powerless; those who had more power would hit. And those who had the greatest power only used a few cold and correct words.

Now, in any case, he had been placed as a helping hand in with the car mechanics, had to wash cars, scrub floors, and run errands.

But it was a pity that he was going to lose so much money. They had a lot to do on the job now; Mikael could vouch for that.

Stig and Henning looked for a corner to themselves, had a lot to talk about. Stig's band had already played a few times at the meetings of the boys club. Now there was the spring party. They would sell tickets to that, earn money on it. It was best to play mostly easier numbers, the ones that would entertain most people. "Lambeth Walk," was still definitely being played a lot. And then they had a swing number that they liked to take, "Tiger Rag," that Ragge Lätt had played so often at the weekend cottage exhibition at Skanstull a year or two ago. Henning nodded in agreement.

Gun sashayed past them time after time. She had such a teasing manner. If Henning happened to be seated next to her at the dinner table, she sat and rubbed her knee against his or gave his leg little pinches. If he tried to do it back, she might scream ouch so loud that everybody would wonder what was wrong with him.

She was impossible. But, at the same time, she was the only girl that he actually knew. There were only boys in school, the same with the club. Maybe all girls were like Gun, in which case pretty difficult. But still attractive, an unknown part of his environment that sooner or later ought to be discovered. And consequently his cousin was the closets, and, in spite of everything, most accessible part of the unexplored continent.

Gun had grown a lot during recent years, was taller than Henning now. She had finished eighth grade almost a year ago. Had worked as a trainee in a department store and would surely become a salesclerk. Since she had begun working, she had started wearing powder and putting rouge on her lips. The light powder and the bright red color made her face look like a mask, he thought.

In every way, it seemed like Gun was older than Henning. It irritated him since he was actually the older one. Almost two months separated them.

She teased him and attracted him. And he was probably a little afraid of her, too, precisely because of that unknown element, because she was a girl.

Since there had been talk of Henning's schooling, Maj told them that Erik was going to help so that Henning could continue his studies. She had only mentioned it to Jenny and Emelie before. But it was nothing that could be kept a secret in the long run, and they understood that she could not afford anything like that on her own.

Maj looked at Elisabet a little anxiously, in hopes of being able to check any acid comments. And for once, Elisabet refrained from bristling when she heard Erik's name. She just said it was a good solution. Studying seemed to suit Henning.

But it would take a while before he would be able to help out and earn anything, Mikael said. Though he would earn even more later on instead.

No one appeared to have any objections; everyone was in accord about it being good for Henning to continue his studies.

Emelie remembered when it had been about August once upon a time; it had almost been seen as a betrayal of his class. In that respect, circumstances had changed as well. The boundaries between classes had softened. But if anyone wanted to study, it was, of course, still necessary to have someone who could pay what it cost. And that would certainly never change.

Elisabet sat and observed Lennart. Small, light wrinkles spread across her brow. It was like a weak spot for him, a scarred wound. Lennart never broke free of the dream he had had; his old school books lay neatly stacked in a dresser drawer. Sometimes he took them out. He might feel like he had relinquished his studies for her sake. He had dreamed of becoming a teacher. He would have been cut out for that.

Even if they felt happy now, she had to ask herself: What kind of world did they have?

They had been children during the First World War, had to grow up on makeshift provisions and war years' rations. They finished school in time to be thrown into the unemployment of the crisis years. And then a few years came along when they could let the wounds heal. And now? Did it not seem as if there was a new war being planned? For the time being, the dictatorships were digesting the bites they devoured—Abyssinia, Spain, Austria, the Sudetenland. But they were already crying for more. Mussolini wanted to have Tunisia and the Suez; Hitler was reaching for the remains of Czechoslovakia, for Danzig and Memel.

Was it not as if her generation had lived all its years in a borderland, between war and peace, between economic crisis and growth? They had never been allowed to live in security, not been allowed to turn their dreams into reality.

Deep inside, she had always had a drop of bitterness. Because she was aware of being born at the wrong time?

This Sunday, it was Mikael who was the spendthrift: He invited the four youngest ones to the movies.

Elisabet and Lennart left pretty early, had a long way home. Jenny disappeared to the theater; Maj wanted to get home to prepare for the coming week.

So there were only three of them left. Beda and Mikael at Emelie's. It grew so quiet and peaceful. Emelie put the coffee on again; they were sitting at the kitchen table since Emelie preferred not to stay in the other room when Jenny was out. She saw the room as Jenny's and the kitchen as both of theirs.

They talked about Tyra's children. Mikael about Allan, and Beda about Gun. And Emelie about Stig: He was living with his father, who was home again, as long as it lasted. Strangely enough, it seemed like Stig was getting by pretty well.

But they never heard from the youngest, Per. He knew that he was welcome but never came. And his brothers did not say much about him either. That was not a good sign.

Allan and Gun appeared to be developing into quite normal people. Far from perfect but still somewhat within the borders. Circumstances might naturally carry them over to the other side; none of them had a particularly strong character. But if their circumstances were reasonable, they would still probably manage in any case.

With Stig, it was different. He had something his siblings lacked: a will and a goal. Maybe he did not carry out his job as a security guard more than mediocrely; it did not mean enough for him. Music was what he focused on and wanted to sacrifice everything for. Now he had both a trumpet and a clarinet, but no overcoat, though it was the middle of winter. As long as he did not destroy himself; he had to think of his lungs. Emelie had given him a sweater that she had knitted, and this he wore under his sport coat. But, of course, it could not warm and protect like a coat.

Stig got by, apparently also succeeding in maneuvering his father in one way or another. Mikael believed that the boys living at home had staged some sort of revolt and done away with his role as father. David probably did not get far when there were two of them. Per was evidently a hard-nosed kid, one who they could likely be glad they were not trying to take care of.

Emelie did not want to admit that any young person could be a hopeless case. But now she knew that she did not have enough strength or capacity to do anything about him. She had to be satisfied with what had happened.

The younger family members walked from the movie theater to the street corner where Allan was going to be picked up by his military buddy who had a motorcycle. "Number one hundred six" drove him to and from the barracks in exchange for Allan buying him coffee at the canteen.

The January evening was cold and windy. Since Gun's brothers were completely uninterested in the fact that she was cold, she tried to huddle against Henning, used him as a shelter from the wind, stuck her hand under his arm. He tried to push her away, but when she asked so sweetly to be able to stay there, he gave in.

Then number one hundred six finally arrived, rolled up to the curbside. Allan hopped into the sidecar. Stig asked if he could ride along a little way and got to sit on the passenger seat.

Allan saluted as if he was saying farewell to a general. Then the vehicle drove away with Allan hooting and waving in the sidecar and Stig sitting huddled up and trying to hold onto his hat and cling tight at the same time as he held his jacket closed for protection from the wind.

And then Henning and Gun suddenly found that they were standing there alone. She glided quickly aside, away from him.

"Tomorrow is another day," she said, as the grown-ups usually said.

Yes, he agreed with her. And he was going to have a test, too.

"That you even have the energy to study," she said.

"It gets you a good job later," he said in defense.

"Bye then," she said and left.

And he went off in his direction, without looking back at her. But he thought of the possibility of giving her a real nip in the leg next time he saw her.

SPRING OF VIOLENCE

The strong one made demands. Would strike if he didn't receive. The cautious or the weak one gave, gave in and sanctioned.

Hitler turned the rest of Czechoslovakia into a German protectorate and let himself be celebrated in Prague. He appeared a few days later with a naval squadron outside of Memel and occupied the previously Lithuanian region. At the same time, the pressure on Poland was stepped up, the aim being Danzig and the corridor.

On Good Friday, Mussolini invaded Albania. After thirty hours, the fighting was over. And the dictator could weigh down his emperor and king's head with yet another crown.

The petty offenders seldom got to work undisturbed like the major offenders; for the small fry, there was a functioning police force. For Per, the police were not enough; he had Aunt Dora as well.

But even if Dora Berg was strong and tenacious, it was hard for her to steer her family. She was so alone, alone in trying to hold the whole thing together. She was helpless against her daughter, blinded by a mother's love. She could not do much about her father and her brother, two wrecks. And it didn't help to talk to Per either, who she was now saddled with.

All day long while she was out working, those four hung out at home. But when she came home, they were usually out, all except for her father, who insisted that he was sick and wanted his dinner in bed. He was not too sick, in any event, to help David bootleg liquor.

With Stig, it was different; in spite of his living there, he stayed outside of it all. He worked in the daytime; Dora woke him up before she left. In the evenings, he was out playing and usually came home late. He slept at their place but otherwise was not part of the household. He caused barely any trouble, was hardly of any use either. Well, he paid his way, of course.

The four daytime loafers were a little afraid of Dora; in any case, that helped some. Ever since David had been arrested for having bootleg liquor in the kitchen sofa, she kept her eyes on them, did not tolerate having anything at home that might interest the police. They had to keep their stash somewhere else.

But then Dora managed to slip on one of the stairs she was scrubbing, broke a leg, and was taken to the hospital.

It wasn't exactly the intention that they were going to have a party because she had gone to the hospital; it just happened that way. There was no one holding them back, only a lot of freedom that had to be made use of. David fetched one of the last bottles he had left; Rutan fried some pork, Per bought some beer. The old man got so excited that he had to get out of bed.

They ate and drank and howled until the neighbors knocked both on the ceiling and walls. When the old man wanted to crawl into bed, he got orders from Per to lie on the kitchen sofa, which was usually Dora's sleeping accommodation. Per shut himself in the room with Rutan.

Stig got home around two o'clock. He felt dead tired, longed to throw himself in bed and sleep a few hours.

His father was sitting in the kitchen, sleeping with his arms stretched across the table; his grandfather lay on the kitchen sofa.

In the room, Rutan and Per were lying in the bed that the brothers normally shared.

He had to stand still a minute and calm down. Wanted to rip the blanket off of them, throw them out, scream his fury. Was he now going to have that whore in his bed, too? But he knew that he did not have a chance, Per was much stronger. Maybe Rutan, too. It was he himself who would be thrown out if he tried to cause trouble.

Rutan's doughy, puffy, white face twitched. She was twenty-seven, almost ten years older than Per.

Stig felt for a moment a mighty urge to somehow violate her. But disgust for the whole thing took the upper hand. He walked over to the closet, took out the suitcase he had when he came back from the sanatorium, packed the little he owned.

Goddamn swine, he wrote on a piece of paper. Now I'm leaving and not coming back again. You can all go to hell.

He felt reluctant to write his name underneath. It felt wrong, like breaking the style. He satisfied himself with printing an S.

The tenements on the hill above the garbage dump lay gray in the gray morning mist. The spring evening's chill still lingered.

Where to? He had no money, not enough for a hotel room. Tonight, it was too late to sleep anywhere. Later, he could always sleep at a friend's. Until he could arrange something.

Aimlessly, he walked through the streets. He had not ever felt this alone before. He regretted suddenly that he had placed the piece of paper right on the kitchen table. His father would believe that it was mostly aimed at him. His dad was, of course, just the way he had always been. Though let him read it. He could have tried at any rate, at least tried…

The suitcase felt heavy even though there was not much in it; he put it down for a bit. He lit a cigarette and coughed violently. Gradually, he could stand up straight again, stood on the street corner and saw the street lanterns fade away in the dawn.

The spring night felt dead. Empty and deathly cold. And he stood there himself like a runaway in the emptiness, as if fleeing home and the sanatorium. They would not get him back in the tenements. But he could not avoid the sanatorium in the long run.

Play, he said to himself. Play your lungs out. You have no chance of surviving in any case.

Dora's absence perhaps gave freedom—but it did not give bread. If they wanted food and drink now, they had to pay for it themselves. They could not even think about credit; in the stores where they were not unknown, they were notorious. And now Stig had disappeared, the last remaining one who had an income.

The bottles were empty; there was nothing to sell. Nothing to buy with either, and these kinds of deals could only be made with cash.

Rutan and Per could maybe arrange something. But there was no solidarity there; they only thought of themselves. They just told you to shut up if you dared approach them.

Now it was not easy to be called David Berg. With Dora away, Per dominated even more. He drove his father and grandfather out of the kitchen to be able to sit there with his cronies and drink.

David did not understand what had gotten into the boy. The other kids had had their sides, but they had a certain respect for their father. But Per only threatened to hit him if he did not do as he said.

Completely without consideration. And worse: without caution. He clearly did not care if everything went to pot. He bellowed and shouted so that the neighbors complained, he let Rutan bring her men in there. Then they had to sit there, quiet as mice in the kitchen, while she had her "meeting" in the other room.

Afterward, Per would take the money she earned. When she first tried to refuse him, he had hit her. Now she obeyed.

Per and his gang were preparing something. David did not know what. But he had the feeling that he was living on top of a powder keg that could explode in the air at any time. One day—or rather one night—it would explode. And then it would not be long before the police were here again.

May Dora come back soon.

He had never believed he would wish for that. But now he understood that Dora was their only salvation. Everything had to be kept within certain limits, even that which occurred outside the limits of the law.

Some of the guys from the gang came and got Per. For once, they were silent, suspiciously silent. They did not drink more than one beer apiece before they disappeared.

If there had been somewhere to escape to, David would have done it. If he could have gotten Dora home by going up to the hospital and telling her how things were, he would have done it. But he could not go to the police; you did not do that sort of thing. And Per would be able to tell them a whole lot about him in any case.

So he sat there and slept at the kitchen table. It was just as well to be prepared when the cops arrived.

But it was only Per who arrived. He had a suitcase with him that he locked in the closet. Then he took the key and stuck it in his pants pocket.

When morning came, David went out and spent fifteen öre on a newspaper. But he found nothing that could be connected to Per.

He went home again, carefully unlocked the door. Per had woken up and gone out. The key was still missing from the closet. But it was a completely ordinary key. David tried the key from the pantry; it fit.

The suitcase was standing there.

He checked himself. He was not a nitwit. There were not going to be any fingerprints on this suitcase, not David Berg's at least. He found a pair of gloves that belonged to Dora on the closet shelf. They were quite small but he forced his hands into them. He fumbled with the catch.

Some work tools. And wrapped in newspaper some bundles of bills. Large bills. But some small ones, too, fives and tens.

The big bills were maybe marked. Maybe counted as well. But they probably had not bothered with the small bills. If he took two tens, there was probably no great risk.

He showed his character by not taking more. Wrapped up the paper again, closed the suitcase and the door.

The old man sat crouched on the kitchen sofa, had probably guessed what was going on.

"Well?" he asked.

David showed him the bills.

"There is a whole suitcase full of them in the closet," he said. "At least several thousand worth. This can never come to a good end."

"You had better tell the boy to take it away from here," the old man said. "Otherwise, we will all go to jail."

"Get dressed, and we'll go to the tavern," answered David.

When Per came back, he had bought a new suit. He locked himself in the room, opened the closet and took out the suitcase. He counted the money. That damned old guy was just the same—he could not even steal, just pinch. Petty and pawing, no grip.

He moved the money over to the new suitcase he had bought. Started to laugh; opened the old suitcase and wrote in big letters on the inside of the lid: "You got zero."

He imagined seeing his dad fiddling with the catch. Now those old devils could sit and starve. They had gone straight to the tavern for sure.

They could have a little something as thanks for their hospitality. He went out to the kitchen, looked around. He swept down the jars from the kitchen shelves; flour and sugar got mixed in with the blankets. He kicked and broke a couple of chairs. He would have liked to crumble everything he saw to bits, crush every single window. But it was best to get out of there as fast as possible, not attract attention, if he was going to get any pleasure from the money. Rutan was waiting at Central Station.

He pulled the new hat down over his forehead, grabbed the suitcase.

I'm never coming back, he thought.

A week later, he was caught with Rutan by the police in Copenhagen.

A SUMMER OF GRACE

Yet another warm and beautiful summer. And Sticken Berg's Quartet played. The rumor spread: they were good for being so cheap—amateurs with something of a professional style.

They did not earn any great sums. But they had been forced to buy an old car to get around with their instruments. The drummer was the only one who had a driver's license; he drove a company car by day. They still had their jobs, all four.

Stig felt like he lived in a perpetual hurry. There were late nights; they didn't always have time to eat as they should. The lack of sleep and food, the fever that was probably inside him—he grew so tired that he stumbled along.

Craziness maybe, he would think. It will do me in; it can't go on like this for long. But, still, this was how he wanted to live; in fact, this was the first time he had lived. And, therefore, there was nothing else to do than be prepared to pay the price.

It was his first real summer. And now that he had it, he would certainly have to be satisfied. Though, of course, there was a lot he wanted to have time for, now that he discovered how rich existence was.

He lived so intensively with and for the band that he barely had time to think of anything else. He seldom went to Emelie's on Sundays. He still got to hear some of the news about the family—but it barely concerned him; he forgot most of it. The family belonged to a past that he no longer had time for.

The one who came with the news was Allan. He popped up from time to time at the outdoor dance floors where Stig played. He kept track of where his brother was, proud of knowing the guys who were playing.

Otherwise, it seemed as if he was trying to learn to dance and found it convenient to locate his practicing as far from town as possible. Perhaps he did not make any major progress; more than one girl had stopped dancing and left the floor when Allan had asked her to dance. He did not take it so hard; he was not pursuing those bitches either. He got to be a little sly in spite of everything; he would ask mainly the ones who seldom got to dance and therefore would put up with him.

Allan had finished his military service now and was working again. It was primarily on Saturdays that he took his bicycle and rode out. Whether the goal was three or eight miles distant didn't make such a big difference; he pedaled away until he got there. He danced, joked with the girls, talked to the guys in the band. Followed them to their car when they went to drive home again. But once they had gone, he would take his bicycle, ride a little way into the closest woods, sit down to eat in peace and quiet, and then fall asleep under a convenient branch. The next morning, he would swim if there was a lake nearby and then ride home so that he got to Emelie's in time for dinner.

He was very pleased with his summer program, thought he had come up with an ideal solution. And besides, it so happened that Daggan's parents had a summer cottage where she stayed all summer long, so it wasn't worth sticking around the city looking out for her.

Allan had tried to get Henning to go with him on his Saturday outings, but Maj would not allow it.

But when Henning wanted to go out trekking with Arne Asplund, she felt like she could not say no. Arne was seven years older than Henning and lived in the same building. He was also the leader of the boys club.

Trekking sounded healthy and wholesome, not dangerous. Two youths with backpacks walking along the road.

They started on a Saturday morning and, when evening fell, they were a little beyond Eskilstuna. They had hitched a ride for most of the way, of course. When it began to grow dark, they went up to a farm and got permission to sleep in the barn. But they had to hand over their matches.

They sat in the barn doorway and looked out over the field that was beginning to disappear in the August dusk. Beyond the field ran the road; one after another, cars glided past with headlights shining powerfully.

Everything seemed so calm, so safe. They lay close to houses, the light from the farmhouse windows, the field. The scent of hay wafted around them. The farmer came walking out of the darkness, stopped for a while, and talked.

They met many friendly people, such as the ones who picked them up in their cars and let them sleep in their barns. They stopped in small stores and bought the cheapest food they could find: milk, bread, margarine. They foraged for mushrooms and fried them and ate them till they were stuffed full, picking blueberries for dessert. The world was a friendly world; even nature was generous.

They passed across the border into Norway, sat one evening up in a protective rampart at the top of of Fredriksten Fortress at Halden and fried sausage. The steam floated in small gray clouds out over the hills and away to the monument to Karl XII.

Later on, they would often wonder how it had looked at Fredriksten Fortress, after what subsequently happened in Norway.

While Henning was away, Emelie was invited to August's old summer house on Stora Essingen.

The last visit. He had already begun to plan the demolition. The house was old and decayed. But the lot was good; he was going to build many nice, single-family houses.

It would probably feel a little strange when the old house was no longer there. The first time he had come here was with his parents, his real parents. When Papa had worked as a herring packer at Bodin's; at that time, of course, you took a boat out—over sixty years ago. That trip ended up being the reason the Bodins adopted him later on.

August's fate had been decided here, he said. In more that one way; he had met Ida here, too.

To tell the truth, August would have liked to retire and take it easy. But just now they were in one of the most enormous construction booms he had ever experienced. Even if his son was beginning to be familiar with most things, it was still an inopportune time to stop. Karl Henrik would need some help henceforward.

"But you should take it a little easier," Ida advised.

"Well, well. I am trying to take care of myself."

Emelie was not really sure if she envied August or not. Of course, she had missed her job. But eventually she had gotten used to having more time. She was not as quick as before, she felt. Not much got done. She had two old sick people she helped regularly and then her home. Now she could hardly take a job if she was offered one. Who would help those two then? Though it was difficult to make her pension cover everything, and once you landed at the pawnshop, you did not get out of there. When August came to visit, she was always a little worried that he would want to see Annika Bodin's piece of jewelry.

While Ida was in the house seeing to dinner, August and Emelie took a walk around. Previously, there had been so many paths and fine flowerbeds. In those days, there had been a gardener to take care of it all. Now it was too expensive; it had grown in again. When they were out there so seldom, it was actually a waste to put down time and money, in fact, almost a waste to own it and let it stand. So what was happening was best, that the place would come to real use.

So the sweet peas bloomed by the gables for the last time and the old fruit trees bore their last fruit.

Henning came home to start his new school. Södra Latin. For Stig, there were a few calmer weeks; crayfish parties and summer dances were over. Allan thought it had grown too cold and not fun for sleeping in the woods—and besides, Daggan had moved back to town; he had to keep track of what she was up to. August and Ida moved in from their summer house, Sommarro, they had to get an extra moving van to take everything away. They had barely had time to leave it before the old decayed walls began to be torn down.

Jenny was happy that the season at Tanto open-air theater was over; it had begun to be a little dark and cold in the evenings. And

Emelie was also glad—now she could get together with a fuller family circle on Sunday afternoons.

Summer was over. And one could ask: the last summer?

The Germans and Russians had concluded their trade agreement and non-aggression pact; the old enemies had grown polite with each other. This might mean that the road to war had now been opened; Hitler could invade Poland without risking opposition from the Soviets.

In England, they imposed a blackout in London, as if they were expecting a sudden and unexpected attack. Even in Sweden, they prepared for meeting a state of war.

At dawn on Friday, the first of September, German troops crossed over Poland's border. And Adolf Hitler declared that he had put on his gray field uniform and would wear it until he had either declared victory or died.

INSIDE THE DARKNESS

So the long-awaited war had begun. And the proclamation of something like mobilization went out very quickly, so quickly that one could assume it had been lying ready for dissemination.

Proclamation of military duty. Reinforced defense readiness is commanded. The first day for reinforced defense readiness is Sunday, September 3, 1939.

It was the same day that Prime Minister Chamberlain, with a gas mask on a strap over his shoulder, declared that a state of war existed between his country and Germany.

Allan was one of the ones who was called up in the first round.

Mikael felt sorry for him when he left. Allan, who usually took most things so lightly, was silent and downcast. He had not been free for very long. And who could know how long it would last this time?

Allan had gone and talked to his buddy, "one hundred six," who was called Elof in civilian life. They would go to the barracks together. But now they had to take the streetcar; a driving ban had already been put in place for motorcycles and private cars.

On the way to Elof's, Allan passed the building he had lived in earlier, where Daggan still lived. She was not in sight. Just as well; he had seen her in company with another fellow. And, as someone called up, he had no chance against a rival. It was surely an army reject she had gotten hold of; he already felt the conscript's bitterness toward the ones who had escaped being called up.

Everywhere, people were talking only of war, at home at Loffe's as well. Loffe's father invited the conscripts for a schnapps apiece; the old guy was a little tipsy himself. And talkative, as if the war had put him in high spirits. He sounded as if it were a boxing match he was talking about. He'll be the devil to make juice out of that Hitler. The Pole fell right on his face… and just wait till Hitler starts to waltz about with that guy with the umbrella, too…

Loffe's father laughed at the thought. He sounded so confident, as if he were completely assured of enjoying the whole battle from the ringside seats.

Allan and Elof did not have such an easy time laughing. Last spring, they had whooped with joy at getting to demobilize, had imagined they never would have to return to the barracks. And now it was time again.

Elof had brought out the toothless comb decorated with tassles that he made before his demobilization. Now, he broke it to pieces and threw them in the garbage pail.

They arrived at the barracks. They had believed that they would get to keep on working at the car garage now as well—but they were not wanted there. Apparently, they had read the proclamation wrong; they were supposed to go down to the harbor at Stadsgården and eventually board a boat bound for the archipelago. Before the boat set sail, it had begun to grow dark. They stood in the stern and watched the lights from the city grow dimmer and finally disappear in the darkness.

There were not as many as usual at Emelie's on Sunday afternoons. Gun began to go out with her friends from work, and Mikael had a bad back and stayed lying in bed at home a lot. Allan had been called up and, in October, it was time for Lennart as well.

Elisabet looked sad and lonely when she arrived. Jenny asked if she wanted to move home again while Lennart was away. But she did not want to. She did not really know where Lennart had ended up; he could not write it in his letters. He was "somewhere." It sounded as if it were on an island.

Stig came quite often now that the summer season was over. He looked sick and tired. Emelie talked with him, asked if he shouldn't go to a doctor and be examined. But he was going in for a routine check-up in a few weeks and so it would have to wait till then.

He and Henning took a walk after they ate. It felt good to get away from all their cares for a while. They walked down toward the harbor.

They were dynamiting day and night in the hill at Henriksdal for the new wastewater treatment plant. There also would be some military stockpile inside the hill. There was a shortage of air raid shelters of all types. At Hötorget, they had banned the merchants' stalls and begun to blast away under the square.

The lights from the Luma light bulb factory shone between the hoisting cranes and Hammarby harbor. The cranes were standing still, like high gallows. From over at Folkungagatan could be heard a streetcar's piercing singing sound. Otherwise, everything was silent.

What was waiting in the silence?

Poland had capitulated, been divided by Germany and the Soviet Union. Once the deed was accomplished, Hitler had given the western powers his offer of peace. But now the scorned little man with the umbrella had said no, did not believe in Hitler's willingness to make peace any longer.

So the war continued. Though hardly anything had happened at the front in the west, as if both parties were avoiding initiating what could no longer be avoided.

Rumors buzzed. Despite, or perhaps thanks to, all the urgings to remain silent: Bite your tongue, and you do your country a service; do not believe in any rumors; a rumor is a dangerous weapon.

The Germans thought, of course, that Stalin laughed too much in his photographs, as if he had fooled someone. And Russia had, without a doubt, started to move. It had taken its share of Poland, forced Russian bases and troops on the Baltic states. Now they were approaching Finland with their offers, had questions to discuss, as it was called. It did not sound good.

The darkness was filled with rumors, presentiments, anxiety. And when people turned the radio's dials, they could notice how the music had been moved aside for words. The ether was crawling with words, words, words.

On Wednesday evenings, the boys club had its meetings. Stig usually was there since his band contributed to the entertainment quite often. But, on this day, they had a hard time concentrating on the club's business when so much was happening outside it.

Today, the Nordic countries' flags had flown over the city. The king had called his neighboring countries' rulers to a meeting that would express Nordic unity and community.

It was as if some of the late summer sun was still left; it shone on the fluttering banners. The dream of the Nordic countries as the peaceful oasis. Maybe the Nordic countries, by some unfathomable mercy, could be spared from yet another world war.

They were gathered at the castle now, the sovereigns. King Gustaf, King Christian, King Haakon, President Kallio. And the Stockholmers came by the thousands, maybe the hundreds of thousands. To pay homage to the symbols, show their solidarity? Or maybe just to take part when something was happening?

Norrbro was filled with people who almost trampled each other; the open space in front of Parliament was also a dark billowing sea of people.

Shadows were seen in the palace windows, people guessed their names. Massed standards swept past. Film companies' spotlights shone light, giant torches against the dark sky; suddenly, King Gustaf's shadow was cast unnaturally large over the opera house on the other side of Strömmen.

Then the cries began, at first spread here and there, then collectively and in time: We want to see our king… Kallio, Kallio, Kallio…

Cheers, shouts of hurrah, applause. And then they sang A mighty fortress is our God, a bulwark never failing…

Stig and Henning wondered what this meeting might mean, discussed the possibilities. They were saying, of course, that the Finns were being threatened. Maybe they had decided now that Sweden would go along if the Finns went to war?

The light that was dancing across the sky, the cries of hurrah, the enthusiastic people. One felt so strong when everyone was standing tightly together, everyone subject to the same excitement. So dangerously strong, so easy to entice.

Stig did not say very much. It was mostly Henning who talked, asked, came up with capricious ideas. Somehow the whole thing did not have an impact on Stig any longer. The day after tomorrow he was going to the doctor, and he suspected the outcome; it would have to be the sanatorium again. Worry before what felt like his impending doom drove him out. He could not sit home alone; he had to experience what was left to experience before it was all over. But at the same time, it was as if he lost feeling, could not experience anything any more. Everything had become so terribly insignificant.

At the end of October, the first rationing cards appeared. It was only a preparatory card for eventual necessity in the future. They were similar to the rationing cards from the previous war, a ghost that walked again. And they became the reason for people to begin hoarding goods like sugar, soap, and flour.

It still seemed uncertain if there was going to be a real war. The Germans and the Allies continued to hold their strongly fortified lines, as if locked in place. One could speculate as to whether negotiations were perhaps going on quietly since both parties seemed so unwilling to strike.

Then the blow fell—but not on the western front. The last day in November, Russian planes bombarded Finnish cities without making any formal declaration of war. And the next day, a message was sent from Moscow that a new Finnish people's government had been built in Terijoki beside the Russian border to the Karelian peninsula.

Finland was at war.

A people in danger. You can help. Finland's matters are ours. Finland is calling—get behind it!

A volunteer corps with an enlistment bureau was set up. A string of collections was begun. Once atheist authors traveled around and spoke in churches for Finland; previous Communists underwrote fundraising efforts. And many spoke for "courageous rallying at their brother nation's side."

Among Henning's friends in the club, there were those as well who were gripped by the enormous wave of enthusiasm. Two of them enlisted as volunteers.

On Christmas morning, the two traveled by the same train toward Haparanda.

Many of their friends gathered at Central Station. In the middle of the gang stood the volunteers. People pressed their hands, gave them boxes of chocolate and books.

Would they ever see them again? Or would they fall over there in Finland?

Fall. A new word, a word one had never thought of before in connection with anyone from the gang. Esbjörn was a corporal after all.

One of the ministers from the parish was there at the train. He struck up "A Mighty Fortress is Our God."

They were still singing while the train began to roll away from Central Station. They waved and sang. And then the train disappeared in a cloud of whirling snow. The pastor pulled his fur hat over his ears and nodded farewell.

Henning stood and felt the temptation to become a hero. He could imagine standing there on the train while the pastor lead a farewell homage and Mama cried. He could see himself, his face hard and coldly determined.

But he was not going away, of course. He was too young, had school. And did he even want to?

Letters arrived from Finland, many from Rolle and some from Esbjörn. Rolle had been there during a Russian bombing and seen a little girl running in a snowy street with her arm half off. Blood had streamed after her in the snow. He had run over to help but had fainted. Another day, he had seen how they made neat piles of Russian corpses frozen solid.

If they were to believe the letters and the newspapers, things were going well for the Finns. The Russian soldiers stank of filth; when they were whipped on by their commissars, they made the sign of the cross and then went on the attack—like a flock of animals—to be mowed down. Those who were captured thought they had it so good that they asked how they could get their wives and children to Finland. And Mannerheim had said that if only Sweden and Norway could give him one hundred fifty thousand men he would capture Leningrad. He should be given that, thought people who said it was shameful to be Swedish now, a betrayal by Sweden to stay out of it. People blamed the new coalition government for this unwillingness to intervene; it was clearly not the government that the nation felt it needed, wrote its critics.

Major Finnish victories were reported. People learned names like Suomussalmi and Salla.

Still, perhaps people should have understood that it was an impossible fight, that the uneven odds were too tilted, that there could only be one ending. Now the tough peace came like a shock.

Henning received *The Volunteer,* the newspaper of the Swedish Corps, from Rolle. The whole front page was framed in black for mourning. *Finland's matters were not ours. Our Sweden that we loved betrayed our brother nation.*

For us life is crueler than death,
We do not own more than our native soil.

But Rolle and Esbjörn still seemed glad to be home again, Henning thought.

THE COOL HEAT

The war changed the city. Air raid shelters were built; large cement pipes were laid in the parks, seen as shelter for those who did not have time to find anything better. Bank and store windows were hidden behind coverings of boards.

The shortage of fuel became apparent and, at the same time, the cold was unusually harsh. During the coldest weeks, many churches were closed; schools had to give their students a "coke* vacation." Warm water disappeared after one last big bathing day in the beginning of March. Coffee, tea, and sugar were rationed.

Even if there was plenty of work when so many were called up, a sort of paralysis spread. There were fewer immigrants. Bus traffic diminished and cars disappeared more and more even if some furnished with coal gas units appeared. Residential construction dropped sharply. There were still lots of available apartments; in some suburban communities, every tenth apartment stood empty. The insecure times and the draft caused people to squeeze in together.

In some previously all male professions, uniformed women were seen: streetcar conductors, mail carriers, and ticket collectors on the railroad. They filled the slots of the many conscripts.

On the ninth of April, the Germans had made a surprise attack on Denmark and Norway. Denmark had been occupied immediately. Fighting was still going on in Norway.

Barely a month after Finland had gained peace, there was now war once again in the Nordic countries.

Now it seemed as if all the enthusiasm had been exhausted when it came to helping their brother nations, as if the faror had been extin-

---

*Coke was used as a fuel source for heat. To conserve their fuel, they would sometimes shut down the schools during the coldest weather.

guished by the Finnish war's bitter end. Opposition might seem meaningless. It was a different enemy now as well, one stronger and more dangerous. At the same time, perhaps viewed with greater sympathy or at least understanding by many among those who had seemed most eager for the efforts in Finland.

The threat had come so close, so close that no one was calling out any longer.

Without any new proclamations being given, something as good as a mobilization was being carried out in silence. Even older conscripts, who earlier on had not had any training, were taken, and a home defense was created.

It was just recently that Henning had begun to see his mother with different eyes from before.

It was not until now that he had begun to understand that she was not only his mother, but entirely her own person with her own thoughts and her own life. And with her own secret.

That every person had his or her own secret was a new discovery he had made. That one never got so close to anyone that there would not be something left, something hidden. He did not know if he was happy about this discovery or not. It scared him and gave a feeling of aloneness: One never got further than shell against shell. But there was also a safety, a hiding place for the innermost self.

He noticed such things now that he had not noticed before. Like that part about his mother's calm, something that was just a given before—she was an adult, would give security. But he also noticed the limits of her calm. When it came to her relationship with his father, there was a crack in her assuredness. Not in anything she said, but he could notice it in the expression she took on when someone talked about Papa. She looked like she wanted to flee, hide away.

But that thing about Papa was an exception.

It was now, during wartime, that he began to observe her calm. Maybe simply because her manner was so different from most. They talked so much, grew heated. They hoped for and believed so much.

Far too much, it often turned out.

Never her.

But he knew that there was a strong heat under the cool surface. She saw what happened in a more serious light than others did, saw human fates where others might be talking as if about a sporting match. And she could understand and forgive that people were weak but not that they were evil.

Sometimes she had told him about her childhood, about how she had been a tomboy who had always hung out with Papa and Uncle Bengt. The weakest one who could not show her weakness, who could not cry if she hurt herself. Instead was obliged to sort of make a shell for herself, she said.

But, of course, all people had to do that, though maybe in different ways. He felt like he knew this now.

For many years, Maj had not been able to be free of Erik, the memory of her time with him, the irritating thorn that stayed put as a last reminder of their love.

She was convinced that she had acted rightly, that it had been necessary to break away. Not least of all for Henning's sake. If she had continued on, their child would have had to grow up in a poisoned atmosphere.

Still, it had been hard. They had only been children when they had begun going out together. He was the only one she had loved, the only one she had had. Though he had had so many, even during the time they had been together.

She did not miss him, had no thoughts that they might be able to get back together again. The anxiety she felt when she thought about him had its origins in just the fact that he had been the only one, that there was no one else for her to fasten her memories onto.

She had met a man whom she liked, whom she could love if she dared to and allowed herself to. They were work colleagues. It depended on her if anything was to come of it. He had reached out his hand; she hesitated about taking hold of it.

Her indecision was out of concern for Henning, worry for how he would react. Now he was almost seventeen at any rate; a few more years and his schooling would be over. Then it would surely turn out that he would find a girl and get married. And then she would be alone, terribly alone.

Already the loneliness began to creep over her. Henning made more and more acquaintances, schoolmates, club friends.

In fact, he had way too much going on as far as school went. But it was hard to prevent him; he was so engaged, lived so intensely. She remembered how it was when she herself was in school those last years, wartime then also. How she, evening after evening, took part in the demonstrations, though they were all so worried at home. It was Erik, of course, mainly for his sake that she was so eager to get to go.

Just because Henning was out so much... because it maybe required so little for him to disappear completely with others. Just because it was necessary for her to be at hand when he needed her, to sit and wait until he came. She helped him a little with his homework, too, though it was beginning to be more difficult when he was studying things that she never took; Latin, for example.

If the new man meant that she risked driving Henning away from home—then it was impossible.

Maybe they were just silly dreams. She tried to diminish her feelings, get them to become as light as possible before she placed them on the scales. But they stood there and trembled in the uncertain position of equilibrium, as if refusing to make a decisive verdict.

She did not feel a lot of the calm that her son detected in her.

She would have liked to talk to someone, but she believed no one would really understand. Not her mother; Jenny would only encourage her to think of her own happiness, for heaven's sake. Maj's happiness could not hurt the boy! And that was too optimistic, too simple. Maj feared that one person's happiness always injured someone else. It was an awful thought, as if happiness could only be stolen.

It went against Maj's nature to not act after a clearly thought-out plan. Thus, it was indeed a measure of her uncertainty that she allowed herself to be drawn in.

It happened when Henning had a coke vacation, when they closed the schools to save on coke for heating, and was at a camp that the club had organized for a few days. When she did not have any pretext to refuse.

John asked if they couldn't go out and eat dinner together. He had asked several times before, but she had always been in a hurry then to get home to Henning.

They had, in fact, eaten lunch together quite often. But they had never gone out like this. Had never walked side by side like this either, she thought. Like a couple. They stopped in front of a window, their reflection in the glass. A not completely young couple, middle-aged. They seemed quite sedate and peaceful, not as if they were out doing anything wrong.

While they ate, they talked only about the usual, about the firm, the war, about the rationing. But over coffee he lowered his voice.

"You know, of course, that I like you a lot. That I would really like to get together with you more often."

She just nodded. He saw that tears welled up in her eyes.

"Do you believe me?" he asked. "Is there anything for me to hope for?"

She nodded again.

"It's Henning. Just so that he won't in any way... feel abandoned." She could not get out any more. It was so hard to sacrifice Henning and herself to a third person. Even if it was John. It went against her natural tendency; it was she and Henning who belonged together first and foremost.

He sat quietly a moment.

"I don't want you to sacrifice anything for my sake, risk anything," he said at last. "But maybe we could try to move forward. Eventually, maybe I could meet your Henning. And we are not giddy young people who have to rush off. We can take it easy and go along carefully so that we don't ruin anything. If it doesn't seem to take... then I will just disappear."

That was John. Such was he. Calm, good, considerate.

"You are kind," she said and took his hand.

"I like you," he answered and placed her hand in his.

He walked her to the streetcar; she did not want him to ride with her. There was always the risk that people would see them and begin to talk. Henning had friends and acquaintances in the building, too. When or if something was to be said, she wanted to say it herself.

John Sjöberg was the warehouse boss, forty-nine years old. A quiet man who managed his job conscientiously, even if it was not what he may have dreamed of doing. Like so many others, he had been forced to take what there was and had gotten stuck. He was handy; once he had thought of becoming an upholsterer and setting up his own business. Now he worked in a warehouse with furniture and furnishing fabrics, close to the old dream but still so far from it.

He had been married for a few years, a long time ago now. Since they had not had any children, it had been natural for them to go their separate ways when they found that they did not get on well together. It had been painless, an inexpensive failure. He had moved back to his mother's and lived with her as long as she had been alive. During the worst years of crisis and unemployment, he had also been among those affected. When he had started working for the furniture company afterward, it had felt like being rescued.

Maj and he had a lot to do with each other, and, over the years, they had become good friends, begun to address each other in the familiar form, gone out to lunch together sometimes. They liked being together. And then he realized it was more than friendship he felt for her.

At closing time the evening after their restaurant visit, he took his hat and coat and locked the warehouse. He walked across the vestibule to the office, opened the door and stepped aside for some of the office girls who were on their way home. They smiled and nodded, but he wondered if there wasn't a little glint of curiosity in their smiles, if they guessed...

She was still there alone, had just closed the safe. It had been a busy day, and they had not had the chance to exchange more than a few words. But it was clear that she was waiting for him to come.

He always felt a little strange in the office; it was not his realm. He stood by the coat rack, waited while she locked her desk and took her purse, turned off the lamp over her table.

When she came toward him, he thought he felt a wave of warmth and, in the middle of that wave, there she was; so light and cool, the light hair around the narrow face, the blue dress that revealed how slender she was.

It felt like it was the first time they were alone and unseen, as if he was a confused and shy boy who for the first time had made a date with a girl.

Her gaze in his. The glitter in her eyes.

Then she was in his arms.

Henning observed his mother.

Something had happened with her; she was different. Happier, as if lighter. But also strangely preoccupied sometimes. Not really quite as effective when it came to testing his homework and keeping track of where he was going. One evening when he came home, it dawned on him that she must have been crying—but oddly enough seemed just as happy anyway.

When she had behaved peculiarly before, it had had to do with Papa. But then she had only been sad.

There was something, but he did not want to ask. Besides, he was so caught up in his own things. School, the club. And then he had gone with Arne Aspman to something called Fighting Democracy. Ture Nerman had given a talk, and he and Arne had signed up as members. He had received a bundle of *Despite Everything!* and was going to sell the newspaper door to door at the neighboring buildings.

It was exciting, and he wondered what the Germans would do with him if they came to Sweden. Didn't Mama understand how dangerous it was? But she only said that if he did not neglect his studies, then it was a good task he had taken on. For Nazism was something that had to be worked against, something thoroughly evil.

He smiled when he noticed how it seemed to start the sizzling in her, how some of the heat began to make its way up through the cool shell. It was this way he liked her best. Sometimes it had seemed as if she had given up, then she would grow silent and cold, a little irritated if he had been out too long and or not attending to his studying. But in recent weeks, it was as if she was going around bubbling inside. She was not watching over him slightly anxiously like before either, but he thought that was completely natural. He was going to be an adult soon. On a Wednesday when she knew he would be going to the club, he received money to go out and eat at a snack bar beforehand so he would not have to rush home so fast and prepare food. This was also something new, a new freedom.

It was the same day, on a Wednesday in May, that the German front rolled into Holland, Belgium, and Luxembourg.

TO DARE NOT LEAVE

Spring arrived, despite everything. Despite the bitter winter, despite the war. It arrived while the German divisions rolled farther into France, while Belgium capitulated, and the English shipped out from Dunkirk.

August Bodin stood on the streetcar platform and read the evening paper, tried to skim the latest news as well as he could without using his glasses. The streetcar shook and swayed; it was one of the old, open trailer cars that had been enclosed. Almost all the streetcar equipment was worn out; since before the war, they had planned to phase out the streetcar and go over to buses. But now it was lucky, of course, that the old streetcars were still there.

August was not really used to having to be shaken around this way. Naturally, he was spoiled, had had his own automobile. But it was up on blocks in the garage waiting for the war to be over. It might be soon; the Germans seemed like they couldn't be stopped. But it would probably be a troubled world, too, in the future if that Hitler was going to play the starring role.

A seat became vacant, and August took it. He felt tired, overworked. And what could you ask for when you had gotten to be over seventy. Besides, it was hard times for people in construction. Hard to get money, hard to get permission, materials, everything.

Just because he thought it was so hard he felt he could not leave the firm. Although, in truth, he wanted to, although Karl Henrik would surely be glad if he could take care of the whole thing. Karl Henrik was forty-five, maybe not so strange that he was beginning to seem a little impatient.

August played with the thought that he should retire. He fantasized about the day Ida and he would perhaps move to a small town and try out how it felt to take it easy. Though they ought to keep the apartment in Stockholm; it wasn't sure that they could be happy anywhere else. He would probably like to have the firm close by in any case. He could step in if Karl Henrik got stuck and needed help.

It was only a few years till it would add up to fifty; August had been in charge so long. It had not gotten easier with the years. Now, maybe it was more difficult than ever. It was not only the building contractors who were upset about all the government intervention; the workers were as upset, too. All these regulations, this insufficient understanding that a construction business, too, needed continuous operation. A crew was broken apart when one could not hold them together. Many construction workers looked for work in defense installations out in the country. Or in other professions where they could get steady work.

As it was, it would probably not be so easy for Karl Henrik to manage it all.

Maybe it would have been better if August had left the leadership to Karl Henrik during the good years just before the war. But at that time, they had instead had such unbelievably big opportunities. The opportunities that August did not dare let go of, that he feared Karl Henrik would not have been able to take advantage of.

Didn't he believe enough in his son? Was he unjust toward Karl Henrik? It sounded sometimes as if Ida thought so.

"You have to dare to hand over the responsibility," she said. "Even if Karl Henrik chances to commit some mistakes, it is from mistakes that one learns."

Easy to say. But mistakes were so costly in this insecure profession he did not think that they could afford to make any now.

Sometimes August thought of his adoptive father: How had Fredrik Bodin actually been constituted to dare place the whole responsibility in a twenty-five-year-old boy's hands? Even if the company had been a smaller size at that time. But poor Father had been sick, of course. Or to tell the truth: a real alcoholic.

At the time, August had been ready to take over, filled with the desire and the willpower to take up a struggle for the firm's continued existence. And he had succeeded, though things had looked grim in the beginning.

The trouble with Karl Henrik was that he had never really had that desire and willpower. To be sure, he had wanted to take over the leadership. But not for the sake of the task, not because he was filled with the desire to work. If anything, it was to enjoy the fruits, to make things easier, escape his father's control.

Perhaps Karl Henrik would have fit in better in some other line of work; he was not really a building contractor. Not a manager. He was too easily irritated, would flare up; conflicts would arise so easily.

He caught a glimpse of an old dream: Imagine if both sons together took charge of the company. Gunnar with his practical experience, his knack. And Karl Henrik. But Gunnar had his own company, of course, that was probably doing quite well. Besides, it was so apparent that Karl Henrik did not want to work together with Gunnar; he wanted to be alone.

If only the war would end and conditions become normal again. Then everything would be easier, then Karl Henrik would doubtless be able to get by.

Wasn't it unusually warm in the streetcar? The sun shone in through the panes, spring had arrived. August unbuttoned one button in his coat. But not out of joy at the spring's warmth. As if it had gotten harder for him to breathe, as if he needed air.

The streetcar rolled across Norrbro, onto Gustav Adolf's Torg. Here he was going to get off, go up to the office. He looked at his watch. Everything took too much time. He had only meant to make a quick visit to see about a lot. But the owner had been so talkative, so long-winded.

When he stepped off at the stop, there was someone shouting his name. An old acquaintance, a master house painter he had done a lot of business with.

The master painter was standing there enjoying the sunshine, his overcoat on his arm, his watch chain glittering on his well-rounded stomach.

August was obliged to stop and talk a while, though he felt like he was in a hurry.

The house painter had retired, was only in town for a day, had a cottage in the archipelago where he mostly stayed. He was surprised that August did not arrange things as well for himself. There was no one who would say thank you for working yourself to death.

"Let's go to the Operakällaren Café and drink a whiskey and soda," said the master painter.

But August shook his head. Unfortunately, he couldn't. They were waiting for him at the office. But another time.

They parted; August looked at his watch again. It was no lie that they were waiting for him. Karl Henrik and he were to have a meeting with a representative from a cement firm.

August was punctual about being on time. Maybe now even more punctual than before because Karl Henrik was sloppy about it sometimes. But if one came too late, it meant lost time for many. A firm should function perfectly like clockwork. The head of a company as well. Letting people wait was an expression of nonchalance.

That would have been just great if he had gone and sat at Operakällaren! Even if it would have been fun to go on talking for a while. It would have to be another time. He could have telephoned, of course, and let Karl Henrik receive the salesman alone. But it was probably good to be there anyway.

Terrible how many bicycles there were in the city! And the way they zoomed through!

He hurried across the roadway. His coat was pretty warm; he understood why the master painter had been carrying his own coat over his arm. And then across Fredsgatan; yes, he could certainly make it ahead of that truck. But wasn't his watch wrong? It couldn't be that late.

On Drottninggatan, there was always a lot of traffic. Buses and bicycles and trucks that crept along and had to maneuver and jockey to be able to pass and get by each other. He looked up toward the building on the other side of the square; Karl Henrik was standing there looking out. August waved to show he was coming, but it did not seem as if Karl Henrik took notice of him.

No, now they had to let him across!

He walked out behind the bus that had just passed. He had time to take a few steps before he became aware of the car that was coming from the other direction. It beeped angrily. He had to take a leap to get up onto the sidewalk and save himself.

In the middle of the leap, the pain came, as if he had leaped straight onto an invisible spear. There wasn't anything more, he did not have time to feel anything more. He only took another short, staggering step, and fell.

Karl Henrik had seen August's leap to avoid the car. So typical of his father, to rush like that just because he was two minutes late. The sales representative had not arrived yet.

Someone started to shout. Had something happened?

He opened the window to be able to see the sidewalk below. He saw the body lying there, the hat that had rolled aside, the people who were beginning to gather.

His father was already dead when he came down.

He leaned over him, tried to listen for a heartbeat, for a sound of breathing. He held his hand against his father's cheek so that his head would not fall over. It was already difficult to recognize him, he was someone else, a dead man.

The ambulance arrived; Karl Henrik went along to the hospital. He received the doctor's confirmation.

While he sat there and waited for his mother and sisters, he felt the sorrow. And also how abandoned he felt, like a child alone. But somewhere inside him was also another feeling that he felt like he was supposed to chase away, deny. Something of a liberation. He was his own person now, decided things himself. How would things have gone if his father had continued living? Papa would never have dared hand over the responsibility. He simply believed that no one else could carry it.

But it had not had to happen this way. So fast, so cruelly. Or so mercifully easy? Papa had avoided suffering at least. Been able to be active to the last.

At Operkällaren, a master painter was paying for his whiskey and soda. Then he wandered slowly down to the boat at Blasieholmen, stood and chatted with the captain in the warmth of the afternoon sun, made sure that he got his usual table in the dining room.

So, August Bodin was still at it. Maybe there lay a little bit of envy in his thinking. But nice to take it easy, too, of course. Before he traveled into town next time, he would call Bodin and arrange to get together. But Bodin would naturally not have an opening then either; that was the way it was when one was in the thick of things.

As soon as the person who called said his name, Emelie guessed what had happened. She had not seen Karl Henrik for many years, not since he had gotten married and left home.

He told her how quickly it had happened. His mother was so affected by the occurrence that she was unable to call. But she would surely get in touch, as soon as she felt a little better. So far nothing had been decided about the funeral. But they would let her know later.

Emelie laid down the receiver, stayed sitting in the chair. She did not feel like she had the strength to get up or even speak. But when Jenny asked, she had to answer, "August is dead."

Alone. The last of the siblings. Except for Gertrud over there in America.

They had not gotten together so often, of course. August had not had much time. But still, they had lived like siblings again after the years they were apart. And during the recent years, she had grown so attached to him. They had talked so much about their childhood, about the years before the siblings were separated. Now there was nobody left she could ask: Do you remember? Do you remember Mama, Papa, our home?

August. She thought how he had stood on Norrmalmstorg once

and greeted her so politely, very elegantly, when she arrived on the streetcar. And how he had walked out there at Sommarro, that was now torn down and gone, almost like a boy with his shirt open at the throat. And the last time she had seen him—at her seventy-year-old birthday a month ago, when all the relatives were gathered and both August and Ida had come.

He had been so kind to her, truly a brother. And he never grew arrogant though he had such good fortune.

She got to thinking about Karl Henrik: He had sounded a little fumbling and unsure about how he should address her. Then he had said aunt. In some way, it was as if Karl Henrik had acknowledged her now. She was not sure if he had done it before.

Among the row of portraits that Jenny had hung up in the room was one of August. Emelie had received the photograph, but it was Jenny who had placed it in a frame.

Emelie fetched the photograph.

"May I place it in the kitchen window a few days?" she asked.

It did not matter how many times Jenny explained that they certainly should have the apartment together, Emelie did not really want to consider the room as hers.

"I am going to go and buy flowers and place them beside it," Emelie said.

"I will come along," said Jenny. She felt like she did not want to leave Emelie alone now, as if Emelie needed protection.

They walked together down to the flower shop and bought two Easter lilies, placed them in the window beside August's portrait.

A while later, Gunnar came. He also had learned of what had happened and left work to come to Emelie's.

Through the sorrow and missing him, she felt solidarity's warmth, kinship. With August, with Gunnar, with Jenny.

RETURN

Paris was occupied. France capitulated; Hitler returned to Germany and made his victory parade through Berlin. Perhaps some were tempted to believe that the war was over.

But in the city, the war still set its stamp on everything. More air raid shelters were made ready, new blackout drills were held, new defense organizations were built. And the draft continued.

His shoes are too big and his hat too tight
his pants too narrow—and his coat too long
but that doesn't matter because he is my soldier
somewhere in Sweden.

Gun knew the song by heart—it returned constantly to the radio's gramophone program—and she sang it for Allan when he came home on leave. But he asked her to stop bawling, he was tired of it now.

Emelie heard them. But it was as if their talk had nothing to do with her in the same way any longer. It was so hard to get away from what had happened to August. And now she was supposed to go up to Bodin's office tomorrow. Why, she did not really know. She had been to Ida's home earlier in the week but had not gotten any more information as to the reason for this meeting.

"You'll see that you are inheriting something from August," Jenny said.

No, that would be the last thing. Emelie grew almost angry. August had a wife and children, of course; it there was anyone besides the Bodins themselves who ought to get anything, then it was Gunnar. Though he had actually received his inheritance from his father in advance, in connection with August helping him start his carpentry business.

Think again, thought Jenny. If August had only guessed how much it was needed. They had had a very hard time for a while. Emelie had such a small pension and, as for herself, Jenny had scant work again, could not help out like she ought to at all. And Maj and Elisabet did not have more than what they needed themselves.

But Maj had bought herself a new dress. She looked younger than usual. And happier. The slightly sorrowful expression was gone; sometimes it looked like she was sitting and thinking about something completely different from what they were talking about.

It couldn't be about some man? Jenny felt like asking. Her question was already on her tongue when she swallowed it. Maj would not like that at all, least of all when Henning was listening.

Jenny had never really understood that serious streak in her daughters. She herself had lived life in another way. A little lighter, happier, never so weighted down by responsibility.

"That is an awfully pretty dress," she said anyway. "You look so young in it."

"You have to have something new sometime..."

Maj looked a little guilty, felt like the dress gave her away. She could have just as well worn the old one this evening, when she was not going to see John anyhow.

Jenny felt really excited. Now she would have liked to interrogate Elisabet a little; they had been married for over nine months after all. But it was not worth asking her anything either. Nothing was visible at any rate.

But Emelie looked so little and sad this evening. Jenny had to try and cheer her up a little, not just think of herself and her daughters. Though it would be fun if Maj in some way loosened up.

"I think we should get some more coffee," she said.

At least no one could take offense at that.

"So, finally," Allan said. In one week, he was going to be demobilized at any rate.

He sat silently a moment, tried to picture how it would feel to be free again. Among the first things he'd do would be to swing by the old place where Daggan lived. He wondered if he would catch a glimpse of her, if she was still together with that guy he had seen her with. When he was discharged, he would be able to take up the battle.

Gun served him more coffee. And even though he had eaten so that he was stuffed, he could not resist taking one of Emelie's delicious buns.

Gun came out to the kitchen with the coffeepot and put it down on the stove. Henning was sitting alone at the kitchen table leafing through an old newspaper.

She squeezed herself down beside him on the kitchen sofa, hissing: "Move over!"

But he did not move. She ignored him, leaned her elbows on the table, and looked at the newspaper.

He did not think that Gun was good-looking, in fact, just the opposite. But she smelled good, as did her fair hair that almost tickled his nose now. It smelled of powder, too. And he felt her warmth and softness, her closeness. He pulled up his hand that had gotten stuck when she had squeezed in beside him, felt her stocking's garter beneath the cloth of her dress. He fingered it for a moment; it did not seem as if she noticed what he was doing. Then he pulled her dress up a little and put his hand under it. But when his hand advanced farther, she hissed in a whisper to him: "Someone might come!"

Maybe it was lucky that they called for the coffeepot in there in the room. Gun got up quickly, tugged on her dress.

When she came back, he tried to pull close to her again, took hold of her waist. But she freed herself, took a step away. Then she turned around and looked at him thoughtfully. He did not know if he was ashamed or what it was, but he did not really like looking into her face. It was not as much fun any longer either when he had to say to himself that she was not at all good-looking.

"You don't care about me anyway," she said in a low voice.

He tried to protest.

"Don't give me that," she said. "I know it perfectly well. And it can just as well stay that way."

Nothing more was said because Allan came in, wondering if

Henning wanted to walk with him a little way, down toward Stadsgården where the boat was waiting. Allan had gotten a big parcel of sandwiches from Emelie.

Henning nodded. He looked at Gun. Was she intending to go along, too? But she was not and it was probably easiest that way.

They walked through the blue summer evening, stopped a while by Katarinavägen and looked down at the boat that Allan was going on. A number of military personnel was standing there on the quay, in small groups. Some had their girls with them; one could just make out the sheen of light-colored dresses in the shadow of the hoisting cranes.

"Now I hope it's the last time I go back to that hell," Allan said. "And Mikael says there is a job for me when I get out. They have saved the job of drudge for me."

Allan laughed at the thought; he did not really much believe that part about the drudge job. It was quite the contrary; they had left a place for him, they had not filled it with anyone else, but had instead waited for him.

"And then I will tell the truth to that damned Daggan, too..."

Suddenly he started to laugh again, that laugh that Henning had not heard for a long time, a snorting, bellowing laugh that made people walking by jump in the air with fright.

It was clear that he was going to be discharged soon. He was on his way to becoming the old normal Allan again.

Now that Emelie was not working any longer, she did not go down into town very often. She felt insecure, not at home in the same way as before. And the errand she had increased her insecurity. She had not been up in August's office so many times. And now, when August was no longer alive, she felt even more out of place.

What could Karl Henrik want of her? She had said hello to him at the funeral. At that time, she had barely recognized him. He had changed a lot, was forty-five now, of course, but almost looked older. Thinning a little on top, had started wearing glasses.

The office was only one floor up, so she preferred walking to taking the elevator. She stood a minute and caught her breath before she took the door handle. Yes, evidently she should just walk in. Before, there had been a receptionist in an anteroom. It was still that way.

The girl said she would tell the building contractor. As if August was still there. But now it was Karl Henrik.

He came out and greeted her, asked her to come in. And introduced her as his aunt to a man who sat there in the room and waited. Emelie grew a little worried and did not comprehend what the other man's name was or who he was.

The room looked the same as before, she thought. Except the old sofa that August had was gone. Now there were some armchairs around a table instead.

The strange man was clearly a lawyer. He read parts of a document he had in front of him aloud, and which evidently was August's will. Gunnar would get a share, how much was difficult for Emilie to understand since it was not a question of money but of stocks and bonds. And then the part came that she was maybe beginning to expect but could hardly believe: To his sister, Miss Emelie Charlotta Nilsson, he wished, as a little thanks for all her help during years past, to will to her a sum of five thousand kronor to be paid in cash.

She started at the amount.

"No," she said. "I cannot accept that, so much money."

"Yes," said Karl Henrik. "I know that Papa wanted you to. He would have actually liked the sum to be larger, but most of what there is is so tied up in the company."

She received a receipt to sign and five large pink thousand kronor bills were spread out on the table before her. The lawyer took her hand and said good-bye, he was leaving.

Emelie was so overcome that she hardly knew what she said or did. She sank down in the chair and wept a little at the thought of how kind August had been and how she missed him. But then she tried to gather her forces again; she could not sit here and trouble poor Karl Henrik. She stood up and thanked him, asked him to say hello to Ida and thank her as well. If she really could accept this, if it was not too completely crazy that she had received so much money.

He assured her that everything was as it should be. And asked if he shouldn't ask the receptionist to call for a cab for aunt.

Cab? For a second, she wondered what he meant. He maybe thought she had so much money now. But she was not going to fritter away August's money by riding in a cab.

"No, thank you," she said. She would certainly take the streetcar.

But once she got out on the street, she almost regretted it, felt unsure, reeling, in fact. And to sit on the streetcar and walk through the streets with such an enormous amount of money in her purse. Couldn't people see in her face that something had happened, guess that her purse was full of money? What if she was assaulted?

There was a tobacconist's close to the office. She called home to Jenny from there and asked her to come. Jenny was ready right away; they would meet at the stop on Gustav Adolf's Torg.

Emelie looked back at the office building she had just left. There, on the street outside the door, August had died, where people now were walking past free of care, without having any idea of what had happened. And up above was the office that she had now probably seen for the last time.

She shook her head. And slowly began to walk toward the stop. Surely, there used to be a park bench there. She felt the need to sit a while, just sink down somewhere and calm down, try to get her nerves to relax.

Jenny saw Emelie from the window of the streetcar. A small black sunken figure on the bench. With both hands, she was holding tightly onto the new purse she had received for her seventieth birthday.

Emelie spread out the pawn tickets on the table. One might well think she and Jenny did not have so much of value to borrow against, but almost a dozen tickets had accumulated. She took them one by one, counted out the interest and wrote it and the amount of the loan in the little accounting notebook she had recorded her accounts in. Then she went to her notes about loans. She had had to borrow a little from Jenny's daughters to be able to buy clothes for the funeral. She had intended to pay that back with money from her pension. Otherwise, all she had was a big debt. Gunnar had helped out when it had come to Tyra's illness and funeral. Gunnar had said that he did not want the money back; Tyra was his half-sister after all. But Emelie could not accept that, so the almost six hundred kronor still stood as a debt in her notebook.

With Jenny's help, she began to put the pawn tickets in such an order that she would avoid going too far out of her way when everything was to be brought home. Since she was ashamed to go back to the same pawnbroker, the sources of the loans were quite spread out, and there were many places to visit. But this time it would feel really good.

If August had not been so kind and thought of her, she would have been obliged to die leaving debts behind.

Then she had to weep again, at the thought of all the goodness she had been the object of.

She did not understand how she had become like this, she who had almost never cried before. But this thing with August had hit her hard; she was not herself any longer.

It was warm, at the height of summer, quite lovely to be out. Every day, she walked with Jenny between the pawnshops and home. One evening, they traveled out to Gunnar's. He was just as stubborn as Emelie; finally, he accepted two hundred kronor anyway since he understood that Emelie absolutely wanted to share the costs when it came to Tyra.

Much that had been gone for a long time was brought back now. Presents she had received for her birthdays a long time ago. The Chinese dress fabric Mikael had brought when he came back from sea. Annika Bodin's piece of gold jewelry; that was the one she valued most highly among her pawned goods.

Everything came back home again.

Emelie would never make use of such a fine piece of jewelry so she gave it to Maj. And Elisabet got the dress cloth.

Finally, Emelie also brought out the almost falling-apart old envelope she had kept the money for her funeral in. It was covered with numbers that showed how much she had placed in and taken out of it, and when she had done it. It could be read as a history, to remind her of the good times and the bad. But she did not want to put money back in the envelope again; she did not want to have it any longer and instead tore it into tiny bits. It was better to put the money in a savings account; it was way too much to put in a drawer.

That she would experience owning a bankbook as well. It was unbelievable and never would have happened if August had not…

In the middle of the beautiful summer, Emelie felt longing and desolation.

EXPANDING BORDERS

The world was closed, the borders blocked off. Even if the big showdown on the western front had ended with an overwhelming German victory, the war was not over. The fighting on the ground had been followed by fighting on the seas and in the air. The fight for England had begun; the "Blitz" had been launched.

Of course, Henning sometimes felt like he lived in a closed world, the walls were closing in. The German terror in the occupied countries escalated. Central Europe had become a prison, England a fortress under siege; Sweden lay like a closed-off and wind-whipped island in a sea of brown.

But it was during these years that he stepped out of childhood and into youth. It was now that he was beginning to discover the world around him, expanding his own borders. For this reason, he was able not to experience these years mainly as the time of war, but as the time when he was young. Even if his world might seem dying, his time was still filled with life.

Now he experienced the Word. The enormous possibilities of conversing your way to a contextual awareness that you had not even suspected existed before. The moment when an image one has had of one's existence is suddenly erased and disappears like smoke. There were visions perhaps, of towers and scaffoldings that rise up in a sort of haze and could be more sensed than seen.

Henning used a different name from "word." He said, "talk." This talk went on in the little café where they usually gathered after club meetings. Talk with schoolmates during breaks and on the way to and from school. Talk with Stig, who had been released from the sanatorium again and had returned to his job and his band. Talk that made it hard to part at the end of the evening because there was so much to talk about.

The all-embracing talk. That began with the program for the club meetings, or the result of the English test. That continued with the war and Nazism, or the programs at the movies and the football results. And that could end with dealing with girls or about God, about death or about the soul. When Arne Aspman had read a book called *The Conquest of Happiness,* they talked about work and someone quoted Aldous Huxley: "You've got to spend eight hours out of every twenty-four as a mixture between an imbecile and a sewing machine." Another evening, it was Stig who spoke about youth's so-called revolt. It didn't make sense, said Stig; youth was reactionary, sat in a little, blue-painted cell, indifferent to the fate of the world around.

The talk might sometimes billow out across vast expanses, encompassing everything. And other evenings it could fasten on a single unimportant detail, such as establishing the line between running and walking. This was when the big nationwide walking competition was current.

In organized conversation, a formal discussion, Henning still felt too unsure of himself to dare participate, even if sometimes he went with Arne to some debate in Fighting Democracy. Henning waited to express himself once they were on their way home.

Previously, he had not liked coffee particularly well. Now the coffee tasted worse than ever, pure "makeshift," as the connoisseurs said. But that was part of it all, especially when the club leaders got together. And he got used to it. Drinking coffee and talking went together, characterized that time. The smell of the little, smoke-filled café, the smoke from his friends' cigarettes. They leaned forward and listened, stirring their coffee with their spoons.

This was camaraderie. Though it might seem so quiet and uneventful, it was still the adventure he was living. Though he only sat in a smoky café and drank surrogate coffee, it felt like he had broken through the borders and was wandering out in the previously closed-off world.

Some of Henning's classmates were going to participate in nationwide walking. Since he had not planned anything else for Sunday afternoon, he decided to go along.

During the spring, a few hundred thousand Swedes had taken to the roads to walk their kilometers and get the bronze badge.

The Sunday of the last week of September turned out to be unusually beautiful. Many people showed up. His classmates gathered on one of the marked-out tracks south of the city. One of the boys had brought along his sister; she had been alone and really wanted to go with him. The girl, who was named Karin, smiled a little at the group of boys.

There was a line in front of the registration table the whole time; more and more people were arriving, entire families. Bicycles lay in clusters in the ditch.

They got their start times noted down on their cards and left. Some of the boys had set out to break the record and pulled away ahead of the others. Karin's brother, who was one of the class' best sportsmen, was one of them.

Henning took it easier; fifteen kilometers was long, and it was a question of not wearing oneself out in the beginning. He gave himself the time to exchange a few words with Karin, asked which school she went to—it was Schuldeis' close to Götgatan. She was in her last year there now. So she was probably a year younger than him.

The sun was beating down pretty hard; he unbuttoned his jacket and pushed back his school cap. When he came, he had thought he would push himself to the best imaginable result. Now it was not as important anymore.

They walked silently for a while; their steps ate up meter after meter; he felt like he was working like a machine.

Some of the ones who had been bringing up the rear began to go faster. They would have to increase their speed if they were going to get silver badges.

Karin straggled behind. Henning thought it looked like she was limping a little.

"I think I have a blister," she said.

It was good now that Mama had stuffed that little tube of foot tallow in his pocket, though he thought it was a little wimpy to carry it with him.

They sat in a ditch beside the main road and she began to unbutton her stocking.

"Turn around a minute," she told him.

Then she showed him her foot. It was red but there was no hole. If she put the tallow on it, things would probably be all right. He helped her smooth on a good layer, shook out her shoe so no grains of sand would land in the tallow.

She pulled up her stocking again and since she forgot to ask him to turn around, he saw her leg and a little of the white skin above the stocking.

"Now it's my fault if you don't get a silver badge," she complained.

"I don't care about the silver badge," he said. "Bronze will have to be good enough. I will finish at the same time as you. I am not a slave to the second and decimeter race."

He came up with the quote from Arne Aspman. They had had a discussion about sports in the club. Arne was against sports and had put up the "free hikers in the woods" as an ideal.

She laughed at him.

Things went well for a while, but soon her foot began to hurt again. But by then they could already see the finish line. She leaned a little on him, and he was happy to oblige. In this way, they got through the last part. She hopped more than she walked.

He made the bronze by a minute; it had taken one hour and twenty minutes. And her time wasn't good enough for more than bronze either.

They sat on the wooded hillside to wait for the others. She borrowed the tube of tallow again and applied it while Henning stood down on the road at a candy vendor and bought a bar of chocolate. When he came back, he had to see her foot and found a clean handkerchief that he helped her put on it.

"We don't have to sit here right on the road," she said.

But wouldn't the others surely be coming soon and perhaps wonder where they were?

Oh, they had seen that she was beginning to limp. And probably thought that they had gone home early.

They found a road that disappeared into the woods and followed it a ways. There was a large woodpile there that they could sit with their backs against. The sun shone between the tall pine trees.

He offered her some of the chocolate bar, and she broke off a row of squares.

"Shall we see who gets the most? We each eat from our end."

She placed her teeth in the piece of chocolate and leaned toward him. Astonished, he looked at her, wondering if he understood right. Then he felt her mouth against his for a second—and then both the mouth and chocolate bar were gone.

"I won," she said. "But you get revenge."

Bewildered, he broke off another row of chocolate squares, looking at it thoughtfully. As if she had just fooled him—but maybe he could fool her back. Now he was faster than before. And his mouth reached hers. But this time he did not pull back.

She pushed her hair back from her forehead, straightened her jacket. Sounded a little unsure when she said: "It was my fault. I should not have said that."

Was it wrong? He did not know. They hardly knew each other. Now he could almost imagine that what had just happened meant something decisive.

"Was it really, truly wrong?"

"I don't know," she said. "What do you think?"

When he saw her smile, he suddenly felt so sure, reckless. He put his arm around her. And she rubbed her cheek against his.

"We have to test to see if it was wrong or not," he said with his cheek still against her cheek.

"You are crazy," she said. But she was immediately ready. And now she held onto him, held him tightly. When she slid down on her back in the moss, he followed her. She did not let go of him until they had to separate their mouths to catch their breath.

He looked at her, felt like he had not seen her before now. And thought for a moment of Gun, of how much prettier Karin was.

Then she pulled him down to her again, pressing herself hard against him. And eagerly he reached for her.

"We are crazy," she finally said. "We are hugging each other to death."

She sat up, straightened her clothes. He still lay there and looked at her. Wondered how far she had gone with other boys. Even though she was a year younger than him, she was more experienced than he was, he felt it.

"I have to go home now," she said. "Brush me off, will you?"

He brushed off the moss and pine needles. He wanted to put his arm around her again, but she held him away.

"No," she said a little crossly. "We can't start all over again. I have to get home in time for dinner."

So there was not just the word, but the unsayable, what maybe could not or should not be said.

He got together with Karin a few evenings. They went to the movies, stood tightly intertwined in the park afterward. He felt like they were eating each other. But the more he ate, the hungrier he became.

Then there was not much more. She claimed that she did not have time to go out. He guessed that she was seeing other boys. Still, strangely enough, he was not unhappy.

He did not like her brother. Rune was one of the Nazis in the class. And he understood that a lot of things would have grown difficult if he and Karin had continued to see each other. Her family had a nice big apartment, plenty of money. He himself was the son of an unwed mother and lived in a building owned by a foundation.

In spite of his having been so close to her, they were strangers. Almost enemies, he thought when he remembered that she was Rune's sister.

Still, he felt grateful to her. She had taught him something about life that he needed to know. She had expanded his borders.

TURNING POINT

The war grew; more and more nations were pulled in. On midsummer 1941, the Germans and their allies attacked the Soviet Union. The front stretched from the North Sea of ice to the Black Sea. Finland was once again at war.

In December, Japanese airplanes attacked the American base, Pearl Harbor, and the war had definitively been transformed into a world war.

The Japanese conquered the Philippines, Singapore, and the islands of Indonesia. The Germans planted their flag on the highest peak of the Caucasus and reached all the way to Stalingrad. The Allies could also point to successes, principally in East and North Africa.

In Sweden, defense preparedness claimed its victims. A ferry loaded with conscripts capsized at Armasjärvi, a gunpowder factory exploded in Björkborn, three destroyers sank at Hårsfjärden.

From the occupied countries, alarming reports arrived of increased terror. Terboven executed Norwegians; in Czechoslovakia, the village of Lidice was destroyed after the German protector there was murdered. Issues of Swedish newspapers that criticized German brutalities were confiscated by the government.

Even in the countries that were neutral, people felt that developments were soon reaching their culmination, that the crucial moment was lurching forward.

Behind the big headlines and the big tragedies was everyday life with its more paltry troubles. More and more goods were rationed until practically all food had to be bought with a card. Clothes, shoes, wood, warm water—there seemed to be a scarcity of everything. The earlier surplus of housing changed over to a substantial shortage.

The winters were colder than usual. The city's parks and streets were filled with enormous supplies of firewood, which, to begin with, gave off a fresh scent of the woods but soon became refuges for rats. The supplies seemed like they would last a long time, but it had still been decided that the country's twenty-year-olds should go out into the woods to chop down more.

Henning was from one of the years that had been designated, those who were born in 1923.

He had taken his high school exam the previous spring and in the fall had begun college, since his father had promised to pay for some additional years of study. For a long time, he had felt unsure of what he actually was going to specialize in.

But during the last half year, it had begun to crystallize. He had written a couple of articles that he had managed to sell, some contributions to the eternal debate about youth. And now he felt like he knew: He wanted to be a journalist.

Though it took time before one could begin to work; society had big demands. Not least on the "forty-threers," his class' year. When he was done in the woods, he had his military service that awaited him.

Still, he felt like he had reached a point in the road when he finally knew what he wanted to be. Now he had a goal to focus on. Everything became simpler. He was free of worry over his own uncertainty as to choice of career.

He was the only one so far in the family who had gotten to continue his studies, except for the Bodins, of course. It was an advantage that sometimes could feel like a burden. It was like it held him back; he was still treated like a schoolboy.

However, he had grown too old to be able to live in the foundation house anymore. Just in time, before the housing shortage had set in, they had gotten a little apartment on Åsögatan, where the cosmetics factory had once stood.

A few times a week, John came and visited. He had been at Mormor and Aunt Emelie's, too. And that, of course, was a sign. Henning guessed that his mother was thinking of marrying John, maybe as soon as he himself moved away from home. Their consideration irritated him a little.

"Get married!" he wanted to say to them. But the result might be instead that his mother pulled away from John, that he ruined things for them. The only thing he could do was show his regard for John. And that was not hard.

One afternoon when Henning was on his way home from a lecture, he saw that a lot of people had gathered at the newsstand on Odenplan. The evening papers had arrived. He cut diagonally across the street, read the news placards.

After almost five months fighting around "the bottleneck of the Volga," the Germans in Stalingrad had surrendered. Perhaps it was anticipated, but still the news felt like a shocking confirmation that the war had turned, that they could begin to anticipate the end.

REMAINS OF TIES

A streetcar on the number four line rolled into Odenplan. It aroused a certain amount of attention since it did not look like the other streetcars but was instead an experimental model with a stationary conductor. It was an old streetcar with a motor that had been rebuilt according to the principal of circulation, which meant that people got on at the back of the car and off in the middle or the front.

That was why Henning looked at it especially attentively and noticed Allan, who was standing farthest forward in the car. Henning jumped on board, went out of his way for friendship's sake.

Allan had just finished a job on a house out in Enebyberg. Now he had gotten the idea that he would go and see how his dad was doing. He did this from time to time.

He had news for his dad as well, Allan said, and tried to look mysterious. But Henning knew that it would not take long before he, too, would find out what it was. Allan was not the type to be able to keep quiet when there was something weighing on him.

"We are getting married, you see," came out the next minute, as predicted.

Henning was not especially surprised. Allan and Daggan had been together a few years, and there was not really more to expect than their getting married at last; they seemed so mad about each other. Allan had brought Daggan with him up to Mormor and Emelie's some Sundays, and the whole time he had had Daggan on his knee and sat there patting her. But it was so harmless that not even Elisabet seemed to get annoyed.

"She has a bun in the oven," Allan whispered so that it could be heard through half the streetcar.

He was proud and happy, no doubt about that.

While Allan recounted the possibilities of obtaining one thousand kronor in a housing loan, the streetcar glided across Västerbron. In a gray mist, the city lay encircling the water beneath them, a wreath of pale light anchored to the darker curves of the shorelines. On the other side of the bridge, Långholmen Prison stuck up, and the profusion of light-colored scaffoldings could be made out on Reimersholme.

The streetcar rounded Hornsplan and continued onto Hornsgatan. Allan had grown quieter now, pensive. This was his old neighborhood; he had gone to the small movie theaters here—Chicago and Strix and whatever they were all called—as a boy. During the troubled years, when he had waited to be gotten and taken away, when there had been neither justice nor mercy.

A little of the old anxiety always came back when he returned. As if everything that had happened since then suddenly would prove itself to be but a dream, as if the social worker from the child welfare board was still waiting for him.

He was probably still a little afraid of his father, too, even if he was coming voluntarily. He was afraid of getting caught and sinking back in. There was something in the air and atmosphere, something that drew him to it. But, of course, he could deal with it, he could certainly resist it, he had his job, and Daggan and Mikael, who helped him.

His father was always expecting more than he got. He was expecting a ten instead of a five, expecting Allan to stay instead of just coming and paying a visit. It was undoubtedly this that made it feel like he was sneaking, too, when he came.

They went up deserted Rosenlundsgatan, across the railway, between dilapidated shacks. But on old Rackarberget where Negro Village's miserable shantytown had stood, the immense Söder Hospital was being built. Though not so far away—on the hills around Skånegatan—tenement housing still stood. It was there his father lived. But his grandfather had moved one hundred meters away, into the old age home. And Rutan had gotten "the clap" and been taken in at Sankt Göran's Hospital.

Allan nodded silently to Henning and got off.

As soon as his father opened the door, Allan saw that Papa was in a good mood.

His eyes were twinkling; his voice was proud and strong. He was not sickly any longer, as at the last visit, but a successful businessman who a little condescendingly received his insignificant poor stripling of a boy.

It took a while before Allan had time to get used to the change; he dug in his pocket for a five but even before he found it, he realized that it was not fitting. It was not needed; his father would take it as an affront.

Evidently, big business was under way. Allan knew from experience that it was illegal. Everything that was permitted was too much trouble or earned too little for his father to deal with.

"You look chipper," said Allan. Before, he had not addressed him with the familiar form, but, from now on, he was doing it. He used it with Mikael and all the other old guys on the job.

"Oh yes…" answered his father. He always kept his bad stomach at the ready; business could, despite everything, always turn bad. Just fine was how things were anyway.

Allan was invited to have a beer. He could have had a schnapps as well, but since he was going over to Daggan's that evening, he declined. He looked at his father, who was sitting opposite him at the kitchen table and felt clumsy and inferior, so childish. His father was so elegant now; Allan himself had come directly from work.

And his big secret… Now it was also like coming out with a shameful admission instead of imparting big news.

And his father grew almost indignant, shook his head. Getting married and having children—and in these times, too. When there was such a shortage of everything. But not that Allan was so sorely obligated to…

But probably he could help Allan a little in a pinch. Expecting a child. He dug in a box he had in the closet. He had to hide things a little because of Dora, you see. He threw a bundle of ration cards on the table. Butter, bread, meat, sugar. Even tobacco and coffee.

He had come across some, had his connections, of course. As Allan could see. He leafed through the bundle.

"You eat out most of the time?"

Allan nodded, though he ate at home just as often. Mikael and he usually made a little something for themselves in the evening.

His father shoved some restaurant cards over to him, gathered up the bundle again and stuffed it in his jacket's inside pocket.

"If you get too hungry, you can get in touch."

He was going out. Hopefully, before Dora came home, Allan understood. It was as if he was pushing his son away from him. Whenever his father was up to something, he always got this agitated and eager, he could not sit still, had to be out and in action. Then the tavern awaited him in recompense; that contributed a lot to the hurry.

They kept each other company for part of the way. At Götgatan, his father turned down toward town. Allan stayed standing there a moment and watched him disappear into the crowd.

Stig and Gun had freed themselves, they seldom talked about the past, never called of their father. If they ever said anything about the old times, then it was their mother they talked about.

For Allan, it had sometimes felt as if his father was some kind of link to his mother. Although their father had never really been capable of being interested in them, he had still been part of their home. To cut that tie was like forgetting his mother. When something important happened, Allan felt like he had to look up his father and tell him. As he had told his mother before.

He felt a little crestfallen and rejected, as if his father had picked up the scissors and cut him off.

The cards he had received lay in his pocket. He wondered if they were forgeries or were real. Probably real, it was probably hard to make forgeries. And that meant they were stolen from somewhere.

They were probably dangerous to have. What if someone came across them in his pocket, asked how he had gotten them. He could not send his dad to prison. Then he would go to prison instead, would lose both his job and Daggan.

Maybe he was being shadowed? Maybe someone was standing and watching the house and had followed him and his dad? That one in the trench coat? Or him in the brown hat? He began to walk faster.

He had to get rid of those cards in a way that no one would see. Somehow, it felt difficult; they were, in any case, something he had received from his dad. He tried to recall if he had ever gotten anything from his father before. It was always Mama who had done the giving.

But he had to do it to save Daggan and his job, to save himself. Everything that had to do with the future. He felt that if someone came and interrogated him now, he would betray his father. For this reason, he was just as worried for his father's sake as for his own. It was a question of saving them both.

He half ran up into the White Hills Park, into the shadows. The social worker and all the police and functionaries of the whole society ran after him. He stopped and caught his breath while he stared into the darkness. He could not see that anyone was following him, not a person was in sight. Then he sank down on the ground, took the cards out of his pocket, looked at them by the light of the lantern beside the summer tea pavilion's fence. One restaurant card for butter and two for bread. They seemed real. But for safety's sake they had to be destroyed anyway. He tore them up into small pieces and poked them down in the ground beside the fence, dug up the dirt and laid it over them.

Like burying them.

He stood up. Still, the park seemed deserted. He ought to be able to feel calm. Yet he was shaking, fear like sobs in his throat. He wanted to live decently, of course, live so that no one could accuse him of anything. He wanted to marry Daggan and take care of her and the kid. Was it necessary to cut off all the old ties to be able to do it?

Right now, it felt like he would never dare visit his father again, as if he risked everything by doing it.

When he had calmed down, he walked in the direction of home. It had grown chillier toward evening, or maybe it just felt that way. As if the cold was freezing off what lay behind him. His mother who had died and his father who he had to flee from, the torn-down tenements in Negro Village and the memory of the reformatories.

But before him, light was shining through the window. Mikael had come home, had probably begun to get the food ready. What if he had gotten a message from Gunnar, if Gunnar had found an apartment? Allan started to hurry.

His anxiety subsided; now he was just eager to have enough time. He forgot what lay behind for everything that lay ahead of him.

DAUGHTERS

The streetcar thundered away down Erstagatan, squealed when it slowed down for the stop on the street corner. Even though Emelie was so used to the noise, she still started, could never learn, no doubt, that their old quiet street had been transformed. Now that she had such an abundance of time, she sat more and more often and sunken into the past, remembering people and houses that had disappeared long ago. Then she could imagine that everything was as it had once been, when the small cottages still stood here and there was a tree in the middle of the hill and a piece of fencing to divide the street's two levels from each other.

And then the streetcar would sound, and with it all the new things that she had forgotten about for a while.

Emelie had gotten a letter, had read it many times. She always did this with Gertrud's letters. Really wanted to imprint on her mind what her sister wrote—and then the letters were not so easy to read either. Gertrud had never really had very good handwriting, and with the years, her Swedish had also become more and more peculiar. It was American that Gertrud tried to turn into Swedish when she could not remember the old real words. Then Emelie had to ask Henning for help.

It had been so many years since Gertrud had left home, the year of the general strike, 1909. Ever since Rudolf had died, she did not have anyone to speak Swedish with either; the children were married to Americans and, of course, completely Americanized. All except for their oldest daughter who had had her fiancé from Sweden with her. But they lived in another part of America now.

Gertrud had sent a picture, too. Of herself together with her second oldest daughter and her daughter's daughter and her daughter's daughter's daughter. They had become four generations now, over there in America. Greta, the second oldest daughter, had been seventeen when they left. But Emelie had never seen Greta's daughter, who was a little over twenty now, and the little youngest one, and would certainly never get to see them either. The papa of the little one had been drafted and was fighting against "the Japs," Gertrud wrote, on an island with the strange name of Guadalcanal. And Greta was a sedate, middle-aged woman now, and Gertrud a plump little old lady.

Now that August was gone, there were only Gertrud and Emelie left of the siblings. And here they lived each on their own side of the globe. Emelie remembered how Rudolf's parents had complained of his moving so far away, when they had moved to the Vanidislund part of town, in Siberia, as they said then. Then it had not taken many years before Rudolf had dragged the family as far as he could get them to go. He had worked on the streetcars in Stockholm and gone all the way to New York to become a streetcar conductor there. Collector was what it was called in American.

Gertrud—there was not much left that reminded her of her sister now. Emelie regretted that she had gotten rid of the old, pull-out bed she and her sister had slept in when they were little, "the accordion bed," as they had called it. But it had been so old and dilapidated, not much to save—and so it went out with the attic cleaning. Now there was actually only the old dresser that could remind her of Gertrud, that their mother had been given when she got married and that Gertrud had been given when she moved to Siberia.

Emelie had to go in and look at it. It was a little clumsy with its thick blocks for feet. But their mother had gotten it as a wedding gift from her mother. Mama had chosen to receive a dresser instead of a bridal gown with the money that her mother had saved.

They had been so poor. So Mama had surely chosen well. The dresser was still in use. It was outright beginning to be an antique, August had said once.

And August was dead now. He, too.

Jenny wanted to talk about her daughters, was a little concerned about the girls. What worried her most was, of course, that they were so unlike herself. One should live as if one were playing in a comedy, Jenny said—but the girls behaved as if they were auditioning for the leading rolls in tragedies.

Now she was worried about the girls' ways of treating their men.

Maj could not be getting it into her head that that poor John should go and wait for however long she took, could she? Now, when Henning was so grown-up, she certainly no longer needed to relinquish John for the boy's sake. It was perfectly clear, by the way, that Henning did not have anything against John. It was only a pure penchant for self-torment that governed Maj.

Well, John did not seem offended, he seemed satisfied and happy, Emelie said. They did not have to be in such a hurry.

"Life is short," said Jenny. Oh, so well she understood Allan and his funny girl, who could not keep their hands off each other, who were so natural, so real. In some way, her own girls were too well brought up, however that had come about.

Maj ought to get married to John. And Elisabet ought to have children, had been married over four years now.

Everything had seemed so fine when Elisabet had gotten married. But now it was as if she had gotten back that ill-humored streak, as if she was not satisfied with her existence. Elisabet had difficulty being satisfied, demanded too much. Jenny was afraid that her daughter demanded too much of Lennart as well. He was still at the printer's where he had begun after the years of unemployment, but Elisabet had moved around among many offices, and every time gotten better conditions. Even if it was a good profession Lennart had, Elisabet probably hoped he would advance. Become a foreman or whatever they became in such places, and then change jobs and become something even more at another printer's. Elisabet saw it as an obligation. It was not enough to fulfill the tasks one had been given—one should go further, to new and bigger tasks. Never stop in one's development.

That criticism Jenny had certainly felt many times, even if Elisabet had not said it straight out. Elisabet was so quick to put down the comedies that Jenny appeared in. And it was clear that a lot of it was trash; no one admitted it more freely than Jenny herself. But comedies made people happy and were Jenny's livelihood, and no more reasons were needed.

Jenny thought it seemed as if Lennart had been shrinking back lately, as if he were slipping away and trying to make himself invisible. He had never been especially colorful, but now he was grayer than ever. As if he himself thought he had failed. And accepted the failure.

If one could only talk to the girls, Jenny sighed. But they were so impossible, so stubborn, so easily hurt. And, in any case, they would never be guided according to what she said.

Just as Jenny was talking, the telephone rang. Emelie tried to not listen in, but it grew more difficult. Jenny sounded so strange, as if altogether blown away. Finally, she said yes to something, whatever it was, and thanked them several times.

Then she hung up, standing there at the telephone. Emelie waited.

Suddenly Jenny did a violent pirouette, twirling around several times, sank down on a chair and began to laugh.

"It cannot be true!" she shouted. "It is impossible. I am dreaming."

She had been offered a role in an operetta that was going to be on at Oscar's Theater in the fall. Only a minor role, but still. She who had toiled her whole life in outdoor theaters and small music hall performances. But someone had seen her and said that she would fit perfectly.

"At Oscar's Theater..." Emelie said. "Imagine how exciting the girls will think it is."

Maj came up for a while that evening, and Jenny got to tell her. Maj became so interested that she almost forgot that she herself had something to tell.

Well, she hadn't forgotten. But it felt good to get to hide her own news behind her mother's. She had never really liked discussing anything about herself.

In any case, they had decided now, she and John; they were getting married. She had talked about it with Henning before he had traveled to his school's lumber cutting; he had thought it was good. Otherwise it was for his sake, of course, that she had waited, and maybe in fact had wanted to wait longer. But John and Henning got along so well that there was no reason to delay it any longer because of Henning.

They each had their own apartment, she and John. It would not be hard to exchange them for one so big that Henning could have his own room. He needed it now that he was studying.

They agreed with her about that, even Emelie who, in her whole life, had never had her own room.

And here Jenny had sat and thought that everything was so gloomy. Shouldn't she run down to the bakery for some pastries so they could really celebrate? But the others didn't want any; it was only Jenny herself who was so fond of sweets. Though to tell the truth, they would like coffee, without any "makeshift" in it.

Jenny had a hard time falling asleep that night. She came out to Emelie in her nightgown, had a bottle of red wine and two glasses with her. But she had to drink alone, of course. She sat at the kitchen table and talked with Emelie, who lay on the kitchen sofa. She smoked some cigarettes.

Like this, in the summer light, Jenny still looked like a girl, Emelie thought. So thin and supple. No one could believe she was over sixty.

Now everything would take care of itself, Jenny said. She had worried needlessly. About Maj, maybe about Elisabet as well. All people looked a little tired and worn out at times, you could not place too much importance on that. And Elisabet and Lennart had known each other so long that they ought to be able to overlook each other's weaknesses.

Elisabet slept. But Lennart lay awake.

He was a little afraid of her, maybe because he felt that she was not really satisfied with him. Even in her sleep, there was that expression of severity still in her face, as if she did not dare to relax. Her demands on herself and on the world around her were hard. She was so effective, preferred not to understand that others might lack the strength she herself had.

She knew her weakness. Insecurity and fear. This fear of failure that made him a failure.

He could have at least applied for that foreman's job. Elisabet had clipped out the advertisement and placed it on the desk. And became unhappy that he did nothing about it. But he would have never gotten it anyway. Though Elisabet did not understand this. That not everyone feels like chancing it on something new. This was something unnatural and incomprehensible to her.

He had no desire to seize the more difficult tasks. He would rather satisfy himself with those that were simpler, those that he knew he could manage. He had no need to remind others of his existence. He only wanted to be tolerated. That was enough. He did not ask for more, only to be tolerated.

It was also difficult to show real interest in a job when one knew the whole time that there was, in fact, something else that one wanted to be doing.

"Well, then prepare yourself for that other thing," Elisabet would say. "Begin studying again. I can probably take care of supporting us until you are done."

Though it was too late, and he would probably not succeed anymore either. At that time, before, when he had had dreams—then he had wanted to become a teacher. But now he was over thirty years old. It was not at all sure that he would be suitable as a teacher anymore. You had to be young for that, and it would take many years for sure until he was done.

She had to despise him. Be ashamed of him. Feel deceived. It was, in fact, his love of reading that had once made her interested in him. And what had become of that reading? Nothing.

He suffered from his own lack of enterprise. But it only paralyzed him even more. At the same time, he became even more vulnerable, took both silence and words as reproaches. And drew even further back, even more into himself.

Sometimes he might wonder if it was Elisabet's fault that he had become the way he was. If it was because her demands on him felt so high that instead of trying to reach them, he gave up, sank down.

TAKE RESPONSIBILITY

Despite the war and all the curtailments it brought, the city grew faster than ever. It spilled over across all the old boundaries, into what previously had been woods, fields, and meadows. Westward they had reached almost as far as they could go. New incorporations were being discussed. Now the road rolled southward, into Enskede and Brännkyrka.

Maybe it actually was not until now that the big small town became a small big city. With new and large projects. New traffic routes were needed to transport people between the center of town and the new suburbs. And all of old Norrmalm had to be recreated to form a new city.

But no matter how much they built, the lack of housing only grew bigger.

Henning came back from two months' work in the woods. He was sunburned, had gotten calloused hands. Somewhat more broad shouldered as well, he imagined. It felt like he had the strength to carry more on his shoulders than before.

Certainly he could say that he had lost time and had to work really hard for the kronor he had earned, unused to physical labor as he was. But he also had to admit that he had gained something. Learned to adapt, take care of himself without his mother's help. He thought he had become an adult.

His mother and John had not gotten married yet; they were waiting for the right apartment. If not before, they would succeed in finding something by the first of October. At that time, some people would undoubtedly move since it was the customary time to move.

One of the first evenings Henning was home, he went over to Allan and Daggan's. Through Gunnar, they had succeeded in finding an apartment on Hammarbyhöjden. A bus went there, but Henning bicycled. He bought some flowers to bring along for Daggan. He had not seen her since she had had her baby, a girl.

They were expecting guests when Henning arrived. But that didn't matter; it was only Gunnar and his wife. And then Mikael was coming. He dropped by now and then.

Stig had had a hemorrhage of the lungs, Allan said. He never was careful, he was impossible with his trumpeting. Now he was in the hospital again. And it was critical this time. He might never come out again.

Allan and Stig were so unalike, had not hung out together so much during recent years. Still there was a strong tie between them, and now Allan was worried, quiet and subdued. Though when he showed off his little daughter, he, of course, forgot everything else. He shone with pride and held her with a carefulness that one would not have believed of him.

The baby was hungry, and Daggan sat down completely unabashed at the coffee table and took out her breast—it was only homefolk there, she said. Her breast was like a big white sack that the baby ate out of.

Allan stood behind Daggan's chair with his hand on her shoulder, proudly guarding and protecting his family.

Gunnar and Mikael talked about work; they did not see each other very much during the days now. Gunnar was working mostly with store interiors, which was their specialty, Mikael with digging and foundations for small houses, which they also built. Gradually, Gunnar's carpentry business had evolved into two companies. Still, he was trying to keep it as small as possible; did not want to hire more people and take more on himself.

But Karl Henrik had big plans, he had heard. And for Bodin's, it was a different situation. Gunnar thought Karl Henrik was doing the right thing when he wanted to expand; such were the times. The big companies with their large offices and many employees had to be run in a completely different way from a little carpentry business.

Gunnar had done a certain amount of interior work for Bodin's, since the time when August was alive. Now Karl Henrik had invited him to lunch to discuss working together. Gunnar was not so pleased with wasting work time to eat, but, on this occasion, he had to accept. Besides, he was quite interested in hearing what Bodin had to say. When August at one time had wanted to get Karl Henrik and Gunnar to work together, Karl Henrik had not seemed so keen.

"Maybe he wants to cancel working together now," Mikael said.

So let him do it. But Gunnar hardly believed he would do it. If Bodin wanted to expand, then he would probably need all the help he could get. It was hard to find capable folk when so much was being built.

Allan listened to them, smiling contentedly. He had worked for Gunnar for eight years now, saw that he could count himself among the capable ones. The ones there was a need for, who were of value. Surely, he would take care of himself and his family.

Karl Henrik Bodin looked at the portrait he had had painted of his father. For being done from a photograph and without the artist having seen Papa, it was an astounding likeness, he thought. Though Mama thought he looked a little too stern and authoritative. But she had not seen him in action at the office; here they recognized him. Of course, Papa had been kind and decent, but strength and willpower he had certainly not lacked.

It would have been nice, in fact, to have portraits of the earlier Bodins as well. His grandfather, Fredrik, his brother, Leonard, and their papa, whatever his name was, who had built the company at one time. Though in those days they only sold herring. But if one took the herring firm's beginnings as a starting point, then the Bodin company would turn one hundred in the year 1949. One should think of putting together a celebratory publication in honor of this.

He said and thought grandfather out of habit. He knew otherwise that his real grandfather—his father's and Aunt Emelie's father—had only been a herring packer in the firm. That great-grandfather would likely not be included in the jubilee volume, it there was one. It would have been nicer if they had been building for one hundred years rather than spending half of the time selling herring. That part about the herring was not really much to be reminded of. Hadn't an old masonry foreman yelled out "herring strangler" at Papa once, as a matter of fact?

He looked at the portrait again. A fine and stately gentleman, a little severe. Hard to imagine that he came from that poverty-stricken little cottage on Söder. And that he once, young and careless, had gotten a slut with child. Papa who was caution itself, only all too cautious.

However things had been with Gunnar's mother, Karl Henrik had full respect for Gunnar himself. A skilled carpenter with a good little business. Papa, had wanted the two half-brothers to work together, maybe take over the firm together. But Karl Henrik had tried to avoid it. He was young then, so inexperienced. And Gunnar six years older. It would have been like having someone over him; he would not have been able to hold up his own against Gunnar's professional expertise. Besides, in many ways, Gunnar was the very image of Papa, just as cautious.

Development was heading toward industrialization of the construction trade. The construction industry was the nation's largest industry, yet there were many who insisted on seeing construction as handiwork. And people built without plans, often on such small lots that they really did come down to the handiwork scale.

However, in the new suburbs, they were not building on small individual lots, but on whole blocks, even whole city sections, at one time. One could really speak of industry there, and then one could work with new methods. They did not let in the small craftsmen to potter, each with his little house; rather they built in series. And it became a question of money.

Papa, with all due respect, still had a little of the herring dealer's point of view in him. Afraid to invest big. And afraid to leave the least little responsibility to anyone else.

There was nothing to say about it; it was only a bygone time's way of seeing and working. Now they had to go about it another way.

They had arranged to meet at Rosenbad, in the grill room. It was close by and good for Karl Henrik, he was well-known there, a regular customer. He liked the old-fashioned and dark room with the smoke-imbued, brownish red plaster wallpaper, the buffalo hide covered sofas and chairs, and the multicolored lamp globes that gave the impression one was looking through a kaleidoscope.

Gunnar had already arrived, was waiting in the vestibule. He was big and strong beside Karl Henrik, reminded him a little of his father in his bearing and his gait.

Karl Henrik showed him the way to the table he had reserved, a quiet corner where they could talk unconstrained.

That Karl Henrik did not want to break off their collaboration was something Gunnar had sensed. But he had not expected this.

Building contractors had been building completely without plans, Karl Henrik said. Without bothering to ask what they should be building. They had never done any research as to what was needed and what people wanted. When there was plenty of money, they had built too much—and become destitute when all their newly constructed buildings had stood empty and rents had to be lowered. They had been forced to creep into their winter lairs and go without food while their employees looked for other occupations. Until it was time again and all the stupid things were done all over again. And there was surely no other profession that was shaken by so many crises.

That last statement Gunnar recognized; August had said it many times.

Now a number of analyses had been done; they had something to follow. Even if the state, in an unjust way, had favored the so-called public utility undertakings, the municipal and the cooperative businesses, one could, in spite of everything, work more effectively than before. And there had to be enormous opportunities; this was about a line of business where the demand was much bigger than the supply.

Many years in the future there would be a housing shortage; they could count on that. And it was clear that people's demands grew with every year that passed; they were not satisfied with leaving things as they had them. How many people had grown up sharing a room when Gunnar was a child? Now every kid would soon have his or her own room.

A construction company had to become like a factory; they had to assemble houses in the same way that cars were assembled on a conveyor belt. Some specialists in collaboration would accomplish this miracle.

And now he came to the question: Did Gunnar want to be a part of this?

Gunnar felt the temptation; much of what Karl Henrik said sounded right. But if he went along, he would be obliged to specialize more rigorously than now, and, in addition, he would have to enlarge his company. Both the chances and the risks would increase. A company of the kind that Karl Henrik imagined would probably become vulnerable. The one Gunnar had now was small but secure, so elastic that it could completely adapt to the demands of the day. If only he did not expand it too much, stretch it so thin that it lost the ability to quickly shrink back.

He was tempted by the offer, felt honored as well, would have liked very much to meet him halfway. But still he said no. He would prefer to continue to collaborate to the same extent as now, could perhaps increase it somewhat. But not in the way that Karl Henrik wished.

Karl Henrik did not persist—and Gunnar realized that Bodin's had several carpentry businesses in mind. Surely, there were those who were interested. It could be a fine piece of business.

Maybe he had acted foolishly, if one looked at it purely from a business perspective. But he was not a real businessman, only a carpenter who wanted to live relatively quietly. He did not seek larger responsibilities than he could handle. He saw no value in growth for growth's sake. There was plenty of work now, and room for many companies. No reason to take on more than what he himself could keep an eye on. He lived simply, did not think he needed to earn more than he did.

Karl Henrik maybe had something of a commander's ambitions, but not Gunnar. Maybe it was the old socialist inside Gunnar that held him back, that somewhat reluctantly could accept that he was a petty capitalist carpenter but never that he became a big capitalist industrial practitioner.

He thanked Karl Henrik for the offer, for the outstretched hand. And he should be sure that Gunnar would truly like to continue with the same collaboration that they already had. But he did not dare and did not want to go along with something that demanded so much more.

His answer was given, and the conversation could touch on the events of the day.

Karl Henrik admitted that he felt quite confused over the international political situation. He had been strongly engaged in Finland's matters, and still was. But he could not approve the Nazis' ideas and ravaging.

Now it looked as if Hitler was going to lose the war. The Allied forces had landed on Sicily, and Mussolini had been removed by Marshal Badoglio. It was only a question of time before Italy would seek peace. The German cities were being exposed to heavier bombing raids. German desperation was growing—it was noticeable, especially in Denmark, where a state of emergency had been declared. And the Russians were simply forcing the Germans ever farther westward.

Karl Henrik was a little worried by the Russian successes, would have liked to see the Soviets beaten down before the other allies conquered Germany. If the Russians stood as victors in the war, they would occupy Finland, reach all the way to the Swedish border. Who could guarantee that they would stop there? In any case, they would swallow Finland and all the brave resistance the Finns had put up would be in vain. He did not believe that the Russian terror would be any less severe than the German.

Gunnar did not feel the same dread. When the war was over and

Germany conquered, the wish to keep the peace would be big and deep, not least of all in a country that had suffered as much as the Soviet Union. The Russians would not risk a new war by coming up with too big of demands. Though, when it came to Finland, he was afraid that the Finns would bitterly regret that they had participated in Hitler's assault.

But they had only wanted to take back what they had lost, countered Karl Henrik.

Maybe so. But with Hitler's help. By taking that help, they also placed part of the German guilt on themselves.

Karl Henrik did not want to admit that.

It does not help to brood, he said. He himself tried to lessen the anxiety he felt by burying himself in his work. One could at least make oneself believe that what one accomplished would yield results that would last. That one was not building houses that would be bombed, but that would perhaps still be standing one hundred years into the future.

Despite all the imperfections and troubles in their line of business—was there anyone else who was creating such large and lasting value? He felt that previously people had not realized what value there was in what the builders did, what responsibility they had.

DEFEAT

Italy capitulated. One million tired and frozen Germans dragged themselves back through Russia to the Polish border. But in the occupied nations, German desperation fought its way in ever less concealed terror.

In Sweden, the German setback led to political concessions being replaced by protests. A ban on the transport of Communist newspapers was lifted.

Dora did not experience much of what happened out in the world. She saw the news placards flutter past with their headlines about victories and defeats but barely read them. She didn't buy newspapers. And ever more clearly she saw that she was toiling in vain.

She had tried to help her brother, David. But what thanks had she gotten for it? Now the police had swooped down on him again, arrested him in her home and found bundles of stolen ration cards there. Her home had been turned into a hiding place for stolen goods, unbeknownst to her, to a place where the police went when something disappeared.

This time it would be a good while before he got out again. Dora would not miss him; all too many times he had broken his promises.

"Keep him," she had shrieked. "I don't want to have him here anymore. I don't want anything to do with his dealings."

Ever since Tyra had died, there was only misery and crime around her. Per was in Hall Prison again.

But what did she care about David and Per? If only things had gone well for Rutan. But first the girl had taken off with Per and gotten a suspended sentence around her neck. Then she had caught a shameful disease that she had been hospitalized for, and now they had moved her to an institution for vagrant women.

Dora felt like she could hear how all the tenement housing was filled with whispering, all the tittle-tattle of what had happened in her apartment. Finally, she couldn't take it; she had to exchange a one room plus kitchen for a single room in an old stone building. She was sitting there now.

Never again would she help anyone, never again believe anyone. For more than thirty years, she had toiled for Rutan. To think she had been such a blockhead that she had not demanded that her daughter go to work and pay her way once she had become an adult. Now there was an end to it; now Dora could do no more. She had written this to Rutan. But she had not gotten any reply. Not even a letter telling her off. Nothing.

But David wrote begging for money and packages. This time, it was Dora who did not reply.

"I don't want anything to do with whores and thieves anymore," she said to the empty room.

She didn't cry. She worked just as hard as before. Lived just as frugally on her own. Now that she no longer had all of those around her who sucked it out of her, she found that there was money left over. She had begun to go to Salvation Army meetings and put the money in their collection. No one would find an öre left when she was gone and get drunk for joy that Dora finally was dead. For that was what she believed of them. She knew that they had organized a drinking party the night she had gone into the hospital for her leg.

Misshapen and ugly, poorly dressed, haggard from hard work and worries. She liked to mutter to herself as she walked huddled against the wind through the streets. She would sit on one of the outermost benches at the Salvation Army hall. She did not care so much about the speaking, but the singing somehow soothed her, gave her some courage and strength to go on living. But mostly she came to get rid of her money, to be really assured that there would be nothing left for those who had been given everything before.

Jenny appeared in the operetta at Oscar's Theater. Her role was not big, but she had received a few favorable lines in several newspapers, so it was still a big success for her.

Jenny was really funny; Emelie and Maj and John could vouch for that. They had gone together to the theater. Elisabet had not had time to go yet. Jenny asked—it was noticeable how much she wished Elisabet could come, too.

Elisabet was plainly not in a very good mood that Sunday. She answered so brusquely, almost hostilely. She had always had a hard time keeping her temper. She used to lock herself in the bathroom, and sit there and sulk during the period she lived at home. Then Emelie and Jenny would stand and knock and make a fuss for a long time to get her to finally come out of there and let someone else in. And the way she snapped at Tyra sometimes…

Jenny decided not to ask her any more times; Elisabet could do what she wanted. Though it felt a little hard. Now Jenny was appearing for once in a good piece in an elegant theater. And it was just what Elisabet had always wished she would do.

Elisabet felt irritated, thought her mother was nagging her. In truth, she had not wanted to come today, but Lennart had apparently taken it for granted that they were going. And he was right; they ought to have said in advance if they were not intending to go.

Despite everything beginning so well at one time, something had gone wrong with their marriage. It did not feel like it was any tangle they could sort out, but rather an insoluble flaw. They were drifting away from each other. She knew inside herself that she was difficult at times. But he got on her nerves. Was so compliant, always gave in. To her or to anyone else who wanted to walk over him. If he noticed that she was sore at him, he tried to stay away. If she argued with him, he answered by admitting that she was right.

Of course, she had nagged him many times. Not least of all regarding his work. But it was for his own sake. He wanted something else, something more. But he stayed where he had landed, among all the same old men who had been standing there at the printer's when he got there. Who really just talked about their families, their half-liters, their trivial problems.

While he had stood still, she herself had progressed. Continued her education, followed what was happening in the world, tried out new environments, been given greater responsibilities.

Now, he could just do what he wanted, she was tired of nagging. But she thought he had gotten stuck somehow. Not just at work, but in his development in general. Before, she had liked to listen when he talked about what he had read, thought it was interesting and worth talking about. Now, she had a feeling that she recognized it, that he droned on, stuck in whatever he had been occupying himself with for what would soon be twenty years, ever since his years of unemployment.

He read a lot still. But seldom anything he had any use for. Philosophers that nobody cared about any longer. And in a notebook he wrote down what different things were called in Greek—but he doubtlessly didn't know how the words were pronounced.

All this was surely fine and good. But it was only to dig yourself down in a world that had disappeared and been gone for a long time. She felt like he had disappeared and died there as well.

He was not awake in the present. And he was so uninterested in how he looked. He went around in the same old suit, the same hat and coat. She had to wonder what her work colleagues would think if they saw him. They would probably think he was strange.

Elisabet would certainly admit that she was particular about her appearance. Now she had more resources than before; with the larger responsibilities, she had received larger salaries. She tried to be well-groomed, went to the hairdresser a lot, was careful to be perfect in every detail—whether it was visible or not.

Though it was not easy to dress well now during the war. What was mostly for sale was rather drab, price-controlled clothing, affected by the shortage of materials and by the fact that so many of the world's women were wearing uniforms. Strict and severe. Elisabet kept to the style they tried to dictate from occupied Paris, small waist and wide skirt. That suited her best; she had such a naturally narrow waist.

They were standing and waiting at the streetcar stop; the streetcar was late. A taxi driver had stopped his cab and was stirring around in his pot of coal gas.

"If you are tired, maybe we can take a taxi," said Lennart.

She only sniffed—indulge in taking a taxi all the way out there!

Some young men wearing the big hats and long baggy jackets of swing dancers walked past. Actually, they were not offending anyone, but she grew angry just at the sight of them. Young people had no style any longer. Take the young girls at the office, for example. They whined about their salaries, though they didn't know anything and didn't do anything useful. The reversal had come too quickly; it had become all too easy for youth. Now, of course, they didn't think that a job was worth anything anymore. She, who had been there, could tell them a thing or two. At that age, she had had to be content with being an errand girl. Only through hard work had she been able to reach where she was. They wanted to go out and have fun when evening came, didn't want to ruin their free time by learning something.

It felt like it was an injustice that had been perpetrated. So much had been asked of her.

She was a private secretary now. She knew regarding herself that she was competent. Never forgot anything, already knew what her boss wanted even before he said it, always prepared to work overtime if it was necessary. Sometimes, she wished that they would place higher demands on her, that the work would be more complicated than it was. Everything she lacked an outlet for at home she wanted to put into her work duties.

That was why she had an advertisement in her handbag. She had answered it but not gotten a reply yet. They were looking for a really clever private secretary for varied and interesting assignments.

Finally, the streetcar arrived, and they could begin the long trip home. While she sat and looked out into the darkness, she felt how a headache crept over her. It had gotten so noisy on Sundays. With Allan and Daggan and their kid. Allan held onto the tradition. He seldom missed. And had begun to take the whole family with him, took it for granted that everyone was welcome. They were, too, of course.

But Elisabet certainly thought it had become rambunctious company.

At Tegelbacken, they changed to the number two which had to stand and wait a long time for the lowered gates at the railroad crossing while a train with rows of lighted-up windows rolled past.

She wanted to go to bed as soon as they got home, complained of a headache.

He helped her make the beds. But he said he thought he would sit and read a while in the kitchen, if he didn't disturb her.

While he was looking for his books and notebooks, she got undressed. He saw her pass by close to him, undressed, in bra and panties. Her legs were so long and slender in the dimly shining stockings. He became painfully aware of how beautiful she was and how much he liked her, that he wanted to have her. But also that she was displeased with him. He thought a lot about how he could change, become whatever would make her like him as she had before. He could not come up with anything other than that he was the way he always had been, while she had changed, sort of grown away from him. She had become more beautiful, more refined, cleverer. And impatient with him, who still remained among the old things. It was almost irremediable. Even if he had gotten that foreman's job, he would have been the same person anyway; it would not have changed him. In fact, she would not have even noticed it in him, if he had never told her about it.

He guessed that what maybe irritated her most was the knowledge that he was broken for all time. That he had lost that firm belief in his own ability. But one cannot escape one's experiences. The years of unemployment had taught him how little a person is worth in certain situations, how low a value might be placed on himself.

He took his books, looked at her. She had gotten her nightgown on now.

"Good night then," he said. "Try to sleep off your headache."

"Good night."

He went out to the little kitchen and closed the door behind him.

He put down the books on the kitchen table, looked to see that the lead pencil was properly sharpened.

But it was difficult to read, difficult to sink into the world he longed for, the calm adventures on the pages of the book, the discoveries, the connections that one suddenly could surmise.

Just to find a word's origins and actual meaning, to ponder over how it had been changed and distorted, just to do that... It was something he would have liked to tell Elisabet. But he could not do it so that it would captivate her.

He tried to read but had to break off. He could not get away from his thoughts about Elisabet, rumination over what he was going to do so that everything would be good again. And longing for her. Their beds stood only a few decimeters from each other, but there was something like an insurmountable chasm between them. When she was upset with him, he could not come to her. He would just fail at that, too.

He was looking for an expression he read once, something he couldn't really remember anymore. Something about love's essence: To love was the same as to suffer. That the one who loved was at the mercy of pain.

Naturally, everything would be simpler if he didn't love her. But as for now, when he did, then the pain was unavoidable.

AFTER THE PARTY

Elisabet got the position and began her new job the first of February. It was a so-called popular movement company, but that it was so closely allied with the one Erik worked for, she had known nothing about. It came as an unpleasant surprise. But, she thought, her opinions about Erik certainly ought not place obstacles in her path. It wasn't him she was working for either.

He ran into her sometimes at the office, when he came up to meet with her director. He was a little teasingly polite but not as disagreeable as before, she thought. Rather elegant, a little gray at the temples, not so slim anymore, of course. According to what she understood, he was very competent and well-liked.

In the spring, a company party was arranged for the two collaborating companies. It was light outside and beautiful weather, and it was held at a restaurant outside of town. Erik was her table companion. It might have been because she was the secretary of the other director or because someone on the party committee knew that she and Erik knew each other.

He was nice. He had a lot of interesting things to tell, socialized apparently with a lot of famous politicians and was well-informed as to what happened behind the scenes. He also had a whole lot of stories about what had happened in the old Socialist Party, in his wild youth, as he said. Now many of his former party comrades were involved in the popular movement's different companies. Kilbom was in charge of the People's Parks, and Einar Ebe, whose name used to be Olsson, was director of *The People in Pictures* magazine. And others…

Elisabet had never been especially interested in politics, and much of what she got to hear was new for her, useful as well. The sort of things one ought to know in a company of this type.

She laughed, felt unusually happy. Maybe part of it was due to what she had been drinking; she was unused to liquor and wine. There were so many who were kind and polite and toasting with her, and then she had to toast back. Erik toasted, too, of course, to their renewed friendship. Though they had never been especially good friends.

There was dancing after dinner. She excused herself for being such a bad dancer; it was so seldom she danced. But Erik insisted that was just talk. She was undeniably a real dancing doll, in fact. And she had to admit that it was easy to dance with him. He led so confidently, gave her such a feeling of security. At first, she thought that he was holding her rather tightly, but then it felt only natural. In fact, quite nice when she grew a little dizzy.

Some people began to disappear, leaving for home; there were some streetcars going into town. In particular, the older people and those who had a long way home. But a loyal group was still staying on when the late night supper came out. Erik went and got hash and beer and schnapps for her and put out meat coupons since hers were all gone. He was so thoughtful and polite.

"Let's take a cab home together. We are going in the same direction after all." She was happy to do that, it would probably feel a little uncomfortable to go out and wait for a streetcar now. It had grown cold during the evening as well.

She felt it when they walked out onto the stairs to wait for the cab. She was too thinly dressed, began to shiver in the cold. She grew grateful when he unbuttoned his coat and pulled her in under it—though it was clear that it wasn't really proper. She looked around, but they were alone. The others were apparently carrying on with the dancing inside.

In the car, he put his coat around her again. And she relaxed, leaned her head against his shoulder. For an instant, she wanted to sit up, push him away from her. But then she sank back against him again, wished that the car ride would never end. That he would hold her the way he was doing now. But maybe also, too, that nothing more would happen.

He wanted her to come up with him a little while and see his apartment. It was worth seeing—with Lake Mälar and Västerbron in front of the window. There was no one home so there was no one to disturb.

She understood what he really wanted. Yet she followed him up. Did she want it herself?

The apartment truly was beautiful, the view as well. He showed her into the big living room, put the nighttime needle on the gramophone to lower the sound, let it play the same waltz they had danced to at the restaurant. They danced a few turns round the room, but the dance soon stopped in an embrace.

"Come," he said.

She had only seen such wide beds in a furniture store. He turned on the lamp at the end of the bed and turned off the one overhead before he began to undress her. Strangely enough, it did not feel like he was divesting her of anything, but more like he was liberating her.

He conquered her totally. Whatever it was that happened, she could never quite explain to herself. It was not just the alcohol, no, it was not the alcohol at all. It was as if he had fanned up a fire inside her, a fire that caused her to throw herself into everything she had shrunk from before. But even if he lit her, the fire was hers.

Then he suddenly turned.

"I want to give you something I have never given a woman before," he said. "And do you know what it is? It's a beating. I want to hit you like hell."

She began to tremble, as if the pain had already reached her.

"Do you want to know, by the way, why you have landed in this bed?" he continued.

"For an old memory's sake. Maybe because you have to learn to know what you do. Because once, many years ago you stood up high on a ladder and knew so well that you were offering yourself to me. In all respectability, right? So, sure, I could see but didn't dare touch. But I don't satisfy myself with just looking in the store window. That's why you came here in the end. Do you get it?"

Suddenly, she was crying. From shame and tiredness, from alarm at what he had brought about.

"Get dressed and get out now," he said. "The show is over. And I'm going to have a whiskey and soda and rinse the whole thing down."

When she came out of the bedroom, he was sitting on the corner of the sofa. He stood up without looking at her: "I'll call a taxi."

He didn't follow her out, let her leave like a beggar.

When she had gone, he filled his glass, opened the door to the balcony and went out. He saw the taxi with Elisabet in it rolling away westward. And the lights from the arch of Västerbron between its dark abutments.

He had really behaved horribly toward her. But she was going to get it for all the old stuff. And maybe that was what she needed. Somehow, someone had to get the sanctimoniousness out of her at any rate, for her own sake.

Tomorrow, she would probably arrive just as perfect as always. Maybe he would draw a little blood anyway, go up to her and say hello and very smoothly thank her for a pleasant evening.

Lennart woke up when she came home, asked with a sleepy voice if she had had a good time.

"Yes," she said quickly. "Though it went so terribly late. I have to hurry to get some sleep."

She crawled into the sofa bed, pulled the blanket over her, tried to hide herself as far against the edge as possible. She felt Lennart's hand on her shoulders.

"Good night," he said.

"Good night."

She had wanted to grip his hand, beg him for forgiveness, cry out all her humiliation to him. But did not dare do it now, had to sleep first, think first. Had to understand herself what had happened.

Maybe it was best for Lennart if he never learned of it? Or did she have to treat him so badly?

He began his day so early, was gone before she woke up from the alarm clock ringing.

She remembered what had happened in a different light from before; it turned so grotesque, so ugly. Erik had fooled her the whole time, somehow punished her. Gotten her to believe that it was a question of some sort of love—no, not so much that, but some sort of feelings in common anyway. And then he had just taken his revenge, like he was standing outside of himself and observing her.

She had to wonder if she had been insane. Or so very drunk?

If someone else had behaved the way she had, she would have had an easy time condemning him or her. Possibly she would have understood the man who acted like Erik—if it wasn't Lennart—but never the woman who had behaved in the way she had done.

For the first time, she had to condemn herself. There were no mitigating circumstances.

Now, they would certainly see through her when she got to the office. Everyone must guess what she had been up to. Some would have surely noticed that she and Erik went home in the cab together. She would have liked to stay home. But that would be feeding the gossip even more.

She drank a cup of coffee but was incapable of eating anything with it. She sank down on the wooden chair at the kitchen table. Now there was no security or safety left anymore. Now anything could happen with her.

Lennart's books still lay on the kitchen table; he must have sat there and read and waited for her as long as possible. And his notebooks, page after page with notations, but hardly anything she understood. He had created his own world that she did not know anything about. And now she felt so sorry for him that she wanted to cry again.

She left later than usual, at the last second. At the office, there was no one who seemed to notice anything. They were only talking about how successful the party had been, such good music and such a nice atmosphere.

Erik came in the afternoon. She grew so upset that she was shaking but kept herself under control and greeted him as usual. He thanked her for the day before as if nothing had happened.

Then he leaned toward her and said in a low voice so no one else would hear it: "Forgive me if I behaved all too horribly. It was not so completely ill-intentioned as it may have seemed."

And in a lighter tone: "Shall we have lunch together? We could use a pick-me-up."

"No," she said. "We won't."

She told Lennart everything that evening. Not the details—but still what had happened and what Erik had said.

"If you want to drive me out now, then do it," she said.

"Do you want to leave me?"

"No, but you can never forgive me. I can never forgive myself. Nor understand myself."

"Do you still care about me then?"

"It's not what I think that means anything now."

"Yes," he said. "It is the only thing that means anything. I have liked you the whole time and still do. There is no one else for me but you. For this reason, the only important thing is if you can accept me, such as I am. A failure maybe, boring, a bad lover, I suppose."

"That's not true," she said. "You are not all those things."

"Yes," he said. "And you have probably thought it at times."

She knew it was true.

They lay quietly in the darkness. Then she asked him: "Can you manage to still have me then?"

"Only if you can manage," he answered. "Then we will try again. Try to live a little better than we have."

THE MEMORY OF A FRIEND

The world waited. In the west, the big invasion was being prepared; in the east, the Russians pushed ever closer to Germany's borders. And the hurricane of bombings of the German cities grew in strength.

Out of this waiting, anxiety in the occupied nations grew as well. The pressure mounted severely. From without, from the increasingly desperate Germans and their sympathizers. And from within, an unbearable longing to finally get to experience the end of the terror.

Henning did his military service. He resigned himself listlessly to the everyday routine that seemed so divorced from reality in this dramatic time. He got accustomed to the thought that this would be his life for a whole year. It felt difficult at times, like a big sacrifice.

On Saturday afternoons and Sundays, he often got to go home. His mother and John now had three rooms and a kitchen in a relatively newly built apartment house on Ringvägen.

He felt like a stranger when he stood on the open space outside Central Station. The city functioned so well without him; he seemed superfluous. Vast streams of cyclists flowed southward; the offices must have closed by now. Streetcars rolled past and got held up at Tegelbacken where the big trains for the suburbs had their final stops. People swarmed everywhere, and he did not recognize any of them. Though he had been born here in the city, was at home in the swarm, still suddenly he was so alone.

Did he feel this way because he was going to bury a friend? Or because he was still a little unused to the new apartment, did not see home really as his since his mother and John had gotten married?

He had not been there for the actual moving. Instead, he had come to a new apartment that he had not seen before and was different in so many ways from the old one. John's furniture was here as well and some they had bought new. Such things he could not consider his. But he was careful not to show he felt lost. In truth, he did not feel he missed the old place either. More a certain relief. His mother would not have to be alone; it would have undoubtedly been rather empty for her during Henning's long conscription if she had not had John.

Now he did not need to feel the same responsibility toward his mother as before. He was free, and if he wanted to move away from home one day, it would not be so hard to do it. Possibly he might think that there was a little more of a hurry for him to find a girl to live together with. So there would be a thoroughly good reason to move. And that way maybe also give his mother and John increased freedom.

Stig's long fight against tuberculosis was over. Ever since he was a child, he had wandered in and out of sanatoriums. Now he had not been home for half a year. He had gotten to live twenty-four years in any case, one more year than Henning's grandfather, who had died of the same disease.

They assembled at the churchyard at Skog's Church on the last Sunday in May. Henning stood and thought about how Stig had once spoken about the boys in the old Negro Village. He had named them by name one after the other, and listed up where they had ended up: Söderby, Långholmen, Skrubba, Hall, Wenngarn, Svartsjö, Sidsjön, Ulleråker, Skog's churchyard. There were not many who had avoided any of the end stations. A large part of a generation had just been swept away, disappeared inside the recesses of prisons and nursing facilities or buried in churchyards. Even if the dilapidated houses in Negro Village had been especially hard hit, there were surely some victims in almost every house on Söder. The years of crisis had taken a heavy toll.

Consumption was what it had once been called.

Emelie stood there, too, and thought back—about her father and her younger brother, Olof. Both had fallen as victims of the disease. Back then it had still been an epidemic, a national disease. "The sickness of the proletariat," they had also called it. Now it was a disease among all the others; there were those who believed that one day it would be conquered. But it had taken Stig. He had naturally never taken particularly good care of himself. In Stig, Emelie had seen a lot of the same restlessness and self-destruction that she had seen at one time in Olof. The same hectic hurriedness, as if they always knew how short their time was and had so much to accomplish before it ran out.

Now the coffin was being lowered slowly into the dug-out hole. The flowers on the lid of the coffin swayed.

They walked over to the grave. Last came the three who remained of "Stickan Berg's Quartet." One of them spoke a few words in thanks. Otherwise, there was no one who spoke, except for the minister.

David Berg was there and followed his son to the grave. Allan asked if his father didn't want to come over to his place for a little while; the others were coming. But David couldn't; it would have to be another time.

David just lifted his hat, bowed and went his way between the graves and the trees newly in leaf.

He could have gone along. But still he did best to let things be. Everyone certainly knew how things were with him, that he could never be of any help to his children. It was probably just as well that he did not get to know them any better, that he barely remembered what Tyra's relatives looked like. Then he would not be tempted to go to them and ask for help some day. Then he would not ruin anything more for Allan and Gun.

Now, he was completely alone. Not even Dora was there any longer for him. He helped Allan and Gun the most by keeping away from them. He was afraid of Per. But he had wanted to be there when Stig was buried. Perhaps to ask him for forgiveness.

Stig was the one who was to get his accordion, he had thought sometimes. But the pawn ticket for the instrument had expired many years ago, and now Stig was no longer there either. Nothing turned out as one thought. Never had. But he still had one big and fine memory from his life, something they would never be able to take away from him: Tyra.

Tyra would have mourned Stig. But it would have made her happy that things were good for Allan and Gun. She had been especially worried about Allan at times.

Since, for once, David was on leave from his institution and had to eat somewhere anyway, he went to a tavern. He felt the temptation to take "French leave," drink himself silly and not bother returning to the institution on time. But there was something in him that resisted. This time he would try to conduct himself better; another time it might be different.

Allan and Daggan invited everyone for coffee. People conversed in low tones. The mood lightened a little when Daggan came in with the one-year-old girl. She seemed especially fascinated with Lennart; when he held her, she grabbed hold of his ears and crowed delightedly.

Allan stood at the window and pointed out where the Russian bombs had fallen a few months ago, at the old outdoor theater in Eriksdalslunden. He had heard the first explosion and rushed to the window and seen the light and heard the explosions. The windows had rattled so he thought they would break. But they had been all right here; in the buildings alongside Ringvägen, lots of windowpanes had broken.

Allan had calmed down now, but his eyes were still red. He had been the last to leave the graveside.

They did not stay very long. Henning walked home. It felt good to walk alone, to not have to talk to anybody. Stig was his first friend to die; he could feel the reality of death in another way from before: It had hit so close, among his contemporaries. He thought how if he himself grew old, Stig would still remain eternally young. He might forget how his other contemporaries looked since he would see them changing. But Stig would always be twenty-four years old. And he saw the narrow face under the hat brim, the fringe of dark hair, heard the somewhat hoarse voice that seemed to spit out its sentences.

It was hard to fathom that he would never hear that voice again, that they would never meet again at a little café and sit there and fantasize about the world and themselves. It was as if the image of Stig was floating in the cigarette smoke of the café, in the sparkles of the sun as it played on the waters of Hammarby Canal.

A little more than a week later, the invasion came. Early in the morning, on the sixth of June, the Normandy landings began and continued all day long.

Would it end with a new Dunkirk or would they succeed in breaking through the German Atlantic Wall? Hitler had said that if Churchill wanted to attempt an invasion, his troops were welcome; they would get to land but would not get to stay there more than nine hours. Things would end up like they had in Dieppe.

But now the hours passed, turned into days. The first cities were captured by the landed troops. The Atlantic Wall seemed no more impossible to penetrate than the Maginot Line once had. The moat to "Fortress Europe" had been forced, the western front retreated.

The Germans tried new weapons; robot bombs were dropped on London. They wrought great devastation but did not seem to have any direct importance on the development of the war.

The Nazis grew obviously more and more desperate. Horrific descriptions came from France about how the village of Oradour, along with its population, had been destroyed, how women and children had been driven into the church, which had then been blown up.

Somewhere Henning read a description of how a young French resistance fighter had been executed. The condemned man had stated that he was dying in peace, in the assurance that he belonged to tomorrow, while his executioner was already part of the past.

Henning imagined that that young Frenchman looked like Stig, just as thin and dark-haired, with the same fiery defiance and that same hissing contempt in his voice.

Stig had never seen himself as any sort of martyr. He might curse at his existence, but he never complained. Stig would have spoken like that if he had stood in front of the firing squad. He had shocked many also by not being afraid and humbled before his fate. Stig had never stood humbly before death, instead waited for the unavoidable with a bitterly scornful smile: Here I am!

It could just as well have been Stig who said he belonged to the future, while all the cautious and surviving ones sank into the past.

Henning could hear him say it. And it felt like a consolation, as if Stig had spoken the truth, as if he was there and walking into tomorrow. Always just as young, immortal.

BEACH IN AUGUST

The sandy beach created a soft arc between the two promontories. Light, small waves rippled in and pulled quickly back again, wetting and darkening the outer edge of the light strip of beach. Against the light, the rocks stood dark in contrast to the dazzlingly shimmering water. The sand shone a warm yellow beside the waves' narrow white strip of froth.

Above the beach, the pinewoods began, the straight, glistening brown trunks rising over blueberry bushes and lingonberry sprigs. Splashes of trembling light made their way down between the green treetops. The path between the trees was covered by a brown layer of dried pine needles. And in there, in a glade in the woods, lay the cottage.

They were coming down from the beach. John walked first; he was carrying the oars across his shoulders, had slung his bathing suit over one of the oars. Maj had a picnic basket in one hand, swung her bathing suit in the other. It was bright blue and gleamed like a happy little signal.

She had never experienced the archipelago like this before. As if they two were the only people in the world and as if this was the world.

John had told her about the cottage he owned; it was an inheritance. He had asked if they couldn't take a vacation there, though it was small and uncomfortable. It lay several kilometers from the main road and more than ten kilometers from bus and grocery store. That was why there were not many people who went there, when you could not get there by car or motorboat.

Maj had felt rather unsure at first, had never lived in a summer cottage before, only small private hotels. She wondered if it would be any really restful vacation. But for John's sake, she had said yes.

She had barely had time to do more than see the place before she became attached to it. And now she almost had to reproach John that they hadn't ridden out every Saturday and Sunday since the cottage had become his. It wasn't so hard to get here either, with the help of a bicycle.

The beach was the biggest adventure. They didn't own it, but it was there anyway, waiting for them.

They hung their bathing suits over a pine branch. He placed the oars against the wall of the cottage, sat down on the step and filled his pipe. She came and sat down beside him, shutting her eyes against the sun. The ring of trees around the glen broke the wind, but she could hear its gentle sighing up in the treetops.

She felt the sunlight through her eyelids. Thought how the beach had been there all these years without her knowing about it, as if it was waiting for her. Just like John had been there without her knowing about him. The years that had passed might well feel lost, but maybe also necessary; they had brought her here. Maybe one had to journey across the troubled sea to reach the peaceful shore. Though now, afterward, she had a hard time imagining how she had managed.

They walked along the road through the woods with their bicycle between them; closest to the cottage it was hard to bicycle. But then the road grew more even and firm, and Maj could sit up on the baggage rack. They glided along between the sparse tree trunks and came out on the country road where John could increase his speed.

Elisabet and Lennart were going to come out for a few days. And on Saturday, Henning was going to come as well; then it might get a little tight in the cottage.

Beside the bus stop stood the store. They shopped and then sat down at the edge of the ditch to wait. They had not met a car the whole time. After a while, the big yellow bus came rumbling along, and Elisabet and Lennart stepped off. They had some fully laden suitcases with them, and Lennart had brought along his bicycle as well, unhooking it from the bus.

The guests looked a little pale and proper, like city folk beside their hosts. Maj and John had had time to get suntanned; John was wearing workpants, and Maj had on shorts and one of Henning's old shirts instead of a blouse. Lennart and Elisabet were dressed for the city; he was wearing a jacket and tie and she a flimsy, light skirt.

It took a while before they had loaded everything on the two bicycles and figured out how Elisabet would be able to sit on the baggage rack without getting grease on her skirt or ruining her stockings. But eventually they did get underway, rolling along a little precariously down the hill from the bus stop. The road to the cottage took longer this time; Elisabet's shoes were not exactly intended for walking on a country road, and she had a hard time when she had to walk uphill. But she took the inconvenience with unusual aplomb. In general, she had been milder and friendlier lately, Maj thought.

When they reached the cottage, John had to go and fetch water. He took the pails and left. Maj began to get ready for dinner. The guests changed. In Lennart's case, it only meant that he took off his jacket and tie; he had traveled in an old, cast-off suit. But Elisabet changed her blouse and skirt for a sunsuit she had bought, and pulled out socks and sandals. She was still the most elegant; looked more like she had gone to a private hotel instead of a primitive cottage. When she helped Maj set the table, it happened that they stretched out their bare arms over the table at the same time—and had to laugh at the image. The one arm so light and the other so dark. And it was the same with their legs; Maj had had time to get really brown while Elisabet was almost white.

John and Lennart placed boards on sawhorses beside the picnic table, and John got beer and a little bottle of distilled vodka out of the cellar. The sun had begun to sink down behind the trees, but still glimmered through them between a few sparse branches. The evening was warm. And they sat out there for a long time.

John and Lennart got along. They were both calm and a little quiet, they could talk together and be quiet together and the whole time feel a certain camaraderie. In a way, their camaraderie was greater than Maj and Elisabet's. The sisters had not been together so much and then they were so different. Quite often, they had grown irritated with one another; the ten years between them had felt like an abyss, as if they belonged to different generations.

Now it was no longer so; it was as if they had become more the same age. Ever since Henning had grown up, Maj was not the continually anxious and concerned mother any longer; she had a little more time for herself. And her marriage with John had also undoubtedly made her happier and calmer, Elisabet thought. Even if Elisabet herself might have thought John was a little quiet and boring.

Elisabet had not gotten over that episode with Erik yet; the shame, the regret, the feeling of guilt. She was afraid Maj would have gotten wind of something; she saw Erik sometimes. Erik was certainly the type who could say anything, probably was not afraid to expose her. Even if he didn't say anything, if Maj didn't suspect anything—she still felt that what had happened must in some way stand between her and Maj.

It could be an obstacle, something that separated them. But also something that united them. And now she thought she felt a greater solidarity with Maj than previously. It had nothing directly to do with Erik, more with the summer evening's mild warmth, the twilight that slowly settled, the feeling of calm and stillness, of closeness. People came closer together when they sat like this outdoors, with the darkening woods surrounding and the empty sky above.

They walked down to the inlet, the path at first like a tunnel under the leafy trees and then a lighter ribbon between the trunks of the pine trees. The water was still light and shining though it was beginning to grow black by the rocks. Light waves rippled in. Elisabet went barefoot and walked at the water's edge. It was warmer than she dared believe.

"Can't we swim?" she asked.

"You two swim," said John, "and Maj and I will go up and see if we can find some sheets and blankets."

They undressed, stood like two light shadows in the descending darkness. She began to shiver a little now. And then they ran out into the shallow water, threw themselves in and began to swim.

"It's not cold once you are in," she exclaimed with a gasp.

But when they came out again, it felt cooler. She borrowed Lennart's shirt to dry off with. Just as they were about to leave, a boat came, far out on the water, casting streams of light across the estuary.

"Just imagine if we could get someplace like this," she said.

"We could maybe rent something at least."

They walked slowly back toward the path. He held her. And in among the dark tunnel of trees, they stopped and he kissed her. She pressed herself against him and asked as she had asked so many times: "Can you forgive me then, can you really do it?"

"You know it," he said. "You know it."

The windows of the cottage shone among the trees. John had lit the kerosene lantern. It was planned that Lennart and Elisabet would sleep in the kitchen, but there were no extra beds so they had to lay mattresses on the floor. They were prepared for this, and it would, of course, be fine.

They sat a little while and talked in the other room; some wood logs crackled in the stove and the firelight flitted over the floor and on the walls. Outside it was dark now, completely black. The trees had drawn closer and the glen in the woods disappeared. When they opened the door, they could hear the waves rolling in against the shore. It was blowing a little more now. The sky above them was fully dotted with stars and a crescent moon had begun to rise above the pines.

The next day the sky was just as blue; the wind had slackened. Elisabet could feel how her skin was beginning to burn, and she smoothed on some of the oil she had brought with her. She and Lennart lay on one of the rocky ledges by the water. She had taken off her bathing suit to get really tan.

She was just as slender, just as girlish and just as beautiful, he thought. He remembered their first morning, when she had stood under the shower and her skin had glistened with the many small drops of water. And he remembered, too, how happy he had been then.

Then—but now? Even now, on a day like this, he could feel something at least resembling happiness. Though it was different from the happiness he had felt before, more resigned. Maybe because he knew so well how brittle it was, how vulnerable and easy to crush. Just a few words, maybe only a gesture—that was enough.

Of course, he had forgiven her. He had said that, meant it, too. Though he maybe wondered if what had happened was actually something one could forgive. Not that she had done something unforgivable, not that he was mad at her. Just that forgive was the wrong word. A feeling perhaps cannot be forgiven, is nothing to ask forgiveness for. And if the action was merely a consequence of the feeling...

To forgive someone else was to say that he was right. But his fault was just as big as hers. He had disappointed her, not been the person she thought he was. It was his deficiencies that had driven her to what she had done. But once it had happened, she had come back to him. As if the fiasco had brought her down to his level, so that she could accept him.

"Lennart..."

He looked up. She had placed the beach towel over herself now, leaned her head forward.

"Yes?"

"If you want to—then I want us to have a child together."

"Do you really want to?"

"Yes. I am certain. I have thought a lot about it. Before I didn't want to. But now I think it's right, that we would be happier, too. But you—you maybe don't want to—anymore?"

"Yes," he said. "I would really like to, as long as you want to."

They walked along the beach, past the boat where some fallen red balloons lay and shone from the gray bottom. The sun was not as strong any longer; it was shining a little at an angle across the rocks they had just been lying on.

It was Saturday afternoon. When they reached the cottage, Henning had just arrived; he had bicycled the whole way from town. Maj was getting dinner ready, John was chopping wood. Henning was going to take a quick dip before eating and rinse off the dust from the country road.

Elisabet wanted to dress for Saturday dinner, went into the room and took off her sunsuit. She saw how red her skin was and realized she would suffer from it tonight. But it didn't matter; it had been wonderful. She put on a light-colored dress, combed her hair out in front of the mirror. She looked a little scrappy and wild from the woods anyway. She came closer to the mirror, as if she was looking for a secret in her face.

A child, she thought, I want to have a child. She felt a touch of fear, faced with the nine-month burden and what would happen next. But also felt that she was ready for it, that it was something she wanted to give Lennart. That maybe it was a way to pay a debt, to receive forgiveness.

She felt happier than usual, showed it, too. She laughed at all the small jokes, talked more than she usually did. But grew quiet and listened when Henning and Lennart talked, when it turned to what Henning was studying at college. Everything Henning touched on and that neither she nor John nor Maj knew anything about, seemed to be completely familiar to Lennart. And Henning said: "You know so much more about that than I do. I have only read what is in the textbooks."

Everything Erik paid a lot of money for so Henning could learn—Lennart knew. Everything that she had thought was so silly and useless. So it was worth something; it was not just a strange hobby. And she had to admire his tenacity, that he had the energy to keep on though no one had asked about it and no one had encouraged him. And though he had no use for it at all.

The sunburn made her grow a little cold in the dusk, and she snuggled closer to Lennart.

Before they fell asleep, they walked down to the beach one more time, stood a moment in the cool wind and heard the waves slowly roll in, like breathing.

"Yes, I want us to have a child," she said again. "And I hope it will be a boy and that he will be like you."

THE PAST AND THE PRESENT

When Emelie had retired, it had felt like a catastrophe at first, a disaster along the same lines as the general strike and unemployment. But during the years that had passed, she had begun to grow used to being free. She had helped some sick neighbors for a period; they were dead now. And now she was so old herself that she did not have the strength to be so useful. Next birthday she would turn seventy-five.

She was without question old. But she was healthy. And maybe more interested in the life around her than before. Before, it had been so hectic; she had never had time to think of anything other than those closest to her. And felt like she neither could afford nor had time for newspapers. Now, a newspaper arrived in her box every morning; it was Gunnar who had subscribed to it for her. In the beginning, she maybe read mostly out of duty, to take advantage of the gift. It would have been ungrateful of her toward Gunnar not to do it. But once she had really begun to read it every day, her interest was awakened. All those cities and nations and generals and politicians that she never had the opportunity to keep track of before—now she began to think that they were all old acquaintances. She still had Elisabet's student atlas, and she looked up places in that, took note of where they lay. Now she knew exactly how far inside East Prussia the Germans were positioned. And where Paris and Brussels and Antwerp were located—the three cities had been liberated by the invading forces to the west. And the Finns had lost Vyborg and requested negotiations and gotten peace at last. But in Warsaw, which had risen up against the German oppression, General Bor had to surrender to the superiority of the German forces.

She discussed war events with Jenny, who had foggier notions about the whole thing. Jenny did not read the newspaper so carefully. Sometimes it was also maybe a little hard for Jenny to understand what Emelie meant—since Emelie pronounced most foreign names the way they were spelled. In such cases, it was not worth correcting her; it was easiest for Emelie to keep track of the big picture if she read everything exactly as it was written. And she did not want to pretend that she spoke foreign words when she didn't. In which case Jenny could laugh as much as she liked.

It wasn't until she was old that she began to know anything about the world beyond her. Earlier, the city had been her world. Well, not the whole city, but the neighborhoods where she had lived and the streets she had walked on to and from work. But on the big overview map of the whole world, the city was barely a dot and all of Sweden just a little patch.

She read the newspaper now the way she had done her job before, thoroughly and without sloppiness. It became something of a duty.

Now she had laid aside the paper to tidy up. Jenny declared, to be sure, that it was as tidy as it could get, but Emelie still found one thing or another that could be improved. Then she set the table in the living room with coffee cups and bread plates.

It was a dear guest she was expecting, also someone she saw rather seldom—her sister-in-law, Ida. Ida had, of course, been here with August a few times, but it was the first time she was coming alone. They had talked about it for a long time, but during the summer it had not been possible. That was when Ida had been in the country with one of her daughters. Now she had come back to town and telephoned Emelie.

"She's coming now," said Jenny, who was standing at the window and saw a taxicab stop outside the door. But it took quite a long time before Ida had walked up the two flights; there was no elevator in the building.

Ida was panting with the exertion. She was two years older than

Emelie and had, over the years, begun to have a hard time with stairs. They were "heavy-chested" in her family. Karl Henning had a sensation of this, too; already as a boy he had grown so tired when he tried to run.

Ida liked to talk about Karl Henrik; time after time she came back to him. She was proud of her son. August had surely been a little needlessly worried about the boy, perhaps not really understood him. She wished August could have seen how well things were going now, how well Karl Henrik was succeeding with the firm. Around them in the new suburbs you could see signs with the words "Bodin's is building here."

Ida had entered the picture at the time when August was young and taking over the firm, talking about the shock when he had discovered that the company was actually falling apart where everything had seemed so solid. How she had been able to help him go through the books and how they had found the grim truth but also the possibilities for avoiding a catastrophe. Those years had still probably been her happiest, when she had gotten to work together with August and live through their success.

Emelie knew fairly little about the years in August's life. Their parents' friend, Thumbs, had more or less driven August away, called him a traitor to his own class. And so it had happened that Emelie did not see August for several years. What Ida told her was new to Emelie; it gave, in part, a new picture of her brother. It had not been so simple that he had just gone to the Bodins and been given everything. He had also had to work hard, he had had to be anxious and unhappy.

In exchange, she could tell Ida about August's childhood, about their home out on Åsöberget a few blocks away. About their parents' hard work, about their father's illness and death. She showed Ida the old bureau and told her the history of it. And from one of the bureau drawers, she took out a little flat package, the only tangible memento that was left of her and August's father. On the outside of the paper was written in childish handwriting:

Gift from My Father on My Birthday 1878.

She had turned eight then and received the handkerchief with its embroidered E and forget-me-not. Papa had bought it from one of the packers at Bodin's—it was the packer's wife who had sewn it. And from Mama, she had gotten a bun and coltsfoot flowers around her morning mug of milk. At that time, August was still living at home and going to school down in Malongen at Nytorget. A few months later Papa had come home and told them that August was invited out to the Bodins for the summer.

So it had begun, so had August Nilsson become August Bodin. Such a long time ago.

So long ago that the little handkerchief had become completely fragile. Emelie hardly dared open it out; the thin cloth had begun to fall apart at the folds.

Ida also told about herself. How she had met August when they lived at their summer houses on Stora Essingen, how her father had gone bankrupt, and she had begun to work in an office, and how she had met August again after several years. And Emelie understood that even if Ida had lived in another world and another circle of people, she had not been spared either. It brought Ida closer; the distance that had been there and certainly still was there had diminished. They became just two people who both had had their difficulties and setbacks but also a lot of happiness. Happiness and sorrow, that was life. It was good, and it was hard, but it was not insignificant. They had lived, they had taken part. Ida had her children and grandchildren. Emelie had her siblings' children and their children and the unfortunate Bärta's children and grandchildren. And among Bärta's children was Gunnar, of course. Gunnar was probably more like August than Karl Henrik was, so very much that Ida had given a start when she saw him at August's funeral. And Emelie told about Bärta, how she for all those years had wanted to keep the secret from August that Gunnar was his son. Until her need for alcohol took the upper hand, and she exploited Gunnar's existence to extort money from August. But Emelie had learned the truth early on.

It wasn't hard to talk about it now, during later years. August had often spoken with Ida about Gunnar. Neither Ida nor Emelie felt any bitterness toward the past.

Yet they had a harder time understanding the present. The growing city felt more and more foreign to them; it was not as easy for them to get out as it had been before, and when they missed the daily contact with life outside their windows, then that life was no longer theirs. Even if Ida felt pride and joy over the new buildings that Karl Henrik constructed, she still preferred the old ones. And Emelie was almost frightened when she saw how a big cluster of pointed buildings grew up on Klippan where the windmill had stood before, and how the bridge, Skanstullbron, that she had crossed when it was new, landed in the shadow of an enormously high bridge that was under construction.

It was not only the city that was changing. People were transformed too, becoming so efficient, were in such a hurry. Those who were old could not keep up, meant nothing anymore. Those who had needed their help before took care of themselves now. Ida's grandchildren were so big that she never needed to help out taking care of them anymore, and no hungry kids gathered around Emelie's dinner table. It wasn't needed. And if it had been needed, they would hardly have had the strength.

Emelie realized that Ida, despite all her children, was probably lonelier than she was. Emelie had Jenny, and through Jenny, Maj and Elisabet and their husbands. And then she had Mikael, who needed her help sometimes. And Allan came, of course, with his family as good as every Sunday. He, who was not family with them, probably had the strongest family feeling of all.

But Ida lived alone, and her children had their families to think of. Ida undoubtedly had a lot of time to sit alone and remember. Emelie wondered if maybe Ida didn't read the newspaper thoroughly enough, but she didn't want to ask. The newspaper was in many ways a consolation.

Contrary to her habit, Jenny sat silently. She said a few words at times but otherwise satisfied herself with listening. She was more than ten years younger, still involved in contemporary life. She had a script she had to learn, though it was put aside now that they had a visitor; she was going to play in a revue in the fall. It was a time of hard work with late evenings; she was also beginning to feel that she was not so young anymore. But she was not worrying about it yet.

Maybe she was keeping quiet because she had her own life to think about, her own family members. Elisabet seemed calmer and happier now. And everything was fine with Maj and John, and in the spring Henning would be done with the military. The girls had gotten over their periods of trouble now; everything would take care of itself.

They were so unlike each other, Maj and Elisabet. Maj had always been ready to sacrifice herself, never thought of her own comfort. Elisabet was different, she thought mostly of herself.

But they did have different fathers, too. Julius had forced himself upon her, and she had married him only so Elisabet would be born legitimate. Many times she had said to herself that she had to be fair to the girls, that she should not blame Elisabet for anything because of her father. She thought she tried to treat them the same, even if she was closer to Maj.

Maybe Elisabet had felt it; maybe in the past, there were things that had harmed her. Jenny didn't know.

But it looked like everything was going to be fine for her girls at last.

When Ida went home, it had begun to grow dark. Jenny called for a cab, and Ida rode through the streets tinged blue with the evening. Voting posters were still hanging on the endless woodpiles, Per Albin Hansson's slightly sorrowful face above the text, "Vote for him!" and the right's, "Freedom or Coercion—decide for yourself." Per Albin had been elected again, of course, but the election had been a big setback for the Social Democrats. The big victory had been won by the Communists, who had taken twelve parliamentary seats, maybe an echo of the Russians' enormous successes on the battlefield.

Streams of people trailed home from their jobs, an anonymous black mass with display windows as background lighting. Unknown people in an unknown present. Ever since August had died, it was as if it was not as important to live any longer. So they would have to forgive her if she longed to go to August. Life had run past, away from her. And she lay like a fish who had landed in a pool on the side, gasping, tired after the struggle.

But it had felt good to get to talk to Emelie, like coming back to life for a while—in the past life, the real life.

EQUALITY AND FRATERNITY

During the war years, enormous new residential areas had been created; the city had grown faster than ever before. The housing shortage meant the increasingly more distant fringes had to be settled and transformed. The clearly defined, concentrated city would not exist in the future. It would be replaced by a vast city landscape with countless cities within the city.

Such a city landscape called for different communications. They counted on tunnel traffic in the future, and the streetcar line to Ängby was built so that it could also be used for a subway train. Means were appropriated for the beginnings of a subway between Kungsholmen and Hötorget. A new general plan for the whole city area was to be worked out and the re-creation of lower Norrmalm into a new city was being prepared.

On other levels as well, they were preparing for peace. Within the labor movement, a committee had been set up to work out a post-war program. In the spring, the committee had laid out a proposal of twenty-seven points, which over the summer had come out in book form. It was being discussed now in trade unions and labor unions.

Full employment was one of the main points, employment for all. Reasonable and equitable division of joint proceeds from work, raised living standards. Increased security.

Peace could and would give everything. And now it was obvious to everyone that the German defeat could not be far off. Hitler himself had declared that all of his allies had betrayed him, and in the German SS newspaper it was being discussed what the best way would be for facing an Allied occupation.

Erik belonged to those who studied the post-war program especially carefully. It fascinated him; there was such a socialist tone in it that he almost believed the Social Democratic Labor Party had lost. Even that maybe he himself had lost, but now was drawing him back again.

Actually, he had not had any intention of playing any political role. But he did go to his local parish association meetings, and however it happened, he always had a hard time not expressing his views whenever there was a discussion. He was a good speaker, he knew that. He could get people on his side. And now it was pretty clear that he would land in an electable position on the list next time they held municipal elections. There were still a couple of years until then. But it was as if he was establishing himself for it, preparing himself.

He had spoken on the post-war program in his association. The talk had hit home; there had been an unusually lively debate. Apparently, the report of that successful speech had spread. Now he was invited to speak on the same subject in one of the suburbs southward.

He felt a little nervous on the way out. Even if he was sure of himself and his abilities, he was not used to going out like this anymore. He had hardly done it since he was in the Kilbom party. Irene went with him and wanted, of course, to talk along the way, but he asked her to be quiet.

The association in the new suburb seemed lively, a lot of people, mostly young people. Most of them had surely lived on Söder as children and moved south of Söder when they got married. It woke an old mindset inside him; he felt at home.

His brother Bengt was there with his wife, Britta. They had moved out to gain more space for their kids, Bengt said. They had three now.

It had been more than ten years since the brothers had seen each other last; it was the night the old Katarina elevator had been torn down. Bengt was still an electrician with the streetcars.

Bengt found Britta and brought her over: "This is my little woman."

Britta looked very ordinary, poorly dressed, too, Erik thought. But Bengt's salary did not allow any for extravagances. Beside Irene, she looked plain. But she did not seem any older than Irene, actually younger. Really two contrasts. Britta fair, a little mannishly gaunt, against Irene's dark, heavy womanliness. The one marked by work, the other by living well.

But it was the same for him and Bengt. Here he was, standing roundly rosy and doing well, beside his brother, who so visibly had had his thorns in life.

Erik might have felt a little guilt, thought that maybe he had had it too easy at times. Of course, he had had to work for his success; of course, he had had his lean years. But he had never gone out for physical labor, had never worked in the same way that Bengt had. But should he feel guilt over that? That one had been successful in life was nothing one should go around with feelings of guilt about. Still there was something shameful in the fact that life was so different for different people.

And for this reason, it was necessary to do what one could so there would be a change. He should really speak in favor of this post-war program.

And he spoke, more convincingly than he ever had done, he himself thought. He began by reminding his audience about their impoverished childhoods, about how it had looked in this city during and after the First World War—when the bourgeoisie had been in power. He reminded them of the hunger riots and living conditions of squalor. He talked about the time of economic crisis and the shooting of the workers demonstrating in Ådalen, about the difficult years of unemployment—indeed, about everything that no one would wish back again. No one except for a few who had profiteered on want, and who would certainly go and suck it out of people once again if they got the chance.

Now a new future was expected soon, when the Nazis' barbarism was over. Would they have to experience the same disappointments as after the previous war? No, he answered. Now the labor movement was preparing a new program for taking advantage of the opportunities of peace and reshaping society in a socialist direction. This time, it was not the bourgeoisie who was going to decide, now there was universal suffrage and a labor government. Now it was a question of assured full employment, it was a question of an elevated standard of living, a more equitable division of the welfare that increased production could yield. It was a question of security for all.

He felt how the memories of injustices and hardships welled up inside him, how he was gripped by his own words.

A little more, and it will become a real salvation meeting, he thought, and tried to calm down a little. But he felt how his audience was still with him, even when he went through the twenty-seven points and talked about things that were less easy to make engaging. He had aroused the memories of the past in himself and his listeners. He felt how determination grew within them: What happened last time was not going to happen again. The twenties and thirties were not going to come back.

He had never received so much applause before. A little dazed, still moved, he sat down. And a little embarrassed. Everything he had said he had meant, but—it was just that he himself had always escaped the worst of it. If he had had to suffer and toil more in the past himself, in such a case it would have been more honest.

But not even Bengt seemed to have anything to object to. Just the opposite. He was more enthusiastic than Erik had ever seen him, even went as far as expressing himself in the debate afterward. Only voicing agreement that, in fact, did not give any new points of view. But still—Erik had never heard his brother say anything publicly before.

"It is people like Erik Karge that we need within the movement," the chairman of the meeting said in his farewell remarks.

"That was the best speech we have had as long as I have been a part of this association," Bengt said.

"It has been such a long time," said Erik. "Now let's go eat together, all four of us. My treat."

They went in town to Slussen, took the elevator up to Mosebacke.

Bengt and Britta were unaccustomed to going to restaurants and did not know what they wanted to eat. Britta maybe would have most liked to have a cup of tea and a sandwich. They had eaten dinner at home before the meeting, she said. But Erik said they should eat something small and tasty. Eel with scrambled eggs or salt-cured salmon? And beer—and schnapps for each of them, of course?

No, Britta did not want to have schnapps. Even though she saw that it was frightfully expensive, she did not want to shilly-shally any longer and chose the salmon. And drank beer, though she did not like beer at all. She hoped Bengt would not drink too much—he was so unused to it, and it could easily become a bad habit. But she saw that Bengt was having fun. The brothers had so much to talk about, everything that had been revived by Erik's speech. Britta and Irene listened mostly. Irene had not even grown up in Stockholm.

Erik returned to what he had talked about: the new era and its opportunities, the post-war program. There was so much left to do. Such as reshaping schooling, giving everyone the same chance for education. He had helped Henning go on to higher education. Very soon, schooling had to be made so that everyone had the same chances. At last, they had come so far that there was a possibility of realizing dreams of liberty, equality, and fraternity. He himself had not had much, neither of the one nor the others. Now the thing was to give children a better society than the one they themselves had had to take over.

The children—Britta began to grow worried. It was beginning to grow late, and tomorrow was another day.

It was not easy to leave; Erik and Bengt would have preferred to sit a little while longer. But they broke up anyway. They took the elevator together down to Slussen, and Erik found a cab for himself and Irene, while Bengt and Britta walked down the stairs to the streetcar that was standing at the mouth of the tunnel.

The taxi went across Slussen, down toward Kornhamnstorg. A few small cargo boats lay like dark shadows in the inlet, and the railroad bridge became a black band over the water.

"Life can be so strange," said Irene. "That you two are brothers.

And live in such different circumstances, that they should have to be so badly off…"

"That was what I was talking about," he said a little irritatedly. "That conditions have to improve for everyone."

"Yes, I know," she interrupted. "But I wonder if some people are not always going to have it better than others, no matter what you do. Because some people can work things out for themselves while others have to take it as it comes."

He did not answer. Her words felt like a reproach. Although it was surely as she said. Life worked that way and even socialist societies had their upper classes. And he knew that Bengt would never be able to take as much of what was offered as he himself. Bengt was not one of those who took, he received. While Erik himself always had been able to place a price on his own work, could demand what he saw himself as being worth.

"Any total equality will not be attainable," he said at last. "But we can raise the level and reach the place where everyone gets the same chances. Though it has to be up to them to take advantage of them."

When they got home, Irene hurried in to the girls to see of they were asleep. Erik opened the door to the balcony, stayed standing out there a while.

He looked toward Söder, Långholmen's and Skinnarviken's dark, cold rocks, and the lights in the brewery at the edge of the water. Far away over there, behind the hills and masses of buildings, his brother lived in the new suburb. And everywhere, in all the dark buildings, there were people who were toiling and working without gaining especially much for their trouble. Of course, conditions had been improved. But much still remained. That had to be achieved when peace came.

Some little contribution he ought to be able to make at any rate. As a payment—on his debt. So if they truly wanted him to offer himself as a candidate for city council, he would not pass on the offer.

SPRINGTIME WANDERER

Spring arrived early. And Henning, who finally had been released from military service, was out and strolling through the streets as good as every evening. He was enjoying being home again, in the city. The fantastic play of lights, the blue mist that enshrouded the water and buildings and gave him a feeling of wandering around in a painting by Eugene Jansson.

The blue light, the silence, and the stillness—everything became so unreal, like walking in a dead city. But there was nothing frightening in the silence, only an almost unnatural serenity. It seemed completely incomprehensible that a war could be going on in Europe, not even one thousand kilometers from here.

Maybe it was frightening in any case. That one could be living so peacefully while all that was going on. As if one was closing one's eyes to what one had to have the strength to see, one was sleeping and dreaming.

Of course, the newspapers were telling them, one could certainly understand something of what was happening when one watched the newsreels at the movie theaters. Still, it was as if there was a membrane in between, something that protected them but also concealed.

Right now, one was obligated to see without protection, he thought. It was necessary to feel how far a person could be driven to something, how inhuman a human being could become. Any person at all? Me myself? Or only a Nazi, a German?

In truth, it was terrible that one had to say: maybe me as well. If I were afraid enough, if I were forced to, if I had not learned to stop in time.

Now that the victorious armies were pushing into Germany from the west and the east, all the truths about the concentration camps were being unmasked. They were impossible to escape; only the accomplices could declare that it was all lies and anti-terror propaganda.

Belsen, Buchenwald, Dachau, Mauthausen, Ravensbrück, Sachsenhausen, Auschwitz, Birkenau, Terzin, Treblinka, Majdanek.

Man could be that cruel. So dishonest that he could live as neighbor with the crematorium without smelling the smoke. So insensitive that the murdering of innocent fellow human beings was only a duty among all the other blameless government duties. So compliant and obedient that he participated without protesting. So lacking in imagination that he never could imagine that a government order could be a crime against humanity. And it was not always the case that the accomplices unwillingly allowed themselves to be driven there. There were those who hurried forward to take part.

When they knew it. When they were aware that this could happen in the middle of civilized Europe. After so many centuries of sermons about Christian love, after all the talk about humanity and fraternity.

It was at that point it was not easy to dream of a better future. At that point, they knew too much about man's evil. At that point it became hard to dare believe in his possibilities.

And yet he believed, yet he dreamed.

He wandered alone through the springtime, tried to fit once more into city living, life in general. During the long time he was away, he had grown away from his friends. Many were already married, had their own lives. Eventually, he would see them again. But it felt like he first had to find himself again and the life he had lived before his military service.

If it was there to be found, if it existed anymore. He was a different person from the one who had once enlisted. Had he simply gone through his trial by fire, as it was so poetically called? Or had he crawled in dirt it would be hard to free himself of? He himself was unsure. He had learned to kill. That was part of it, was the point. To hit the heart with the shot, to stick the bayonet in the belly, to consider a person an enemy. He had also heard and participated in sex talk that could take on totally grotesque proportions. Kill the men, rape the women—the teachings could be summed up this way.

Yes, he had become someone else. To think for yourself could be a breach of discipline. You stayed silent and obeyed orders.

And he had to wonder: Wasn't this the beginning of the procedure that brought the executioners to the concentration camps? They had taken and obeyed orders. Where did the boundary go between shooting the unknown person who had been driven into the death camp and twisting the bayonet in the belly of the unknown person on the battlefield? Between killing children in the gas chamber or by bombing the houses where they lived?

He was no pacifist. He himself had spoken for defending democracy and fighting Hitler, he had rejoiced at the successes of the Allies and the defeats of the Germans. Still, he was frightened now, felt like the concentration camps' guilt rested to some degree on him as well, on all who were prepared to keep quiet and obey—and kill.

The city he wandered through was still as blue and as silent, dreamed just as sweetly. But now his feeling of alienation grew, his experience of unreality. As he walked along the quays and looked out across the empty water, he felt disappointment. This was not the life he had longed for, the one he had now come home to. He could ask if life even existed at all, if it wasn't just an illusion. Such as this whole unconscious and sleeping city.

But the following morning, the city was living its booming life, and he walked through the streets down to the newspaper editor who had answered his application and learned that he could work there as an intern during the summer.

Then it felt different, as if the city was real nevertheless, as if this reality waited for him.

One afternoon he went up to visit Mormor and Aunt Emelie. He stayed a few hours and talked, mostly with Emelie since Mormor was in the middle of studying her role; she was still playing in revues.

Henning was surprised at how well Emelie kept track of everything that happened, both out in the world and at home. She talked about Roosevelt's death and about the Americans' and Russians' meeting on

Elba. But also about the Swedish jitterbug championship. Gun and her fiancé had taken part, though without any great success. And Elisabet was expecting a child sometime in the summer.

Existence was a strange soup—death and birth, battlefield and jitterbug. Everything personal seemed small just now.

Emelie talked about her father, too, the Henning who had come wandering to the city eighty-five years ago. No photographs had ever been taken of Emelie's parents and especially as far as her father went, she had a hard time really remembering what he looked like. But she wondered if Henning didn't look a little like him. And then she had realized that her father would have turned one hundred if he had lived.

She was going to turn seventy-five in a few days. She did not say this—but Henning knew, of course.

While they conversed, someone rang at the door. Mormor and Aunt Emelie wondered who it could be, hurried to tidy up.

It was Henning's father who had come.

His father's visit was completely unexpected. Erik had not come to see them since when he and Maj had been together. He had only kept in touch via telegram or sending flowers on bigger occasions. This time, he had been reminded of Emelie's birthday by Bengt and come to congratulate her, though it was a few days too early. He preferred not to bump into all the others. He had a big flower in a pot and a gift card with him. It was for a whole hundred kronor, and Emelie didn't know if she could accept it. But he said that he wanted so much to thank her for the years long ago. It was surely thanks to Emelie that they had gotten by as well as they had, both he himself and his siblings. He wanted so much to show that he had not forgotten her, even if circumstances had become such that they did not see each other.

Naturally, they had to make coffee again and talk about old times. And also tell any news there was. Erik thought it was nice that Elisabet was pregnant, that was no doubt good for her. He had seen her before when he had errands at her company, but now she had stopped working there.

He could not stay any longer, had only slipped away from work for a short while, he said. Henning accompanied him a little way. He told him about the internship he had gotten for the summer. He was going to begin his studies in the fall again.

His father had no objections. Get in touch if you need any help, he said and pressed a ten into Henning's hand. He hailed a cab.

So Henning walked through the streets again, aimlessly. He was over at Götgatan and looked in at the café where they used to sit sometimes in the evenings, but now there was no one there. He took Folkungagatan back over toward the tollgate, climbed up the hill toward Fåfängen. He found his way out to the edge of the hill and sat down there.

He heard steps on the gravel path above and looked up. It was a girl standing there; she had stopped when she caught sight of him and was apparently thinking of turning around. But then she smiled in recognition and said hi.

It took a minute before he recognized her. She was the sister of Rolle in his club. He had seen her at some of the club's parties, but that had been several years ago, and she had been just a kid then. Her name was Barbro, he suddenly remembered.

She sat down beside him. She was also free, had been sick. Now she was on sick leave for a few weeks before she was to go back to work again. And she was out walking around without any goal.

Just like himself. They had both gotten a furlough from everyday life. He told her about his military service, that he was free now and was going to work at a newspaper for the summer. And then study again for a while, one year at the most. Then he had to be through. He was managing to grow old before he even got going. Twenty-two soon. She had turned seventeen, he found out.

Only a child. But it was still fun to talk to her, to have someone to talk to at all. And he felt like a kid, too, as he sat there. He suddenly remembered how he had sat here with Karin once upon a time. The chocolate bar... But that was the difference, of course. Then he had only been seventeen himself.

Rolle was married now, she told him. Lived in Årsta.

Yes, he knew. Many of the old pals. Arne Aspman, Esbjörn. But he was loose and free.

She laughed. Wondered if that was some sort of invitation.

Only a declaration, he said. Maybe a warning. It was best she watch out.

But she did not look especially afraid.

He followed her down the hill and over to Renstiernasgatan where she lived. They decided to meet the next day.

He told them nothing at home; there was nothing to tell. Though he did say he had been up at Mormor's and that his father had come.

"That was nice of Erik," Mama said.

There was no longer any anxiety or insecurity in her when she talked about his father, more a little indifference.

Henning had not counted on anything other than beautiful weather. When he woke up and saw it was raining, he wondered if Barbro would come. Actually, it didn't really matter, he said to himself. Still, he felt a little disappointed.

He left so that he arrived too early, thought that she would not have to wait in the rain—if she now came. She had been sick too, of course.

She came, a few minutes before the appointed time. She had turned up the collar of her coat. But had no umbrella. She looked pretty when the raindrops ran down her cheeks.

Where could they go in this weather, she wondered.

They took shelter in a doorway for a minute while they thought. It began to look like it might clear up.

"We can go up to Skansen," said Henning. "I think it will be fine weather soon." The money he had received from his father the day before had made him feel like spending.

And when they got to Skansen, the rain had stopped and the sky had begun to clear. They walked around in all the cottages until they grew tired and found a bench sheltered from the wind.

Now the sun was shining and she unbuttoned her light-colored trench coat. She had a wide belt around her slender waist and the same woolen sweater as yesterday. It was a little tight across her chest, and he thought that she was not entirely a child at any rate. Not in her mannerisms or speech either, he had noticed. They had had fun together these days. Actually, he would have liked to kiss her but refrained from doing so. Maybe she didn't want to. Some of the pleasantness came maybe just from there being two people who got together and enjoyed each other's company. Nothing more. Nothing was said, and nothing had happened. They could part with a happy goodbye and never see each other again.

While they sat there on the bench leaning against the gray cottage wall, he told her how he, unsure and lost, had wandered around to sort of find himself again. And how empty and dead the city had seemed, almost indifferent.

"Until I found you," he said—suddenly rallying a little. "Then it came to life again."

She laughed. And now he would have kissed her anyway—if an old man had not come tottering along and sat down on their bench. The old man had nuts with him, and the squirrels came scampering.

Henning and Barbro stayed sitting where they were and watched. But they sat much closer to each other, and it was perhaps not only to make room for their neighbor on the bench.

Then the days arrived when the whole world seemed in the grip of spring's delirium, and of the furiously fast development of events.

They had long been waiting for the war's end, and now it was clear that the moment soon would be there. In the evening on the first of May, the news on the radio announced that Adolf Hitler was dead. The next day the resistance ended in Berlin. On the fourth of May, the Germans in Denmark, Holland and northwest Germany surrendered; on the fifth of May, Montgomery's parachute soldiers were carried in triumph through Copenhagen. But in Norway, they were still dreading a bloody final battle since Quisling's minister of police had urged them to fight.

IN A CITY TRANSFORMED

They had been walking along Djurgården's shoreline and sitting down by the water in the sunshine. From Bellmansro, they took the number fourteen line in toward town.

At first, everything seemed normal, a normal beautiful spring day. But when the streetcar reached Strandvägen, it was as if the city outside their windows was transformed and had become another city. The people who had been walking between the trees in the plantings on the street looked so happy and excited. And when they arrived at Nybroplan, a party of people arrived that had put whole bouquets of flowers in their buttonholes.

They began to guess what had happened. But they did not yet dare believe it. They hurried off when the streetcar glided into the stop on Norrmalmstorg, half ran to the newspaper kiosk and squeezed in among the people.

The news placards' large lettering shone in their direction; the evening newspapers had come out with extra pages.

Unconditional German surrender 1:00 today
Firing ceased throughout Europe
Peace throughout Europe

Peace! The long war was over.

People began to wave and shout, scream the news out loud to each other, strangers wildly embraced each other. A tobacconist had hung out old leftover Christmas tree flags in the window, and people streamed in there and bought Norwegian and Danish and Swedish flags that they hung on themselves.

They were completely caught up in the atmosphere, were pulled along with the streams of people on their way toward Kungsgatan.

All of Kungsgatan had been transformed into a billowing sea of people. Cars, streetcars, and buses got caught in the throngs of people. They danced and hopped and howled with joy. Flags waved from windows and were raised on the buildings' flagpoles. Office workers in the buildings along the street emptied wastepaper baskets on the crowds and pulled paper rolls out of adding machines to use as serpents. The air grew white with paper, as if it was snowing enormous white flakes. When the waste paper was finished, they began to empty whole cartons of unused writing paper.

Trucks with hurrahing Norwegians and Danes on their platforms tried to get through between the crowds. People sang, "Yes, We Love" and "Tipperary" and blew on toy trumpets. Boys with news placards on their backs and stomachs teetered along on their bicycles. On one of the balconies above the street, champagne corks popped.

Kungsgatan had to be blocked off to traffic. Offices closed, and more and more people streamed toward the center. But in front of the German tourist bureau's windows hung large, concealing cloths, and police were posted outside.

Small demonstrations plowed through the throngs, refugees on the way to their embassies and legations. Youths with student singers at their head paraded toward Banérgatan to honor the Norwegian ambassador. They sang and shouted, "Europe free! Europe free!" Then they continued on to the castle, but the king was at Drottningholm and talked from there on the radio. The crown prince and his wife came by car on Birger Jarlsgatan and were surrounded by huge multitudes of people who followed the car to Blasieholmen, where it stopped outside Prince Carl's residence on Hovslagaregatan.

All the restaurants were filled; people rushed in with flags in their hands to eat festive meals. The curtains were lifted from windows, and people hurrahed and waved to each other through the glass panes.

Henning stood in the middle of the delirium on Kungsgatan with Barbro in hand. He felt for a dizzying moment that life was his—that it could and would begin now. That feeling of meaninglessness that he had had ever since he came home had finally let go. He was free! The future was his; life awaited!

He snatched up a news placard and let it flutter like a banner in the wind.

Peace in all of Europe

MAIN CHARACTERS AND FAMILIES IN THE STOCKHOLM SERIES

NILSSON

Henning (b. 1845, d. 1879) and *Lotten* (b. 1848, d. 1889) have the following children:
August (b. 1868, see Bodin), *Emelie* (b. 1870), *Gertrud* (b. 1871, see Lindgren), *Olof* (b. 1879, d. 1902). Olof marries *Jenny* Fält (b. 1881); their daughter is *Maj* (b. 1900), has a child with Erik Karlsson, *Henning* Nilsson (b. 1923). With the singer Julius Törnberg, Jenny has a daughter, *Elisabet* Törnberg (b. 1910).

LINDGREN

Thumbs (Ture, b. 1845, d. 1924) and *Matilda* (b. 1845, d.1910) have three sons:
Rudolf (b. 1868, d. 1924) marries Gertrud Nilsson. They emigrate to the United States in 1909. *Knut* (b. 1870) moves with his family to Göteborg. *Mikael* (b. 1875) is unmarried.

BODIN

Fredrik (b. 1835, d. 1898) and *Annika* (b. 1846) adopt August Nilsson as their son; he receives the name Bodin.
August marries *Ida* Wide (b. 1868); their children are:
Karl Henrik (b. 1895), *Charlotta,* (b. 1897), *Anna* (b. 1898), *Fredrik* (b. 1900), and *Elisabet* (b. 1904).
All their children, except for Fredrik, who died young, are married and have children. With Bärta (see Karlsson), August has a son.

KARLSSON

Johan (b. 1870) and *Bärta* (b. 1868) have the following children:
Tyra (b. 1895), *Beda* (b. 1897), *Erik* (b. 1899) and

Bengt (b. 1900). With August Bodin, Bärta has a son,
Gunnar Karlsson (b. 1889), who marries
Hjördis Ekstrom (b. 1892). They have two children.
Erik Karlsson, later Karge, has a son with Maj Nilsson (see Nilsson).

BERG

David ("Yellow David," b. 1879) and Tyra Karlsson
have the following children:
Allan, (b. 1918), *Stig* (b. 1920), *Per* (b. 1921), and *Gun* (b. 1923).
David's sister, *Dora* Berg (b. 1883), has a daughter, *Rut* (b. 1912).

In *City of My Dreams,* the years 1860–1880 are depicted. *Children of Their City* covers 1889–1900; *Remember the City* spans 1900–1925; and *In a City Transformed* 1925–1945. One more novel follows in the Stockholm Series.

55813406R00203

Made in the USA
Charleston, SC
09 May 2016